W9-AUJ-124

THE COMEBACK

THE COMEBACK

ELLA BERMAN

THORNDIKE PRESS
A part of Gale, a Cengage Company

LIBRARY OF CONGRESS CIP DATA ON FILE.
CATALOGUING IN PUBLICATION FOR THIS BOOK
IS AVAILABLE FROM THE LIBRARY OF CONGRESS.

ISBN-13: 978-1-4328-8291-4 (hardcover alk. paper)

Published in 2020 by arrangement with Berkley, an imprint of Penguin Publishing Group, a division of Penguin Random House, LLC

Printed in Mexico
Print Number: 01   Print Year: 2020

THE COMEBACK

The Comeback

Things I remember from the accident: his voice — low and gentle, despite everything else about him. The feel of his hand on my leg just before I do it. A familiar something prickling through my body, too complex to label. The full moon hanging cleanly in the sky for the first time in a while. When I finally turn to look at him, he laughs because he doesn't think I'll go through with it. If I really think about it, this is what makes me do it. One small jerk of the wheel and then that perfect in-between moment just after we clear the road but before we start to fall. The sound of Tom Petty's voice as we crash down, down, tumbling to the bottom of the earth. A piercing, jagged tear, and then nothing but stillness.

■ ■ ■ ■

BEFORE

■ ■ ■ ■

BEFORE

CHAPTER ONE

Six Weeks Earlier

They recognize me when I'm at CVS buying diet pills for my mom, the only kind that don't make her lose her mind.

"Aren't you Grace Turner?"

The woman is pleased with herself, a red flush climbing her neck and bursting proudly across her cheeks. Her companion is smaller, wiry, with narrow eyes, and I already understand that she's the type who will need me to prove it somehow, as if I have anything left to prove.

"Grace Hyde," I correct, smiling politely, *humbly,* before turning back to the staggering array of options in front of me. The one my mom likes has a cartoon frog standing on a set of scales on the box.

"Do you live around here now?" the first one asks hungrily. She's already terrified that she'll forget something when she recounts the story to her friends.

"I'm staying with my parents." Maybe I'm in the wrong section.

"What was your last movie, anyway?" This from the smaller one, obviously. She's scowling at me and I find myself warming to her. It's hard to find a woman who still believes that the world owes her anything. Her friend, who has been shifting from foot to foot like she needs to take a piss, jumps into action.

"Your last film was *Lights of Berlin.* You were nominated for a Golden Globe but you'd already disappeared."

"Top marks," I say, forcing a smile before I turn around again. Then I put on a truly award-worthy performance, this one of a former child star in a supermarket, dutifully shopping for all of her mom's health care needs.

"Were you needed back at home?" The woman puts her hand on my shoulder, and I try not to flinch at the unsolicited contact. "I'm sorry. It's just how you . . . you disappeared one day. Was it because your parents needed you?"

Her relief is palpable, hanging off each word. And there it is. Because not only has this woman recognized me despite my badly bleached hair, ten extra pounds, and sweatpants from Target, and not only have I validated her very existence merely by being in the same shitty store in the same shitty town as she is, but also, after a year of waiting, I have restored her faith in something that she might never be able to articulate herself. This woman can leave the weight management aisle today believing once again that people are inherently good and, even more important, that people are inherently *predictable*. That nobody on this planet would walk out of their own perfect life one day for no discernible reason. And all this on a Monday afternoon in Anaheim no less.

"Can you do the bit? From *Lights of Berlin*?" she asks shyly, and the way her mouth tugs up more on one side when she smiles reminds me suddenly of my dad.

I look down at the floor. It would be so easy to say the line, but the words get stuck at the back of my throat like a mothball.

"You have pasta sauce on your T-shirt," the smaller one says.

CHAPTER TWO

I take the long route home, walking down identical streets lined with palm trees and fifties-style suburban houses. My parents have lived here for nearly eight years now, and I still can't believe that such a place exists outside of nostalgic teen movies and suburban nightmares. It's the kind of town where you can never get lost no matter how hard you try, and I end up, as I always do, outside my parents' neat, pale pink bungalow. It has a wooden porch in the front and a turquoise pool in the back, just like every other house on the street.

The smell of bubbling fat hits me as I step through the front door. My dad is cooking ham and eggs for dinner, with a couple of broccoli spears as a nod to my former lifestyle. I didn't realize how badly they'd been eating until I came home, but it turns out there really are a lot of ways to fry a potato. I arrived back in Anaheim a vegan, but as I watched my dad carefully prepare me a salad with ranch dressing and bacon bits on my first night, I knew I couldn't remain one for long.

My mom is watching TV on the sofa with a slight smile on her face, and I know without looking that she'll be watching the Kardashians, or the Real Housewives of anywhere else on earth. She used to be a semi-successful model back in England, but now she's just skinny and tired for no reason since she rarely leaves the house. Instead she lives for these shows, talking about these women as if they are her friends. I try to apologize about the diet pills, and she just shakes her head slightly, which I take to mean she doesn't have the energy to discuss it. It's this new thing she's doing, rationing her energy and refusing to spend it on anything that either displeases her or causes her stress. She's selective with her energy but she'll watch hours of the Kardashians each day.

I sit next to her, carefully avoiding the pink blanket that covers her lap. I tuck my legs underneath me, and my dad passes each of us a tray with a beanbag underneath so that we can eat from our laps. My mom's tray has a watercolor picture of poppies on it, and mine has sleeping cocker spaniels.

He takes a seat on the green corduroy armchair next to my mother, and I know that he will be watching her with an affectionate look on his face. The one that annoys her when she catches him doing it. Weakness has always repelled us both, which is somewhat ironic given my current state.

I eat the broccoli first from the head down to the stem, and I wish I hadn't made such a thing about salt being the devil. It's overcooked to the point of oblivion. I coat it in ketchup instead until it's nearly edible, and then I start to cut the ham. The Kardashians break for a commercial, and my mom mutes the TV. It's her way of beating the system — she will never buy a mop just because some newly promoted advertising executive thinks she needs one.

I watch my mom push a piece of ham around her plate. We all know that she's not going to eat any more than a third of it, but she keeps up the charade for my dad.

"Good day, everyone?" my dad asks, studying a cut on his thumb.

"Excellent," I say, and my mom lets out a small laugh.

"Just sublime," she says, before turning the volume back up. I stare out the window and watch my parents' neighbor Mr. Porter arranging a Thanksgiving display at the end of his drive, soon to be replaced by an elaborate nativity scene. I already know he will back his car into each one at least three times before the New Year and will blame everyone else for it. At times like this, I can almost understand why my parents never left Anaheim. There's a comfort to be found in the inevitability of it all.

I arrived on their porch nearly a year ago, with a camouflage duffel bag filled with all the things in the world I thought I couldn't live without, most of which are now long gone. I was seven hours sober after six months that I remember only in gossamer fragments, and I saw how bad it had gotten in my parents' faces before I ever looked in a mirror.

Despite what I told the women in CVS, I haven't really been Grace Hyde since I was fourteen, so I had to work hard to make my return as seamless as possible for my parents. I observed their habits carefully before slotting myself into their schedule, drifting into their spaces only at breakfast and dinner, never in between. I even matched my rootless accent to theirs again, pulling back on my vowels wherever they did to remind them of who I was before we moved here. I,

17

too, have learned how to worship at the altars of TV dinners and reality shows, all the while pretending to be like any other family deeply entrenched in the suburbs of Southern California.

In the middle of the day, when my dad is at work and my mom is painting her nails or watching QVC, I walk the streets of Anaheim, generally ending up at the same manicured park with a pink marble fountain in the center. I am rarely approached here when I go out, and if I am, I politely decline to take any photos. People in small cities are different — they need less from you. I thought it would be hard to disappear, but it turns out it's the easiest thing in the world. Whoever you may have been, you're forgotten as soon as you pass the San Fernando Valley.

For my family's part, they don't question my presence. Awards season came and went, and we all pretended that my eight-year career never existed. Maybe they're respecting my privacy, or maybe they really don't care why I'm here. Maybe I lost that privilege when I moved away, or that first Christmas I didn't come home, or maybe it was all the ones after that. When I'm being honest with myself, I understand that I only came back here because I knew it would be like this — that as much as I don't know how to ask for anything, my family also wouldn't know how to give it to me.

19

CHAPTER THREE

The air feels crisper than it has in a long
time when I wake up, and I'm feeling okay,
about to go for a walk when my mom stops
me.

"Grace, shall we go for a drive?" she asks.

I stand in the hall, confused because this
isn't how it has worked for the last 360 days
that I've been home. My parents drive to
the supermarket for a food shop once a
week, and I supplement this with trips to
the drugstore for all the products my mom
refuses to buy in front of my dad, even after
thirty years of marriage: her diet pills and
panty liners and my tampons. Every other
Sunday we go for lunch at the Cheesecake
Factory and my dad orders three Arnold
Palmers and extra bread before we've even
sat down. My parents share the fish tacos,
while I alternate between the orange chicken
and the pasta carbonara. Very occasionally
my parents will drop in to a mixer at a

neighbor's house, and afterward my mother will act as if she spent the entire evening being waterboarded, as opposed to just engaging in polite conversation about the best local schools or how to circumvent Anaheim building code regulations to install a sauna in your guesthouse. We do not go on drives together. It's funny how easy it is to become a creature of habit, even when those habits are not your own.

"Do you need something?" I ask, trying not to sound suspicious.

"If you have other plans, then just say," my mom says testily, and I shake my head.

"No I don't, obviously I don't," I say as she gathers up her navy quilted coat and slips her feet into a pair of old UGG boots. The ankles cave inward heavily over the soles and I look away, focusing on zipping up my jacket instead.

When we get to her car, she hands over the keys, even though I can't actually recall ever having driven my mother anywhere in my life. I pull out of the driveway before switching on the radio, which she immediately turns down.

I glance over at her and she frowns.

"Watch the road, Grace, and stop rushing. Remember, one stop sign at a time. Who taught you how to drive?"

I try to remember who did teach me to drive, but it's lost somewhere in the blur of faces and locations that make up the latter part of my teen years. It wasn't her or my dad, is the point she's trying to make. I slow down extra early for the stop sign, to make her happy.

"So, next week it will be a year you've been staying with us." My mother rifles in her bag for something as she talks.

"So it will be," I say, rolling through another stop sign.

"And obviously your sister will be back in a couple of weeks for Thanksgiving break."

"I'm aware of that too," I say, even though I hadn't remembered. My sister, Esme, returns home from her boarding school in Northern California four times a year, and we are all forced to spend the duration of her stay pretending to be marginally higher functioning than we are, with nightly trips to various chain restaurants, where slices of anodyne predictability are served up alongside the pizza. Everything we say has to be bright and constructive, and I have to try not to feel envious of the way my mother disguises her indifference to us all only for Esme's benefit, her interest fading again the minute my sister's left.

"So, any danger of you having figured

your life out by then?"

"I'm taking a break, Mom," I say. "Who would pick up your HRT if I wasn't here? Esme can't drive."

My mom raises her eyebrows at my tone and I eventually have to turn away. I wonder if this was her big idea, to lure me into a confined space with her so that she can interrogate me about my future.

"I thought you'd like having me at home."

"This hasn't got anything to do with us," she says. "It never has."

I can't say anything now because she has played her best hand early: I was the one who left them.

"You know it's actually not healthy being back at home when you're grown up. It's called arrested development. Cynthia told me about it."

"Mrs. Porter told you about arrested development?" This surprises me, mainly because I'd always assumed this particular neighbor was borderline senile. She wears a thick bathrobe covered in fluffy yellow ducks when she waters the plants lining her drive. "You know some of the Kardashians still live at home. At least I left and *then* I came back."

"That's not even slightly true. Kim and Kanye moved in with Kris while they were redoing their house, but even the younger girls don't live there anymore. Kylie bought a house in Calabasas and flipped it for three million. Plus, she's a *mother* now."

"This is really sad, Mom. You know too much about them. You shouldn't even know where Calabasas is."

"Turn left here," my mom says, ignoring me.

I take a left, promising myself that I can turn left again in three blocks. Thank god for the grid system. I slow down to let an old woman with a walker cross the road. My mom makes an impatient noise and I try not to smile.

"Grace, you have a house in Venice and you made 3.2 million dollars on your last movie. You can't actually be telling me that you're happy here."

"How do you know that?"

"Google," she says.

"Great, well there's taxes and commission on that, you know," I say, rubbing my eyes. "And you moved from London to a house the color of Pepto Bismol in Anaheim, but you're telling me that you're happy here."

"We're older than you. Happiness is no longer relevant," she shoots back, and I wish she hadn't because the phrase settles somewhere deep inside me. I open the window, and for once it's cold enough in Southern California that I can see my own breath.

"Okay, little miss sunshine. Let's try this. Tell me one time you've been happy since you've been back. And I'm talking genuinely happy. If you can do that, and I believe you, then I'll leave you alone."

I pull up at a traffic light and turn to look at her. My mom's hair is still red, but it's finer now and dusted with silver at the roots. Her beauty has become slightly distorted with age, as if her features are now too big for her face.

"I was happy last week when we went to Costco and they had the giant version of that hot sauce we both love."

My mother looks at me like I'm insane, and I shrug.

"Can you pull in here?" my mom asks, pointing to the parking lot of a health-food store I've never been in, and after a moment I oblige.

"I'll be two minutes," she says, and I watch as she walks into the store. While she's inside, I stare at the window display, where the same photo is repeated at least twelve times in various sizes. The photo shows a man holding an iron dumbbell, his neck swollen with engorged veins and his body angled into a deep squat. They probably could have chosen a different position.

My mom opens the car door and slides back into the passenger seat.

"They don't have my pills here either," she says.

"Okay," I reply, unsure of what else to say. My parents do not like change. It's like they decided that the move from England would be their final adjustment in life so they just buckled in instead, waiting to grow old and die. It's easy to forget that neither of them has even turned fifty yet.

I reach out and touch her arm. She pulls away instinctively, and I realize I can't remember the last time we touched each other on purpose. Before I moved to LA, I guess.

"So are we going home?" I ask.

She nods, and tunes the radio to a country music station.

"You know those pills are basically speed," I say after a moment. "They're not good for you."

"Are you sure you're qualified to give me a lecture on drugs, Grace?"

"I don't know. Why don't you just skip a couple more meals and then we'll talk," I say reflexively, and she pulls away from me as if I've bitten her.

I keep my eyes fixed on the road ahead,

and I spend the rest of the journey home thinking of all the things I could have said instead of *that*.

CHAPTER FOUR

When the anniversary of my return to
Anaheim comes and goes without further
comment from my mother, I wonder if she's
forgotten our conversation about my future.
It's almost entirely out of character for her
to drop something so easily, but she has
spent the last few days in a state of neurosis
preparing for my sister's impending return,
dusting the ten-year-old studio family
portraits that line the green walls of our
hallway with military precision. She's already cleaned Esme's room twice, even
though my sister isn't due home for another
week.

For my part, I've spent the last few days
proving how content I am by smiling like a
maniac whenever I'm in her presence, even
though it turns out that being happy all the
time is exhausting. I have no idea how the
Mormons keep it up. I stay out of my
parents' way as much as possible, even skip-

ping the morning coffee ritual despite knowing it means I have to walk four blocks to the nearest Starbucks for my Americano.

I am woken up one morning by a particularly loud front door slam, and the thud of something being dumped in the hall outside my bedroom. As I stretch in bed, I can hear hushed voices drifting under the gap in the door and perhaps even the sound of someone crying. It's early, and I could probably fall back to sleep, but I'm mildly interested in what's happening, as it's not following the blueprint of my parents' usual morning routine.

I slip out of bed in my gray tracksuit and an old Winnie the Pooh T-shirt, stumbling over a large purple suitcase that has been dumped in the hallway outside my bedroom door. My parents are in the living room, sitting around the table we only use on the rare occasions we have company. A bunch of yellow tulips are arranged in a vase, and the pink sparkly mug nobody is allowed to touch when Esme is away is laid out in front of an empty chair.

"When did you start drinking coffee?" I ask as my sister walks into the room from the kitchen. Her black hair is pulled back into a ponytail at the nape of her neck, and her skin has gotten worse since I saw her last, sort of tender and raw where she's been picking at her spots. We hug briefly but, as always, we don't quite fit together right, and her shoulder digs into my throat. I pull up a chair opposite her, and nobody talks for a moment.

"What are we talking about?" I ask.

My dad picks at a rough bit of skin on the back of his hand, but my mom is already frowning at me. Something is definitely off. I've always known how to read a room, even if I don't always adhere to the rules.

"I've been suspended until the end of the year," Esme says after a moment in which it becomes clear my parents aren't going to tell me. She's attempting to sound bored, and my mom flinches. I can't imagine how much she'll hate that I'm here to witness the decline of yet another of their progeny.

"What for?" I ask. The suspension is interesting to me for a few reasons, not least because, to my limited knowledge of Esme as a teenager, it is entirely unprecedented. Always a thoughtful kid, my sister has grown up into a solemn teenager, cocooned both by my parents' adoration of her and her advanced placement status in everything she does at her elite boarding school. Even her pale skin seems too vulnerable for the unflinching Southern Californian sun when she's back, as if she's somehow remained untouched by anything harsh up to this point.

My sister takes after my dad, aesthetically speaking, which would be a euphemism unless you'd actually met my dad. Growing up, before I realized how it worked, how sometimes the thing that you were always told was a blessing can actually be a poison, I would feel guilty when people complimented me on my hair or my perfect white teeth, and Esme for her grade in math or her piano playing. I thought that it meant I was better somehow, and that my parents were only overcompensating for her plainness by loving her more, when in reality Esme was probably just kinder than me, less slippery, less attention seeking. If I thought about it too much, I could feel jealous of her, but I think she could say the same about me.

Esme stretches her arms above her head and then shrugs, a movement that reminds me so much of myself that I pause.

"I don't want to talk about it," Esme says, her accent more pronounced than ever. I try to find the sister I once knew in this American sixteen-year-old, but it feels like a lost cause. I remember how, when she was younger, Esme used to break anything she loved. She'd take apart her favorite American Girl doll or the Transformers car she got for her sixth birthday just so she'd know how to put it back together again if the worst were to happen. The floor of our house in England was always strewn with abandoned limbs and random rubber wheels as a result, but she never once faulted her own logic.

My mom exhales helplessly next to me, and I feel sorry for her even though she's probably already working out how it's my fault. I do the math and figure that we wouldn't have left England if it weren't for me, so the connection shouldn't be too much of a reach for her. It never is.

"What was it, bad grades?" I ask, trying to lighten the mood. Even when she was a kid, it was clear that Esme was smarter than the rest of us put together.

Esme shakes her head.

"Did you finally set fire to that vile uniform?" Esme frowns at me, and I realize too late that she's still wearing the green pleated skirt underneath her wooly sweater. I remember now that my sister has this way of looking at you as if she can see through you to your blood.

"Alcohol?" I ask. "Not drugs?"

"I'm not you," Esme mutters, just loud

enough for everyone to hear.

"Well, I highly doubt that it's sex," I say, stung that she mentioned my sobriety in front of our parents, even though I already understand that I deserved it.

"Grace!" my mother says, before preempting Esme's tears by taking her hand. I push my chair back and walk into the kitchen, debating whether or not I need to apologize already. I don't know when it became so difficult for me to have a civil conversation with another human being. I pour myself the end of the jug of coffee, the part with the sludgy grains that get caught in your teeth, and figure I'll probably just head back to bed instead.

I'm flicking through some old photographs when my mom knocks on the door. After less than a second she's standing in my room, and it's the first time she's been in here since I moved back.

She hovers above the bed, and I move my legs so that she can sit on the end. She does so, folding her hands on her lap and leaning against the sparkly purple wall. This already feels too intimate for us, and I squirm under the sheets, wishing I wasn't tucked back up in bed like an invalid.

"Who are these people?" she says, squinting at one of the photographs on the duvet.

"Her name was Anna." I point at a pretty dark-haired girl standing next to me, flashing a peace sign at the camera.

"Oh yes, you did ballet with her. I remember her mother. Their TV was practically bigger than their house," she says as she drops the photo back on the pile. This used to mean that they were low-rent, tacky, but I think she's forgetting the sixty-two-inch screen she has hanging above the electric fireplace downstairs. She shifts her position on the bed, and I can see how thin she is underneath her cotton shirt.

"Esme's had a rough year, you know," she says.

"She's barely been here," I say. "How would I know?"

"You're one to talk," my mom says, and I realize too late that I walked right into her trap. Because I'm the one who made them move across the world and then left them behind, and the only way they knew how to punish me was to make their world smaller and smaller until there was no room for me in it anyway.

"I get it, I'll apologize to her," I say after a pause, just in case I can change the course of this conversation for the first time in my life.

My mom shrugs, as if I'm missing the point.

"I meant what I said the other day. You can't hide here forever."

"Mom, do we have to do this? I'm not a kid anymore."

"Says the girl in the Disney pajamas, making her sister cry," my mom says. "You never had to want for anything, that's why you're like this."

Say what you like about my mother, but she's never missed an opportunity to get a good dig in.

"I spent the majority of my teenage years alone on a film set, so don't tell me what I've wanted for," I say, trying to be calm but hearing something in my tone that I can't control. Fighting with her is like muscle memory. The smallest thing used to set us off and we would spar back and forth, neither of us really caring what the other one said until suddenly we did. We say a lot of stuff that means nothing, but it's like a coin-pusher game in an arcade, each insult edging us a little closer to the edge until all hell breaks loose.

"If you have something to say, then just say it," my mom says, narrowing her eyes at me, but I look away, ignoring the adrenaline that is now coursing through my body. She shakes her head. "You had everything."

"And I would still swap places with you in a heartbeat," I say, and then we both realize what I've said, how small her life is because she had to accommodate mine, and how much more she would have given up for even one-tenth of what I have.

"You've always been selfish, Grace. It's nice to see you haven't changed," she says.

"You know, I don't expect you to give me any special treatment, but I thought you could at least pretend to like me," I say quietly. "I already said I would apologize."

We sit there for a few moments before she stands up. I think she's going to leave but she starts to speak again with her hand on the door, her gaze unflinching.

"Do you want to know the truth, Grace?"

I shrug, because she's going to enlighten me either way.

"I don't think you're a good person for your sister to be around right now."

And there it is. Can you hear it? That's the sound of coins clattering into the gutter. I stand up, suddenly needing to be anywhere on earth but here.

"Gosh, I have no idea how that could have happened," I say as I drop the Polaroid I'm holding onto the bed. The photo was taken at Disneyland when I was twelve, just before our lives were transformed. My dad and I are grinning on either side of a life-size Pluto. My sister is holding my dad's hand, shyly peeking around him to squint into the camera. My mom is on the other side of me, her arm around my shoulders and a pair of sequined Mickey Mouse ears on her head. I wonder now whether her dislike for me crept up on her so slowly that she couldn't see it happen or whether it happened all at once, like an earthquake.

"You know, you never asked me why I came back," I say, and then I push past her, walking out of my bedroom, out the front door of the pink house, down the porch steps, until once again I am under the endless blue sky, racing past miles and miles of stucco bungalows flanked by 4×4s on one side and rippling American flags on the other.

CHAPTER FIVE

When I was thirteen, a casting director came to my school in London to find an unknown actress for a trilogy about a trio of teen assassins at an international spy school. We all put our names down to audition for the part, and the other girls giggled and rehearsed all morning, arguing over who deserved to be in the film the most. I ignored them, and the casting director's appraising eye, instead staring down at a well-worn copy of *The Catcher in the Rye* that I carried around because I thought it made me seem complicated. I had long, glossy cinnamon-colored hair, one blue eye and one green, and dimples, all of which meant I was already popular so I could afford to be pretentious. Dimples are the kind of thing that matter in a state school in London, and everywhere else, it turns out.

For the first thirteen years of my life, our basement apartment in Islington was filled with my parents' friends, the only obvious grounds for an invitation being that my mom found the person interesting in some small way. The adults drank a lot and had loud, unruly debates about everything from Princess Diana to Marxism, and although my dad was engaging enough in a hardworking, salt-of-the-earth kind of way, even then I understood that mom was the reason people kept coming back. She could be searingly funny, due to a combination of her razor-sharp perceptions and occasional callousness, and she was also beautiful, with thick auburn hair and eyes the color of a swimming pool under a thin layer of ice.

As I got older, people would say I was her doppelgänger, and I knew they said it because I sort of looked like her, but mostly because I worked hard at it, copying the way she laughed, the arch tone of her voice, so that people would know not only that we were the same, but also that we were better than everyone else. When my sister was born, I was surprised to find that even though it didn't seem like she should be a threat to me, pale and solemn as she was, it didn't stop my mother from loving her more. It turned out they'd been trying for another baby for a while, and Esme was the grand prize.

When the lunchtime audition came around, I stood on the stage in our main hall next to the other girls, embarrassed by my sameness and disguising it as boredom. The other girls were bouncing on their toes, excitement distorting their voices when they said their lines as they tried not to laugh at their friends who were pulling faces and waving at them manically from the seats.

When it was my turn, I completely blanked. Of course I hadn't rehearsed anything, had just expected to deliver it all seamlessly and walk off, maybe stick my middle finger up to make the other girls laugh. I stood onstage, trying not to piss myself because I knew that even I would never live that down, and I realized that I had never wanted anything as much as I wanted this, and the futility of realizing it at exactly the moment I was ensuring it would never happen made me burst into tears. Everyone around me froze, because I was too old to be crying that way, so shame-lessly. When I finally managed to get the line out, it was through heavy, juddering sobs and barely intelligible. That same night, the producers called my parents to ask if I could be flown out to LA to screen-test. The way my parents looked at me changed from that moment on, and, for the first time since my sister was born, I figured out how to hold on to their attention. Looking back, I feel ashamed of how much I wanted it all.

CHAPTER SIX

When Disney offered me a lifetime pass for shooting a movie with them, I didn't imagine I'd use it even once, let alone once a week for the entire year I've been back in Anaheim. Every week, however, I leave my parents' house in the morning and walk to the resort hotel we stayed in when we first visited California, before we ever imagined we'd be moving here. Even though I know it's weird, sometimes just being somewhere so entirely engineered to make you believe in something makes me feel better. It would be embarrassingly reductive to say it reminds me of a simpler time, so let's just say I go there for the buffet and the Mickey Mouse waffles.

Disneyland is also the only place I can get away with wearing pajamas and a pair of Converse at eleven a.m. on a Thursday, and, after being seated at a small table near the kitchen of the Storytellers Café, I join the line for the buffet. I fill my plate with the usual: three Mickey Mouse waffles, two pieces of green melon and a cup of black coffee that I already know will taste so ashy I'll actually look for a cigarette butt floating in it. I sit back down at the polished table and watch the kids tripping on maple syrup around me. They're standing on chairs and howling or they're barreling through the gaps between the tables, knocking glasses and milk jugs as they weave, physically vibrating with adrenaline. When I watch them I can almost remember what it was like to know I was happy at the exact moment I felt it, as opposed to only after the moment has passed.

I've eaten two of my waffles when Sleeping Beauty walks into the restaurant and, after pausing at the entrance to scan the room, sits down in the chair opposite me. I'm surprised because I have been coming here for a year, always wearing my sunglasses and a baseball cap pulled over my bleached hair, and, until today, nobody has either recognized or wanted to talk to me.

"Are you okay, honey?" Sleeping Beauty asks in a high voice. She has a hint of a southern accent, and I try not to stare at the cakey foundation caught in the corners of her mouth.

"I'm fine, thank you." I smile at her politely and then turn back to my waffles, hoping she'll move on to another table. There is a prepubescent boy at the table next to us gazing intently at her.

"Wow, I didn't realize you were British," she says, blinking heavily under the weight of her false eyelashes. "I've seen you in here before. I like your movies."

"Oh. Thanks. I like your . . . movie too," I say, unsure of what the Disneyland rules are for adults, whether I might offend her if I don't play along.

"Oh, you're sweet for lying," she says, and I wonder if that's something you start to care about when you do her job. My last movie was a biopic about a sex worker who murdered seven of her former clients, and I think I would still experience a visceral reaction if someone criticized her right now. It always surprises me how willing we are to forgive someone once we think we understand them.

"If my only friends were a bunch of vermin and three senile bitches, then I'd kill the person who bothered to wake me up," Sleeping Beauty says as she adjusts her wig slightly. Her hair is dark underneath the synthetic spun gold.

"It's itchy," she tells me. "So do you want

44

a photo?"

"I don't have a camera."

"You have a phone though. Everyone has a phone," Sleeping Beauty says, narrowing her eyes.

"I actually don't have a phone," I say, patting my pockets. I nod at the boy at the table next to us who is now staring at us with unconcealed interest, his Mickey Mouse–shaped PB&J sandwich hovering in the air. "Maybe that kid will want one."

"I doubt it, they want to meet Anna and Elsa now. I'm left with the creepy dads."

"Sorry to hear that." I push my sunglasses up on my nose. Sleeping Beauty plays with the packets of sugar, shuffling them in the pot so that the Sweet'N Low is mixed in with the brown sugar and the stevia, but she doesn't show any signs of leaving.

"Look, I don't want to be rude, but I really just came here for the waffles," I say, pointing to my plate.

"Well, there's no need to be a bitch about it." Her voice is lower now, grittier, as she pushes her chair back and stands up.

"You know the hotel manager asked me to talk to you because you always look so sad that you're, like, freaking out the other customers. They've had meetings about how to handle you."

45

She waits for me to say something, and when I don't, she sticks her middle finger up at me before walking away. The kid at the next table stares after her, his jaw slack and his eyes wide.

I return to the house dragging a seven-foot Christmas tree behind me, even though it's too early in November to have bought one. The encounter with Sleeping Beauty has cheered me up, and it might even be something my mom would find funny if I can tell it right. I'm feeling something close to exhilaration after our fight, as if it could have finally cleared the heavy air that's been hanging between us since I came back to Anaheim. Perhaps I can even show her a tiny bit more of myself, loosen my grip slightly. At the very least, this is familiar territory for us. We've both always been on our best behavior after our very worst, and I figure that if everything plays out like it used to, there will be no need for apologies and, in fact, no need to mention this ever again.

When I was sixteen, during one of our worst fights, my mom told me she'd been pregnant with twins but that I had killed my twin in the womb before we were born. I asked my on-set tutor about it, and it turns out that the other fetus would have died

46

early from natural causes, and that I may have absorbed her fetal tissue due to the fact that we were sharing a womb with limited space and disposal options. The phenomenon has a name, vanishing twin syndrome, but to hear my mom tell it, I took up too much space before I was even born. I've never told anyone else the story, and not because I was traumatized by it or anything, but because I know exactly how it sounds. It wouldn't be fair to define anyone by such an appalling moment, let alone your own mother.

I nod at my parents' other neighbor, Donna, who is leaving her house dressed head to toe in velour, and I drag the tree up the porch, dropping pine needles as I heave it into the hallway. My dad stands just outside the kitchen with his hands in the pockets of his corduroys. I lean the tree against the wall, and he just stares at me for a moment, looking uncomfortable. My mother comes into view, and I can see that she's been crying. I take a deep breath and try to stem the resentment already building in my chest.

"I meant to ask you, did you see that Donna got a new dog?" I say, making my face as open as possible to show I've for-given her. "I think it's a rescue, or maybe

47

she was saying she rescued it from her daughter. The one with the OxyContin problem. Also, is it just me or has she had something done to her lips?"

My parents lock themselves in the kitchen as Esme and I dress the Christmas tree, filling each branch with garish, flashing baubles, each more hideous than the one before it. My dad found a crate of decorations in the attic, and when he brought them down, I had to try very hard not to think about the first Christmas I didn't come back, or any of the ones after that. I would like to say that I've thought about it before, but I would probably be lying.

As we work, I hum Christmas songs to drown out the sound of my parents arguing, even though Esme is still refusing to talk to me. It's a throwback to when we were younger, back when our parents' arguments used to be loud and fiery instead of ice cold, always when they thought we were sleeping. Esme would wake up and climb onto the foot of my bed, turning to face the wall so that her forehead was pressed against it. While our parents fought over my mother spending twelve pounds on a moisturizer, or going out dancing with her friends when the water bill still hadn't been paid, I would make up stories or songs about a pirate-fighting mermaid called Patrice to distract her. Esme was young then, only eight when I left, and I think I thought of her as mine for a while.

I steal glances at her while we decorate, and it strikes me as so strange that I don't know this serious, dark-haired teenager any more than I know my parents' next-door neighbor. She has rings of violet underneath her eyes and a small gap between her front teeth that she must either love or despise.

As a result of what has been happening in the kitchen, dinner consists of defrosted hash browns and boiled hot dogs, with a watery pile of spinach in the middle. Esme takes one look at her plate and announces that she needs to lie down in her room. She's usually the definition of polite, so this is entirely unprecedented. There is this moment where my dad stares helplessly at my mom but they let her get away with it, and I can see how it starts, how someone can slip through your fingers even when you care so much it hurts.

I settle down next to my mom on the sofa for an episode of Real Housewives. My dad hands me the tray with the poppies on it by mistake, and my mom and I wordlessly swap before we start to eat. I open with the spinach and work my way to the hot dogs, leaving the hash browns until last because they're the best part. I really like hash browns. How can my mom say that I'm not happy?

"Grace . . ." My dad cuts across the show at a pivotal moment and I frown at him slightly. My mom mutes the TV.

"I know your mother tried to talk to you earlier, and I wanted to say that I support her 110 percent. Whatever she said, I agree." He seems like he's in physical pain with the effort of having to involve himself in this, but it's still not enough for my mom, who makes a small sound.

"Great, me too. We are all on exactly the same page then," I say brightly. My mom keeps her eyes fixed expectantly on my dad. I frown at the TV but they don't turn the sound back on even though the show has restarted. We stay frozen like this in a silent showdown for a couple more minutes. I could do this forever, but I also kind of want to know how the episode ends.

"What was the scale?" I ask eventually. My dad just looks at me, confused, but my mom shakes her head because she knows what's coming.

"You said 110 percent but I have no idea what the scale was. It devalues the whole system. What about 500 percent? You could even support her a million percent if you tried really hard." I think I can hear Esme snort from her bedroom down the hall, but maybe I'm imagining it.

"Grace," my mom snaps, and I sink back into the sofa.

"I don't want to have to remind you that I bought you this house. So this is actually my home," I say, hating myself more with every word that comes out of my mouth.

"You guys can obviously stay as long as you want," I add graciously.

"Grace, please," my dad says, and I feel horrible because I think he's going to cry. Sometimes I wish he could just figure out how to repress his emotions like the rest of us.

"This is ridiculous," my mom says, throwing her hands in the air. "You can't pretend that your life there never existed. That it doesn't *still* exist —"

"*Mom,*" I interrupt, and then I count to five in my head. "Can we talk about something else?"

I walk over to the TV and turn the sound on manually. One of the Real Housewives is upset that her friend said she had an alcohol problem. I let her voice wash over me as my heart rate returns to something close to normal. It never occurred to me before, but maybe this is what people outside of LA and New York do to meditate.

"You know, I heard something today about the Independent Film Awards," my mom says after a moment. I keep my eyes trained on the TV, even as my heart rate picks up.

"Where did you hear about that in Anaheim?"

"It's a figure of speech, Grace. I saw it on Facebook. Anyway, Able Yorke is being honored. They're giving him a lifetime achievement award for his commitment to the industry. I thought you'd want to know."

I swallow hard but I don't lift my eyes from the TV.

"Not really," I say, then I collect her plate on top of mine and put them both in the kitchen sink.

I watch the rest of the episode with my parents before excusing myself, but I know my mom will think she has won anyway. Because surely that's what she was doing — appealing to my engorged celebrity ego, thinking that I would never be able to resist the slithering pull of awards season. Surely I would never miss seeing Able win for his body of work that couldn't have existed without me. That this entire time I've been pretending to rebuild Grace Hyde, we all knew my alter ego was always going to win in the end.

I try not to think about his papery skin, the copper smell on his hands, but the memories slide and distort behind my closed eyes until they fuse together like a time-lapse film. I open the secret drawer of my old jewelry box and pull out the orange tube of pills I haven't touched since I left Los Angeles, running my thumb across the smooth label. Percocet: a prescription for yet another version of myself, the one you may find in a heap on the bathroom floor. I quietly pour two pills out onto my sweaty palm and swallow them dry. After a moment I swallow one more because they haven't kicked in quickly enough to stop the shame clawing at my insides, and I don't think I can risk what comes next: the involuntary mental checklist of all the ways I've ever failed anyone.

I sit against my bedroom door and wait for the numbness to melt over me, for the present to replace the past, to be aware only of the blessedly tangible: the texture of the carpet beneath my fingertips, the hum of the dishwasher in the kitchen, the canned laughter from the TV down the hall. Just as my muscles start to melt, my heart rate slowing down to normal, I hear my sister's voice, calling out for my mom from her bedroom. I slip into the bathroom next to my room, and I stick the plastic end of my toothbrush down my throat, vomiting messily into the stained porcelain basin as hot tears streak down my face. Afterward, I curl up on the bath mat and rest my cheek against the cool linoleum floor. Maybe my mom was right about me when she said I wasn't happy, but what she doesn't understand is that since the age of fifteen, I've never even dared to want to be happy. I'm just trying to stay alive.

CHAPTER SEVEN

For the first time in months, sleep eludes me entirely. It becomes something slippery, just out of reach, and I know that it has started all over again. Able has crept into this house and I will start to see his face reflected next to mine in the bathroom mirror, the outline of his profile in a slice of burned toast. My mom may have been the one who said his name, but I'm always the one who leaves the door open for him. He was never supposed to exist here, but now that he's here, he comes after me like a flood.

I already know what happens next if I stay, because it's the only part that ever comes easily to me. Worse than the numbness, worse than the bending and yielding to fit myself into a place I no longer belong, I will become resentful, bitter, and it won't be long before I'm drinking again, mixing vodka with my pills and blacking out in an effort to forget my own name for just a minute. My parents will no longer be able to ignore what I've become, and neither will my sister. I understand that they have all just been tolerating my presence since I got back, waiting for me to get sick of them and leave again. I don't think I can even blame them for it, as much as I want to.

As the sky begins to lighten outside, I pack up my things, dropping the clothes and books from my drawers into my small suitcase without looking at them. I arrived at my parents' house with little, and I'll return to LA with even less.

I peek into my parents' bedroom on my way out. They seem older when they're asleep, on their backs with their mouths tugging down at the corners. I feel a shift somewhere deep in my chest, so I close the door gently behind me and creep toward the front door.

"You weren't going to say good-bye?"

My mom appears in the hall behind me, one hand gripping the wall. She's like me, a useless automaton version of herself until she's had a cup of coffee.

I shrug, the key she gave me hovering next to the lock. "I'll visit soon."

"You'll miss Thanksgiving," she says matter-of-factly.

"We barely celebrate Thanksgiving," I say, smiling slightly.

"Will you be back for Christmas at least?"

"I don't know," I reply.

My mom runs a hand through her fine hair, and I wonder for the first time if this is hard for her too. I remember how much I used to worship her before we moved here, and I know that I would take it all back if I could, and if I could just figure out how to tell her that, it might be the most honest thing I've ever said.

"I just wanted to be normal for a while," I say quietly.

A flicker of a smile.

"You could never be normal, Grace, you just don't know it yet."

I don't say anything as I turn back to the door.

"You don't want to say good-bye to Esme?"

An image of Esme as a young child appears in my mind, but I shake my head. I've always been good at leaving; it seems strange for her to have forgotten already.

"Grace?" my mom says when I'm halfway down the front porch steps, but her next words get lost in the sound of a lone car speeding past us.

"What did you say?" I ask, and suddenly

something is pressing on my chest, making it hard for me to breathe.

"I said, watch the traffic around the 710," she says, louder this time.

I nod wordlessly as she closes the front door.

CHAPTER EIGHT

After my audition, arrangements were made for me to screen-test in LA over the summer break. My parents left Esme with a friend, and we boarded a flight without her for the first time since she was born. I held my mom's hand during takeoff, and even though I could see how clunky a metaphor the ascent into the clouds was for how I was feeling (even my insipid English teacher would have circled that one in red), it did nothing to stem the growing feeling I had that all the other passengers on the plane were just along for the ride. While my parents slept for most of the flight, I watched a garbage movie about vampires that I had never been allowed to watch at home, and I wondered if I'd ever feel grounded enough to sleep again.

Our flight landed in the late afternoon, and a black town car was waiting to take us straight to our hotel. The production company had booked us a suite at the Four Seasons, and I knew as soon as we arrived in the perfect, marble lobby that the new pair of Reebok shoes my parents had bought me were all wrong.

Everything in the hotel was a beautiful, rich cream color with gold accents and little touches we never even knew we were missing. My mom and I ran around our suite, calling each other over to feel the luxurious bathrobes hanging on the back of the door, or to touch the embroidered cover of the book of dreams tucked in the drawer next to the bed. My dad trailed behind us, already off-balance by the whole experience. The studio had left a giant hamper filled with American sweets on my bed, and my mom and I tore through Tootsie Rolls and Twinkies as we flicked through the TV movie channels. I felt mildly guilty that Esme wasn't there to see any of it, but it was also the most attention I'd received from my parents in a long time. I hadn't let myself realize how much I'd missed it.

I had three auditions over the next week, and each time I read the lines I felt more connected to them, as if they were bubbling up from a place inside me I never knew existed. I didn't even care when the adults behind the table interrupted me to order

Mexican food or whisper notes to the assistant standing with a clipboard behind them. I think my parents were worried that I already wanted it too much, but it never felt like a risk to me because I had a feeling the role was already mine.

Sure enough, the night before we were due to fly back to London, we were invited to dinner at Nobu with Able Yorke and his wife, Emilia, along with Nathan and Kit, the two men who would become my agent and manager. I had been introduced to all of them at various points over the week, but at the time I had lumped them all into the same category, filed only under "adults I need to impress." As we walked into the dark restaurant, my mom reminded me that Able Yorke was the person I needed to win over the most.

Able was beautiful in the most obvious sense of the word, but I was beautiful, too, so I didn't dwell on it other than to clock his two perfect dimples, just like mine. His wife was easier to overlook at first, less shimmering, less glamorous, except for her hair — creamy blond and thick, unlike anything I'd seen before. I could tell she was pregnant from the soft swell of her stomach underneath her cashmere sweater, and the way she instinctively touched her bump whenever she spoke.

My dad was wearing the same black suit with shoulder pads that he wore on his wedding day, and his trousers were bunched up over his Clarks shoes. As I watched him stab at the rolls of sushi and soft-shell crab with one chopstick, he seemed to belong to a different generation than the other men at the table, even though they were all around the same age. My mom wore a tight velvet dress that she had found in a thrift shop on Melrose earlier that week, and I went from feeling so proud of her beauty to mortally embarrassed as soon as I saw Emilia's jeans and sweater, and the looks on the other diners' faces as they stared at us. I didn't know why or how, but I knew that my parents had gotten it wrong, and I couldn't understand why they didn't realize it too.

I held my breath as Able offered me the job right there at the table, even though, for some reason, he was looking at my parents when he said it. He spoke quietly, so that they had to move closer to hear him, and after a while I realized that he appeared to be convincing my parents to let me take the role, something I had assumed was a given since we had flown across the world for it. I watched as Able assured my parents that if we moved to Los Angeles to do the trilogy,

I would be completely looked after, that my education would actually improve under world-class, private tuition. He said that he wasn't just talking about this one project — he wanted me for longer. Able had identified the inevitable road bumps in the career of any young actor and was removing the variables. He wanted Marilyn without the overdose, Winona without the shoplifting, Gwyneth without the health shit. I wouldn't waste my time or reputation on any trashy projects because I would work solely with Able. He would be my filter, my translator and my protector all in one. I wouldn't go looking for any trouble because I would have everything I ever wanted given to me.

My parents listened in awe as Able laid out his plan, and, perhaps noting their implicit consent, Able subtly adjusted his rhetoric from the hypothetical to the concrete. The people around the table that night would perfect everything about me — my backstory; my classic, insouciant style; even my sarcastic interview manner — before my face ever appeared on a screen. They talked about changing my surname to Turner, evoking images of two Hollywood icons, Lana Turner and Grace Kelly yes, but also to separate my two identities so that I could always return to who I had been

63

before. I would be reborn, and the best part of it was that it was a no-risk situation. There would be so many people watching over me, people personally invested in my career, that nothing could go wrong. I would have Able and Emilia to protect me in my parents' absence. I would never make a sex tape or shave my head or be caught drunk driving, because I was in on the act: I had never really been Grace Turner at all.

I'd like to say I didn't understand what I was agreeing to, but I think it would be a lie — even back then I knew I was giving a part of myself away. Only, sitting there that night, watching these glossy strangers talk about me as cool, buttery sashimi slick with soy sauce melted over my tongue, it just didn't seem like the worst choice in the world. What I couldn't have predicted was how people would want more and more of me; I didn't yet know how closely praise is linked to punishment, how I would never again determine my own value because I wasn't so much a person as an idea, shaped not only by the people around the table with me that night but by the millions of people who would pay to watch my movies in the years to come.

My mom behaved strangely at dinner, laughing loudly at the wrong moments and fluttering her eyes at Able like a marionette. Emilia smiled reassuringly at me whenever I looked at her, but I could tell she pitied me for my mother's theatrics. I frowned at my mom and watched as my dad stared somewhere over my manager's head for most of that first dinner, and all of the subsequent ones.

In the end, it didn't matter anyway, because these strangers were all only tolerating my parents to get to me. I tried to be lively and entertaining whenever they spoke to me, and I told myself that I was doing it for all of us, to let these men know that we were in on the joke, when I gestured to my parents and apologized for bringing the Addams Family. The men erupted into laughter, Able whacking the table repeatedly even as he apologized to my dad, and Emilia allowing herself a small smile. My mom seemed confused at first, but then she joined in, grinning and laughing loudly along with them. I hated to see her make a fool of herself, but the men, who had been studying me closely since I arrived, were charmed, and that was what we had all dressed up for, wasn't it? She'd been so excited all week, and I told myself that I could give all of this to her for the rest of her life if tonight just went well. I tried not

65

to notice the growing patches of sweat underneath her armpits, or the way she kept licking her lips before she spoke.

The more she drank, the more revealing her stories became. We were all used to her being the heartbeat of any group, but it turned out she didn't know anything about this new world I was joining, and she told embarrassing stories that always circled back to her modeling career. At one point she described in excruciating detail exactly how her career had been hindered when she married my dad instead of moving to Los Angeles as a teenager herself. Able listened patiently and asked the right questions about my dad's construction company, but even then I realized that he was just handling them both. For the first time I saw my parents through someone else's eyes and felt embarrassed for them. I interrupted them both after that, cutting across their stories, and in doing so I understood implicitly that I was giving the men permission to do the same. My mom stopped talking as much, and I tried not to see the disappointment in my dad's eyes. After a while, it just became easier not to look at either of them.

My parents' role in the plan was laid out from the start. All they needed to do was create a loving and stable home environment for me to return to, and since their role was to treat me like a regular kid, it was better that I didn't associate them with work in any way, or vice versa. As soon as the visas were sorted, my family obediently scuttled away to their new home. Anaheim was the only place in America we'd ever visited as a family, and I guess my parents liked the convenience of being so close to Disneyland or something. Or maybe it was the relentless sunshine and right-wing politics. I don't know, I have no idea why they chose Anaheim, but I'd rarely slept more than five nights in a row at their house until last year. From that first movie on, my mom and I fought like rabid dogs, or like two people more similar than they would ever admit. As far as I knew, my mother never tried to find modeling work in California, and they certainly didn't make any effort to find new friends. I never knew if she was bored, lonely, envious or a combination of all three, and I didn't hang around to find out. Of course I understand that I was the one who'd left them behind, but I also understood that they'd let me. By the age of fifteen, I was more used to being alone on a movie set than with my family, in theory watched after by a guardian, but in reality tethered to absolutely nothing at all.

I tried to keep in touch with Esme, sending her gifts when I remembered, but soon after moving to Anaheim she applied to a boarding school for gifted children, and she gradually turned into just another person around whom I had to play a part, only this time I was pretending that I was still her big sister.

Able was the writer and director of that first movie, and every movie I made after that, except for one disastrous horror movie that was sold to me as the new *Scream*. It was supposed to set me free but it tanked, and, under the advice of my agent, my manager, my parents and basically every single person that I met in the street, I ended up back with Able. My fate was more sealed than ever before — I was his muse and he was my Svengali. His work was at its most brilliant when I was in it, and, for my part, I glowed onscreen like nobody else around me. The other two assassins faded into adolescent obscurity after the second film, but not me. I was untouchable, unstoppable, hurtling down a path to immortality so rapidly, so immaculately, that not one person stopped to question how it all worked so well, a fortysomething man and a teenager being so inextricably linked.

CHAPTER NINE

I arrive back in LA as the sun is rising. It's easy to forget the things you loved about a city that has ruined you, but I always liked this one small window of time when Los Angeles just looks like any other city in the world. It happens only once the streetlights have stopped twinkling in the dark, but before the golden sun begins to light the city like a movie set. It was the only time of day that LA ever felt like home to me.

I pull up outside the glass house in Venice. I don't have the key anymore, so I ring the bell. There is a cactus next to the door that I don't remember being there before. I reach out and touch it, but it's softer than I thought it would be, and my fingernail leaves a wet, crescent-shaped mark.

My husband opens the door wearing a white T-shirt and a pair of boxer shorts. It's what he wears to bed every single night, and he somehow looks both exactly the same and entirely different from how I remembered. I try not to think about when we first met, when we were just two teenagers staying up all night in his apartment in Los Feliz, drinking tequila as we talked about all the people we'd left behind to be there. For me it meant leaving my parents and sister who had moved across the world for me, and for him it was leaving a close-knit family in a town where fireflies lit up the sky and people kept guns in their glove compartments. When he had to leave the room to throw up from the tequila, I slipped quietly out the front door, leaving a note in my place that read *you're perfect* in lowercase, drunk letters that didn't touch each other at all.

"Shit, Grace," he says, trying to look at me before he has to turn away. He already looks lost. When I was away, I only ever pictured him smiling, his bronze eyes crinkling at the corners like linen in summer, but now I remember this face too. I follow him into the house.

"Welcome home, I guess," he says, and we both know that the house is mine only in the legal sense. It even smells like him, slightly sour and woody. I don't know whether to laugh or cry when I see that Dylan already has a Christmas tree up too, and that it's not even the kind an interior designer puts up for you. It's decorated with hundreds of swinging multicolored baubles and paper cut into crude animal shapes with lollipop sticks for tails. Nothing matches.

"You're a little early with the tree," I say, peering past him. "Did you get a wood burner put in?"

A woman with long dark hair and freckles is sitting on the sofa in plaid pajamas, holding a mug of coffee with her legs curled up underneath her. I can tell instantly that she is better than me from the way her entire face lights up when she smiles at me, and from how quickly it happened, as if her default setting is only ever .3 seconds away from elation. I don't feel sad when I realize this, just a strange, muted relief that in some way, my expectations have finally been met.

"Where's Doina?" I ask, looking between the woman on the sofa and Dylan. Doina was our housekeeper.

"She's gone, Grace," Dylan says, shrugging. "You should have called."

"Now or a year ago?" I try to make a joke, but it turns out I still have the ability to hurt him, because he flinches.

"I'm exhausted," I say, staring upstairs in the direction of the bedrooms longingly.

"It's the morning," Dylan says slowly.

"I'm Grace," I call past him to the woman on the sofa.

"I know! I'm Wren. It's great to meet you."

"She seems lovely," I say, to nobody in particular, and then I walk upstairs to the master bedroom because I know that Dylan won't have slept in there once since I've been gone.

The room is lifeless, untouched. When I turn the main light on, dust particles spin in the air around me. I pick up a framed photo from our wedding day that still sits on the bedside table, wanting to recognize myself in it. We got married in Big Sur in January, the night I turned twenty-one, and during the ceremony I gripped my bouquet so tightly that I pricked my finger and it bled onto my white jumpsuit. I could taste metal for the rest of the night, but it didn't matter because I read a poem by Richard Brautigan to my new husband while people held sparklers shaped like hearts, and for the first time I saw myself as everyone else saw me.

I left within the year.

CHAPTER TEN

I spend my first morning back in LA drifting in and out of sleep, waking eventually to the sound of someone tapping lightly on my bedroom door. My mouth feels dry and tacky, and I can smell my own sweat on the sheets. The sun is right above us and all I see is the blue, blue Pacific Ocean through the floor-to-ceiling windows. I remember how I once thought that being close to the water made me feel as if I could breathe again, but now I find myself missing the flat suburban sprawl of Anaheim, the sanitized public spaces and the flags floating lightly in the wind. I feel exposed being back in LA, and I wonder what it would be like to actually know how I feel about something before I've already lost it.

The door opens gently, scraping across the top of the carpet, and I grab the tube of pills from the bedside table, shoving them underneath my pillow. Dylan stands at the foot of my bed, looking anywhere in the room but at me. His eyes eventually settle on the movie poster for *Breathless* hanging on the wall above my head.

"I called Laurel. She's downstairs waiting for you."

"Why? You hate Laurel." Laurel was my sometime friend, sometime assistant, always outrageously ineffective sober companion.

"I don't like Laurel, but you don't seem like yourself," he says slowly.

"You haven't seen me for a year, remember? This is what I'm like." I pull at my shoulder-length hair with the greasy dark roots and the blond ends.

"I'm not talking about your hair."

"Do you like it? Stripper chic, n'est-ce pas?"

Dylan exhales exasperatedly. At its best our relationship was based on me saying and doing stupid shit to make Dylan laugh, but I understand that what I did to him means that I have lost the right to that too.

"Sorry. Laurel. Please can you tell her to go away? I'll call her later."

"All right, but what meds are you on?"

I shake my head.

"Drug- and alcohol-free since the day I left LA."

It's almost the truth, but it just makes

74

Dylan look more disoriented than ever.

"What's up with you then?"

I stare down at my hand, turning it over and realizing that Dylan will notice I'm not wearing my ring. I don't know if I need to feel bad about that or whether it would be stranger if I were still pretending. I tuck my hand back underneath the duvet anyway.

"I'm still getting used to being myself."

I stay in bed for another hour, watching how the sun glitters on the surface of the water and trying to feel anything other than numb about that and everything else in my life. You know those days when you're soaring and every single thing you touch is so immensely, undeniably perfect, and the best part is that you made it like that all by yourself, just by being so shining and lucky and brilliant? Well, those days don't exist when you're not on drugs. They're no longer an option. And that may have worked out when I was with my parents in Anaheim, where life drifts slowly along a baseline, but I understand that people in LA are going to want something from me that I don't know how to give them. They're going to want an explanation, a reckoning or, best of all, some Hollywood sign of an emotional breakthrough. I have none of the above. Time stood still while I was in Anaheim, and maybe that was why I chose to go there; I always knew that I could walk for miles each day and still end up back at the exact same spot.

When I come downstairs to find coffee, Wren is sitting at the dining table with a boy who is about eleven or twelve years old. Or he could be fourteen; I actually have no idea. Wren holds up a card with a photograph of a teenage girl on it, and he pulls the same face I do when I'm expected to know anything about technology.

"Okay, Barney, try this one next. If Amy says to you, 'I don't believe you,' and she's making this face, what do you think she really means?"

Barney studies the photograph carefully. Amy is grinning in the photo and she looks like she's being a bitch, but I manage to refrain from joining in the conversation.

"Ummm . . ." Barney frowns and holds the card at a variety of distances as if it's one of those Magic Eye puzzles.

"It's okay, take as long as you need. Do you remember the first clue we look for?"

I walk into the kitchen, where Dylan is grabbing a box of water from the fridge. I guess people are drinking water from boxes in LA now.

"What's Wren doing in there?"

"She's a speech-language pathologist."

"Cool."

Dylan looks defensive. "I said it was all right to use the house for her pro bono cases."

"Of course it is, that's fine."

"I wasn't asking, Grace, you haven't been here for over a year."

We're both silent while I figure out what to say next. I take a banana from the fruit bowl in the middle of the kitchen island, then realize I didn't buy it. I did pay for the bowl, however, and the marble island. I turn the banana over in my hand and try to work out what to do next.

"Do you think your new girlfriend can teach me about nonverbal cues? Or is the catastrophically self-absorbed actress a lost cause?"

Dylan shakes his head but I can tell he's trying not to smile.

"You're not catastrophically self-absorbed, Grace. Humans have just never been your strong suit. It's different. And she's not 'new.' "

I think of all of the questions Dylan has every right to ask of me that I know he isn't going to because he doesn't want to hear the answers. Dylan packs up his laptop and a camera I haven't seen before, and puts them in his camouflage backpack.

"You still dress like a teenager," I say.

"The kids at work call me sir," he says, and he's smiling slightly now.

"You're not even twenty-four."

"I'm working with sixteen-year-olds all day. I'm an old man," Dylan says.

"More surfers?" When I met him, Dylan was making a film about surfers in Malibu. He spent three years following a group of kids, and then he turned it into a Sundance-winning documentary about teen suburban malaise and prescription drug abuse.

"The same ones. It's harder. They're hyperaware of their online presence and, like, their 'aesthetic' this time around."

"And nobody has been maimed yet." I can't resist. He never denied that his first documentary would have been less gripping if one of the surfers hadn't gotten into a car accident while high and lost a hand during the shoot. No pun intended. I hate puns.

Dylan stops by the door, and something flickers across his face.

"What are you doing today?" he asks.

"I've got an NA meeting this morning." The lie slips out of my mouth easily, a throwback to a former version of myself.

Dylan nods, relieved that I'm not going to be pouring out lines of coke in front of autistic children in his house.

As soon as he's gone, I walk up to the pool on our roof. The water has a layer of something oily on the surface and a cluster of dead insects floating in one corner, but I get in anyway so that I can lie on my back while the winter sun explodes behind my closed eyes. I feel weightless for the first time in a while.

I arrange to meet Laurel at Gjelina, a restaurant on Abbot Kinney Boulevard. I stand in front of my untouched closet for nearly half an hour before I leave, stroking the silk dresses and cashmere sweaters that hang from the bar across the top. I pick out a rose-gold, floor-length Calvin Klein slip dress that I wore to the Met Gala on my eighteenth birthday, an evening I mainly spent hiding in the toilets to avoid the lethal combination of small talk and selfies — not because I thought I was any better than anyone there, but because I didn't understand them.

I pull the dress on over the stained Winnie the Pooh T-shirt I'm still wearing, and then I stare at myself in the mirror until it's time to leave. I walk to the restaurant with my skirt trailing on the ground over my Converse, picking up pine needles and dirt. Everything seems too bright.

Abbot Kinney is the same as when I left, only more. It's a ten-minute walk from the coast and it has transformed from a local neighborhood with a few restaurants into a bourgeois, farm-to-table influencer heaven — Beverly Hills by the sea. I push past teenage girls posing with brightly colored juices outside storefronts painted pink just for them, while women with bodies like Victoria's Secret models line up for coffee outside the minimalist spot with the amphitheater seating. There are fewer stores selling healing crystals, more stores selling $800 shirts, and men with full beards wandering aimlessly at eleven a.m. on a Friday, holding babies with names like Hudson and Juniper in slings around their necks.

When I get to the restaurant, Laurel is exactly as she always is, short black Afro, her obnoxiously skinny frame draped in layers of organic cotton. Only the crease between her eyebrows has changed. I resist the urge to reach out and touch the smooth, waxy skin.

"You need a project," she says almost as soon as we've sat down. A wave of mild resentment washes over me, and I wonder if I liked having her around before because she reminds me of my mother.

The server comes over to take our order.

"Can I have the flatbread with goat cheese and caramelized onion?"

Laurel looks horrified. "What the fuck?"

It turns out it's totally okay to drink so much that you have to be carried out the back door of a strip club, but the moment you order carbs for lunch, you're certifiably insane.

"You know they call it a flatbread but it's really a pizza. A *pizza.* Do you want me to take you to an Overeaters Anonymous meeting? I've heard that everyone goes to the one in Silver Lake."

"Jesus, Laurel."

"Okay. But let me know."

I pour some sugar into my black coffee, but I don't mix it because I like the warm sugary paste that collects at the bottom. Laurel is watching me closely. I forgot that this is how everyone looks at me here, as if they're waiting for me to break.

"So should I start telling people that you're back?"

People. She only knows people because of me.

"No."

"Okay, no problem. You need to settle in. Do you want me to speak to Maya about starting up barre and Pilates again?"

"I don't want to do barre or Pilates."

"Okay, sweetie." Laurel raises an eyebrow and looks somewhere over my shoulder like we're on a reality TV show and I'm being unreasonable. Then she starts to flick her hand at me, pinching the air around me.

"Stop adjusting my energy," I say irritably.

"I'm cleansing your aura. Why did you come back, Grace?"

The waitress brings my pizza over, and I inhale the scent of melted cheese. Why did I come back? I think of everything I've ever left behind, of the memories that come back for me just when I think I could be safe, and I feel a kick of shame somewhere deep in the pit of my stomach. *I came back because I was drowning there, too, Laurel. I came back because I have nowhere else to go. I came back because I wanted to start over, but now that I'm here, it's like I've forgotten how I ever pretended to be normal.*

"Because my mom made me," I say, but Laurel doesn't smile.

"How was it with you guys?" she asks seamlessly, as if she remembered all along that my mom and I don't get on.

"Okay, I guess." I shrug. She reaches over

and covers my hand with hers. She's wearing large crystal bracelets, and they rest uncomfortably on my wrist. I resist the urge to move my hand.

"Are you on something?"

"Why is everyone asking me that?"

Laurel frowns at me. "Do you think you should go to a wellness retreat or something for a while? Or you could join that church everyone goes to? With the tattooed pastor? He wears cowboy boots."

"What?" I say, squinting at her. "What about cowboy boots?"

"Trust me, it's a real thing."

"I am not joining a church," I say slowly, "because it's a *thing*. Anyway, my mom's half-Jewish."

"What's that got to do with anything?" Laurel says. "Look, I'm just worried you're not ready to be back in LA. People are going to want answers."

"I don't have any answers," I say, and then I shrug again. "Being back here, I don't know. I feel numb. It's not the worst."

"Numb isn't good for people like me or you," Laurel says, but she can't quite frown in the right way because of the Botox. "Where did you go, Grace?"

CHAPTER ELEVEN

A good memory, this time. One of the few that I cling to as if it could slip away at any moment, as good things have the tendency to do.

Six months after I landed the role in the assassin trilogy, the studio held fan events in three key cities — New York, Beijing and London. The movie was a remake of a comic book, so there was already a network of die-hard fans that came with the territory. They seemed desperate to stake their claim on this new incarnation from the start, devouring and sharing every piece of information from the moment the franchise was announced, so the studio took advantage of it.

The London event would be my first-ever public appearance. We were warned in advance that it would be broadcast live online, and potentially picked up by TMZ and E!, as well as other media outlets. This didn't mean a huge amount to me at the time, other than it being the driving force behind Able's decision to put together an impromptu hair and makeup team, saving me from making any major mistakes so early on in my career.

We were given a hotel room close to the venue, and I sat in front of a large mirror as my new "glam squad" set to work. A Black Eyed Peas song played from the hotel radio, competing with the sound of the football coming from the TV my dad was watching, and I tried not to sneeze every time the woman doing my makeup dusted something over the bridge of my nose. My mom proudly stood watch next to us, instructing the makeup artist on my best features, while Esme curled up on the sofa next to my dad, watching us all over her copy of *Anne of Green Gables*.

"Your collarbone is a work of art," the hairstylist said to my reflection as she brushed out my hair. My mom nodded her agreement, and I tried not to show my surprise. Up until that point I'd barely been aware that my collarbone even existed, let alone that it was something to be championed. I moved the strap of my sky-blue top to see what they were talking about, but they'd already moved on to something else.

"Have you seen her philtrum?" my mom said proudly. "It's been like that since the day she was born."

The makeup artist turned me around and squinted at my lips. She squealed with delight. "The most perfect cupid's bow. You are so lucky," she added seriously.

Philtrum. I memorized the word to look up later.

"I would just kill for the amount of collagen you still have." She sighed then, and I tried to catch my sister's eye in the mirror, but she was already ignoring us all, her face obstructed by her book.

My mom watched as the makeup artist ran a soft brush over my face, turning the apples of my cheeks into shimmering globes, and the hairstylist pulled my hair into braids that would wrap around my head like a crown. Afterward, I tried to remember every other compliment the women paid me, but somehow all I could recall was the five-minute conversation on how best to "approach" my nose.

The women asked me question after question as they worked, and they both laughed hysterically as if they were genuinely enthralled by each response I gave. I'd never really been able to hold an adult's attention before, not like that anyway, and I found it unnerving until I realized what was happening: their jobs were dependent on me liking them. For the first time in my life, the adults around me had something to prove to me, and I wondered how far this extended — whether a day would come when Able and the rest of my new team needed me more than I needed them, or maybe even my parents. I didn't do anything with the knowledge yet, just tucked it away somewhere to come back to later.

When they were finally finished, I got changed into an outfit that a stylist from Los Angeles had chosen for me: a white denim dress and sparkly trainers. I lent Esme the pink beaded bag I had been begging my parents to buy me for years, which, like most things I've ever owned, had lost its appeal almost as soon as it was in my possession. The makeup artist took a photo of the four of us before we left, and I smiled so widely I could feel my lips crack.

We got into a car with blacked-out windows and made stupid jokes about rerouting to McDonald's to ease the tension that was building because none of us had any idea what to expect. We pulled up outside the venue, an old fire station, and I thought I had my nerves under control until I climbed out of the car. My stomach dropped to the floor. There was a crowd of fans outside, chanting something I couldn't decipher, all of whom seemed to know exactly who I was already. I was too disoriented to look any of them in the eye so I rushed past without stopping to sign any comic books or pose for photos.

Once we were inside, we were immediately led past the rows of waiting competition winners and into the VIP section: a champagne bar where people from the studio and production company were hanging out, as well as a few reality TV stars and models who had been invited along for the photo op. People started to slink over to introduce themselves and I shook their hands, my palm firm in theirs, even kissing some of the women on each cheek like I'd seen my mom do. Everywhere I turned, people were either looking at me or deliberately not looking at me, and it felt as if everyone was talking about the unknown girl about to be rescued from a life of mundanity in England and dropped into the heart of Hollywood.

I had made a point of inviting my old school friends along, even though they had all stopped speaking to me as soon as I won the role, effectively freezing me out for my final months in London. I wasn't surprised to see them in the crowd anyway, sitting in a row still wearing their identical yellow puffer jackets. I waved to them quickly as I made my way to the stage and they sat slack jawed, too impressed to even remember not to seem it.

I was miked up and then led onto the stage to sit on a couch next to the other two assassins and the actor playing our mentor in the film, a veteran action star from the nineties. I tried not to notice the number of cameras swinging in front of me and that they were manned by actual humans whose only job was to make sure that every single sound I made was caught and transmitted to God knows how many people watching from home.

Once the crowd had settled down, a famous TV personality introduced us, starting with me. I was fourteen but I looked younger (in the movie I would play a twelve-year-old), and on the whole I was still treated like a child by men like the host. It would be another year before the double entendres and winks would start, or even the questions about boyfriends, the cutesy references to puppy love and first kisses on set.

I was sitting next to the older actor, who smelled like beer, and as I looked out at the rows of expectant fans, some of them more than twice my age, I felt my confidence grow exponentially. I never once felt like I didn't deserve to be there. I answered the host's questions with stories I had already fed the researcher, and I quickly worked out that even if the crowd didn't respond to my words, all I had to do was giggle after I spoke and they would laugh along with me. I felt a strange sense of calm when they did, a warmth spreading through me that made me feel like I was finally good at something.

When the host asked me about my parents, I pointed them out in the crowd and told him that I'd just bought them a house with my first-ever paycheck.

"Wow, you're fourteen years old, and you already bought your parents a house. How does that feel?" he said, and he was so close that I could see the makeup clinging to his wrinkles.

I paused for a moment and looked out at my parents again. My mom was smiling and my dad was leaning forward with tears in his eyes. I could see Able sitting a few seats down from them, too, his eyes trained on me. I flashed him a quick smile before turning back to the host.

"I mean, the house is in Anaheim," I said, deadpan. "It's kind of the armpit of California."

The crowd roared with laughter as the host pretended to be horrified. I followed my words with another giggle and instinctively checked whether Able was pleased with my response. He nodded once and I felt invincible.

When the Q and A ended, the girls from school came running over, bubbling with excitement and asking me endless, inane questions about various things I had ascribed no importance to, like how long it had taken to braid my hair for the event, and whether the male assassin was as cute up close as he appeared onstage. While they were talking I felt a vague disappointment, as if I'd worked myself up for a battle that wasn't worth it in the end.

I left the event flanked by my parents and Esme, and the fans waiting outside went wild for me all over again. My dad had located the car and was already opening the door when my mom grabbed my arm and leaned in close to me.

"Wait," she said, her breath warm and slightly sour from the champagne. "Just wait a moment, Grace."

She pointed to the crowd, and I understood what she meant. My mom wanted me to stop and take everything in, to preserve the moment and store it somewhere so that

I could look back on it when I was old and no longer beautiful, and perhaps had forgotten what it felt like to be loved by people I'd never met. So I stopped, my arm still interlaced with hers, and we gazed out at the crowd together. Goose bumps traveled up my arms as I tried my hardest to absorb every tiny thing about the moment. It was the first time I could remember seeing my mother this proud of me, and now all of these strangers seemed to want to love me too. I smiled and waved at them, and their voices only got louder.

When we eventually got into the car to go home, the sound of the fans' chanting still ringing in my ears, I finally figured out what it was they had been saying all along:

Grace Turner, Grace Turner, Grace Turner.

They shouted it so many times that it had morphed into something else entirely.

CHAPTER TWELVE

When Dylan comes back from work, Wren and I are sitting next to each other on the sofa, sharing a bottle of red wine and watching *Scarface*. Wren knows all the words and has been murmuring along with Al Pacino the whole way through. Dylan stands in the doorway with his hands by his sides, looking between the two of us.

"Grace? Can I speak with you in the kitchen?"

Wren's eyes remain fixed on the TV. I wonder if she really doesn't realize how weird this is or if she's trying to show Dylan how cool she can be with the situation. Either way, I figure she doesn't know what it is to hurt or be hurt yet.

Dylan leans on the island, shaking his head slowly.

"So you're drinking again."

"Well, I was until you came back," I say, rolling my eyes, but he doesn't smile and I

93

instantly regret it.

"Half a glass of red wine, Dylan. It's not a big deal."

"Addiction isn't something you can dip in and out of. It's all a big deal. Wren shouldn't have been drinking in front of you."

I forgot he'd started going to the Nar-Anon family meetings before I left. Being back here, I can remember what it felt like to have the weight of his expectation crushing me every day. There are an infinite number of things that are better than knowing exactly when you're falling short of someone's expectations and still being unable to stop it. Toward the end I think I did it on purpose, just so we'd both have a reason to feel as bad as we did.

"Can I tell you a secret?" I climb onto one of the breakfast stools and rest my chin in my hand. My blood is already warm from the wine, and I don't want to admit it but I already feel calmer, steadier. I study Dylan's face, taking advantage of the fact that he can't seem to look directly at me. He nods, his face tight as he stares down at his hands.

"I don't know if I was ever addicted to any of it. It just seemed easier to say than admitting that I actually liked forgetting who I was for a few hours."

"That's still destructive," he counters.

"Using it to forget who you are."

"I don't know, it's actually been one of the higher functioning relationships in my life," I say, immediately regretting my choice of words.

"Grace," he says, and suddenly my chest hurts.

"Fine," I say, pushing the glass toward him. I make a mental note to hide the bottle of Percocet somewhere other than just under my pillow. Dylan was there when I was first prescribed the pills following a subtle tweak to my nose (a *finessing* more than anything), but he never knew how many times I'd topped up my prescription since then.

"Don't just do it for me though," he says, visibly relieved. Laurel used to call him Dylan the Saint, and he's still the only person I know who never even has to try to do the right thing, it just comes naturally to him. I look over his head, at the fridge where five colorful stick drawings of Wren are pinned up with magnets. Dylan is pretending he's already built the big, perfect family just like the one he left behind.

"Would you mind not saying anything to Wren?" I ask.

"Whatever you want, Grace," he says, but I can see that there are a million things he

95

wants to be saying instead of that. Eventually, he finds one of them. "Did you come back to make it official?"

Dylan looks me straight in the eye for the first time since I've been back, and I feel a familiar kick low in my belly.

"I don't know," I say again. "If you need to for Wren, then we can start —"

"Don't put this all on me," he interrupts, shaking his head. I know there's nothing I can say that will fix anything. People only want to hear the truth if it also happens to be what they want to hear. There is no way of telling him that he never stood a chance with me.

"Can you just explain one thing to me? Because of all the things that went wrong, there is this one thing in particular that stands out for me —" He breaks off, and this time his hurt is drawn so acutely onto his face that I'm the one to turn away. He takes a deep breath and stares up at the industrial chandelier we chose together. "You never called. Not even once."

"I thought it would make it worse," I say, while he stands opposite me, looking as if I have come back solely to set his life on fire all over again.

"Are you happy, Dylan?"

"What's that got to do with anything? Fuck."

It's the last thing that the Dylan I knew would have said, and we are both quiet for a moment.

"It was nothing to do with you. Why I left." I know instantly that it was the wrong thing to say. Dylan takes a small step back as if I've punched him.

"Well that's just fucking great."

His dark hair is sticking out where he's been running his hands through it, and he looks at me differently, as if he's seeing me for the first time. My heart twists in my chest, and I know that he's finally going to ask me why I left, and if he does, I know that I have to find the words to tell him.

He takes a deep breath and speaks slowly, saying instead, "You took your wedding ring off."

I look down at my bare hands, and I know I shouldn't be as surprised as I am. We were always living different versions of the same story.

"Where did it go? I would have taken it back. You knew it was my grandma's."

Where did it go?

It was my first night back in Anaheim. I was fragile, sober for the first time in months, and I felt as if I was absorbing everything around me, but instead of weighing me down, I was lighter than ever before, as if I might float away and nobody would know how to look for me. I went to bed early and I reached for the locket that Dylan had given me just after we met, but it wasn't there. I tore through my suitcase, and when I still couldn't find it, I hid beneath the covers of my childhood bed, my body racked with grief for the death of everything I had tried so hard to be. The next morning I woke early and gave the rest of my jewelry to the first woman I saw on the street, a cleaner for one of our neighbors. It was raining as I handed it over and I told her to give it to her kids, or grandkids, whoever she wanted. A few months later I watched as a bored cashier at CVS bagged my tampons while wearing my old wedding ring.

I look at Dylan and understand that what I say next is important. I'm about to tell him the truth, when Wren starts singing along with a commercial in the next room. Dylan is waiting, staring down at the floor with his jaw clenched, and I think about the infinite number of things I could say to let myself off the hook, the whole while knowing I would only end up hurting him again, and again and again, until neither of us recognized ourselves anymore.

I take a deep breath. "I sold it."

Dylan breathes out heavily, and he can barely bring himself to look at me. We always did have our biggest fights in the kitchen. We were two kids pretending to be adults in an $8 million house with nothing of our own.

CHAPTER THIRTEEN

A story about Dylan, or maybe just a sentence. Dylan looks like Johnny Depp in *Cry Baby* but he says *okeydokey* and does a dance to make me laugh when he's brushing his teeth. No . . . another one. When I first met him, Dylan had a framed print of David Hockney's *Pearblossom Hwy.* hanging on his bedroom wall. He'd had it for years and never once noticed the trash lining the side of the road. I felt bad after I pointed it out because before me he'd only ever seen the endless blue sky and the open road leading to anywhere you wanted to go. Cut Dylan open and he will most likely bleed America and maybe some puppies.

Dylan and I circle each other warily in the house, but somehow I settle into a routine that, if not thrilling, is gently gratifying in its mundanity. I spend most of my time wandering the serene Venice canals. The houses lining the water defy all rules of architecture: a pink Tuscan villa with purple Tudor turrets stands next to a mid-century craftsman bungalow with a photovoltaic canopy on the roof. It's the same way all over LA, as if to belabor the point that you get to choose who you want to be in this beautiful baby country. One morning, I watch a couple row a boat from the dock outside their house to their friends' house, waving a bottle of champagne wrapped in pages from an issue of the *Hollywood Reporter.*

A lone paparazzo half-heartedly waits outside the glass house, but I escape through the back on foot, trailing down to the beach and then cutting back up to Abbot Kinney Boulevard or Rose Avenue. The residents of Venice have always been respectful of my privacy, but I still look at the tarmac, the sky, anywhere but the faces of the people I pass. At night we eat at home, ramen that Wren makes with thick shitake mushrooms floating on the oily surface. Wren never eats much of hers, tipping her slimy noodles down the sink once we're finished, while I pretend not to notice.

"Happy Thanksgiving," Wren says cheerily at the start of one of these meals, my sixth or seventh night at the house. She holds her wineglass up and I clink it lightly with my water glass.

Dylan avoids looking at either of us, staring instead into his bowl of ramen as I realize too late that this probably isn't the Thanksgiving he had planned. He usually goes home to Ohio, and I wonder briefly why he didn't bring Wren back this year, before figuring that he didn't want to leave me by myself. I can only imagine that Dylan's parents already love Wren. Even I can see that she is perfect for him; she probably greets his parents at the airport with fresh-baked cookies and bracelets made by the children of convicts. I try not to think about it anymore, or about my own family at home, eating some god-awful sodium-free bird that my dad will have incinerated beyond recognition and my mom will barely touch.

"Nathan called again. He sounded even more pissed this time and told me to remind you that you're still very much under contract with him," Wren recounts, once we've started eating again.

I swallow a mouthful of soup, trying to disguise the fact that I flinched at the mention of my agent's name even though Dylan is never looking at me anyway. Nathan, Kit and Able. The only holy trinity allowed in my life.

"John Hamilton also called. He wanted to know if you can have lunch together tomorrow. He said you could choose where. He has a project, like this beautiful, powerful love story set in space, but, you know, with a feminist edge, that he needs to talk to you about."

Wren takes a long gulp of wine before adding, "It sounds *super* original."

"I don't know, it could be interesting," Dylan says, sounding anything but interested. John Hamilton directs big-budget action movies, essentially 120 self-indulgent minutes of car chases and half-naked women, so I know he can't really be listening.

"Oh, come on. Hollywood's version of feminism is a Victoria's Secret model knocking men out while wearing a Lycra bodysuit. Right, Grace?" Wren rolls her eyes at me and I smile back at her. Dylan frowns and I realize two things at the exact same moment — one, that I like Wren, and two, that I could probably stay here forever, in this house where nothing is ever asked of me, but that if I do I'm going to ruin everything for Dylan, and probably myself, all over again. I put down my chopsticks and pick out a piece of spongy tofu that drips down my fingers.

"I've been meaning to tell you both that I'm going to move out this week," I say, once I've swallowed it. "I figure it's time to try something different."

Wren looks to Dylan for her cue before she speaks, but the expression on his face makes her stare back down at her lap for a moment before she reassembles her features and smiles at me.

"Are you sure? I can look for somewhere . . . This setup wasn't ever permanent, my lease just came up a couple of months ago so we thought . . ."

. . . *that Dylan's wife had left him a year ago without so much as a working phone number so it should be fine* . . . I finish the sentence for her in my head and resist the urge to laugh.

"No," I say loudly instead, and they both stare at me.

"I'll look at some places tomorrow. Or . . . Laurel will. Venice is *so* over anyway, right?" I say, trying to make Dylan smile with my impersonation of her. He doesn't, and I start clearing away our bowls instead, my obnoxious words hanging in the air like a noose.

Happy Thanksgiving.

■ ■ ■ ■

I meet Laurel at the Butcher's Daughter for brunch the next morning, and she doesn't even raise an eyebrow when I order the egg sandwich with a side of potatoes. I offer her the same courtesy when she orders a glass of rosé. I'm relieved that we're not pretending she's my sober companion anymore, particularly after Dylan told me he saw her hounding everyone for coke at some party he'd been to in the hills just after I went away.

"Have you spoken to Nan? You're everywhere, and not in a good way," Laurel says as soon as her wine has arrived. Nan is — or was — my publicist. Big teeth, a lot of hair, and looks simultaneously as if she could have been a member of the royal family and like she might retire and start breeding Labradors at any given moment. She was very good at her job in an uncompromising way that I know should have impressed me more than it terrified me.

"Not since I've been back. I'm everywhere?"

"Honey, it was okay for you to be clueless when you had a full team around you, but now that you're clearly desperate to do

105

everything on your own, you have to at least let me in on your plans."

"I don't have a plan. You don't *always* need a plan," I say, just to cover up the fact that I only seem to remember I don't have a plan when somebody reminds me. I feel unexpectedly angry that, along with everything else, my time isn't even my own to waste.

"You know you'll be starting from the beginning again if you leave it too long."

"How are you so sure I want to act again?" I ask, frowning.

"Because you were good at it. And because you don't know how to do anything else, unless you've learned the ukulele since I last saw you?"

Laurel taps something out on her phone and then passes it over for me to see. It's a story from a gossip site I don't think I've heard of before. The headline "Drugged and Alone" sits over a photo of my pale, bloated face that must have been taken as I walked through the canals the other day. I look like Charlize Theron in *Monster,* but I tell myself it's just the angle. I should probably wash my hair tonight though.

"The Snap Online has posted about you being back in Venice, living with Dylan and his new girlfriend," Laurel says. "They have a source swearing you spent the year being treated for an opioid addiction in a Nicaraguan rehab. It's getting picked up everywhere."

"Why now?"

Laurel stares at me in confusion.

"Like why didn't they do any stories back when I actually left?"

"When you left you could have been anywhere, shooting a movie in Canada or the Ukraine, recording an album of Scottish pirate metal songs, I don't fucking know. The press isn't going to ask the questions if the fans aren't asking questions. But now you're back and you've got nothing to show for it, and nothing to say about it, and people are starting to notice. You're also dressing like my great-aunt Meryl, and not to be rude, but you're borderline chubby."

"Wow, Laurel," I say, trying to will some tears into existence to make her feel bad. "I never stood a chance with friends like you."

"Do you think you could have Lyme?" Laurel asks, frowning at me.

"I don't have Lyme disease."

"Okay, you have to help me then. What are we doing here? Are we doing 2007 Britney? Or a Marilyn thing? Because you're smarter than this, Grace."

"Why is everyone more worried about me

having a breakdown now than when I was actually having one?"

"Because at least your hair was good then," Laurel sniffs, and I stick my middle finger up at her. I don't hate her as much as I should, which probably says a lot about me.

"Honestly? I just want to be normal, Laurel," I say, but I can hear how cliché it sounds now that I'm back here, and how holing yourself up in your husband's house with his new girlfriend probably isn't the best way to go about it.

"No you don't, Grace, you just think you do," Laurel says, looking disappointed. "Shall we ask our server if she wants to swap places with you? Do you want me to ask if they're hiring here?"

"I'm figuring it out," I say, ignoring her.

"You don't get to choose when to be normal. Don't you realize that?" Laurel says, shaking her head. "That was the deal."

I watch over Laurel's shoulder as a woman in a Lakers T-shirt asks a man at the table next to her something about me. He shrugs, embarrassed when he catches me watching. I reflexively peel my lips back into a smile.

"I'll message you the link to the Nicaragua story," Laurel says. "And you can tell me how you want to respond."

"I still don't —"

"You still don't have a phone. Of course you don't, you little freak," she says almost affectionately. "Okay, I'll print it off for you and give it to you next time I see you, or maybe I'll transcribe it and train a carrier pigeon to drop it off to you, since there seems to be no urgency whatsoever on your part to read it anyway . . ."

Our server places my egg sandwich down in front of me and I watch as Laurel pulls out another phone, this one black.

"Why do you have two phones?" I ask as I chew a mouthful of bread and egg dripping in harissa mayo.

"I have one for play and one for work."

"What . . . what's your exact job at the moment?"

"I'm a life coach. I specialize in pivoting career goals so that they reflect your strengths," Laurel says, completely seriously.

"Have you ever had a career, other than being a career adviser?"

"Of course I have," she says, making a face like I'm an idiot. "You."

After that I finish my sandwich in peace because Laurel seems to have forgotten I'm here, rapidly firing off some emails and texts instead. Despite the glass of rosé, she does seem to have got her shit together since I last saw her.

The soft egg yolk drips down my fingers, and I lick each one before cleaning myself up with my napkin. Laurel is eyeing me with disgust.

"Don't be mad just because you haven't eaten a meal in ten years," I say, and she starts to laugh.

"There she is."

I smile at her, but I'm already bored of our sparring and bored of the couple next to us who are taking photos of me when they think I'm not looking, and bored of this lunch but also bored of anything else I could be doing instead.

"So, this house thing," Laurel says, watching me closely now. "I've pulled some options together for you. Two of them are near me in Silver Lake, and two of them are on the beach. I know you want to be away from Dylan and what's-her-bitch, but you can't let them drive you out of the entire Westside."

"Wren. She's actually a delight."

"What happened to you at home? Are your parents loving or something?" Laurel asks, and I forgot that she could occasionally make me laugh.

"Something like that. Let me see the beach houses."

I wait as she pulls them up. There are certain things that nobody teaches you when you have people who are paid to do everything for you. How to be alone is one, and doing anything useful online is another. Or at least it was for me. My agent and manager picked up on the fact that I'd never been allowed a smartphone as a kid, and decided to project an image of me as an extinct species in the age of the overshare — a millennial without a social media presence. No hawking of detox teas or dating apps for me. Instead, they curated a portrait of a reluctant young indie actress trying to live a normal life in Venice with her talented documentary-filmmaker husband. Much was made of the fact that I used a flip phone and had never posted a selfie anywhere. In reality, my movies were never real indies and I was never really cool, but that didn't seem to matter. Working with Able was supposed to give me the exposure I needed, without having to force myself on the public in other ways to stay relevant. It was a luxury I always knew I was lucky to have, despite everything else that came with it.

I had two carefully chosen brand partnerships — one with a French fashion house and one with a company who made instant film, and I walked in fashion shows in Paris and London only if I knew the designers and they asked me. Other than that, self-promotion was kept to a minimum. As planned with my team, I went to my own movie premieres and showed up at awards shows if something I was in was nominated, but I made sure to seem as uncomfortable as I could (without appearing ungrateful) about having to do either. It helped that Dylan wasn't famous in the same way I was, so we were left alone by the press most of the time. We didn't go to any of the new clubs or restaurant openings in Malibu or West Hollywood, and I was never photographed on a yacht in a bikini or at a certain pop star's New Year's Eve party. All of my bad behavior was carried out behind the closed doors of private residences in Venice and the Hollywood Hills, and, as a result, I was exempt from much of the tabloid mauling my peers experienced. I was on another planet to them all, and even though it hadn't been my idea, I thought I liked it that way.

"So even though Venice is almost over, I've found one place. It's beautiful, and the security system is next-level shit. Some Russian oligarch lived there before he disappeared." Laurel shows me her phone. The house is angular, imposing, heavy on the cement.

"That used to be a drug dealer's house," I say, shaking my head.

"You're right. Bad vibes. And we should know. Lol." I forgot that Laurel occasionally says *LOL* out loud.

"Okay, so this one could work, but it's a weird location. It's right next to that mobile home community in Malibu. Do you know which one I mean? I think the guy who played James Bond moved there when he had that B12 deficiency and lost his mind."

The house is a Cape Cod–style bungalow with white clapboard and navy shutters, and a small white porch with three steps down onto the sand. I scan the information below the photographs.

"Coyote Sumac?" I ask, trying to keep my voice level.

"Yeah. I once woke up at a house there, and the guy actually had a glow-in-the-dark mural painted on his bedroom walls. He was a grown man. Creepy as hell. The houses are right on the beach though. I think it started as a cult in the eighties, and Malibu developers are still so pissed because it's the most *prime* real estate, but it's just full of burnouts smoking weed and surfing every day and, worse than that, *talking* about smoking weed and surfing every day." I

113

hand Laurel her phone back and she shakes her head. "You're right. You don't need that shit. And there isn't a single photo of the interior, so it's probably a sex dungeon inside."

I know exactly where the Coyote Sumac community is, I just didn't know the name of it until now. Three years earlier, at my lowest point ever, I had looked down on the perfect, wisteria-framed houses and wished more than anything in the world that I was hidden safely inside one of them. I try to focus on the next house Laurel shows me, but when she talks, each word floats into my ears like a sound I've never heard before.

CHAPTER FOURTEEN

The day before I'm supposed to move into a house on Laurel's street in Silver Lake, a woman turns up on the doorstep of the glass house. She rings the bell in the late afternoon, wearing a navy silk wrap dress and pumps, her dark hair pulled back, no jewelry, no makeup.

Dylan is on his way out when she arrives, and he finds me standing by the door in my old white bathrobe, staring at the security monitor. We watch her on the screen for a moment, shoulder touching shoulder for the first time in over a year.

"Want me to tell her to fuck off?" he asks.

"Do you know who she is?"

"Nah, she looks like a reporter though."

"I'll speak to her."

I open the door and Dylan slips out, tapping the side of his head at her as he does. The woman nods at him briefly and waits for him to pass before she turns back to me.

"My name is Camila Amri. I'm working on a story for *Vanity Fair* that I think you could be interested in."

I turn around, leaving her on the doorstep with the door wide open.

She follows me through to the living room, every step hammering a small mark in the wooden floor. She carries herself in the way that people who were overweight as children do — as if they can't quite get used to their impossible lightness.

I sit on the sofa, peeling my feet out from the sticky Japanese slippers I'm wearing, and tucking them underneath me. Camila sits opposite me on the green velvet armchair that appeared in the living room one day, around the same time all the expensive art was hung on the walls. People were always scuttling around me and rearranging things, but I never thought it was weird because it just felt like another movie set.

"I like your Christmas tree. It's very . . . authentic."

"Thanks. The decorations were made by real-life, authentic kids."

I watch Camila as she works out what to say next. The Christmas tree has thrown her.

"Aren't you supposed to speak to my publicist before you turn up on my door-

116

step? Or my manager?"

"Do you still have either?"

"I'm not sure."

"I'm not going to lie to you. If we do this right, it could be huge for us both," Camila says, but she's frowning now because this already isn't going as planned. I keep my face neutral and maintain eye contact, which unnerves her even more.

"Why did you leave LA?" she asks, shifting in her seat.

"Aren't you supposed to be a rising star in journalism?" I ask as she wipes her palms on her dress, leaving a damp pattern on the silk.

"I don't understand the question."

"You just asked me the same question the guy at the gas station asked me yesterday."

"You know I have to ask it," she says quietly. She rearranges her hands in her lap, and her cheeks are flushed.

"Did you used to be fat?" I ask, and because I'm almost fat now, I sort of think I can get away with it.

"Have you done all of this so that you won't be objectified anymore?" she says quickly, pointing at my lap, and I look down. My bathrobe has creased and is exposing the soft, white part of my stomach and my beige underwear thick with pubic hair.

"I'm sorry," she says, holding out her hands, and I can see that I've bullied her into being vicious.

"Women apologize too much," I say.

"Grace. I think you know what I'm about to ask you. Do you want to tell me about Able Yorke?"

I fold my hands in my lap and lean toward her, my chest constricting and exploding at the same time. My breath comes short and fast, out, out, out like a horse in labor. I know what she wants from me, but I can't give it to her because the story isn't going to be what she thinks it is. It never is.

"Get out of my house."

After she's gone, I lock the door and slump against it, pulling my robe tight around me like a blanket. My stomach is knotted, the blood still ringing in my ears when a strange sensation starts to thread its way through the panic. Somehow, this stranger has identified something in me that nobody else could, something that is as much a part of me as my childhood, my marriage, any work I've ever done, but that I've kept hidden in the loneliest depths of my mind since it happened. Even though I know that I will never

118

be able to tell her my story, with all of the nuances, the gray areas I take up, for some reason just the recognition that something may have been wrong, even if it's just a hunch, even if she forgets about it tomorrow, is making me aware that I exist. And not ten years ago, or even five, but right fucking now.

For the first time in a while, I sleep through the night. In the morning I call Laurel to tell her I've changed my mind. I want to take the house by the ocean after all.

CHAPTER FIFTEEN

On the set of the movie, there were three of us, three teen assassins with exactly the same job, but it was obvious to everyone that I was his favorite, his project. Able's beloved grandmother had been British, and he would bring English delicacies to the set especially for me. Once we had a tea party in his trailer with a hamper filled with buttery shortbread and exotic teas he'd had delivered from Fortnum & Mason. The biscuit tin was shaped like a carousel and played tinny circus music while we ate. Able was the most engaging adult I'd ever met, and I idolized him from the moment we started working together. I knew I could do anything he asked because his belief in me made me feel untouchable.

I learned quickly that Able was also tough, resourceful and single-minded, and that nobody could match his extraordinary talent and influence in the industry. He had been an actor before he became a director, and his own history was stranger than fiction, closer to the mythical American dream than any of the films he has directed. As the legend goes, Able was born to a teenage heroin addict in Kansas and spent two weeks on the streets with her before he was adopted by her mother. He moved with his grandmother to Salt Lake City, where he was the sole focus of her love, encouragement and pious affection until his eighth birthday, when she died suddenly of pneumonia. Two months after her death, Able was discovered living alone in the derelict basement of the church she attended, and was placed into foster care until he was discovered again at the age of twelve, this time by a model scout who spotted his teardrop dimples and glittering eyes at a carwash in a town called Lark.

From his first modeling job, Able worked like someone who had promised himself he would never have to eat rats for lunch again. His story became legendary and his face more famous than many of the actors he cast in his films. He was adored by the media and moviegoers alike. When I started working with him, he was already rich in everything that was valued in a man, his beauty only serving to soften the blow of

121

his temper on set. I watched intelligent, powerful women melt at his feet every day, and even though nobody really knew how much of his backstory was real, I realized early on that it didn't seem to matter.

One morning, around halfway through the three-month shoot of that first movie, Able pulled me aside to tell me he wanted me to do one of the stunts myself. Up until that point we had all been using stunt doubles, but Able decided he needed a continuous shot of my face in this particular scene to make it work. Able had made his name shooting gritty, character-driven projects, so this adaptation was a big departure for him, and he often seemed visibly frustrated with the limitations the genre placed on him.

The scene in question showed my character fighting a bomb maker in a New York City apartment, culminating with me being pushed backward off a fire escape. The stunt wasn't advanced — all I needed to do was fall out of a first-story fire escape onto a crash pad below; the problem was that I had been acutely phobic of heights for as long as I could remember. Still, when Able asked, I nodded and listened closely all morning as the stunt coordinator fitted me with pads underneath my costume and taught me how to land the "suicide" fall: on my back, with flat feet, bent knees, and my arms stretched out to the sides at a forty-five-degree angle, making sure to exhale heavily on impact. Once I had perfected the fall on the pit mat, I obediently climbed up the fire escape.

Once I was at the top, I gripped the railing with hands already slick with sweat as Able called action from below. I stood on the edge of the fire escape, swaying slightly as multiple cameras swooped menacingly around me. The man playing my adversary paused to ask if I was okay, but it sounded like he was speaking to me through a crashing waterfall. Panic waded through my veins as I sank down to sit on the platform, resting my head on my knees. My ears were ringing as somewhere below, in another world, I heard Able shout, *"Cut!"* The stunt coordinator made a move to help me down, but Able put his hand out to stop him.

The climb back down the fire escape to the back lot was the most excruciating moment of my life to date. Each step felt like it took five minutes. By the time I reached the bottom, I was trembling all over, and nobody on set would meet my eye. They knew I was Able's problem because that's how our relationship had worked up until then — I had made it clear that I didn't need anyone else. Able called lunch, and the crew dispersed, muttering clichés about never working with animals or children. They knew they didn't owe me anything.

Able beckoned me over to where he was talking quietly with his assistant director. When I reached the two men, the AD took one look at Able's face and headed off to craft services, leaving me alone with him.

"What happened up there?" Able asked, so quietly that I had to lean in to hear him. For the first time, I noticed how his incisor teeth protruded slightly, sharp and shiny with spit.

I pulled away and shrugged as if it wasn't a big deal. "I'm scared of heights. I thought you knew."

Able narrowed his eyes at me and I realized instantly that I had played it wrong, that this wasn't the time for the insouciance, the nihilism, whatever it was he normally encouraged in me. I shifted, trying to become who he needed me to be.

"I'm sorry," I said.

"I don't need you to be sorry, Grace. I just need you to step up," Able said, and even though his words were gentle, his voice was different, as if he was struggling to disguise something I couldn't identify. "Can you do that for me?"

"I don't know," I said, still thinking it was

a question.

Able pressed his lips together tightly. Later, I would become an expert in reading his body language and adapting, but since Able had never been anything but generous and kind toward me up to that point, I had no idea how to navigate what was to come. Behind him, I could see Lorna and Ted, the other two assassins, watching us, and I wondered if I was imagining the satisfaction on their faces. I had never once considered how it felt to be invisible next to me.

"Anyone can be scared," Able said slowly, and when I turned my attention back to him, everyone else faded into the background. "I'm not interested in fear. I'm interested in how we get past the fear. And how do we do that?"

"By doing the thing we're scared of," I said, and Able smiled slightly. I had been listening.

"That's right, Gracie. So do you want to try it again? I'll spot you myself this time."

I stood, frozen at the prospect of letting Able down but equally aware that I couldn't do what he was asking of me. When I didn't reply, Able's face started to change, and I watched as his eyes became flat and his lip curled as he studied me with barely concealed disgust. It was only when it was gone that I realized the extent of his beauty, how safe I felt when he was looking at me.

"Did you forget how lucky you are to be here?" he asked. "It's sort of interesting to me that with all these hardworking, talented people around us, somehow it's you wasting everyone's time."

"I'm really sorry," I said, but the tiny voice saying the words didn't sound like my own. I felt scared, disoriented, as my heart rate picked up in my chest.

"You already said that," Able said, and as he spoke he watched me closely, learning more about my malleability, my eagerness to please with every move I made. "I just wonder if Lorna, or Ted, would like to do the stunt instead. Lorna has been particularly impressive in her scenes. She's grown up a lot in the past few months."

"If Lorna does it . . . will she get my part?" I asked, unsure of how to verbalize what I really meant. My stomach grumbled loudly with hunger at that moment, and I felt betrayed by my body for showing weakness.

"I really can't promise you anything right now," Able said. "A film set is like an ecosystem, Grace, and if you refuse to play your part in it, you're putting everyone at risk."

"Nathan said I wouldn't have to do any

heights," I said, and my voice was raw with the burden of letting him down. "When we signed. He said you would use a stunt double for that."

"I don't care about Nathan," Able said, irritated at the mention of my agent's name. "I care about what's best for my movie."

"Can I just call my mom quickly?" I asked desperately. By this point my family had already moved into the house in Anaheim, but my mom was staying with me in a hotel room in LA for the duration of the shoot. At first, she had seemed to enjoy coming to set even more than I did, but once I was allocated a studio teacher to advocate for me on set, Able told my mom that her presence wasn't necessary anymore. I figured it was just all part of the agreement we'd made with him, the clear separation between work and home, only by the time I was dropped back to the hotel room each night, I was so exhausted I could barely string a sentence together. My mom's questions had long since stopped and the first signs of resentment were already showing, but I still matched the rhythm of my breathing to hers when we went to sleep at night, the air conditioner humming gently in the background.

"You can call your mom whenever you

want," Able said, impossible to read. "But I don't see how that will change anything. She's already aware of this."

"You spoke to her?" I asked, wondering if I'd somehow misunderstood the situation and the disdain I always secretly felt he reserved for her. Maybe she had always been welcome on set by Able: perhaps it was me who had never wanted her there.

"I spoke to her this morning. She promised me you'd be able to deliver on this."

"Is she going to come here?" I asked. My mom knew how terrified I was of heights. She'd had to carry me down from the diving board at our local swimming pool countless times when I was younger. The memory of her warm skin, sweet with sun lotion, made my eyes prick with tears.

"Grace, you know you told me it was too much of a distraction when she visits. I'm trying to understand you right now, but you're not making sense. I've noticed you've been doing this more and more lately — distorting reality so that it fits in with a narrative you've created in your mind."

"What do you mean?" I asked, panicked.

"I mean that it's something we have to watch out for."

I nodded, and my grip on reality loosened with every word he spoke.

"Look, I don't care about your mom, I don't care about Nathan, and I don't care about Lorna," Able said then, his face softening slightly. "I care about you. Do you think I'd ever let anybody hurt you?"

I shook my head, still fighting back tears.

"Because what I'm hearing when you say you don't want to do it is that you don't trust me. Do you remember what I told you? That other people are going to try to get involved and get between us, but it doesn't matter as long as we understand each other?"

I nodded but my legs still felt weak with fear of letting him down.

"I know you better than anyone in the world," Able said. "Do you trust me?"

When I looked up and saw that he was almost smiling at me, my heart rate started to slow slightly. I nodded again.

"So will you try again for me?"

"I can try again," I said, and when he broke into his perfect, famous grin, I felt so incredibly relieved to have made him happy that I figured it may even be worth going up there again.

Despite my trust in Able, my studio teacher, Carrie, still found me crying a little in my trailer at the end of lunch break, as I was putting my padding back on. I liked

Carrie a lot. Her job was to make sure I didn't fall behind with my education, but also to act as my representative and guardian on set. She had a voice like calamine lotion, and when we met she told me that her allegiance was to me, and that she would be my voice on set whenever I needed her. Carrie was the first person in my life who ever admitted to me that things were different for women, particularly in Hollywood, and she was also the first person to ever call me smart. She made me promise I would get my California Certificate of Proficiency, because the industry was particularly rough for the women who men figured they could walk all over. Even after she was long gone, I tried to see my three hours of lessons a day as something more than just an irritating distraction between scenes, despite Able making it clear that they broke my focus and set us back hours each time. After a while he just made fewer allowances for them so that the teacher would have to scramble to make up the required three hours a day in small pockets of ten or twenty minutes between takes.

When Carrie asked why I was crying, I told her. As the words flew out of my mouth before I could censor them, I watched her cheeks turn a marbled pink on my behalf.

After I had finished, she walked up to the trailer Able used as an office, and opened the door without knocking. I hid in the classroom tent, but an assistant soon found me and led me up to Able's trailer, a place that had always been my safe haven up until that point.

Carrie was standing just inside the door with her arms folded across her chest. She had taken off her glasses, and her mouth was set in a grim line. It looked like she'd been crying. Able was sitting by his desk, leaning back in his chair with one leg resting across the other. He eyed me with interest as I approached.

I looked between the two of them and then down at the steel-toed combat boots my character always wore. I already felt disoriented.

"Carrie told me that you've been crying. Is this true?"

He sounded benign enough, but I could hear the real question he was asking: *Don't you trust me?*

"You can tell me what happened. Were you still worried about the stunt?"

I raised my eyes from the floor to look at this person who had changed my life overnight. I thought of what would happen if I got fired from the film — my visa would be voided and my family would be unceremoniously shuttled back to London, my life returning to the bleak monochrome it had been for as long as I could remember. I would have to go back to my old school where nobody was talking to me, and not only would I have let everyone on set down, but it would also mean no more special attention from my parents, no more running around a studio back lot in somebody else's clothes, no more room service waffles with thick syrup and strawberries at midnight, and no more Able. I could barely remember what my world had been like before him, before this movie. I felt strong because Able had told me I was strong, impressive because he had treated me that way since the day I met him. Every single move I had made since then was because he told me to, and I felt frozen with fear at the prospect of it all ending here. Maybe Able was right when he said he knew me better than anyone else — he had always known just how much I wanted it all.

I bit my lip and stared down at the floor. "It's not true."

Able nodded once.

"Are you saying that Carrie is lying?"

I turned to Carrie, and in her bald, stricken face I saw a version of myself that I didn't want to acknowledge existed. I could smell her weakness, and it made me resentful.

"She's lying," I mumbled, without looking at either of them.

"Say it properly, Grace," he said, and I stood up a little straighter.

"Carrie is lying."

It's been hard to forget the way Carrie looked at me after I said that, like she just felt sorry for me. Able let her go on the spot, and she would be the last studio teacher I ever got close to. Over the years to come, Able would repeat the same move with various on-set teachers and guardians and, eventually, with my own parents. The only difference was that the pity on Carrie's face would soon be replaced with a look of betrayal as people became more convinced of my complicity. Eventually it would just become easier not to get close to anyone.

That day, I left the trailer and climbed back up the fire escape steps as if I were on my way to my own funeral. My hands were slipping down the handrails and I willed myself not to cry again. I knew that it was my last chance. When I reached the top, I closed my eyes and told the actor playing opposite me to push me as soon as Able shouted action.

I felt a pair of hands on my chest and then the sensation of falling, of the wind rushing on either side of me, and it was so instantly exhilarating that I had to try not to shriek. It felt like I was flying. When I hit the crash pad, the crew cheered for me, but I barely heard them. The only thing I cared about was that Able had been right all along. The relief I felt was overwhelming: I was at peace again.

Able made me do the stunt over and over again until I got tired and careless and I cracked my head on the railing on the way down. Afterward, Able took me into his trailer and stroked my hair as I cried, while Fleetwood Mac played from his radio. The dull, thudding pain felt rich and delicious because he was being so nice to me again now that I'd shown him just how much he could trust me.

I promised myself that he would never have a reason to doubt me again. After that, whenever I was scared, it was always him I thought to run to.

CHAPTER SIXTEEN

The road down to my new house from Pacific Coast Highway is steep and winding. I can see Dylan in my rearview mirror, driving behind me and wearing the Ray-Bans that I think were once mine but that maybe I stole from him first. We both get out of our cars at the bottom of the track, standing in a thick cloud of dust.

Coyote Sumac is a small, U-shaped community located on the beach underneath a bluff in Malibu. The houses are mostly clapboard bungalows with a few more-modern properties built from steel and glass. Vines of bougainvillea and wisteria frame the wraparound wooden porches, and a few of the houses have golf carts with surfboards strapped onto them parked alongside the Jeeps or pickup trucks in the driveways. Like Laurel said, this is a community for surfers and hippies and, as of now, famous former child actors who just want to be left alone.

My house is set away from the others, closer to the beach, and it is unfathomably dark inside with a damp patch the shape of Russia on the ceiling over the bed. The bungalow came with a TV, a cream leather sofa with grease stains on the arms, and a red-framed double bed in the bedroom. When we saw the inside, after a last-minute viewing with a sweaty real estate agent who couldn't stop apologizing, Laurel described it as "the kind of place an abusive husband rents when he can't accept that he's finally been kicked out of the family home, so he, like, gets this place for when the kids come on weekends, but they never turn up so he hangs himself in the shower to get his revenge. *This* shower, Grace," while acting as if she were planning to commit me at the closest opportunity. Say what you will about Laurel, but she really knows how to paint a fucking picture.

Dylan and I unload the boxes from his car in silence, and when we've finished, he stands in my doorway with his hands in his pockets.

"Thank you, Dylan," I say awkwardly, because here we are — ten boxes containing my only possessions in the world. "I think I can do the rest."

136

"Okay." He nods, but shows no signs of moving. "Look, are you sure you don't just want to take the glass house? I'm serious. I can be out in two days, max."

"No way, I don't want to be there anymore. Too many . . . stairs," I finish lamely. Dylan looks at me for a moment and then surprises me by starting to laugh.

"All right, Grace. We wouldn't want you having to face any stairs."

I grin as he shakes his head. I remember now that sometimes, when Dylan smiles, I would do anything in the world to keep him happy.

"Wren said she'll come check on you in a couple days. You know you should really get a cell phone, it's kind of insane."

"No, I know. I will."

"Ask Laurel. I'm sure she can help you out," he says, without any of the resentment that comment would once have elicited. He turns to leave and then stops again, just before he opens the front door.

"So you're sure . . . you want to do this?" he asks.

"Of course. Why wouldn't I?" I ask. He holds my gaze and then he just shrugs. He holds one hand up and then turns away. "Call me if you need anything."

"Will do."

I watch him walk down the porch without turning back. You could write a symphony with our silences.

When the end came, it was so quiet it was deafening. It was a cool morning last November, only a couple of days after my final movie, *Lights of Berlin,* was released. I was sitting on the balcony outside our bedroom, smoking a cigarette and watching the choppy water crash against the coastline as the sky lightened. I wore a knitted sweater and plaid pajama bottoms, and I had the unfair clarity of someone who hasn't been to sleep yet, mainly because I'd just got back from a party where I was sprinkling Molly into my own drink like it was sugar.

Dylan woke up and found me on the balcony, the tension already marked across his face and in his shoulders. I figured that someone had told him what I'd been doing, even though he wouldn't allude to it directly. He never did and I never apologized. I would just read it in his face, and everything he didn't say. This time, though, he sat next to me and lit his own cigarette, and then he turned to ask me something he never had before.

"Why do we find it so hard to be happy?"

It's me, I wanted to tell him, but some

things are too obvious to say. It was one of those days, weeks, months when I felt the world too strongly. My skin had been peeled away, my chest cracked open, and I was exposed to everything around me in high-definition, 3-D surround sound. The sight of an old man eating ice cream alone or an unhappy silence between a couple I didn't even know would settle somewhere deep within me. The sound of a car horn or siren two blocks away would leave me shaking, and I'd mistake every piece of trash on the floor for a dead animal, my brain contorting and playing tricks on me, just like Able always said it did. Each moment would claim another inch of my mind until, bit by bit, it wasn't my own anymore. I was strung out and so tired of feeling too much that I guess at some point it just became easier to not feel anything at all.

I looked out to the point where the charcoal morning sky met the ocean, and that was when I decided to tell Dylan what it was I had been trying to drown out all this time. What everything always led back to. For the first time in my life, I had realized with perfect clarity that I was fucking something up before it was too late, and I even knew the way out.

"I need to tell you something," I started,

and my throat was thick and tight, as if my body still wasn't ready to say the words I'd never said out loud. Dylan waited.

"When I first got to LA, I didn't know what I was doing. I was by myself and things happened that I don't think should have happened, and I want to believe it wasn't my fault, but I'm too close to it. I don't know if I will ever be able to explain it, even to you, but I know that I want to try, and maybe that's enough for right now."

The sentences were coming out as heavy fragments, but I knew that Dylan could tell it was important from the way he froze next to me. I wrapped my arms around myself and allowed myself to look at him just once more before I started again. I wanted to see the openness on his face, the way his bronze eyes softened when they were focused on me, but instead I saw something unexpected. Dylan, who was supposed to love me more than anything in the world, whom I needed to love me unquestioningly, especially when I didn't deserve it, wanted me to stop talking. He wanted me to save him from the burden of knowing the truth.

"Grace. I can't . . ." He didn't finish but I understood perfectly because he looked exactly how I felt. He didn't want to know because he wanted my story only to be his story, two lonely teenagers who fell in love in the weirdest city in the world and managed to make it work. He didn't want to hear about the story before him, the thing that clung to my back whenever I left the house, or that sat on my chest whenever I tried to sleep.

My heart split into millions of pieces.

When I could speak again, I changed the subject, and we spoke about where we would go on vacation next. Dylan talked about sleeping under the stars in Holbox, just like he used to on camping trips when he was a kid. I already knew that I was leaving, and maybe Dylan did, too, because his words carried an unusual force that morning, as if he were trying to pin me down with them.

The thing was, I could see with uncharacteristic clarity what would happen if I stayed. I would hurt him over and over again until neither of us could look at the other, and this time it would be irrefutably, unforgivably on purpose.

We got into bed soon after that, and Dylan fell straight back to sleep with a slight smile on his lips, the way he always did, and I curled into his back, breathing in his sandalwood smell. After he left for work, I took six Percocets and then curled up in a ball on

141

the cool tiles of the bathroom floor, sobbing like I hadn't since I was a baby. When the world around me finally started to fray at the edges, drifting out of reach, I called Laurel, who arranged for an unmarked ambulance to rush me to the emergency room for treatment.

Two days later, I was back in Anaheim.

Nobody ever thought to ask me why I'd done it.

The rental feels quiet once Dylan has left. I push the thought of him out of my mind in exactly the same way I have for the past year, and I start to unpack the boxes. I didn't know what was officially mine and what was Dylan's, or what he would notice or miss, or think of me when he didn't see, so I brought only clothes with me, even though I've been wearing the same slip dress with college sweaters since I've been back in LA. Wren told me that she's already spotted three women wearing the same outfit in Venice. Maybe they hate the sight of their own skin too.

I step out onto the porch and squint up at the peach house on the hill above. I can't make out whether anyone is home, or even if Able's car is in the drive, and I feel breath-less and weak, my heart twisting like a knife in my chest. My nightmares all orbit around this house, yet somehow I have made my own way back here. I wonder if I thought that being so close might make me feel safer, when the truth is I can't control any of it from here any more than I could from Anaheim.

I walk back inside the bungalow and sit on the sofa, staring at the blank wall in front of me as I try to fight against the familiar feeling of being dragged down to the dark place, dislodging the unruly shadows that have settled within me since I've been back in the city. The most vicious demons have always been my own, and I've never learned how to protect myself from them. I have tried moving quietly through the world, figuring that if I could just forget what happened, then I could move on, but maybe it doesn't work like that. Maybe it's never been that simple.

CHAPTER SEVENTEEN

Everyone kept telling me how grateful I should be that Able had chosen me as his protégé. My agent called it a gift. That's also what Able called it when he first made me touch him, at the age of fifteen, on the last day of that first movie shoot. He placed my hand on his erection over his jeans and told me that it was a secret gift between the two of us, because we had this special connection that nobody else understood.

That's how it went for the next couple of years: he would shower me with gifts and attention during the first half of filming and then would pull back so suddenly that I was left chasing after him, needing his approval and praise in the same way I needed oxygen to breathe. Just like that day with the stunt fall, he would push me to my limit in every possible way. He would criticize everything from my weight to my American accent to my lack of emotional depth in a scene,

144

constantly belittling me on set and pushing me to extremes both physically and mentally before leaving his juniors to deal with me when I inevitably broke. I was exhausted, desperate to please, skinny as a stray dog and covered in sores, but still he would force me to reshoot the same scene over and over again, running well into the early hours of the morning until every single member of the crew hated the sight of me. Then, just as I was giving up hope, certain that my new life was over and he had finally realized that I wasn't the person he thought I was, Able would welcome me back into the glowing orbit around him. If I tried to talk to him about how he'd treated me, he would tell me that I had clearly misunderstood, reminding me that my brain had the tendency to work against me, and that I was lucky he knew me well enough to understand me. As he spoke, relief would flood through me in waves so intense I often found myself crying. He was everything to me — my mentor, my boss, my family — and being close to him made me feel as if I was finally doing something right. Only at that point Able would expect his own reward, too, making me kiss and touch him again on the final day of shooting or at the wrap party. As soon as it happened, I felt sick with confusion, regretting ever having courted his attention. I never told him to stop, and hadn't I worked that much harder than the others to earn his rare praise? Hadn't I felt colder when he wasn't looking at me? I figured that I must be doing something awful to make him act like this, but I couldn't figure out what it was, or how to stop it — I only knew that I deserved it.

I doubted myself and everyone around me, but rarely Able. Everyone had told me about this precious gift, so I took it.

CHAPTER EIGHTEEN

An hour later, I'm driving up the dirt track with my car radio blasting a bad eighties power ballad at an unholy volume because, occasionally, if it's the right song and it's loud enough, music can drown out even the ugliest thoughts in my mind.

The December air is crisp so I roll the windows down, but I have to close them when I end up eating dust from the cars speeding alongside me on PCH. I drive slowly, with no real place to be and only a vague idea of what I want, but I still have to brake suddenly whenever a car in front of me decides to swing into a free beach parking space at the last minute. After a couple of miles, I spot a sign for an independent drugstore, and I signal to turn into the parking lot.

In the store, I approach a girl a few years younger than me. She is standing behind the cash register and playing on her phone.

Her lip is pierced in two places, and she barely looks up when I speak to her.

"Hi, I'm looking for some binoculars."

"Sorry, ma'am, this is a pharmacy." She flicks at one of her lip rings with her tongue. I wait for her to finish. "We don't sell binoculars."

"I understand. Do you know where would sell binoculars?"

"There's a Best Buy kind of near Santa Monica . . . You might want to try there."

I nod but I don't move, and she seems worried for me.

"How far is it from here?"

She furrows her brow. "Don't you have an iPhone, ma'am?"

"Look I'm really sorry, but can you stop calling me ma'am? I'm twenty-two years old," I say, folding my arms across my chest. "And no. Do you sell phones here?"

She shakes her head.

"You can get that at Best Buy too. Take a left out of here. Maybe fifteen to twenty miles?" she says, and when I still don't move, she scribbles down some directions on a Post-it and hands it over to me.

"Thanks," I say, debating whether or not I need to tip her. I feel bad for snapping at her, but when I try to hand her twenty dollars, she seems so alarmed that I stuff it back in my bag.

"Are you okay?" she asks as I'm leaving, and she's looking me up and down. I look down, too, at my sweat-stained Lakers T-shirt hanging over the slip dress, now torn and ragged at the hem, and a pair of promotional Crocs that I found at the house in Venice on my feet. They're lined with sheepskin and they're the most comfortable things I've ever owned.

"I think so?" I say, but I must not be very convincing because she still seems like she feels sorry for me.

I get back in the car and just sit for a moment, sweat pooling on my upper lip. I have let other people do everything for me for my entire life, and most of the time I didn't even know it was happening. Even after I met Dylan, we were only ever pretending to be like any regular college-age couple when really we had a slew of assistants, drivers, wellness coaches and housekeepers organizing our lives. Groceries magically appeared in our fridge every week, and we would stand next to precooked meals from our chef even as we ordered Vietnamese food or sushi to be delivered to our door. I'm not sure I could tell you how to call a cab or make a cup of coffee if somebody were holding a machete to my throat, and what's

149

worse, I don't think I've ever realized that until now.

"I'm looking for binoculars," I tell the first person I see when I walk into Best Buy, twenty miles and three perilous U-turns later. The sales assistant is in his late teens and has an unappealing film of baby fluff covering his upper lip. The rest of his face and neck is clean-shaven, other than one more distinct patch of fuzz over his prominent Adam's apple. When I see how it leaps around when he swallows, I can understand why he was reluctant to shave it. His name tag says Ethan.

"Oh wow. Binoculars. For bird-w . . . watching?" The poor guy is physically shaking. He's already recognized me. I keep having to remind myself that I'm back in LA, where everyone is raised on a diet of *Access Hollywood* and E!, and Oscar nominations are discussed over a bowl of Cheerios in the morning.

I try to seem humble and grateful while Ethan leads me down the correct aisle and waits in front of the binoculars for my response.

"Dolphin watching, whale watching. I suppose maybe some birds."

Ethan nods and passes me a box from the

shelf. While I'm looking at it, he puts one hand inside his pocket, his eyes scanning to check if anyone is watching us, and then he pulls out his phone. After a moment I shrug, understanding that he wants a photo with me. Ethan adjusts the angle of his hand so that we're both in the frame, and just as I'm attempting to assemble my features into something vaguely acceptable, he takes the photo. A flash goes off from the front, startling me. He puts his phone back into his pocket and takes the binoculars from me.

"I actually also need to get a phone, can you help me with that too?" I ask, thinking of Laurel.

Ethan leads me to a different section of the painfully bright store. I request the most basic model, and as he talks me through the setup process, I can see that he is trying to hide that he has an erection underneath his regulation chinos. I feel a vague mixture of disgust and embarrassment for him, and I hope that he isn't going to remember my new phone number and stalk me.

"I can ring you up right here, you don't have to get in line or anything." He picks up a tablet and presses a few things on it. I hand over my credit card.

"Hey, can you . . . can you say the line?"

Ethan asks while we're waiting for the payment to go through, and I know instantly what he means. He's talking about my final line in *Lights of Berlin,* the one strangers demand I send in a voice note to their cousin in Atlanta, or on FaceTime to their dad in Hungary. The one that made audiences burst into spontaneous rounds of applause in movie theaters all around the world as tears dried on their cheeks. The one that never fails to remind me of how much I owe the world, instead of the other way around.

A man in a bright yellow hoodie hovers close to us now, too, waiting.

"I am *so* sorry, but I'm not actually allowed to," I say. "You know . . . for contractual reasons."

Ethan nods and blinks a lot. The hoodie guy moves on.

"Can I . . . ask where you went then? When you were hiding out?" Ethan squeaks, like we're on a true crime show and I'm a missing child off a 1980s milk carton.

"It was an illusion. Grace Turner never really existed," I say, but I can tell that he is confused, unsatisfied with my response.

"I went home. To see my parents. They're getting older," I say, aware as I do that I'm offering up too much information to the kid with the boner in Best Buy. Am I lonely? Maybe I should call Laurel.

"Thank you for your help, Ethan," I say once the payment has gone through, and I hope I'm saying it in a way that comes across as sincere and not like I can't wait to get out of the store and be by myself again. I leave the store with my baseball cap back on and my head lowered, wondering about the kind of person who worries more about hurting the feelings of the guy in Best Buy than their own husband's.

As I enter in the security code, I hear a telephone ring from somewhere inside my new house. Once I'm inside, I locate a white landline plugged in to the wall behind the sofa. I pick the phone up tentatively because I didn't know landlines still existed, let alone that I had one.

"Grace, what are you doing?" It's Laurel. Of course she managed to get my number before I even knew I had a phone. She sounds exasperated with me already.

"I just walked through the door. I've been shopping," I offer proudly, because it sounds like something normal people do. I balance the landline between my shoulder and ear while I try to turn on my new phone. I've already forgotten everything Ethan told me.

"No, I know that. You're all over every-thing looking batshit crazy in Best Buy, al-legedly talking to some kid about your decrepit parents. You know your mom is just going to *love* that, by the way."

"Wait — what?"

"Grace. This shit is *instant,* you have to remember. You don't talk to people you don't know, and you always look at the very least mentally *sound,* because they'll try to catch you off guard. If you need something, just call me and I'll get it for you next time. I told you we needed a plan. For fuck's sake, Grace. Binoculars? They're saying you lost your mind and went bird-watching in the Amazon for the past year."

"Who? I thought they said my parents were old," I say, slightly distracted because Laurel is being so helpful that I'm now wondering whether she's been on my payroll the entire time I was away. I can't remember what we agreed when we met, but life coaching sounds expensive and I don't know when I'll work again.

"They don't care about anything, Grace. They'll say whatever they want. Some kid who served you in Best Buy said you seemed disoriented. What a fucking word."

"The guy in Best Buy? Ethan? He could barely speak. I felt bad for him."

"Don't ever feel bad for them. Rule number one. Kids are different these days, okay? They're not how we were when we were younger."

I'm about ten years younger than Laurel, but I don't think that now is the time to mention it. In fact, there's never a good time to mention it. Once a kid in Starbucks asked if she was my stepmom and she nearly spat at him.

"I'm sure I used to talk to people. Didn't I? This has never happened before."

Laurel is silent for a couple of seconds.

"You disrupted the balance, Grace. You left, and by leaving you showed weakness. It's open season."

"Is that why you're shouting at me now too?"

"Maybe," she says softly.

CHAPTER NINETEEN

Under Laurel's advice, I lay low in Coyote Sumac for the next couple of days, away from the press that she tells me are now circling the glass house like locusts. I order pizza delivery in the evening, thick, chewy dough covered with melted cheese and garlicky meat, and I eat the leftovers for lunch the next day. The only person who sees me is the delivery guy, and I make sure to answer the door in a baseball cap and sunglasses, even at night. He probably assumes I'm recovering from some invasive cosmetic surgery procedure, and he politely averts his eyes when I hand him the cash.

Filling my time is problematic. I find it hard to concentrate on the TV for too long, and the inane reality shows that I could probably just about tolerate remind me too much of my mom for me to watch. I spend the majority of my time sitting in the lawn chair on my porch instead, breathing in the salty Malibu air and watching the peach house through my binoculars. Because of how the property is angled in relation to mine, I can see the roof terrace and the dark blue pool at the back of their house clearly, and each day at noon I watch Able's wife, Emilia, swim lengths for half an hour, emerging at twelve thirty p.m. with her blond hair slick and glittering in the December sun. In a strange way her routine has become comforting to me, as if it is also my own.

I am sitting like that one day, squinting up at the house, when the phone starts to ring inside my rental. I assume it's Laurel, and I'm irritated that I have to lower the binoculars because it's the exact time of day that Emilia likes to go for her swim, but I walk through the screen door anyway.

"I sent a nude," the voice on the other end of the line says.

"Esme?"

"That's why I got suspended."

"Oh Jesus," I say. "How did you get this number?"

"Dylan."

"Oh great," I reply. "I guess I'm the only one who doesn't have it."

"Look, my friend has a therapy session in Brentwood at three today. Can I hang out at yours while she's there?" Esme asks impatiently.

I pause, looking down at the binoculars in my hand. I rarely see Emilia after her swim anyway.

"Sure."

An hour later, a red car roars down the dirt track to Coyote Sumac, and I know instantly that it's Esme and her friend because they're driving in the way only privileged teenagers from the suburbs can: carelessly, unflinching in their belief that they're invincible. I watch from the porch as the G-Wagon pulls to a sharp stop outside my house. The car engine cuts out, and along with it the music, a thin voice warbling shrilly over a synthesized beat.

I almost don't recognize Esme when she climbs out of the car. She's finally out of her school uniform, wearing a cropped striped T-shirt and ripped black jeans. Her black hair cloaks her shoulders, and the heavy powder on her face is a couple of shades too pale even for her. Her brown eyes are rimmed with black liquid eyeliner that has left a mini inkblot test on each of her eyelids, and the overall effect of all that effort is that she seems younger than she is, more vulnerable. I want to reach out and brush some of it off, but even I know that this would be a bad way to kick off our sister playdate.

"Hi, sister," Esme says wearily as she squints up at me, clearly unimpressed by what she's seen so far.

Esme's friend has a shaved head and is wearing a beautiful, sari-like dress with one dangly cross earring. They both stand on the porch and look me up and down for a moment. I realize that I'm breaking all of Laurel's rules at once in a bathrobe and the sheepskin-lined Crocs.

"Hi, I'm Blake," Esme's friend says politely. "Isn't this the cult place?"

"I'm actually pretty sure it's not a cult," I say. "Although I've heard there are unholy sex parties every Tuesday night."

Blake snorts with laughter but Esme glares at me.

"Can you help me with something?" I say, holding out my new phone. "I can't even switch this on."

"I can't believe you're nearly twenty-three," Esme says as she takes it and presses an invisible button on the side. The screen changes from black to gray, and an Apple logo appears.

"She's twenty-three?" Blake says, staring at me closely.

"I'm dressed like a disoriented person," I say, looking down at the robe.

"It's a thing. Apparently famous people are eternally frozen at the age they were when they became famous. Mentally," Esme says to Blake, busily typing something into my phone. She exhales heavily, somehow exasperated with me already. "You've totally fucked this. I need to work on it for a little bit."

"Who told you that about famous people?"

"A girl at school."

"Were you talking about me?"

"God, no. We were talking about Justin Bieber," Esme says, looking at Blake pointedly. "Anyway . . ."

"Okay, I know, I have to run," Blake says. "Can't wait to see what's in store for me today. If I'm super lucky, my hypnotherapist might guide me back to when I was a fetus again."

Blake air-kisses my sister and waves at me before ducking into the car. "I'll be back from my mother's womb in an hour or so!"

"Blake's very funny. Are they a friend of yours from school?" I ask Esme, managing my pronouns clumsily once we're alone.

"*She* lives two doors away, Grace. I've known *her* since I was eight." Esme's

160

scathing-hot tone reminds me so much of my mother that I flinch. I'm pleased that neither of us seems to have inherited my father's affinity for keeping the peace.

"Why is she in therapy?" I ask. "She seems happy enough."

"I guess our particular part of Anaheim isn't quite ready for a trans seventeen-year-old," Esme says, peering past me into my house. "Blake's mom tried to commit her when she found out, but her dad convinced her to try this conversion therapy place instead. Her mom is a total cretin. She's lucky that Blake could basically have graduated high school in fifth grade if she'd wanted to, she's missing so much school."

"Has our mom met Blake?" I ask.

"Mom adores Blake," Esme says, and I wish I hadn't brought up Mom because a defensive silence stretches between us while I rack my brain for something else to say.

"You should call them, you know," Esme says, folding her arms across her chest.

"Look, it's complicated," I say more sharply than I intended, because Esme's face crumples for a second before closing off again. I feel guilty for a moment, but I'm still trying to adjust to this version of my sister.

I turn around and Esme follows me into

my bungalow. I flick the overhead light on, but it doesn't make any difference to the damp, desolate atmosphere in the room. I make a mental note to buy some sort of lampshade. I wonder if they sell them at Best Buy.

Esme looks around wordlessly.

"It's kind of like a cave, right?" I say, and she raises her eyebrows but doesn't say anything. "It's very temporary."

I pick up an empty packet of Kettle chips from the floor and drop it into the huge Dior shopping bag I've been using for trash, in the absence of a real trash can or any liners.

"Do you want to get ice cream or something?" I ask, because the presence of another person in my rental has highlighted to me that I need to buy some basics if I'm going to pretend to be a functioning human being. I take Esme's shrug as affirmation and head into my bedroom to change out of my bathrobe, pulling on a pair of jeans and a white T-shirt with my Crocs. I can't work out whether I care enough to put on some makeup too. I'm not sure what the chances are of getting photographed now, whether the paparazzi know I've moved or if they even care. I wonder if Laurel is exaggerating the threat to make herself more useful because this never used to be a problem for me: I used to give the photographers a couple of staged photo opportunities a year, and in return, they would leave me alone the rest of the time. In the end, I leave the house without putting any makeup on.

"Are you going to go back to work?" Esme asks me once we're in the car and driving up to PCH. She inexplicably appears to be applying even more eyeliner.

"I'm still figuring that out," I say, keeping my eyes on the road ahead. "Apparently I have to start from square one. Audition again."

"Poor you." Esme rolls her eyes, and I'm instantly embarrassed.

"I didn't . . ." I trail off because I'm not sure what I didn't mean to do. Appear ungrateful?

"No, it's cool. I guess it's true what they say, being beautiful makes you lazy. Thank God for us plain girls."

My eyes automatically flick to my reflection in the rearview mirror, and I can feel the disdain dripping from Esme.

"I'd probably worked more hours by the time I was eighteen than most people do in a lifetime," I say defensively.

"You're extraordinary. You were supposed

to tell me I wasn't plain," Esme says, her tone searing.

"You're not plain. At all," I say, too late. "You could do with a little less makeup though."

I pull into the strip mall, swinging into an empty parking space outside the old-fashioned ice cream parlor I spotted when I was at the drugstore the other day.

"Not to be rude, but you could do with a little more. I saw that Best Buy pic. That guy really got you, huh?" Esme climbs out of the car and slams the door. I do the same, and we walk into the ice cream parlor together, except I pull back so that I can study her walk. It's still the same as when she was a little kid: she's always walked on her heels, leaning back slightly.

"He didn't seem the type," I say as we join the queue.

"That's guys online for you," Esme says airily, and it doesn't seem like she's *not* enjoying this. "Get any cretin behind a screen and they think they're Ryan Gosling."

"So it turns out," I say. Silence again, this time stretching as flat and wide as the San Bernardino Valley. I pretend to be excessively interested in the ice cream flavors on offer.

"I'm getting Rocky Road. You?" I ask. Rocky Road was our favorite flavor before I left home, but now Esme looks at me like I've just suggested eating my own hand.

"I'm going to get a kombucha from next door," she says haughtily.

I pay for my ice cream and follow her around Whole Foods until she finds the brand of kombucha she likes — the apple-flavored one made with stevia, *not* cane sugar.

The guy ringing up Esme's drink is only a little older than her, and he's cute in that baby-faced way that never lasts long. He will no doubt soften over the years to come, his features filling out to form something only vaguely reminiscent of his former self, in the way that has happened to most child actors I've worked with. Esme fidgets excitedly next to me anyway, and when I try to give her a fifty-dollar bill to pay for her drink, she bats my hand away, pulling out a credit card I didn't know she had. I try not to smile when her cheeks turn pink underneath her mortician's powder as she says good-bye to him.

We're nearly back at my car when I feel a hand on my shoulder. The guy who was serving us has followed us out. Esme holds her breath next to me, and her obliviousness to what's happening makes my chest feel tight for a moment.

"Did we forget something?" I ask, even though I know what he wants. In the past, it was rare for me to be found anywhere like this. Whenever I spent too long in a public place, I'd start to notice people staring, whispering, and then before long they would approach me with their phones gripped tightly in their palms. It was like something out of a zombie movie; everywhere I looked there would be another stranger sliding toward me, sometimes shyly but more often than not brazenly, hungrily, as if they owned part of me. I could never work out whether they did or not.

"No . . . I just . . . I fucking loved you in that hooker movie. I think I watched it every day for the whole of last summer," he says, grinning widely as if to reinforce the point that he can see my naked breasts anytime he wants. "Do you think I could get a photo with you?"

Esme makes a frustrated sound and is stalking around to the passenger side of the car when he calls after her, waving his phone.

"Hey? Excuse me? Can you take it?"

Esme pauses, and I flinch when I see the expression on her face before she walks back

166

to take the phone from his hand. For just a moment, my sister looks at me as if I orchestrated the entire exchange on purpose, just to show her how much better I am than her. The guy stands next to me, grinning cluelessly as Esme takes a couple of shots. After it's done, she wordlessly holds the photo up for me to check, and, when I shrug, she hands the phone back to him.

"Lights of Berlin," I say over my shoulder as I'm getting in the car. The kid squints at me.

"What?"

"Lights of Berlin. That's what the *hooker* movie was called."

It seems that neither of us is in the mood for conversation during the drive back to Coyote Sumac, and when I pull up outside the house, we both stay in our seats, staring out the windshield for a minute.

"Do you want to talk about the suspension?" I ask reluctantly.

"No," Esme says, unbuckling her seat belt. "Can we just watch TV or something?"

I nod, relieved. Once we're inside, we both sit down carefully on the sofa, and I turn on an episode of *Friends* for her. *Friends* reruns were the only thing guaranteed to be

167

on in whatever country I was filming in, but Esme doesn't appear to have seen it before. She watches quietly, her eyes tracking the characters and then occasionally flicking back to me.

"This show is entirely problematic," she says, once the episode is over. "But I think I don't care."

I'm not sure what to say in response, so I just settle into the sofa for the next episode.

When Blake pulls up outside, beeping obnoxiously four times, I feel guilty about how relieved I am. Esme bends down and pats me gently on the shoulder like a family dog.

"See you next week."

I wash the sticky ice cream off my hands at the kitchen sink, picturing my sister begging our parents to give her permission to come to LA for the afternoon with Blake. It would have taken a lot of convincing, given her suspension from school and their implicit mistrust of Los Angeles. When I was Esme's age, I was living in a soulless hotel in West Hollywood between shoots, and strange men used to follow me up from the pool bar to my room, banging on the door and shouting until I was forced to call my manager from the bathroom to deal with them. The only other people I had contact with back then were either on commission or outright paid to be there, and I spoke to my parents maybe once, twice a month, until the conversation eventually dried up like the Los Angeles River. Like I said, I think I could feel jealous of my sister if I tried.

I turn off the tap and look out the window. The Pacific is glowing fire red in the afternoon sun. I slip out the front door and down the porch steps, drifting toward the water. When the sand becomes damp, I kick off my shoes and then wade into the cold water. There is something calming about the inevitability of it once I'm in, the water icy and my jeans weighing heavy on my hips. I hold my breath as I fully submerge myself, and then I just float on my back for a few minutes.

A small, curling wave approaches. I stand up in front of it, waist-deep with my arms stretched out beside me, my body covered in goose bumps. The water crashes against me, and a piece of seaweed hooks around my jeans. I think about what my sister might want from me, knowing that I will never be able to give it to her. My inability to deliver when it really matters has been my one constant in life.

Another wave starts to gather, this one bigger. It hits me at chest level, salty water splashing up and stinging my eyes. Soon it feels like I am summoning the waves, stoking them until they come faster and crack even harder against me so that I have to bend my knees to remain upright before they snap back into the sea.

For a moment, everything is calm and I face the horizon. I watch a monster wave gathering power until it looms five feet above me, hissing. I hold my breath as the wave crashes over me, and then I am plunged into darkness. Now I am just one other small thing among a million other things, spinning and twisting underneath the water's surface. The water isn't so blue under here; it's blacker and murkier and I'm drifting and my lungs are bursting and it's simultaneously the most alive and the closest to darkness that I've ever been.

CHAPTER TWENTY

When the second installment of the assassin trilogy wrapped, I was offered the lead role in a teen horror movie. As much as I didn't want to admit it, the second shoot had been harder on me than the first, culminating in a monthlong stint in Beirut where I had to endure even longer periods of coolness from Able, periods that often spiraled into meanness at a dizzying speed. On top of the generally disorienting effects of my being sixteen, alone and far from home, Able had made it so I couldn't even trust my own thoughts most of the time. I had learned to be quiet and still around him so as not to set him off, and by the end of the shoot I found I could read his moods better than I could read my own. Afterward, he had taken more convincing than before that I remembered how lucky I was, and he acted like the stuff we did in his trailer was just the price I had to pay for the power I had unfairly exerted over him throughout the shoot. I felt sick, guilty and exhausted most of the time, and I arrived back in California with what felt like gaping black holes in my psyche. I knew I couldn't face my parents in that state, and when I lied and told them I needed to stay in LA for work, they didn't put up a fight.

The horror movie wasn't part of the plan we'd laid out at that first dinner, but I was desperate to fill each second of my time in between shoots, and my agent, Nathan, admitted that Able couldn't do anything about it as long as I was available for the third assassin movie. Even then, even when I was still pretending everything was fine, I knew myself well enough to understand that I had to keep on running. I told myself that I was in control: I was taking the role as a sort of insurance policy, because even I was capable of losing Able's goodwill, but I think I was showing off to him, too, trying to prove all over again how talented I was, how lucky he was to have found me. Maybe Able was right and he really did know me better than I knew myself. Maybe I was deeply fucked up in some irreparable way nobody else but him could see. All I knew for certain was that everything was always part of the same twisted game and I could never keep up with the rules.

In the end, I did the movie without Able against the advice of Nathan, my manager, Kit, and my publicist, Nan. They weren't happy about it, but I was their star client by that point, and they couldn't refuse me. I waited months for Able to tear into me about it, but he never commented on my decision in person. I told myself I was strong enough to handle the silent treatment, but I already felt guilty about wanting too much and seeming ungrateful. As always when I was apart from him, I also felt complicated ripples of shame whenever I thought about the things we'd done.

The actor I was playing opposite in the horror movie, Elon Puth, had come up through kids' TV, shooting five seasons of his own show, *Elon's World,* before calling it a day to take on more challenging roles. I thought we'd have a lot in common, having both started out as young teenagers, but Elon was unpleasant when we met, his eyes scanning my face once before turning away dismissively. He had pale, dry lips and a chin that had the tendency to melt into his neck when he wasn't in front of the camera, and we barely spoke outside of our scenes. I kept expecting the director, Mandy, to pull us aside and confront us over our lack of chemistry, but she never did, and she didn't even seem to notice that we played our characters with a sort of hollowness, just daring each other to feel anything. I could tell from the moment I met Mandy that she wasn't an auteur like Able, and that this was just a job for her, like it was for the people who graded the film or controlled the lights. The movie wasn't ever a *part* of her, like it was for Able. I looked down on her from the start because of this, even though I hated myself for it.

I don't know when we all realized that the movie was going to be a flop, but by the end of the forty-day shoot, the atmosphere on set was pitiful. Elon had only become more petulant as the shoot went on, and by the end he was flat-out refusing to try Mandy's suggestions, occasionally even stealing my lines if he saw them landing better. The director seemed as jaded as the rest of us by then, and at some point she just seemed to relinquish control. I couldn't even blame her: at that point we were all just trying to wade through to the end of the project.

On the final day of the shoot, just when I was counting down the seconds until I was free again, my publicist, Nan, showed up. It turned out that Elon was also her client, and she sat us down in his trailer to talk about the burning wreck we'd all created. Elon watched a baseball game on TV as Nan told us that the studio had suggested we construct a relationship in order to generate some early publicity for the movie. She said that it would help reduce some of the stigma around the release while also showing the studio how committed we were to the project. Obviously we wouldn't actually have to date each other; we just needed to be spotted at key places around LA for a couple of months. Elon shrugged his consent while I slipped out of the trailer to call Nathan.

"Elon is repellent," I said to Nathan when he answered. "This is insane."

"You don't have to actually date him," Nathan said. "You barely have to talk to him."

"Does Able know about this?" I asked. "This was never part of the plan. I'm supposed to be unattainable, not dating some man-child from Nickelodeon."

"Elon wasn't on Nickelodeon. And Able isn't a part of this project," Nathan reminded me. "He doesn't have input in what you do or don't do here."

"He'll care though," I said, instantly pushing the image of Able breathing heavily in my ear out of my mind, just like I always did.

"Please, Nathan. This isn't a good look for me."

"This was why Able came up with the plan in the first place," Nathan said grimly. "So that we could control all of this. You made your choice, Grace. You just have to live with it for a couple more months. Come on, it could be a lot worse. Millions of girls would kill to go on a date with Elon Puth."

I watched as Elon climbed down the steps from his trailer then. He was holding his phone up in selfie mode and was filming himself talking seriously into the camera, as I'd seen him do countless times during the shoot. His videos always started with "hey, guys, so *sorry* for the wait," as if his fans had been lying dormant all this time, just waiting for him to bring them back to life with tales of the offerings from craft services that day, or updates on his sleep cycle the night before.

I thought of Able again, and the realization that everything I had relinquished may have been in vain nearly winded me.

"But why didn't he try to stop me?" I asked quietly.

My first "date" with Elon was at the Arc-

Light in Hollywood a couple of weeks later. We were supposed to look like any regular couple — just like you, but better of course. I didn't actually know what people my age wore on dates, so in the end I chose a tiny red dress and an old jean jacket with some sneakers. Elon picked me up in his orange Lamborghini, and he laughed when I flinched at the sight of it.

"Pretty obnoxious, right? What did you expect?" he asked, and since it was the closest he'd ever come to self-awareness in my presence, I thawed ever so slightly toward him.

I'd suggested we go to the movie theater so that we wouldn't have to talk to each other, but almost as soon as we sat down, Elon started to shift restlessly in his seat next to me, playing on his phone and scrolling through various flashing apps. After about half an hour, he grabbed my arm and leaned in close.

"Do you want to get out of here?"

I shrugged.

Elon led me through the lobby and out toward the car, grabbing my hand when the paparazzi crowded around us at the exit, calling both our names and shouting questions about how long we'd been dating. Elon turned and smiled at me, and his eyes were so warm and enchanting that I wondered how they'd seemed so lifeless throughout the shoot. I smiled shyly at the cameras before holding up my hands to cover my face.

"What are you doing?" Elon asked me under his breath, but I pretended not to hear him. It didn't make sense that I'd suddenly be lapping up this kind of attention after I'd made such a point of being so private in the past. I wasn't going to completely obliterate the image we'd so carefully curated just because I'd made one bad choice.

Elon pulled off as soon as we were inside the car, and we headed into the hills.

"Come to this party with me," Elon said, and just when I was worried he was going to try to blur the lines of the arrangement, he added, "It will look good."

"Whose party is it?" I asked as we drove up one of the winding canyons. I had never been to a Hollywood party without someone from my team, and even then I just dropped in to charm whoever I was instructed to charm.

"Clint Eastwood's lawyer's son," he said, and he frowned when I laughed. "What?"

"Oh, sorry, I thought you were joking," I said, and he turned away from me. I stared

178

silently out the window as the lights of Los Angeles twinkled below us.

The party was in a white palace at the top of Benedict Canyon. Elon knew the security code of the gate, punching it in before holding it open for me. We walked around the house and straight through to the backyard, where water cascaded over terra-cotta boulders into an Olympic-sized swimming pool. A guy in white Calvin Klein briefs threw a shrieking woman into the water, and Elon grinned at me before excusing himself to find the host. People swayed in the water and whispered about me from behind their raised red cups, while I stood awkwardly alone by the sliding doors into the house.

After a few minutes, I let myself into the house and found the kitchen. I opened the fridge and pulled out a bottle of vodka. I'd drunk a little before but never by myself — I was too much of a control freak. As awful as it had been, however, the experience of shooting the film and spending time alone with Elon gave me a sense of independence, and I figured that now could be the time to start making a few of my own decisions. A girl wearing a shimmering white jumpsuit approached me just as I was pouring vodka into a red cup. I quickly topped it up with a splash of orange juice before she could see how much vodka I'd used. When she got closer I noticed that she had tiny crystals embedded in her eyebrows. I took a sip of my drink, wincing as it burned its way down my throat.

"You came with Elon, right?" the girl asked, and she instantly seemed too friendly for one of these parties.

"Yes," I said, smiling politely at her. "I should maybe go look for him."

"Oh, I wouldn't bother," she said, laughing. "He's probably giving someone a BJ in the guesthouse."

"Oh," I said.

"Didn't you know?" she asked, and I shrugged.

"I don't really care," I said, and she laughed again, seemingly delighted with me. I already felt better from the alcohol, giddy almost.

"I'm Alaia," she said at the exact moment I decided that I liked her.

"Grace." I nodded back at her.

"You know, you look like you could use a real party," she said after a moment, and she waggled her tiny, fluffy purse at me. "Wanna join?"

I stared at her for a minute, uncomprehending, and she grabbed my hand, smiling.

"Come with me."

Alaia led me up the marble staircase to a bathroom on the first floor, where a rose quartz bathtub glowed beneath a window overlooking the pool. I sat on the closed toilet seat and watched with interest as Alaia portioned out two neat lines of white powder along the edge of the bathtub. She used her gold credit card to chop and press the powder until it was as fine as dust. I watched as she ran her finger along the card and then put it in her mouth. When she held the card out to me, I did the same. After that, Alaia took a metal straw out of her purse and hoovered up one of the lines in less than two seconds. When she was done she stood, pressing up the tip of her nose and inhaling sharply. The sound was surprisingly guttural, like the noise an animal might make before a fight.

Alaia gestured to the line on the edge of the bathtub, and I slowly eased onto my knees. I took a gulp of my drink, and it was so strong that it made my eyes water. I tried to remember how Alaia had done it as I bent over the powder with the cool straw resting lightly inside my nostril. I inhaled and felt the burn inside my nose. I thought instantly of Esme, and decided that I would call her when I left the party if it wasn't too late.

Alaia smiled at me.

"You okay?"

"I think so," I said, but I was already enjoying how I could really *feel* my brain working in my skull for the first time. It felt as if I could finally control my wayward mind, choosing exactly what I wanted to zone in and focus on with military precision. I felt an immense surge of appreciation for this stranger who had somehow known exactly what I was searching for.

"It's fair trade," Alaia said brightly as she leaned in toward me from her position on the edge of the tub. I looked at her uncomprehendingly. "The coke, I mean. Nobody died to get it to us."

For some reason I found this hilarious, and when I started to laugh, she did too.

"Can we have more?" I asked, sliding back onto the floor. I felt good, clearheaded and alert, but I was also already worrying that the effects would wear off. "Since nobody died or anything."

Alaia smiled and took the bag out from her purse again.

"Have you ever been to Burning Man?"

she asked as she poured more out.

"No, have you?" I asked, running my tongue over the roof of my mouth. The ridges felt numb and foreign.

"Yes. You have to come with us this year. My friend can fly us in."

I nodded, smiling slightly.

"That sounds fun. I'd like that," I said. "I don't have many friends in LA."

Alaia looked at me quickly and then nodded, and I wondered if that had been obvious when she saw me standing alone in the kitchen.

She handed me the straw again, and I bent over to do my second line. I had only cleared half of it when I felt something catch in my throat and I straightened up to swallow. As I did, I happened to glance at Alaia, who was holding her phone at an odd angle in her lap. I stared up at her, and I could tell instantly from her expression that she had been filming me.

"Give me the phone," I said, my voice low and rough. Alaia froze, panicked, and I grabbed it from her lap. The grainy camera was still recording when I turned it over. I realized that I had no idea how to stop it or how to delete what she had done, so I pressed some buttons on the side until the screen went black.

I turned and walked out of the bathroom. Alaia followed me as I stumbled down the stairs and out of the sliding doors to the backyard. People were staring as we passed them, but I stopped only when I reached the edge of the pool. I dropped the phone on the ground next to me and then stamped on it, hard. It crunched satisfyingly under my foot, but I still threw it into the swimming pool once I'd finished.

"That's my phone, you freak," Alaia said, but I just turned and walked back through the house and out the front door.

I sat on the step outside the house, watching a couple arguing on the lawn while I drank a cup of warm beer that someone had left behind. After a while, the door opened behind me and Elon walked out. He stood in front of me, shaking his head distastefully.

"Where have you been?" I muttered. "You're a little late to save me."

He rolled his eyes and then surprised me by sitting down next to me.

"Did you hear what Alaia did to me?" I asked, and Elon didn't say anything for a while. I pulled away from him and stood up. "What the fuck, Elon?"

"It could have been good for the movie," he said, shrugging.

184

"In what way, exactly?" I asked, and even I could hear that I was slurring badly.

"Go home, Grace," Elon said.

"I know you're gay," I said. "Would that be good for the movie too? Is that why you're hiding it?"

The couple on the lawn in front of us stopped arguing long enough to turn to stare at us, and Elon grabbed my wrist tightly. He pulled me up and dragged me further away from the house. I hoped there weren't any photographers lurking to catch this special moment.

"It is not your choice how and when I come out," he said, once he was sure we were out of earshot of anyone else.

"Fuck you, Elon," I said as I slid down the side of a parked car and slumped against it. My red dress was riding up and I was sitting in the dirt, but I didn't care.

Elon eyed me with disgust.

"You're a terrible actress, you know," Elon said. "You ruined that movie."

I shook my head. I knew it wasn't true.

"*You* ruined that movie," I said, jabbing my finger at him. "I don't need this garbage movie. You do."

"Everyone was tiptoeing around you so that you didn't shatter," Elon said, and the look of revulsion in his eyes was so pure

185

that I was silenced for a few seconds. "So what are you, bipolar?"

I stood up and shoved him hard so that he had to grab onto the wing mirror of the car to catch his balance.

"Stupid bitch," he said before he turned around and walked away. I stood dumbly for a moment, waiting for him to come back or for someone to tell me what to do, how to get out of there. Once it was obvious that nobody was coming, I pulled out my phone and looked down at it.

I called the only number I've ever known by heart.

When Able pulled up outside the house, I picked myself up off the ground and climbed wordlessly into his car. He turned the engine off so that we were sitting in the dark, lit only by the streetlight outside. I felt instantly embarrassed about how I looked — overdone as if I'd somehow believed I would be treated like an adult when I got dressed earlier that evening. I noticed then how dirty my legs were against his clean cream interior, but if Able noticed, too, he didn't say anything.

"Are you okay?" he asked quietly, after a moment. My eyes instantly filled with tears.

"I'm sorry," I whispered.

"You don't need to apologize to me," Able said. "You never do."

"I nearly messed it all up," I said, needing him to understand what had happened because now that I was next to him, I wasn't angry at him anymore. I just felt ashamed. I was riddled with guilt that I'd even taken the role in the shitty movie in the first place. Able had put his faith in me from the moment we met, and now I'd nearly thrown it all away just because I was always trying to prove something.

"It's okay. It's okay. I'll handle Nan," he said, once I'd finished telling him what happened, and as he brushed at my tears with his thumb, I thought about how kind it was of him not to say *I told you so*. I promised myself that I would never expose myself like that again.

"None of this is your fault. You should never have been put in this position," he said.

"Thank you," I whispered. Able tapped my seat belt and I fastened it before he pulled off, his headlights illuminating the dark canyon.

"You know, I actually called Mandy before you started shooting," Able said after a moment. "To stop anything like this from happening."

"You spoke to Mandy," I said slowly, trying to understand. "What did you say to her?"

"I made it clear that under no circumstances was she to push you too hard."

I thought of what Elon had said about people tiptoeing around me on set, and my cheeks began to burn. Able sensed my discomfort and his voice softened.

"I did it to protect you, Grace. I didn't want her getting frustrated with you."

"Why didn't you tell me?" I asked before I could stop myself. Able turned to study me, and I could see the indignation building in his face.

"Remember that I know your limits better than you do. Mandy needed to know how easily you can become overwhelmed, and how that affects your processing and judgment, and how it can make you hostile to the people around you. It's not a bad thing, it's a part of who you are, but I knew you would never tell her if something was wrong."

I sat very still in my seat as a warning signal went off somewhere inside my brain. I pushed it back down into the depths of my subconscious and nodded, knowing what he wanted from me.

"Thank you," I said.

"How did you find working with someone else anyway?" Able asked casually as he pulled to a stop at the traffic lights on Crescent Heights.

"It was the worst," I said, and Able smiled next to me. "Mandy didn't care about any of it, and Elon . . ."

"What about Elon?"

"Elon said I was . . ." I started, but I couldn't finish. "He said I was a horrible actor."

Able froze, and even though he didn't say anything for a while, I could feel his rage fill the car around us. When he did speak, his voice sounded thick with emotion.

"Look at me, Grace," Able said, turning my face toward him. I looked at him, my eyes finally meeting his. "That person isn't even worth the ground that you walk on. He'll be working in a parking garage by the time he's twenty-five. This will be the last film set he ever works on, trust me."

I smiled slightly and Able smiled back at me, bathing me once again in his pure light. It always felt so much warmer when he looked at me, I didn't know how I'd forgotten.

"You know I'd do anything for you, don't you?" he asked then, changing tack and catching me off guard again. I sat up a little straighter as the traffic light turned green and he pulled off, the engine murmuring gently.

"Yes," I said carefully.

"Well, you understand that works two ways, Grace. And now you need to earn back my trust."

I felt a thrum of dread deep in my stomach, but when I sneaked a look at him, Able was still smiling. I wondered if I'd got everything confused in the past: maybe Able was right and my useless, burned-out mind meant I couldn't process information like everyone else around me.

"I mean that if our partnership is going to work, we're going to need to trust each other with every single fiber of our beings. There can never be so much as a flicker of doubt between us again. Do you understand that?"

I nodded slowly.

"I trust you."

Able pulled into the driveway of my hotel. He turned the engine off and turned to look at me.

"Now, how about I walk you up to your room, and I wax lyrical about jazz music until you fall asleep and forget this night ever happened. Does that sound good to you?"

I nodded, and as we got out of the car, I felt myself relax into his presence once again, and the decision to do so felt soothing, familiar — as if someone had finally thrown a heavy blanket over a frenzied birdcage.

Able settled in the armchair next to my bed in the hotel room. He picked up a magazine from the floor and flicked through it while I locked myself in the bathroom to change into my pajamas. Once I'd brushed my teeth, I climbed under the cool covers of the giant bed. It felt strange having him there next to me, but, as promised, he played me music from his phone, and, as I lay with my eyes closed, listening to him talk softly about Miles Davis and John Coltrane, I felt lucky to have someone looking out for me again. And this was always how it worked with us — for every time Able took something irreplaceable from me, there was an equal and opposing moment where it felt like he helped me to become more myself. There was never one without the other.

Able's voice rose and fell like a wave that night, and a warm sense of contentment spread through me as I slipped over the line between reality and dreams.

CHAPTER TWENTY-ONE

The sound of screaming water fills my ears, and my shoulder scrapes against something sharp on the bottom of the ocean. I twist, and when I see the sun above the surface of the water, I think that maybe I will stay here forever, until something inside me snaps, like it did that night in the bathroom. I kick my way to the surface, my lungs burning as a surge of adrenaline spreads through me. When I surface I spit out some salt water and let out a shuddering breath, my vision distorted by the brightness of the real world.

I emerge twenty feet further away from the shore than when I started, and the water is as placid as a lake again. I rub my eyes. Someone is shouting my name. I squint at the shore, and somehow both Esme and Blake are standing there, waving their arms frantically. I wave back and, for some reason, I feel borderline euphoric to see my sister again, as if I can make everything up to her right now. I start to swim toward them, and as each measure of oxygen expands in my lungs, I feel lucky for the reminder of how vulnerable we are to depend on anything so much at all.

When I climb out of the water, my clothes are heavy, my jeans sagging on my hips. I wring the hem of my T-shirt out onto the sand as I approach the girls.

"What the actual fuck?" Esme asks, and now that I'm closer I can see that I've misunderstood, that her cheeks are wet with tears.

I pause, unsure of how to respond. I look at Blake but she averts her eyes, embarrassed for me.

"I felt like swimming," I say in the end, because I figure they don't necessarily need unlimited access to my psyche at this point.

"Fully clothed," Esme says searingly. "You are so weird. What is wrong with you? I thought you'd killed yourself."

I try to put my hand on her shoulder but she ducks away.

"I'm sorry. Look, I'm trying, Esme. You guys had left . . ."

"Esme still had your phone," Blake says. My sister still won't meet my eyes.

"Do you want to come in for some tea?" I ask.

Esme pauses, communicating something to Blake with her eyes that I can't read. I pick up my shoes from the sand, and after a moment the girls follow me to my front porch. I try to act like I always go swimming fully clothed even though my shoulder is stinging from where I scraped it and spots of blood are soaking through the thin fabric of my T-shirt.

I leave Blake and Esme in the living room while I peel off my wet clothes in the bedroom, swapping them for a pair of yoga pants and Dylan's Ohio State sweatshirt I snuck into my packing. When I come back into the living room they are both sitting up straight on the sofa. I switch on the kettle and turn back to them.

Esme hands me my phone silently. She's already set the background to a photo of the ocean view from Coyote Sumac.

"Thanks. Can I do anything in return?" I remember the expression of horror on the face of the girl working in the drugstore when I tried to pay her, and manage not to reach for my purse to pay my sister. My transcendental near-drowning experience is already wearing off, and I'm starting to wish I hadn't invited them back into my house, particularly as Esme is still ignoring me and I'm having trouble looking at her, too, her cheeks streaked ash gray from her tears.

The kettle emits a shrill whistle and I take it off the hob, the handle searing the palm of my hand in the process. I ball it into a fist and open a cupboard. Empty. I open another one and then remember that I didn't bring any cups over from Dylan's. I don't even have any tea.

"I don't have any cups. I'm so sorry." I stand in the middle of the kitchen, looking around. I hold my scalded hand out as an offering.

"It's fine, we don't drink tea," Blake says, smiling politely.

The girls show no signs of leaving, even though the silence has stretched well into the uncomfortable zone. I feel exposed, unsure of what to do. What do teenagers talk about? Other than Dylan, and that awful night with Elon and Alaia, I've rarely hung out with anyone my own age since I was in England. I wonder how long they'll expect me to grind out polite conversation before letting me off the hook. My limbs feel heavy, as if they are filled with wet sand, and I want to get back into bed.

"Can I do anything else for you?" I ask. Esme is staring up at the ceiling with her arms folded across her chest. I look at Blake for help, and she shrugs.

"What's it like being famous?" Blake asks, and even though I'm grateful to her for filling the silence, I'm not sure how to answer the question. Should I tell them about the time I had to be dragged out of someone's pool because I'd blacked out while swimming naked with a famous pop star and two men that weren't my husband? Or the morning after, when I went for a painful breakfast with a journalist from *LA Weekly* who described me as having a "childlike innocence, betrayed only by her trembling hands, the keynote topic in countless studio boardroom meetings across the city, no doubt." It was the closest anyone came to referencing the industry-wide open secret of my drug use, and my manager nearly killed me. I spent the following week holed up alone in a bungalow at Chateau Marmont, bingeing on coke and reruns of *I Love Lucy* and ignoring everyone's calls.

I have a feeling nothing I say is going to impress my sister. The few times I've seen her in the years since I moved out, she's never expressed any interest in my job, other than once asking me if it was true that Sean Connery had a job polishing coffins before he started acting. I found out afterward that it was, but I think I forgot to tell her.

"It has its good points and bad, like

anything," I say, cringing at the mundanity of my answer. Esme snorts, which I guess is something.

"It's not real," I say quietly, after another moment. "None if it means anything at all."

The girls are silent, and they don't know what to say because they're still kids, but Esme is at least looking at me now.

"Did you know that Sean Connery worked as a coffin polisher before he started acting?" I ask, trying to lighten the leaden atmosphere I have single-handedly created.

"Do you ever speak to Dylan?" Blake asks, leaning forward and twisting her earring.

I stand up quickly. "Okay, girls, thanks for fixing my phone, but I have some stuff I need to get on with now."

"What kind of stuff?" Esme finally speaks, squinting at me warily. "Drowning-yourself stuff?"

"Grown-up stuff. I need to meditate," I say. Esme nods, seemingly satisfied for the moment.

"My mom does cryotherapy for her depression," Blake tells me helpfully on their way out.

I watch the girls get into the red car, then I remember Laurel at the last minute and shout after them. "Don't tell anyone about the Crocs!"

CHAPTER TWENTY-TWO

I push my silk eye mask up and hold the vibrating phone close to my face so that I can read it through the blur of another heavy night's sleep. The eye mask has been doing its job too well recently, and I'm finding it nearly impossible to get out of bed before midday. When I do wake up, my brain feels furry and strange, as if I'm wading through a swimming pool of thick clay just to form a sentence.

I hold the phone up to my ear as the air-conditioning unit in the bedroom blasts warm, damp air over me.

"Grace, I messed up. Nathan and Kit have been harassing me for your address, and I gave them your cell number. Do you hate me?" Wren asks, sounding upset.

"No, it's fine," I say, stretching slightly and trying to keep the sleep out of my voice because it's eleven thirty on a Monday . . . or maybe it's Tuesday. "I needed to call them anyway so they stop ringing the house."

"Are you going to start working again? Feminist space movie?"

"I don't know," I say. "I guess I'll see what they think."

"Who's the one who talks really fast? Nathan? He sounds pretty pissed."

"I can only imagine."

I assure Wren one more time that I don't hate her, and then I hang up and call my old agent Nathan.

Nathan and Kit were with me from that very first dinner at Nobu. Able brought them on to represent me when I moved over, and the two of them, plus Able and my publicist, Nan, became my team and, in effect, my new family.

Nathan, my agent, is the younger of the two, probably only just nearing forty now, and he hadn't had much success when I signed with him. What he lacked in experience, however, he made up for in arrogance and delusion, two qualities admired above all else by men in this industry. Now he looks after some of the biggest names in the business and has an office with a view from Korea Town to Pacific Palisades to prove it.

Kit, my manager, likes to think of himself

as a more cerebral man. It's definitely an image he has cultivated, playing the role of a beleaguered Ivy League professor who has rather embarrassingly found himself embroiled in our indecent industry. As far as I'm aware, Kit grew up in San Diego and comes from NASCAR money.

We meet at Nathan's office like we always used to. It's been redone again, and everything in the room is now bright white, including Nathan's jeans and his ratty Pomeranian, Dusty. It's like stepping into a seventies insane asylum.

"The prodigal daughter returns." Kit pulls me into a hug even though I've told him at least forty times over the years not to touch me. He gestures to the white leather sofa, and I'm stepping across the shaggy white rug when Nathan grabs my arm and shakes his head.

"Honey, no. This rug is worth more than your marriage. It's not for walking on."

"No problem." I roll my eyes and climb over it dramatically. I've always been on my worst behavior with the two of them, and I naturally fall back into it. I met them when I was thirteen, and it was the only role I ever carved out for myself.

Kit sits in an ivory and chrome chair opposite me while Nathan paces the room in front of the window.

"Someone forgot their Ritalin today," I say, and my first clue that this isn't going to go how it used to is that neither of them laughs. Dusty curls up on the white rug below me, and I look at Nathan pointedly. He doesn't say anything.

"First of all, welcome back to LA, Grace," Kit says, steepling his hands like a Bond villain.

"How was *Anaheim*?" Nathan asks, saying it as if I've been in Fallujah and not a mere forty miles outside of Los Angeles.

"I should have told you where I was," I say courteously.

"You also shouldn't have left," Nathan says.

"That's debatable."

"It's not. Debatable," Nathan says, and I think he's gotten hair plugs since I left. Was everyone just waiting until I left the city to fulfill their cosmetic surgery goals? "You realize we've spent the best part of ten years working with you, right? We have built an entire network based on you being here, showing up and working. Your actions are no longer just your own at this point. You do understand that?"

"Nathan —" Kit interrupts, but Nathan holds up his hand. His lips are slick with spittle, and he wipes them with the back of his hand. When he puts his palm on the desk to steady himself, I can see the glob of saliva on his knuckles, and it makes me feel embarrassed for him. Nathan used to invite me over to his house in Brentwood and his entire family would treat me like I was Beyoncé, calling in the sushi chef from Katsuya and opening $800 bottles of wine that I inevitably ended up knocking over when I got too drunk.

"I just need to check that she understands that if this was any other business, we'd be able to sue the fuck out of her. Because it's not like the CEO of a tech company going missing, or even the lead designer, it's as if the fucking product itself disappears into thin air. Do you get it?"

"Like I said, I should have told you where I was." I fold my arms across my chest and shift in my seat like a child in trouble.

"In all honesty, Grace, yes, you could have sent an email. We looked like retards," Kit adds, and my surprise must show on my face because he shrugs and mouths *what?* at me after.

Nathan stands in front of the window with his arms folded across his chest. The winter sun spills in behind him, lighting him up like an angel. "You know that people very

202

nearly forgot about you. I don't know if that surprises you, but it shouldn't."

"Did you call this meeting to tell me that I'm expendable?" I ask, more surprised than anything.

"Not entirely. But yeah, everyone is expendable. What? I'm being honest," he says when Kit frowns at him.

"I think what Nathan is really trying to say is that what you do next is very important. Have you . . . heard from Able?" Kit asks delicately.

I shake my head as my heart rate speeds up. I don't think I realized it at the time, but Able chose them too. They were nowhere near as successful as he was, so when Able suggested they team up, they probably jizzed in their Calvins at the mere thought. Maybe they don't know who they are without him either.

"Gracie sweetheart?" Kit prompts.

Gracie sweetheart. Said as if I'm still thirteen, fresh in LA in a Minnie Mouse T-shirt and a pair of cream Converse signed by all my friends back home.

"I still don't understand what happened," Nathan says, looking up at the ceiling as if summoning all of God's strength just to deal with me.

I move in my seat, staring past them and

out the window, at the city sprawled beneath us. I've seen this view at least five hundred times, from the highest peak of Runyon Canyon to the rooftop of Soho House, and I have never understood what people like so much about this city. Dylan used to try to explain how much energy he found in the twinkling lights of the valleys and the pastel houses sprouting up in the hills, how much beauty he saw in even the darkest corners of Hollywood and the dusty Topanga Canyon trails concealing rattlesnakes and mountain lions. The problem was, I could never see any of it through the smog.

"Like you said, everyone's expendable," I say coldly.

"Are you sure there's nothing you can do to fix it? You didn't do anything to upset him?" Nathan asks, still desperate to understand just how the well dried up so suddenly.

"Nathan, we've been through all of this. It's over."

Nathan shakes his head, glancing at Kit for support. "Let's see how you feel about that after a year of making holiday movies for Hallmark."

"Okay, there's no need to be mean," I say, frowning as Dusty lets out a piercing yelp.

"He made you what you are, Grace. I

don't know if you can come back from that," Nathan says snidely.

And that's when it hits me that Able still controls it all. He set it up from the start so that he is at the core of every choice I make and every choice made for me, and the best part is, he never even has to think about me. My career, my relationships, even where I live: Able is still at the crux of it all. Maybe he knew all along that without him I would become untethered, floating all alone in the ether of Hollywood. He always knew that nobody else would want to touch me.

"Isn't it your job to figure that out? It seems like a flawed business model to only have one available avenue for your client," I say bitingly.

"Grace. Your last movie came out over a year ago. If you found a project tomorrow, the movie could take up to three years to be released. In that time, even the microscopic percentage of moviegoers who still care about you will have forgotten you. You were one fucking movie away from being a household name. *One movie.*" Nathan slides into the chair behind his desk and places both of his palms in two tiny sandpits on either side of his Mac. He traces his fingers lightly through the sand and then gently rubs them together until his hands are clean again. I raise my eyebrows at Kit, but he just shrugs. I figure that Nathan's feng shui guy has instructed him to do this to calm down in moments of high pressure, and he seems to have nearly achieved it when he catches sight of me. A deep red flush climbs up his baby-smooth neck, and his lips tighten.

"Are you fucking laughing, Grace?" Nathan turns to Kit and points at me, as if he can't deal with me anymore. "Is she laughing?"

"I really am sorry. I know you have families and, like, billion-dollar houses to pay off and stuff. I do understand that. It's hard. It's just, you kind of convinced me I already was a household name?"

"Do you think anyone in Wallace, Idaho, wonders where Grace Turner went?" Nathan asks. "Do you know how hard everyone worked to get that movie out in time to be eligible for awards season because of you? Do you know how much groundwork we laid to try to get you that Oscar nomination? We rented a fucking billboard on Sunset Boulevard, Grace, but you'd already left by the time it went up. We played the entire thing perfectly from the start, and you fuck it up at the last minute by disappearing. Who blows off the Golden Globes?"

Nathan looks at Kit, who shakes his head

sadly, and I wonder how many times they've had this conversation.

"You know, actually, let's talk about the Globes for a moment. We flew sixty-five members of the Hollywood Foreign Press out to Berlin for the wildest party they've ever been to. Most of these guys didn't sleep for the entire trip. Two guys missed their flights home. Our For Your Consideration campaign was so fucking flawless that kids would have studied it in film school for years to come. If you hadn't disappeared six weeks out."

"I didn't know you were doing all that," I say defensively. "Nobody told me."

"Don't play dumb now, Grace. You know, even if by some miracle you'd won that fucking Oscar, *everyone* always knew you needed one more movie to fully cross over. You've fucked it up."

"Nathan, I get it," I say, holding eye contact with him for the first time. "Please. I really get it."

"No, because if you got it, you wouldn't have done what you did. Have you thought about what you're going to do next? Because whatever you do has to be commercial but still have integrity, and do you know who the only person creating commercial stuff with integrity at the moment is?" I can tell that Nathan's about to lose his shit again.

"Can you at least see what else is out there?" I direct my attention to Kit, even though the real battle is with Nathan. "It's pilot season next month. There has to be something for me."

"Sure, honey," Kit says, pulling out his phone and frowning as he reads something. Nathan does the same. They are letting me know they are done with me.

Kit's mouth moves slightly as he types a message.

"Are you making a note of that?" I ask, narrowing my eyes.

"Of course," Kit says absentmindedly.

I stand up, and then I stamp all over the expensive rug to get to the door. I turn around and shake my head. They both ignore me, tapping away silently at their phones.

"You guys are fucking cretins."

The valet at Nathan's office building, Pat, isn't as friendly as he used to be. I wonder whether it's filtered down to him that I'm not someone he needs to impress anymore. I try to remember whether I usually give him a tip for Christmas or not. I hand him a fifty-dollar bill from my sunglasses case anyway and he's a little nicer after that, opening the car door and smiling at me. Pat used to tell me that my talent was a gift from God every time he saw me, but this time he just says, “Happy holidays,” quickly as he’s closing the car door.

CHAPTER TWENTY-THREE

I sit in the car with my eyes closed for a few minutes, trying to ground myself or whatever it was my Transcendental Meditation coach was always trying to teach me to do. I feel uneasy after my meeting with Nathan and Kit and I'm irritated to find that I still care what they think. When my phone buzzes on the seat next to me, I pick it up, staring at it for a moment. I clumsily tap in my security code before opening the message app like my sister taught me.

Don't be mad

I handled it

(It's Esme btw)

Want to know whose little friend this is?

The picture is of a dick, purple and swollen. I slap my hand over the screen and check outside my window to see if anyone is watching me. Fuck, fuck, fuck. What is she doing?

That's right, it's Mr. Best Buy, cretin-in-chief, liar-in-command himself

You're welcome

I delete her messages and throw my phone back onto the seat next to me, banging the steering wheel hard. Then I pick it back up and open a new text to Esme. I type slowly and with lots of auto-correct errors at first.

How did you get that? This is completely illegal and inappropriate.

Esme texts back almost immediately.

It is not illegal. I was trying to help. Don't bother replying if you're going to be dramatic

I rest my head on the steering wheel for a moment, but when I pull out of the parking garage and into the stark sunshine, I'm surprised to find that I'm laughing.

"Sooo, what do you think?" Esme says, try-

211

ing to control the pride in her voice. I press the phone against my ear and sink back into the porch chair.

"I think I could probably get arrested for having that hideous picture on my phone. Is Mom home?"

"They're both out. Jesus, chill, you're not going to get arrested — he's super old."

"How old is super old?"

"At least twenty."

"How did you even get that?"

"Instagram. I started talking to him under a fake account, and he asked me to send a nude first," Esme says defensively. "So I figured he definitely deserved it. He knew nothing about me and he still thought he'd earned the right to see me naked."

"You didn't . . . ?" I ask hesitantly, thinking of the nude she sent at school.

"Of course I didn't. I'm not a total idiot, Grace. I sent him one I found on Reddit, and he sends me his shit back right away, and it was just so gross that it had to be real."

"Oh God."

"Look, I've already been in contact with him to reveal our true intentions, and he's agreed to post something else about you in return for us not sending his dick pic to his boss at Best Buy. So, you're welcome."

"Something else?"

"Something to say he was just trying to get attention by posting mean things about you, and you're actually really normal and non-deranged. Et cetera, et cetera," Esme adds.

"Well. This was all very . . . kind of you, in a way," I say, feeling bad because she seems so pleased with herself. "But that's not going to work."

"What do you mean?"

"It's just not how it works, Esme. Nobody will even bother printing a tiny retraction, let alone a whole new post to say I was behaving perfectly normally on a Wednesday afternoon in Best Buy. That's not a story. Have you ever read that about anyone?"

"That's bullshit," Esme says sulkily, and I feel like I've just told her that puppies don't exist, or that Tom Hanks is a raving misogynist.

"People are saying you have a *problem*. Like drugs or drinking or something," Esme says, and I resist the urge to tell her that it's probably the first time in five years that I don't have either of those particular problems. She doesn't need to think any less of me than she already does.

"Maybe even psychosis," she adds.

"Esme, I appreciate the effort you went

to, but I'm pretty sure that however you got that photo is the last thing I need to be involved in right now. Thank you for what you were trying to do, but can we please just forget about the kid with the boner?"

"But why should he get away with it, just because he's a guy?" Esme says, sounding as if she's about to burst into tears. "Didn't anyone teach you that you have to stand up to bullies?"

I try to remember a time when I believed in rules like this, too, when I last felt owed anything by life. I feel a tug of envy at her naïveté.

"Sometimes real life doesn't work out like that," I say quietly. "Look, you may not know this yet, but there are some bad people in the world, and while some of them get exactly what they deserve, others just don't. I'm sorry to say it, but it's true. This guy might feasibly keep winning, over and over, to the point where you can't even begin to understand how unfair life can be. So the sooner you just accept that, the easier it will all be."

Esme is silent on the other end of the phone, and I shift in my chair to stop my leg from cramping up.

"The Best Buy geek is going to win?" she asks eventually. "What are you saying?"

"I don't know," I reply, exhausted suddenly, and grateful that my parents aren't home to witness the demotivational speech I've just given my sister. "No, probably not."

"So who's going to win?" Esme asks softly.

"Can we talk about something else?" I say, and for some reason I feel lonelier than I have in a long time.

"Why are you just giving up? It's so sad to watch," Esme says, sounding just like our mother.

"I have to go," I say, hanging up the phone.

I lean back in my chair and stare up at the collection of four houses on the bluff over Coyote Sumac. The view of Able's house is even better from here, and when I squint, I can just about make out a figure on the roof, staring out toward the ocean. I know instantly that it's Able. He's at home, standing on his roof deck and waiting for the sun to slip behind the ocean. My heart hammers with fury that he could be doing something so ordinary, something so quietly gratifying as watching the sunset on a Monday afternoon, just like the rest of us. I think of what I told Esme, and how I wish I had been lying. I wish that the bad guys were just the bad guys, that they didn't know exactly how to claw you down with them until your own shame becomes indistinguishable from theirs. As I watch him stare out at the ocean, I understand that I can hide myself away for as long as I want, but it will still only ever be because he made me.

When Able moves inside, a simmering anger bubbles underneath my skin for the first time in a while. The sky casts a deep red light onto the white roof of his house, and the whole ugly thing glows from the inside like it's on fire.

CHAPTER TWENTY-FOUR

Everything with Able changed a couple of months before my nineteenth birthday. I had just finished shooting the last movie where I would play a child, in a World War II film set in a concentration camp, and Able was hosting a party to celebrate at his house, the peach house up on the hill. He had ignored me throughout the entire shoot, breaking the usual pattern, and I had assumed that this time my performance really wasn't good enough, that I hadn't lost enough weight, or that he'd made a mistake by casting me in such an intense role. Or maybe he'd found out about the drugs I was relying on more and more to get through the weeks. The project was the first time we'd worked together since I turned eighteen, and a tiny part of me wondered if he wasn't interested in me now that I was older, but the thought came from the deepest, most unruly part of my mind, the part I had to suffocate in order to do what I had to do, and be who I had to be every single day.

I was surprised when Able excused us from the rest of the party under the guise of showing me our next script, and he led me into his office at the back of the house. Other guests smiled indulgently at us as we passed them, both of us America's adopted sweethearts. I remember that Emilia even waved as we went, before turning back to break up another squabble between the twins.

I floated after him, so relieved that he wanted to talk to me again. A sense of calmness descended over me that made what came next even worse. In the office, Able leaned against his desk and told me that he was finally giving in to me, that he would give me what I had wanted all this time. He unzipped his jeans as he spoke, and somehow, through my fear, I found the words to say that I didn't think it was a good idea. He told me to stop being disingenuous. That everyone knew I'd been chasing him for years. I said I needed to go to the bathroom, but he just looked at me with blank eyes as he forced me down onto the floor and put his penis in my mouth. I started to choke. Thick saliva dripped down my chin and my eyes burned with hot, shameful tears. I was staring at a photograph of Able, Emilia and the twins on the desk behind him the whole time. He didn't even turn it around.

Afterward, I tried to justify what happened. I'd let him believe that we had a special relationship because it had benefited me too. I didn't want to admit that I hadn't had a choice in any of it, and even when the disgust eventually flooded every inch of my body, it was an uninvited, complicated disgust after so many years of believing that his attention meant I was special. Every time he accused me of wanting him or needing him, or making him act this way, a tiny part of me believed him. He'd always warned me that I couldn't trust myself, and deep down I knew I never fought back as hard as I could have.

At some point, I started referring to what happened in Able's office only as "the incident" in my head. I'd had to work harder to repress it than ever before, and it wasn't just because the physical act had been so alien to me. It was what he'd said to me before it happened that really made me feel like I was drowning. In telling me he was finally giving in to me, Able had confirmed my worst, darkest suspicions — that I had some sort of power I had been unintentionally wielding over him all these years. On the rare occasions I did allow myself to think about it, usually if I hadn't drunk enough to blunt the edges of my mind, or if I hadn't topped up my Percocet prescription in time, I decided to believe that there had been a miscommunication at some point, like in one of those sitcoms where everyone's wires get crossed, only instead of ending up on a fancy blind date with my ex-boyfriend, I ended up alone in Able's office. If I thought about it only in abstract terms, without remembering the way I'd brushed my teeth until my gums bled when I got home that night or how I couldn't look in a mirror for three days after it happened, I could tell myself that the incident wasn't quite so bad. I flinched every time someone came near me.

My agent informed me that I had the best part of a year languishing ahead of me while Able developed his new project, the one he had been "showing" me the early draft of that night in his office. At first I was relieved that I wouldn't have to see him, but after a couple of months, when I hadn't heard a word from him, my disgust made way for an all-consuming terror that he no longer wanted me for the part, even though Nathan and Kit assured me that he did. I was so used to our usual pattern — Able's focused dedication at the start of a project, the rare flattery he would display to get me to sign — that I figured I'd done something really bad for him to be ignoring me like this.

For the first time in my life I was filled with both an expanse of free time and an acute, overwhelming awareness of how much trust we put in the hands of other people every single day of our lives. It was a crippling combination. There was no guarantee that the car coming toward me at a crossing was actually going to stop at the red light, yet I was still expected to step right out, and nobody could promise me that one of the many strange, older men waiting outside my hotel with a camera wouldn't just cross that line one night and force his way into my room. It all seemed so fragile to me, the trust we put in others without thinking about it, and once I realized it, the loneliness hit me like nothing I'd felt before.

When I woke up on my nineteenth birthday with my cheek stuck to the dirty floor of a strip club on the wrong end of Sunset Boulevard, watching underneath the toilet cubicle door as the girls adjusted their wigs and stiletto fastenings, I couldn't even lie to myself that I was okay anymore. Something was broken in my brain, and the more I tried to block it out, the worse it was getting.

I texted Nathan to tell him I wouldn't be doing the movie, and that I was done with it all, and I asked him to pass the news on to the rest of my team. Then I turned up at my parents' house in Anaheim much like I have every other time before and since, with my tail between my legs and a duffel bag filled with designer clothes, only this time I sank to my knees the moment my dad answered the door.

For a couple of weeks everything seemed like it was getting better. I told my parents I was recovering from a bad flu and stayed in bed, watching old sitcom reruns on the TV in my room. My dad brought my meals to my bedroom door, and even my mom, whom I'd barely had one civil conversation with since I left home, seemed to enter into an unspoken peace treaty with me. One night, she even ran me a bath filled with bubbles that smelled like rose petals, and in return I listened to her stories about Esme with a fixed smile on my face. I knew it was a fragile peace, effective only until I informed them of my decision to leave behind

222

everything they had sacrificed for me to have, but it still felt better than anything else I could be doing.

One evening, I heard the front door bell ring. I looked out my bedroom window and saw Able's Jaguar parked in front of the driveway. It was low and dark silver like a shark, and it reminded me of another world I had been trying to forget. I closed my bedroom door and sat with my forehead pressed against my knees, my breathing shallow. *I hate you,* I thought, at the same time as I hoped he would come up and find me, tell me he was sorry and forgive me for whatever part I played in what had happened. I was confused, disgusted with myself, but the one thing I understood with perfect clarity was that my parents could never find out about the incident. Whenever I thought about it, the shame would burn through me in rings, then it was waves; before long it became impossible to tell who I was without it.

Half an hour later, I heard the front door close and a car engine start outside. My mom knocked on my door a few minutes later.

"I'm sleeping," I said, but she pushed it open anyway.

"Emilia's just left," she said, standing

223

above me. I looked up at her quickly and knew she wasn't lying. Able hadn't even bothered to come himself, had sent Emilia to assess the damage for him, perhaps even in an ironic nod to the role of protector that Emilia had promised to play when she first met my parents. Only Able and I knew just how short she'd fallen.

Once the twins were no longer babies, Emilia had tried to reach out to me a few times — inviting me to the peach house for lunch or sending me bags filled with new clothes or makeup she thought I'd like. By that point, though, I already realized that whether she knew it or not, Emilia had only been at that first dinner to soften the blow for my parents, as if her presence could make the fact that they were handing me off to strangers more palatable for everyone. It turned out that Emilia rarely visited Able's film sets and that she didn't even enjoy the premieres or awards shows. She must have found it all either intimidating or boring, but I never got the chance to find out which it was, because I never spent any time with her without Able.

"I'm not going back," I said quietly.

"Well, I'm not going to tell you what to do, but she told me to tell you that Able's sorry."

I shook my head, willing her to leave me alone. My mother looked different, affected by Emilia's visit in some way I couldn't identify. I could still remember how she'd acted when we shared the hotel room during the shooting of the first assassin movie — giddy with excitement at first, then stung by my cool response and exhaustion. After that, the fault lines opened up and she grew mistrustful of me.

"Sometimes when people work together creatively for a long time, they can say or do things to hurt the other person," she said mechanically. "It's part of the process."

"Okay," I said, squeezing my eyes shut. Of all the ways I had imagined Able trying to make amends with me, sending his wife to influence my mother wasn't one of them. He was sending me a message, I figured, that Emilia had no idea what had happened. Everything was always a power move with Able.

"Emilia said he pushed you too hard on set this time. Is that true?" she said then, watching me.

"I don't want to talk about it," I said. "Especially with you."

As soon as the words were out of my mouth, I regretted them. Even I could hear the contempt dripping from my voice. I recognized it instantly as the same disdain I'd heard from Able whenever he spoke about my parents, and I was now using it against her. My mom stood up taller and pushed her hair over her shoulder, and I watched as her lips twisted like they had all those years ago in the restaurant when we first met Able.

"I'm sorry I'm not special enough to understand what it's like to be you," she said, and the ease with which she landed on her argument reminded me how close it always was to the surface.

"That's not what I meant," I said warily. I didn't want to engage in the same fight we had every time I came home, because it always seemed to end with me leaving.

"We both know exactly what you meant. I would never understand what it's like to be gifted, or talented, or special, because I'm just a mother, and not even a good one."

"Why are you making this about you?" I asked, and she just stared at me with her mouth open, helpless as a goldfish.

"Don't think that you coming back here is any sort of service to us," she said then, and it made me wonder what it was Emilia could have said to her.

"I wanted to come back."

"Sometimes the past is best left in the

past," she said, and it was only when I looked up and saw the bitterness in her eyes, the strange shape of her mouth, how it pulled against itself, that I understood the full implication of what Able had done to me. How far he'd alienated me from my family so that I could never go back to them, even when I needed them the most. In his most ambitious move yet, Able had turned me into a stranger in my own home.

Neither Able nor Emilia actually needed to say one word to me. I returned to LA the following morning, and almost immediately signed on to the movie. I started drinking more and more, to forget what had happened and everything I'd left behind. I kept my distance from Emilia after that, and, like everyone else in my life apart from Able, she slipped off-screen, fading into the background.

For the first time I let myself believe I was in control of my future, even though in reality everything was spinning away from me, just out of reach. Somehow, when I met Dylan at a party three weeks after my return, I even let myself believe that I could be normal for just long enough that he believed it too. I spent my first year off pretending to be anyone other than myself.

■ ■ ■ ■

When *Lights of Berlin* finally went into preproduction, I had to train for the role of the homicidal sex worker for a further ten months. It was grueling: the incomprehensible German lessons, the Krav Maga training with the former Mossad agent, the hours of body conditioning with the Russian ballet director, the driving stunts Able insisted would only work if I did them myself. I faced him every day, and every night I went home and drank enough vodka or snorted enough coke until I forgot his face. The only thing that stopped me from falling over the edge was Dylan. Each morning I woke up with him still next to me was another small indicator that maybe I wasn't such a bad person. After a while, I even figured that if he believed in me so much, maybe it didn't matter that I couldn't believe in myself. By the time principal photography on *Lights of Berlin* began, we were already married.

The film was shot on location in Europe, and when Dylan agreed to go with me, I thought that I could have broken the cycle for good. I felt stronger, braver, occasionally even happy with my new husband there, and it even seemed as if Able was finally respecting my boundaries. Yes, I was half-naked for most of the shoot, but he didn't berate me on set or make me reshoot scenes unnecessarily in the middle of the night, or make any thinly veiled comments about my inability to grasp the reality of any given situation. He didn't praise or single me out, either, but I told myself I didn't need him to because this time was different. I even almost believed it. I started to think about my next project, believing that if I had Dylan by my side, then perhaps I could choose it myself. There was even already talk of an Oscar nomination, something I had never allowed myself to dream of up to this point. For the first time in my life, my future seemed full of potential, like maybe I could be happy one day, or at least baseline normal.

Then, at the wrap party in a sex club in Berlin, Able pulled me aside and looked me dead in the eye as he told me that he no longer drew any inspiration from me. He thought my work on the film had been adequate, but he could tell from the dailies that I was losing something as I aged. The thing that had once set me apart from everyone else who auditioned for the first assassin movie, the thing that had compelled him to bind his entire career to mine up to that point, the light, the hunger, the talent or whatever you wanted to call it, was gone.

I was always told that the reason Able and I never signed an official contract binding us to each other was because it would have been unethical to do so, but I now know it was just so Able could control the end too. Our working relationship was effectively over, as quickly and unceremoniously as that. I was twenty-one years old, just married, at the height of my career, and still the rejection burned through me like nothing I'd felt before, worse than any other part of it, worse even than that night in his office. I had spent the past eight years living my life in relation to Able, and I didn't know who I was without him. I had been nothing before him, so why would I be anything after him? I could just about handle hating him, but it was the shame that pulled me under, pushing on my chest and making it hard for me to catch my breath. I understood that by waiting until he dropped me, I had turned myself into the least credible of sources. Nobody would ever believe me, even if I could somehow find the words for what happened.

The summer after the film wrapped, I worked harder than ever before to forget who I was for just a second, or a night, sometimes even a week. I chased drug after drug and lied to Dylan so shamelessly that when his ignorance started to feel deliberate, I finally had something to blame someone else for. The way he looked at me used to terrify me. I felt heavy with the weight of his love.

Every so often I try to unravel it again, to see where I can remove my fingerprints, ones that Able marked from the start, but it is still too tangled.

CHAPTER TWENTY-FIVE

I wake up late again, covered in sweat. The bedsheets are damp, and my hair has curled into salty tendrils stuck to the nape of my neck. I dreamed that I was back on the set of *Lights of Berlin* but the entire crew was made up of lizard people, and they were all communicating to each other in a complicated language I almost understood but didn't. In a way, that was how it had always worked, except Able made sure that I was the alien on any film set, the only one who wasn't allowed to understand how the magic actually worked. At the time I believed he was protecting me, but maybe he just needed me to be foreign, uncomprehending, so I depended on him that much more.

I carry my binoculars out to the porch and squint through them, adjusting the focus on the side swiftly, as I have learned to do. The house on the hill is dark, and there are no cars in the drive. Before I can change my mind, I drop the binoculars on the porch chair and walk across the sand until I reach the white wooden beach steps leading to the four houses on the bluff overlooking Coyote Sumac. I'm breathing heavily by the time I climb the last step, and sweat is dripping between my breasts.

I walk through the tall, sharp blades of grass between the back of the house and the road. The house is exactly as I remember it, a sprawling Mediterranean villa with a bright peach exterior and cream roof tiles, surrounded by beautiful, elegant gardens and shaded by palm trees. I think I wondered whether, just by being here and standing in front of it, its power over me could be lessened, but my heart is already beating fast in my chest and my breathing is labored. I know that the memories are about to start and that they'll come in dark fragments at first and then thicker, stronger, until I feel as if I can reach out and touch them. I have already turned around, about to leave, when a car door slams behind me. I step backward, off-balance, as someone calls my name.

"Grace . . . Grace Turner. Is that you?" Emilia asks, her mouth already widening into a smile. She walks toward me and kisses me on both cheeks. "Able didn't tell me you were back in town! He's so thoroughly useless."

My legs nearly give way at the mention of his name, but I recover, forcing a smile that is nearly passable.

"Hyde," I say. "They made me change it to Turner for the films but it was always Hyde. Remember?"

"Of course it is," Emilia says, looking disoriented for just a moment. "I never understood why they did that."

She takes a step back and looks me up and down, smiling again. "Beautiful girl. Well, woman now. What are you doing here? Last I heard you were in Venice?"

"I was just . . . going for a walk. I didn't realize . . . I'm actually living down in Coyote Sumac at the moment. Dylan and I . . ." I shake my head.

"Oh, sweetheart, I'm so sorry. I heard that." Emilia puts her head to one side and pushes out her lips slightly in the universal expression of sympathy for when your marriage has rotted. "You just missed Able, but come in for a coffee?"

Emilia gestures toward the house with her head because she's carrying four canvas bags full of groceries and two huge Fred Segal bags. When she sees me looking, she rolls her eyes, pretending to be embarrassed.

"Christmas shopping. This is conspicuous consumption in action, Grace — it's disgusting, I *know*. Come on."

I follow her into the house.

The front door opens straight into the living room, which stretches all the way through to the back of the house, flanked by a double staircase leading to the bedrooms upstairs. Everything in the house is as rich and ornate as a private members' club, in contrast to the usual expanse of empty white space and driftwood so common to mansions in Malibu. The walls are forest green, surrounding velvet sofas and a hissing, glowing wood burner. First-edition leather-bound books with gold embossed titles line the shelves, punctuated by expensive candles and framed black-and-white photographs of the family on the beach in Nantucket or skiing in Verbier. And the smell — still that suffocating sandalwood, after all these years.

My legs feel like jelly as I follow Emilia, unable to stop. I realize now that I haven't seen her since the *Lights of Berlin* premiere, where I threw up twice in the toilets before the film had even started. She seems calmer, happier than I remember, and I wonder if she's on meds like everyone else with any sense in this city.

The Christmas tree in the center of the room shimmers with gold and white baubles, and thousands of tiny lights on an invisible thread. Hundreds of porcelain carolers stand around the tree, staring up at it, frozen with their mouths half-open and their eyes glazed. The figurines also line every available surface, all dressed in red and green, some holding mini instruments and gifts. Emilia catches me staring at them and laughs quickly.

"When my grandmother died I had this ridiculous fight with my least favorite cousin over who got to keep her collection of carolers. As you can see, I won and am now cursed to display every freaking one of them until the sweet release of death. At this point I don't care if it's hers or mine."

I touch one of them on the head. The caroler is wearing a red skating outfit, and she seems stricken by my touch. We walk past the door to Able's office, and I wonder whether Emilia can see the beads of sweat forming above my lip, whether she can hear the shudder of my pulse as I place my hand on the closed door. I follow Emilia into the kitchen, wishing I'd brought my bottle of

Percocet with me. Sometimes just knowing the pills are in my possession is enough to stop the panic from catching hold like a wildfire.

The kitchen is different. They have redone it since I was last here, and everything is tasteful and overt at the same time, like Emilia. There is no sign of Able's touch left in the house. I lean against the marble island, looking anywhere but Emilia's eyes. Adrenaline courses through my veins and I suddenly, urgently, need the toilet, but I don't want to be alone.

"When was the last time we had you over? I'm always saying how much I miss having you around. It's crazy that we've known you since you were just a kid, really, even though you never acted like one." Emilia unpacks the shopping methodically as she speaks, making piles of similar items and then distributing them among the fridge, freezer and pantry. I take the opportunity to look at her now, taking in her unfashionably thin eyebrows and even thinner nose, her pale eyes the color of the Atlantic Ocean in winter. I realize now that I undervalued her beauty when I was younger — she is attractive in that subtle, fleece-and-jeans, country club way that grows every time you look at her, rewarding you for having noticed it in the first place.

Please be aware that I recognized this as a mistake as soon as I walked through that door. For once, every single level of my consciousness seems to be united and they are all singing at me like a Greek chorus, instructing me to remove myself from the situation immediately, but of course I don't know how. Emilia's composure is unnerving me; I've always believed that the people who feel the most comfortable are the most dangerous to be around.

Emilia picks up a light blue box and hands it to me. "Marrons glacés. We used to have them in Connecticut when I was a child, and they are absolutely the only thing that gets me in the holiday spirit in this furnace of a city. You must try one."

I open the box to find six round globes in individual foil packaging. I unwrap one with trembling fingers, pressing it into my dry mouth. The sweet icing crumbles instantly, coating my tongue so that I don't have to speak. My heart is beating so hard in my chest that I'm surprised it's not visible through my shirt.

"Isn't that just heaven? Able brought them back from Paris for me. He may be useless in every other way, but my beautiful husband would never dare forget my marrons glacés."

"How's the . . . writing going?" I ask, struggling to swallow. Emilia used to be a journalist at *LA Weekly,* but she gave it up a few years ago to write celebrity biographies and brightly colored airport novels. I cough slightly, acrid sugar caught at the back of my throat, and Emilia hands me a small bottle of water from the fridge.

"I'm writing fiction now, you knew that, right? It's total trash but there's something cathartic about leaning into that without any fear. So what if I want to write a book about a vet falling back in love with her high school boyfriend in Montana? I've resigned myself to the fact that my Yale degree will now be utilized to provide comfort for people I'll never meet. And that's okay." While she's been talking, Emilia has whisked three eggs with some cream and salt. She drops the mixture into a frying pan and stirs absent-mindedly with a pale blue spatula.

"Of course Able is mortified. He's always been such a snob, even though he's the one from Utah." She rolls her eyes again and shoves a loose strand of hair back behind her ear. She still has that perfect blond hair — glossy and tumbling, forming a wave over her shoulder and down her back like a

239

cartoon. You can tell everything you need to know about Emilia from her hair, I think now, perhaps unkindly.

I watch as she scrapes the scrambled eggs onto a plate and then stops, frowning. "I'm sorry. Did you say you wanted eggs?"

"Okay," I say, sitting down at the farmhouse table. I feel as if I'm in a dream, watching everything unfold around me without my permission, even though, like always, I'm the one who set it in motion.

Emilia smiles as she passes me the plate and a knife and fork, and then at the last minute she rips into a loaf of sourdough and drops a chunk on top.

"You're young — you can still eat gluten, right?" she asks as she sits down opposite me.

"I'm so sorry, Grace, were you expecting to find Able here? He got rid of his assistant because he thought he could run his own calendar better, but he's just horrible at it. Did he tell you he was away for the next couple of weeks? He's doing reshoots in Utah and promised me he'll be back to help get everything ready for Christmas, but you just never know with him. Do you want some wine? I have the least addictive personality, so I can do things like drink wine at one p.m., but most of my friends can't."

"I'm okay," I say, but I watch as Emilia takes two wineglasses down from the cabinet over the sink anyway. She pours a full glass for herself, then a smaller one for me. She is warm, relaxed, no hidden indignations or insecurities sharpening her angles. Her life is easy, I realize now, watching her.

"Well, I can't be drinking alone when the girls come home," she says, smiling, and it's okay, because I already know I won't touch it. I need to stay focused, alert in this house.

I've never been less hungry, but I eat a small mouthful of the eggs. I can tell instantly that they are perfect, steaming hot and creamy, falling apart as soon as they hit my tongue.

Emilia watches me closely, and I concentrate on eating normally: *chew, chew, chew, swallow.*

"Come on then. Tell me everything I need to know about you. You look great, but then you always did, and Able told me to stop worrying about you even when you became emaciated for that war film."

"He did?" I grip the fork tightly. I manage to swallow something sour at the back of my throat before I stick my fork into the pile of eggs again.

"Oh, you know." She waves her hand. "I think he just knew you so well, knew what

241

phase you were going through and when. I was always an outsider with you two, in the best way."

I focus on pushing the last mouthful of eggs onto a piece of bread, trying to disguise my trembling hands.

"You know, I'm pleased you're here, and I know Able will be, too, when I tell him. The kids would also love to see you — can you wait around until four?"

The kids. Two little girls who cried when they had to go to bed at my sixteenth birthday party. Able's hands clamped on their shoulders in the photo on his office desk. The room fragments around me, fraying at the edges so that I have to place both palms on the table to steady myself.

"I actually have to get back now. I have a meeting," I say, and before Emilia can ask me anything else, I stand up and loudly scrape the chair underneath the table.

"Another time then. The girls are nearly nine, if you can believe it? Silver is very bright but can be a monster when she wants to be, and Ophelia is just a pleasure to have around. Everyone says you don't have a favorite, but my God, do you. Luckily, Able prefers Silver — he's always liked his women complicated." Emilia laughs as she follows me out of the kitchen, seemingly unaware of my urgent need to be anywhere but her house.

When we reach the front door, Emilia seems immediately despondent at the thought of me leaving, asking in a childlike way, "Do you really have to go?"

"Thanks for having me, Emilia," I say. "I'll see you around."

"Gracie?" Emilia calls after me, just as I reach the fountain in the middle of their expansive drive. I stop and face her, the gentle sound of trickling water accompanying her words.

"Take care of yourself," she says, but she looks like she wants to say more. For the first time, I wonder whether she feels guilty about how everything turned out for me. I nod and turn back around, forcing myself to continue slowly, calmly down the hill to Coyote Sumac. When I reach the bottom, I look back up at the peach house. Emilia is still standing in the doorway, watching me.

I'm covered in sweat by the time I reach the sand. Panic is pressing through my veins, and I don't know how to make it stop. I don't know what I was doing, moving here and going back up to the house on my own. Letting Emilia cook for me and say his name ten times. I don't know what I would have done if Able were there with her. Was I planning to confront him? Would I have kissed him on each cheek as if nothing had ever happened? Would I have taken a kitchen knife from the island and plunged it into his neck in front of Emilia, watching the terror in his eyes as they bulged out of his head, crimson blood spraying over us all like something out of a cheap horror movie? What do you do when you can't even trust yourself?

I stand in front of the ocean and try to remember how it felt to be underneath the surface, the burning pressure in my lungs as the need for oxygen tore through me, the sun sparkling just above. I try to remember that I chose to be here. I sink into the sand and breathe slowly, cupping my hands over my mouth and breathing hard as tears roll down my cheeks. When none of it works, when it still feels as if my brain is covered in thousands of scuttling beetles, I text Laurel to ask her to come over. At the last minute I add another line: Bring some of our old friends.

I never said I was very good at protecting myself.

CHAPTER TWENTY-SIX

Laurel pulls out two bottles of Casamigos tequila and a large vial of white powder. She places it all on the glass table in front of the sofa and smiles at me innocently.

"I assumed you meant these old friends, because we hate everyone else."

I look for a couple of glasses in the kitchen even though I know I don't have any, and I can feel the familiar anticipation building in my chest. This is what it used to be like, back when I did this every night. Sometimes I wanted feverish pain and sometimes I wanted blinding euphoria, and then there were the times I just wanted to feel my body jerk and burn as I threw up. I wonder what type of night it will be tonight.

"I don't have any glasses," I say as I sit next to Laurel on the sofa. She pulls the stopper out of the tequila and has a long swig before she passes it to me. I have a smaller sip, and it burns the back of my throat as it hits.

"How are you finding your new home?" Laurel asks, with obvious distaste as she racks up a couple of lines. She remembers how I like mine, skinny and long. I keep my eyes trained on the coke, ignoring her question.

"If Dylan the Saint could see us now," she says when I lean over to snort mine using the straw she passes me. The coke tastes metallic, cut with something petrol-like, hopefully not actual petrol.

"Did you go to rehab last year?" she asks after doing her own line, which is much smaller than mine. I shake my head, wishing she'd stop talking for a minute so that I could feel the adrenaline make way for the strange buzzing calm, closely followed by an intense spike in clarity.

"For fuck's sake, Grace, talk to me."

"I told you, I went to my parents'."

"For the entire year? You were in Anaheim for a year. Less than one hour away. What were you doing there?"

I try to remember. What was I doing there? Now I can feel the coke flooding through me. My skin feels tingly, and I'm already clenching my jaw, so I grab the bottle of tequila and have another swig. It's always a balancing act between the two. Too much coke and you feel on edge, too much alcohol and you feel weighed down.

"I think I was trying to make my parents like me."

"Did it work?" Laurel is talking faster now, leaning toward me. Urgency drills through me, and it's bordering on too intense, and I know that the only way to harness it is to grab it quickly and channel it somewhere. I focus on Laurel, the concern in her eyes that I'm only now thinking may actually be real. I always get everything wrong.

"My mom said it was 'illuminating' spending so much time with me."

"As in, you lit up the entire house?"

"I don't think so."

We drink some more tequila and do another couple of lines each. I forgot this about us; we never knew when to stop when we were together, and the time between racking up lines would diminish until we started moving like a time-lapse film, cutting out all unnecessary pauses as we dipped our heads.

"What did you come back for? Dylan?"

I shake my head. Another line, this one thicker than I like. I wish we weren't in the sticks of Malibu and that there was some-

where nearby I could buy a pack of cigarettes.

"Me?" She puts her hand across her heart
like she's flattered, and I shake my head,
then point at her, acutely, perfectly.

"Definitely not you. You're the worst," I
say, and Laurel is pissed for a moment
before we both collapse into ridiculous,
charged laughter, but I'm only really feeling
10 percent of it. I do another line of coke.

"I came back because I realized I was trying to be someone who doesn't exist anymore," I say, my throat stinging.

"But then when I'm here, I just feel like
I'm letting everyone down all the time too.
I'm never going to be what anyone wants
me to be, you know? Even that little shit in
Best Buy or my own fucking sister — they
think I'm going to be . . . I don't know —"
I search for the right word to perfectly, *ir-
revocably* encapsulate how I feel, the coke
charging through my bloodstream now and
coating every word I say with a thick, urgent
intensity. "*Cool.* They think I'm going to be
cool. I'm not cool. I'm not impressive."

Laurel bursts out laughing again, and
some powder falls out of her nose. She claps
her hand across her nose and mouth, and
you can't even tell that she's laughing
anymore, other than the snorts escaping.

"I fucking missed you. You're worried that people don't think you're cool?"

"No, I'm worried they do think I'm cool."

"You're an idiot, Grace."

We sit on the floor with our backs against the sofa, and everything seems brighter in the room, the lights glowing around us.

"You left me too. You know that, right?" Laurel says. "And I don't think it's better when you're not here."

"I'm paying you, you don't count," I say.

"You think you're paying me?" Laurel looks at me as if I'm insane, and it all suddenly seems so funny that I start to laugh. She doesn't laugh this time, and I can see instead that she's warming up to the idea of having a meaningful coked-out chat, but the tequila and coke both hit me behind the eyes at the same time.

"I thought I was supposed to like myself by now," I say, and now my eyes are stinging with tears because it's finally the truth and it makes me think about how nice it would be to tell her, to get the *thing* off my chest and set it free into the world, to let it feed off somebody else's oxygen, somebody else's bones, but instead I start to gag as the bitter coke drips down the back of my throat. It's too much and I run to the toilet

to throw up, hot messy tears running down
my cheeks while Laurel strokes my hair.

CHAPTER TWENTY-SEVEN

I wake up facedown on the sofa, my mouth tasting like petrol. Every inch of my flesh is covered in an icy sweat as my brain pulses in my skull, knocking against the back of my eyes. I know that sleep isn't an option from this point on, so I stumble through to the bathroom, avoiding looking directly at the mess from the night before. I turn the shower on and make sure it's scalding hot before I step into it, then I crouch on the floor like an animal, my head in my hands as the water floods over me.

I have just wrapped a towel around me when someone knocks at my front door. I stagger across the living room, assuming it's Laurel with provisions, like it always used to be. She would turn up with a bottle of 5-HTP to top up our serotonin levels, a packet of Emergen-C to replace the nutrients we lost, a weed pen and sometimes a Xanax, depending on how much coke we'd done the night before, because we weren't actually trying to *kill* ourselves at that point.

I open the door, and Dylan is standing there with his hands in his pockets.

"Oh fuck," I say, stepping forward in an attempt to shield him from the scene in my living room. Two empty bottles of tequila, my clothes strewn across the sofa, traces of white powder on the coffee table and the unmistakable stench of tequila-laced vomit.

Dylan looks over my shoulder and then back at me.

"Dylan . . ." I start, but there's nothing I can say.

"It's okay, I should have called," he says, backing away. "I just wanted to check how you were doing, but it looks like you're all settled in."

I reach out to stop him from leaving, but he sidesteps my touch and then tries to smile at me to show just how okay the whole thing is. I feel sick as he walks down the steps, and I know that, after everything, he's still only trying to act normal so I don't freak out, which makes everything worse. Surely there must be some limit to how many times you're allowed to hurt another human.

I watch him get back into his car and drive up the dirt track. When his car disappears

252

at the top, something inside me breaks and I slide down the wall of the house, sobbing like I haven't since my first night back in Anaheim. As tears fall down my cheeks, I look up at the peach house, shimmering on the hill above me.

When the beetles take a break from scuttling over my brain, I force myself out of the house to get something to eat. Laurel isn't answering my calls and I don't trust myself to drive, so I walk up the hill to the highway instead, instantly regretting it when I realize that Los Angeles isn't playing fair today. It is fiercely, unfathomably hot, and the ash from forest fires one hundred miles north is coating my lungs. Sweat patches have already formed on my T-shirt, and I can't remember ever having been this thirsty. If this were Venice, I'd already be in possession of a forty-dollar green elixir smoothie promising me beauty and vitality and the cleanest liver in town, but it's Malibu, so all I can do is walk into the first place I come to — a gas station on PCH. I buy some dill-flavored potato chips, a pack of Babybel cheese and a huge bottle of water. As I'm paying, I notice the hot counter next to the till, and I point to a slice of stale pizza, which the attendant drops stiffly into a brown paper bag, all the while staring at me as if I've made some terrible life choices to get here. I grip the bag with sweaty hands and am stumbling out of the store when someone says my name.

"Grace."

I turn around. It's a man around my dad's age, slight, with acne scarring and dark eyes. At this point, it seems like as good a time as any to mention that everyone I meet feels at least slightly familiar to me, so the fact that I think I recognize him means nothing. An example — I meet my driver for the night and become convinced that he also worked behind the cash register in the bookstore I visited the day before. I'm aware that it says a lot about my self-absorption that I think strangers are on some sort of rotating wheel, orbiting my life like something out of *The Truman Show,* but does being aware of that make it better or worse? It's hard to say.

The man in the gas station reaches into his cross-body bag, and now I notice how heavy it is, how much he's trying to blend in with his backward gray baseball cap and white T-shirt. He pulls out a long-lens camera and grins at me.

"This is my lucky day. Welcome home, Ms. Turner. Do you mind?"

"Can I say no?"

He shakes his head, still smiling.

"You know how it works."

I nod and then I quickly turn around, pushing open the door and running as fast as I can to the first crossing on PCH. The paparazzo is only three seconds behind me and I can hear the frenzied clicking of his camera. At this point I have a choice between running across four lanes of fast-moving traffic in my Crocs, or being a sitting target for him while I wait for the light to change. I look down at the sweat marks on my stained shirt, the brown paper bag in my hand with grease spots already soaking through, and I make my choice. The first lane is clear so I run straight through it, slowing to weave in between two cars in the second. A car honks at me, and someone shouts something imperceptible out the window.

"What are you doing, you crazy bitch?" the photographer shouts after me, and even through the traffic sounds, I can hear how much he's enjoying himself. Cars honk at me as they speed past, hot air whipping my face. I wait half a second and then I take the third lane, ducking in front of a VW camper van moving more slowly than the rest. One more lane to go. I can taste the sweat on my lip as I spot my moment, after a black Range Rover with no traffic behind it. I have timed it perfectly, ready to duck behind it as soon as it passes, when the driver spots me and panics. She slams on the brakes and I catch the rear bumper with my thigh. I tumble to the ground but I'm not hurt; in fact, I feel amazing, invincible, like a superhero stopping traffic. I jump up and streak across the road and into the woodland opposite me. I think I can still get down to Coyote Sumac this way, but the paparazzo won't know that's where I'm going.

The wooded area is cooler, shaded by pines and eucalyptus trees. I run through the thicket, navigating the dry, crumbling hill down to my house in my Crocs. Its starting to feel unnecessary, tripping over branches and rocks like I'm fleeing a monster, but I can't risk the photographer finding out where I live and camping out, waiting for me to do something dumb again. The adrenaline is slowly wearing off, replaced by the anxious fog from the night before.

When I get to the bottom of the hill, I realize that I made a shitty decision, running like a wild animal instead of handling the situation. My frazzled, drug-addled brain finally catches up with what just happened when I stop moving and sit down on the steps of my porch. The photographer isn't anywhere near me because he was never following me. He didn't have to because he'd already got what he needed. I open the paper bag in my hand. I dropped the motherfucking slice of pizza when I was crossing the road.

the road

CHAPTER TWENTY-EIGHT

I turn my phone off like Esme taught me,
knowing that it's just a matter of time before
the calls and texts come from Laurel and
Nathan, asking why I so happily exposed
myself like that, running across the road like
someone was threatening to give me a
lobotomy if I didn't make it over at that
exact moment.

I change into a black T-shirt and a pair of
Levi's that I have to leave unzipped because
they don't fit me anymore, and I settle on
my sofa with a jar of peanut butter and a
banana. I am alternating bites of banana
with gratifying spoonfuls of thick, claggy
peanut butter when there's a knock at my
front door.

I wipe my hands on my jeans and warily
open the door. Emilia is standing on my
doorstep, carrying three full Whole Foods
canvas bags. When I see her looking, I pull
the black T-shirt down over my exposed

stomach.

"Oh God. It's worse than I thought," she says, pushing past me and heaving the bags onto the Formica countertop of my kitchenette.

"What is?" I ask defensively.

"Sorry, darling, I didn't mean to sound rude. It's just, I saw how you inhaled those eggs yesterday and I figured you don't have anyone around to . . . do anything for you. I always got the impression that Dylan looked after you. I don't know, the thought of you being here on your own broke my heart."

My face heats up with shame that Emilia would be the person to identify that I'm not coping in some significant, crucial way and would try to fix me. I wonder if Able knows Emilia is here and whether she's already told him how lonely, how tragically incapable, I am.

"I'm okay," I say as Emilia opens the kitchen cabinets. I know that they are all empty except for the one above the sink that houses the dusty thermos lid that was here when I moved in. Emilia pulls out four beautiful peach-colored plates from one of the canvas bags, and stacks them in the shelf next to the oven. While she's doing it, I nudge a pile of empty pizza boxes underneath the table with my foot, and Emilia pretends not to see.

"I've got you some things but we're going to need to order more. Unless you think you won't be here for too long?"

I just shake my head in response, thinking of the look on Dylan's face when he saw the scene in my living room earlier.

"Okay. That's fine. I think this could be great for you. A life-defining moment. I'm going to start unpacking, and you just stop me if you don't like any of it, because Silver will eat it. She'd eat our neighbor's dog if I let her, I swear to God. Just like her father."

She stacks my fridge with mainly green things, kale, spinach, avocados and other dark leafy vegetables, and then she fills my empty cupboards with dried pasta, beans and rice, and cans of organic soup.

"You know, I actually spoke to Able this morning, and, between you and me, he's freaking out about John Hamilton's next movie. They've always had a friendly rivalry, you knew that, right? And everyone is talking about this new project of John's like it's the answer to the great myth of the universe, and it's so different from the one Able's working on that it's really thrown him. I can tell he's nervous because he's asked me to fly out to Utah next week so that I can be there when he shows his new producers the director's cut. Able's already had some problems with them, so he's worried they're going to be difficult about it. You know how protective he is of his 'vision.' "

I note the slight rush I feel at the thought of Able having any sort of crisis in confidence, even though I know it won't last long. I try to memorize Emilia's words anyway, storing them up to devour later like scraps of food.

As she talks, Emilia takes out a carton of eggs, a pint of cream, butter and some salt and pepper in deep blue grinders, and she lays them out on the surface next to the oven. She finds a frying pan in a drawer that I didn't know existed and she washes it in the sink, using her fingers to pull off the flakes of old grease stuck to it. When she's finished, she wipes her hands on her jeans and turns to me.

"Is your boiler working? The water's cold."

"I had a hot shower earlier . . ." I say, remembering the water burning my shoulders as I curled up on the shower floor. I make a note to locate the boiler once Emilia has left, even though I don't know what I'm looking for.

"It should last longer than that. Let me send my guy around to look at it," she says, then laughs. "Listen to me — 'my guy.' It's a plumber, for God's sake. I've been in this city too long."

She puts the frying pan on the stove and lights one of the rings, after a couple of attempts.

"I didn't realize how close you were. We're practically neighbors," she says, dropping a peel of butter into the pan.

"I can see your house from here," I say, but she's not really listening to me.

"When you buy eggs at the grocery store, you have to open the carton to see if any of them are broken, okay?" she says, then glances at me to check whether it's okay that she's doing this. After that she carries on more confidently. "Some people use milk instead of cream when they make eggs, but the increase in calories is negligible when you take into account how much of a difference it makes to the taste. I'm from the East Coast, and we just don't buy into all that crap. If you go into a coffee shop in Connecticut and ask for anything other than full-fat cow's milk, they'll just think you're a millennial snowflake."

She turns back around and starts to stir the mixture with a fork. I pretend not to watch as I lean against the fridge. A strange, adrenaline-fueled disappointment sets in, and I have to force myself not to say anything that will lead back to Able. I forgot how familiar picking at the scab feels, and the realization that this might be what sustains me causes me to burn with shame.

"Did your mom teach you to cook anything?"

"I left home before she really had the chance," I say, and I think Emilia winces slightly. I decide not to mention that when I was back there I didn't want to let on just how incapable I was to either of them, how poor a job I'd done growing up without them.

"You know, I remember that dinner at Nobu as if it were yesterday. It's funny how the mind works, isn't it?" Emilia muses as she stirs with the same baby-blue spatula she used at her place. "Your mom is such a character and so *beautiful*."

"Yeah, I guess she is."

"You look like her, you know."

I try not to think of my mother now — the empty look on her face as she watches TV all day, the bones jutting out of her tiny frame.

"We've had some problems," I say, before I know I'm going to, and I'm annoyed once I've said it. Emilia looks over her shoulder in concern. She drops the spatula onto the countertop and turns around to face me.

"Well, I'm sure it will work out just fine. She's very lucky to have you as a daughter," she says, as confident in her assessment of my abilities as a daughter as she is about everything else.

"I don't think she's lucky at all," I say, shrugging. "She'd say I was the lucky one."

"Sometimes these things can be complicated," she says kindly, and then she steps toward me and pulls me into a hug. My eyes fill with involuntary tears, even as I'm thinking how ironic it is that Emilia is the one to try to help me, after everything that's happened. As she hugs me, I realize how horrified Able would be to know that she was even here, let alone that we had been talking about him. Maybe they will even argue about it on the phone later, and Able will become cold and withdrawn when the fight doesn't unfold exactly how he wants it to. Maybe, without even meaning to, I have somehow started to infect his family the same way he's infected mine. And that's when the thought that has been fluttering in my chest since I arrived back in LA breaks through the darkness, soaring high above me before settling back inside my skin, reborn.

I am the only one in this situation with nothing to lose.

I pull away from the hug under the pretense of checking on the eggs, which are now hard at the edges, curling and brown. I watch the smoke start to pour off the pan, and then I turn back to Emilia, finally meeting her eyes with my own.

"I think you're right," I say slowly. "By the way, next time you speak to Able, please tell him I said hi."

Once Emilia has left, I turn my phone back on to call Nathan. Unexpectedly his assistant patches me straight through and he answers, albeit begrudgingly and sounding just one breath away from telling me he's in a meeting.

"Look — John Hamilton called a couple of weeks ago about a space movie — could we see what that's about?" I ask quickly, trying to lace my voice with the perfect mix of gratitude and authority, always a delicate balance when dealing with an egomaniac.

Nathan pauses, then he sighs heavily. "I'll look into it, but I wouldn't hold your breath. John Hamilton isn't the kind of person who waits around."

"I'm sure he isn't but, honestly, Nathan,

I'll put the work in. I promise. I'll audition, or do whatever I need to do to get that part."

"Okay, Grace. That's good to hear, I guess," he says, and that's when I know I can wear him down if I really want to. I just have to play it perfectly.

"Thanks, Nathan, you've always understood me better than anyone."

"For my sins," he says, and, if I'm not mistaken, I think I can hear a touch of warmth in his voice.

Chapter Twenty-Nine

The paparazzi shots of me running across Pacific Coast Highway are, by all accounts, disastrous. My hair is greasy and clumped together, and my clothes are stained and sweat marked. There is a feral look in my eyes that I don't recognize as I streak across the road, my back curved like a hunted animal. I look so deranged that they would almost be funny if I didn't have to swear forty times to Laurel that I hadn't completely lost my mind, and if Nathan hadn't called me to say only "John Hamilton is out" before hanging up on me.

My publicist, Nan, also rang me when she saw the coverage, and she strongly advised me to release a statement saying I was seeking treatment for exhaustion, brought on by my back-to-back work schedule since I was fourteen. I refused and she quit on the spot, sounding resigned, as if she'd tried every other possible option but I still just refused to play the game. In reality, exhaustion is a cheap excuse, and she would have known that. Everyone knows that it is a euphemism for a drug problem or an eating disorder, afforded only to those privileged enough to have access to a publicist who can barter and lie on their behalf. No, Nan's resignation had more to do with the fact that when I was in demand, she had to work overtime to cover up my transgressions, and that her life would be a lot easier without me now that I'm not. She knew I would never agree to the statement; she just wanted a way out that wouldn't be her fault. I don't resent her for any of it. Conversely I actually envy her if she is able to justify her actions to herself in this way.

Esme is the one who shows me the pictures on her phone, over iced tea on my porch one morning while Blake is at therapy. She's created a whole album of the coverage, and one of the headlines accompanying the pictures was "Crazed and On the Run," which Esme seems to find amusing. She also makes sure to highlight an anonymous tell-all from an alleged former friend of mine, claiming she personally saw me rail an eight-ball of coke alone at a party a couple of years ago. My "friend" ended her statement by saying that even then she could tell I was running from my demons. How poetic.

"So what exactly *were* you running from?" Esme asks once I've read the piece, and because she's still a kid, I'm worried that she actually wants an answer.

"It was really hot," I say.

Two teenage boys are skating up and down the path below my porch, practicing tricks on their skateboards. The younger one falls off, skinning his knees as his friend howls with laughter. I try not to notice that the kid is limping slightly when he pretends to be fine, because I don't want to have to feel sorry for him too. Esme is staring at them, too, but she frowns when I catch her.

"Shall we?" I say, pointing to the water. I've promised to go swimming with Esme, but it's still too chilly to even be outside, let alone in the water. I imagine this is what having children is like, always having to do something you'd really rather not in order to not let them down.

"Not yet," Esme says tersely, shooting another glance at the skateboarders, who are now practicing flips over a piece of driftwood.

"Why are you staring at them?" Esme hisses, borderline hysterical. She's being so dramatic that I have to try not to smile.

"Do you like one of them?" I ask, unsure of the correct terminology because I missed out on all of this. Esme lets out an anguished sound, and I somehow manage not to point out that she's actually drawing more attention to herself.

"All right, it's okay," I say. "Let's talk about something else."

We sit in silence for a few moments, and I'm about to start discussing global warming or something when Esme speaks again. She has been quietly fuming, her fingers curled into fists on her lap. "Do you even have any friends? Because you're always by yourself."

"Wow," I respond, only slightly offended because it's the sort of thing I would ask.

"It's weirder because you're famous."

"I do have friends," I say, thinking about Dylan. "It just gets more complicated as you get older."

Esme opens her mouth, but I shoot her a warning look and she closes it again.

"Everything gets more complicated as you get older," she says, sounding wiser than her years for once. I think she wants to say something else, so I wait out the uncomfortable pause that follows.

"The girls at school don't speak to me

anymore," she says, shifting in the lawn chair.

"What?"

"Do you mean 'what' or 'why'?" she asks, but I can tell she's upset from the way she pulls at the piece of hair falling just in front of her right ear. When she was a kid, she used to twist it so hard that it stopped growing, and for a while she just had this strange mod-style sideburn on one side. I didn't realize she still did it, and a quiet fury that anybody could hurt this person takes hold of me, surprising in its force.

"I liked this guy so I hooked up with him at a party, then he changed his mind about me and told everyone, and now they think I'm a slut."

Esme scrolls through something on her phone, frowning. "And now he goes out with my ex–best friend so none of my friends are allowed to speak to me anymore."

"Is your friend hooking up with him now?"

"Of course," Esme replies witheringly.

"So why isn't she a slut?"

"Because they're committed," Esme says mechanically, without a trace of irony.

"That's stupid," I say stupidly.

"It's how it works, Grace. I don't expect

you to understand the nuances of teenage dating."

"Come on, Esme. This is serious," I say, and Esme folds her arms across her chest. I remember what I said to her about the bad guys winning, and try not to wince.

"Was he also the guy you sent the nude to?" I ask quietly.

"It was fake," Esme says, and even though my sister is partly, mostly, still a stranger to me, I think I can tell that she's lying by the way her eyes dart instantly down to the ground. "But everyone still reposts it all the time, and they write disgusting things on anything I share, even when it's, like, literally a photo of me holding a lizard."

"Right," I say slowly, out of my depth and sort of wishing I'd never asked. "You know, I'm not sure you're supposed to hold lizards."

"Ugh, Grace!"

"If it makes you feel any better, millions of people have seen me naked," I say, but Esme just stares back at me as if I'm missing the point, which I possibly am, but only because I can't explain it properly. I want to tell her that I know all about the power imbalance that exists every time you meet someone who's seen you at your most vulnerable, whether or not it was your choice in the first place. How you have to hope that they don't use it against you in some way, or say something flippant that might burn its way into your sense of self, resurfacing every time you look at your body in the mirror or undress in front of your partner.

"Have you talked to Mom about it?" I ask instead.

"She knows I was suspended for indecent exposure," Esme says, annoyed at the question. "But my school would never admit what actually happened because it makes them look shitty. And it's not like she's going to ask — you know she doesn't like talking about anything like that. She probably thinks I streaked across the football field or something."

"Can you just delete the app?" I ask, and Esme reacts as if I've just suggested she remove her own toenails with a pair of rusty tweezers. "Maybe transfer schools?"

"You don't understand," Esme says slowly. I can hear my fall from grace in surround sound. "My school is supposed to be shaping the most brilliant minds of our generation, but it's just the fucking same as anywhere else."

Esme picks her phone up again and then drops it straight back down next to her as if it's burning hot. "Can we talk about something else?"

"Okay . . ." I say, but I can't think of anything else to talk about. I know that I should tell her that everything will be okay, but who am I to talk?

"Do you still want to go swimming?" I ask eventually.

The boys have disappeared and Esme nods, but she is more subdued than usual, so I stride confidently down the porch steps and onto the sand, trying to set a good example for the first time in my life. Goose bumps are already spreading over my arms and legs, but there's no way we're not going in now. Once I reach the water, I lift my face up and let the salty wind whip my cheeks as I wait for my sister to join me. She follows me, dropping her T-shirt onto the sand at the last minute and carefully wrapping her phone in it.

"I think you're being very brave," I say softly to Esme once we're in the icy water, just before she dives underneath the waves and stays down there for a long time. I think it's the first time I've seen her lost for words.

CHAPTER THIRTY

Dylan answers the door as soon as I ring the bell, before I've had enough time to adequately brace myself. I smile nervously as he stands and looks at me for a moment before stepping back to let me in the house.

"How are you doing, Grace?" he says easily.

"Almost, definitely, okay," I say, and for some reason I also flash him the scuba diving hand signal for *okay*. His eyes crinkle slightly in response.

I trail my finger across the leaf of a cheese plant we bought as a test to see whether we were allowed to get a dog. It's still alive, which is something, but I'm not sure how much I had to do with it.

"Do you remember the video camera?" I ask, and Dylan nods. "Do you know where it is? I'm working on a project."

Dylan breaks into a smile and I have to look away, because of those beautiful fucking teeth.

A couple of years ago I told him about the late-night talk show appearance I'd done when I was seventeen. It was the first one I'd booked where I didn't feel like a little kid anymore, and I was excited to show everyone how much I'd grown up. I wore a short white dress that, naturally, the host made the audience applaud, before he encouraged a bonus round of applause for my virginity, which he then joked had been insured for $10 million. I squirmed and giggled along with him and, at his encouragement, gently scolded him like he was my naughty little brother instead of what he was: a middle-aged pervert. Afterward, everyone told me how well I did. Once again, I had impressed with my amiability.

After I showed him the clip on YouTube, Dylan went out and bought me the camera. He said I could use it to tell whatever story I wanted, and he never even said anything when it sat untouched in our spare room after that.

"That's cool. I can't wait to hear about it," Dylan says, pausing at the bottom of the stairs. I don't give him any more information, and he walks off to find it.

I'm waiting by the front door for him, feeling like a stranger in a home that never really felt like my own, when Wren walks out from the kitchen, wearing yoga pants and a loose tank top with the word *NamaSLAY* printed across it. She is holding a bag of carrot sticks, and I figure she's just finished working out.

"Hi, sweetie!" she says, kissing me on the cheek. She smells of carrots and hummus, and for just a second it makes my chest hurt because Dylan probably deserves to be with someone who smells of carrots and hummus and does yoga every weekend.

"I was thinking, we should go out soon. Do you want to go out together?" she asks, squinting as she holds up the bag of carrots, reading something.

I stare at her, unsure of what she means. "Like to a club?"

"I'd love that, Grace. Maybe next week?" Wren says as Dylan appears at the top of the stairs. He's holding a box and wearing an old gray baseball cap with a faded *O,* for Ohio State, where his brothers all played football.

"You going anywhere good?" I say, a smile breaking across my face because this used to be Dylan's lucky flying hat. He wouldn't get on a plane without it even though I used to tease him mercilessly about it. He had hundreds of these little superstitions, things he half believed in as if he didn't already believe in enough.

He stands at the top of the stairs, smiling down at me, his face half-hidden under the shadow of the brim. Wren is still reading the carrot packaging next to me, and I feel inexplicably irritated by this. I don't understand what she can be searching for when surely the only ingredient is fucking carrots. She catches me watching her and smiles, offering the bag to me. I take a stick mainly because I can't be bothered to decline.

"So, Friday?" she says brightly, and I must appear confused because she shakes her head, laughing. "You and me going out."

Dylan walks down the stairs and stands at the bottom, next to Wren. I wait expectantly but nobody says anything. In the end I reach out and take the box from his hands.

"Grace?" Wren says eventually.

"Great, yeah. Friday," I say, turning the box over in my hands.

I practice using the camera at home, filming in the dark living room. The room is even bleaker on a flat screen. I flip the screen so that it's facing me, and then I talk into it like I've seen the kids on Abbot Kinney do on their phones.

"Hiiiiii, guys, it's me. I just wanted to tell

you about the calorie content of carrots today. Like, everyone thinks carrots are good for you, but in actual fact, do you know how much water is in each carrot you eat? Have you even ever heard of water retention? Because it makes you *fat*. That's what water does. Carrots are disgusting," I say, feeling mean only once I've finished.

I walk out onto the porch and hold the camera up to film the ocean. The sunlight flares on the screen like a shot in a Sofia Coppola movie. I wish I knew how to send the clip straight to Dylan, because I think he'd like it.

I hold the camera up, filming a pelican as it plunges into the ocean for fish, when a car door slams behind me. I flip the camera shut because the sound has already ruined the audio of my shot, even though I don't know what it's for.

"What are you up to?" Emilia asks, climbing up the porch to me. She is impossibly perfect, her hair the exact color of the sand when the sun hits it.

"Just messing around," I say, holding the camera by my side protectively. "What's up?"

"Well . . . my colorist was over and I saw that your car was down here, and I just thought, you know what, I'll see if Grace wants her roots done too," Emilia says, smiling innocently at me. I automatically reach for my hair. She must have seen the tabloid photos of me looking like a serial killer.

"Is that your way of telling me I need to get my roots done?"

"Oh, honey, of course not. I'm sure you mentioned your hair last time, and Margot is absolutely the best person in LA to do blondes, and she's at a loss because she had a last-minute cancellation, which does not happen often, trust me. If I had any inclination to believe in fate, then I think this would be it. She does everyone and she's an absolute sweetheart. She's also a healer and will want to talk to you about all her past lives, which obviously I do not believe in, either, but occasionally I do let her read my energy just because it freaks Able out when I tell him. I swear he's the last person in this city who still semi-believes in God."

"Where is she?" I ask, the irony of her last statement not escaping me.

"She's waiting in the car. Can I tell her to come out?" Emilia says, smiling sheepishly, and, of course, she does it all in a way that makes me think it was all my idea and that I'm actually doing them both a huge favor, because everything she does is seamless, designed to make you feel as special as she is. I realize then what an unusual opponent Emilia would be, the type who could slip under your skin when you least expect it.

Margot has a shaved bleached head and a tiny white tattoo of a shell in between her clavicles, right in the tender part that I will barely let anyone touch, let alone tattoo.

"What are you going to do to my hair?" I ask her as Emilia rushes around my house, pulling up a chair for me to sit on next to the kitchen sink and propping the dirty mirror from the bedroom in front of us, just in case I want to stare at my own puffy face for two hours.

"Oh, I forgot you're really British! Are you from London?" Margot asks as she runs her fingers through my hair. It's the most intimate I've been with anyone for a while, and it's making me feel embarrassingly turned on.

"North London. Have you been?" I ask, shifting in my seat as she clips the top half of my hair up.

"I was a member of the Auxiliary Ambulance Service there in the Second World War. During the Blitz," Margot says seriously, saying *the Blitz* in an English accent.

I'm working out how to respond when Emilia turns around, and our eyes catch in the mirror. We're both trying not to laugh, and for a moment it feels like we're old friends. My face heats up and I realize that this is something else I never learned, how friendship alone can make you feel safe.

"Right. Okay," I say eventually. "That would be in another lifetime, I assume?"

"Of course. Another lifetime, another vessel."

I make a noise that I hope sounds like I'm agreeing with her, thinking that if there's any truth to what she's saying, I better come back as a man next time, one who believes he can do anything, regardless of whether it's true or not. I stop asking her questions, though, because while I can see how believing in some higher power or grand plan could be comforting, it still makes me feel sorry for her and for all of us for needing it.

"So, talk to me. What were you going for with this?" Margot says, holding up a chunk of my hair. The reddish root nearly reaches the tops of my ears now, followed by about five inches of yellow blond, ending just above my shoulders.

"Where was I going?"

"What was the desired result? You must have been trying to say something."

"It's bad, isn't it?" I say, noticing how greasy the roots are again.

"It's less a hairstyle than a cry for help," Margot says, and Emilia, who has been keeping busy arranging a bunch of flowers that have miraculously appeared from somewhere, does laugh this time. "Do you trust me to fix it?"

"I don't think I care enough to have to trust you," I say honestly, because I'm not sure I could ever trust anyone who has a tattoo in the most vulnerable part of their body, or who believes that maybe we were once all just mosquitoes, a thousand lives ago.

Emilia makes a pot of tea and stands behind me. She watches Margot closely, and they both use familiar words in unfamiliar contexts when referring to my hair. After enough *cool*s and *icy*s to sink the *Titanic,* I slump lower in the chair, drifting off only to wake up feeling surprised that I felt comfortable enough to sleep in front of these women.

Emilia is murmuring something to Margot, so I keep my eyes closed.

"I don't know what happened with him. I've been meaning to ask her. She obviously can't live here forever."

"She has a good spirit," Margot says as she massages my hair with bleach, pulling it through to the ends.

"She's a very smart girl," Emilia says, and the pride in her voice makes me feel prickly and guilty, so I wriggle a bit and then stretch, opening my eyes and blinking a couple of times like the Golden Globe–nominated actress I am. Neither Emilia nor Margot seems embarrassed to have been caught talking about me. Emilia leans forward and offers me some more tea, made with fresh mint from Morocco. I have one sip before I place the cup on the countertop and somehow fall asleep again.

Margot taps me gently on the shoulder, and I open my eyes. Emilia is back by my side, and they are beaming at me like proud parents. My entire head is white and crisp with thick, crumbling bleach. I blink, looking between the two women in the mirror, unsure of what exactly is happening. It's getting dark outside.

"Stand up then!" Emilia says, so I do. She whips my chair around and I sit back down, tipping my head into the kitchen sink under her instruction. Margot turns on the water and starts to rinse my hair, stroking it softly with her other hand as she sings something quietly. The water is warm and I have to fight to keep my eyes open again, slightly embarrassed that I seem to have turned into a narcoleptic.

Margot notices my embarrassment and smiles at me. "It's my energy. People fall asleep around me all the time."

I'm back in my chair a few minutes later, facing the mirror as Margot rubs something earthy-smelling into my hair. I can already see that my hair is now white blond up to the root, even though it's sopping wet. I hold a strand and twist it around my finger, trying not to smile. Emilia has disappeared out onto the porch, apologizing profusely before taking a phone call.

"Do you like it?" Margot asks, grinning at me in the mirror. I run my fingers through it, and it feels softer than ever before, even slightly oily.

"It matches your spirit now. You have a lioness guarding everything you do, did you know that?"

I shake my head, knowing that it's just bullshit LA talk, so it has to be the acrid smell of the bleach making my eyes fill with tears.

"Lions are the most courageous of all the spirit animals. They will fight relentlessly to protect you if they need to."

I swallow as Margot straightens up and puts her hand on my shoulder.

"We'll take you back to your natural color next time, but right now you need a blond moment," she says.

"A Marilyn moment," I say, frowning at my reflection as water drips down the back of my neck.

"I was thinking more a Courtney Love moment. Actually, shit — it's your Kurt Cobain moment," Margot says, grinning at me. She has a gold tooth that I didn't notice before.

She leans forward and speaks softly in my ear. "I know that somebody hurt you. Now it's time for you to fuck shit up, baby lion."

CHAPTER THIRTY-ONE

For a while now, I've had this ninety-minute rule. I never spend longer than ninety minutes in someone else's company, whether that's for a work meeting, an interview with a teen magazine or just hanging out with someone at a party. I think that it's easy to pretend to be someone for ninety minutes, but after that you can't help but let your guard down. Maybe you tell a revealing story about your childhood or about a weird dream you had the other night; whatever it is, you end up exposing too much of yourself. Dylan is one of two people I ever spent more than ninety minutes with outside of a movie set, and the other is Able. Ninety minutes is the maximum amount of time I can pretend to be Grace Turner, and after that it's anyone's guess.

Despite my rule, when Emilia invites me back up to hers for a drink after Margot has left, I can't think of a single reason not to. It's Saturday night and my rental feels even bleaker than before the two women arrived, as if the echoes of laughter will now be reverberating off the bare walls around me, mocking me.

We sit in Emilia's kitchen and she pours some vodka into a glass, topping it up with soda water and elderflower cordial. She leaves the vodka out of mine, and I know that she noticed my full glass of wine from the other day and figured it out.

"I've actually been thinking about you a lot, and not just your hair," Emilia says, once she's settled opposite me. Then she lets out a peal of laughter when she sees my face and misunderstands. "Not like that. God, I wish? Wouldn't that be a story. No, I've realized that I never did ask what happened between you and Dylan."

I pause, unsure of what to say that wouldn't reveal too much of myself to her.

"I don't exactly know," I say slowly, buying time before deciding to use my old interview technique of lightly skimming the truth so that my words still feel authentic. "I think what mattered in the end was that I wasn't who he thought I was, and he was exactly who I thought he was."

In a way, it is sort of the whole truth, but

288

Emilia is still waiting, her head tilted to one side. I remember now that she was a reporter for years.

"He wanted me to be someone I couldn't be. I could never live up to his perfect vision because I'd had . . . a life before him," I finish quickly, because I don't know what else I can say.

Emilia studies me for a moment.

"Well, isn't that just the most absurdly *male* quality," she says finally. "So you weren't *saving yourself* for Dylan. They always want to be the first to discover anything. They want to be Christopher Columbus or Neil Armstrong. They want to stick a flag in it and own it."

I look at her, surprised by her tone, and I can tell that she wants a back-and-forth, but the pressure of it all, of having this conversation with the only other woman who may have been able to stop it all if she'd known, is paralyzing.

"I have trust issues," I say lamely, wiping my palms on my jeans.

"Don't we all," Emilia says lightly, but before either of us can dwell on it, she's speaking again. "And what's happening with work? Are you looking for your next project?"

I shrug, avoiding meeting her gaze. Emilia

seems frustrated with my ineptitude, and I have to work harder to pretend I don't care than I do with most people. I know that she's trying to understand exactly what happened to me, but it's the one thing I can't tell her. I need to take control of the conversation, but I can never seem to find the right thing to say around her.

"Grace, I know it seems like I'm being nosy, but I just can't help but feel like we're similar in so many ways, and that I could help you. I've been where you are now, and sometimes when I look at you, I see your vulnerability so clearly that it rattles my insides, do you know what I mean?"

"I guess so," I say as Emilia's pale eyes stare into mine.

"You know, I never said I'm sorry," she says, blinking for a moment, as if to dismiss an unpleasant memory. "I told your parents that I would look after you, but I didn't. Everything after the twins were born is a little . . . hazy. If I'm being honest, it was a shock that none of it came easily to me, and I just had to focus on getting through each day for a while. But you were too young to be alone, and I shouldn't have made a promise I couldn't keep. So I am. Sorry, I mean."

I shrug, staring down at the tiled floor,

not trusting myself to speak.

"And now I'm going to offer my help to you in any way that I can, just on the off chance that one day you may feel like accepting it. It may not feel like it right now, but your life is only just beginning, Grace, and all this is my incredibly convoluted way of telling you that I'm not giving up on you, do you understand?"

Emilia's blinkered faith in me is palpable, a third presence in the room, and I try to ignore the warmth that spreads through me without my permission. I know this sort of promise doesn't mean anything.

"What do you mean that we're alike?" I ask slowly.

"Well," Emilia starts, putting her head to one side. "Do you know that I left my parents behind too? They couldn't have been less impressed when I told them I was moving to LA. They would have preferred I was crawling the streets, as long as I stayed in New England while I was doing it, I swear to God. Good thing they didn't know about the trashy books back then."

"I don't know if I left my parents behind, exactly," I say, because it's always been more complicated than that.

"Maybe you didn't mean to, but we all do in the end," Emilia says, raising her eyebrows. "And for me, it was because I cared too much about what they thought. Not caring at all is so much easier."

"About anything?"

Emilia frowns slightly. "About what you can't control."

"What if you can't control any of it?" I ask, and Emilia studies me then, thinking about her answer.

"You know that at some point you have to make a choice. Life can be cruel and, even worse, random, and if the only way to get through it is to protect yourself, to find the good where you can and just forget about the rest, then is that such a bad thing?"

"I don't know if that's ever been an option for me," I say, staring down at the melting ice cubes in my glass. Suddenly, I feel inexplicably sad to realize that maybe Emilia really does know exactly who I am, and still wants to be around me. That somehow she understands me better than anyone else, and, in another reality, we could have been friends. I can feel Emilia's eyes on me before she drains her own glass, and I realize that I've broken my ninety-minute rule by at least three hours at this point. I've outstayed my welcome and I'm about to dispel the myth that is Grace Turner, if I'm not careful. I take a deep breath and piece

her back together, trying to appear interested but ultimately untroubled by whatever
Emilia has to say next.

"Well, I think we can both agree at least
that you need to start working again, and
whatever it is needs to be so dazzling, so
outstanding, that nobody in the industry
will be able to ignore you," she says brightly.
"I know Able was just devastated when
there wasn't a role for you in this movie. I
saw what it did to him."

"What did it do to him?" I ask, my heart
pounding in my chest.

"Well, it broke his heart," she says, having
a sip of her drink. "Of course it did."

Like hell it did. The silence in the room
feels heavy, but I don't rush to fill it.

"Look, I know Able can be difficult,"
Emilia starts slowly, as if she's reading my
mind. "But it's easy to forget that he didn't
have the traditional upbringing that we had.
Honestly, it still surprises me how insecure
he is, even after all this time. You're probably the only other person in the world that
knows the full extent of it."

Insecure. I roll the word over in my mind
a few times, basking in its familiarity. I
understand better than anyone how tempt-
ing it is to view Able's behavior as the
natural outcome of his insecurity — the

result of some trauma, some life-defining humiliation that occurred in his early childhood. We are all primed to seek order, causation, in this way, but it is only ever to comfort ourselves: Able seeks power because he was born with nothing. Grace is a disaster because she was broken. Grace was broken because she wanted too much. *Be good and dream small and it could never, ever happen to you.* I silently reject Emilia's hypothesis even as I'm nodding at her words.

"I have a meeting, with someone else," I say slowly. Emilia leans forward in anticipation.

"What's the project?" she asks.

"It's the new John Hamilton project," I say, before I can stop myself from lying. "That one you mentioned the other day. It's kind of feminist and subversive, and he really wants me for a role. I think it's a black comedy."

"Grace! That's fantastic. That would be perfect. Subversive and funny would be ideal — I always thought you would be outstanding in a comedic role. You're so funny when you want to be, and it's such a waste not to use that timing."

I smile slightly, because her claims are both generous and wildly inaccurate, and she squeezes my shoulders from behind on her way to the wine fridge. "How sly of you not to have mentioned it the other day! I need to remember what a talented actor you are."

Emilia selects a bottle of Sancerre and turns back to me.

"That's just reminded me actually — I've been meaning to talk to you about something . . ."

I try not to tense as I wait for her to finish.

"You know when you wake up at five a.m. and can't get back to sleep because everything you've ever said or done comes hurtling back into your mind to haunt you?" Emilia asks. I nod but I don't tell her that she's just described every waking moment of my life.

"Well, the other night, that happened to me, and I was thinking that of course you should be the one to present Able with his lifetime achievement award. Doesn't that make sense to you? He always did his best work with you." Emilia leans forward again, taking my hand in hers. Her touch is smooth and warm.

I stare down at the table, my fingers tracking the grooves filled with glitter from arts and crafts sessions.

"It could also be just what you need too. To get back out there after . . . missing it all last year. You know? The show is on January eighth, so you have exactly a month to decide."

"I have to think about it," I say quietly, all the while telling myself that there's no way she knows about any of it, that this could never be Emilia's warped way of assuaging some of her guilt.

"Of course," Emilia says soothingly. "Take as long as you need. A friend of mine is heading up the committee this year and she just asked me who would be most appropriate to do the honors, but if you don't feel ready, then we can always find someone else."

"I don't . . . Did you speak about it with . . . Able?" I ask, wondering if Emilia will notice the uneven edge to my voice when I say his name.

"He thinks it's a great idea," Emilia says confidently, in a way that makes me think she hasn't told him. I wonder what he'd say, whether he'd be able to tell her it was a bad idea without a valid reason or better option. Even I can see that Emilia is right; objectively there is no more suitable, no more press-worthy option for the event than to have me present the award to Able. I try to picture the look on his face as he comes up to the podium. Would he even be scared of me? Or would he never believe in a million years that I would expose him, knowing it would mean destroying myself in the process?

"You don't have to say yes now, but wouldn't it be perfect?"

"It could be," I say, staring into the water in front of me as all of the nerves in my body start to tingle, making me feel as if I could peel off my skin at the kitchen table and step right out of it if I wanted to. "Perfect."

CHAPTER THIRTY-TWO

"So, I think it's pretty simple. You just press this button and point the camera in the right direction," I say, watching as Esme turns the camera over in her hands and studies the back closely. We are sitting in a lobster shack on PCH, and I'm not sure she can actually hear me over the noise of different football games blaring from twenty screens around the restaurant. I had a shower before I came out, and my hair is hanging in wet clumps above my shoulders, dripping down the back of my oversized T-shirt.

"There's a ton more options than that, Grace, but I guess that's the general idea," she says, shaking her head while I signal for the waitress.

"Smart-ass," I mutter as I scan the menu, even though I'm trying not to laugh. We order a small seafood platter to share.

"Why was this so urgent?" Esme asks,

holding up the camera. "I had to bribe Blake to drive me here outside of her therapy schedule."

"I don't know, I just wanted you to have it," I say, already losing faith in my idea. "How's Anaheim?"

"Still Anaheim. The most barren of cultural wastelands," Esme says importantly, as if she heard the phrase somewhere and memorized it. For some reason I think of Emilia, how I could deliver the phrase to make her laugh, even though making fun of where my parents live is always a cheap shot.

"How's Mom?"

"Why don't you call her and ask her yourself?"

"It's complicated," I say.

"Don't bullshit me, Grace. 'It's complicated' is what adults say when they don't have an answer."

"Are you . . . mad at her sometimes?" I ask slowly.

Esme turns her phone over and traces the sparkly Union Jack on the back of the case with her finger.

"Sometimes," she says eventually.

I change the subject before she can ask me the same question.

"How are you feeling about going back to school soon?"

Esme glances at me, then back down at her chipped fingernails, which were once glittery gold.

"Unfortunately, school is the least of my problems. There's a loose behavioral code that most people adhere to when faced with another human. That goes out the window when said human is replaced by a screen."

"What are they doing now?"

"Honestly, Grace? I appreciate that you want to help, but I just don't know if I can explain it to you. I'm totally aware that it's this 'different world' from hearing Dad say it four hundred million times, but it's also impossible for me to put it into perspective for you. Like movies and TV shows about kids my age? If they were actually trying to show our real lives, it would literally just be a bunch of kids staring at their phones. They'll have to stop making movies about kids born past the year 2000."

"It can't be that bad," I say, aiming for soothing but unsurprisingly not pulling it off.

"You have no idea. This is like trying to talk about Bitcoin to someone out of a Jane Austen novel. You're bubble girl," Esme says, eyeing me with disgust. I try not to show my surprise at her anger, and I realize I was probably the same when I was her

300

age. Maybe I still am.

"It's like they forget that I'm a human. Or that they are. This whole generation is screwed."

I want to tell her that she's lucky she has a generation and that she isn't just some weird outlier who can't relate to anyone, but I know it won't work out well for me. Instead, I swirl my straw around in my drink to buy myself some time. I was never exposed to any of the things she's talking about, and I have no idea how different my life would be if I had. Maybe I would feel less alone, but more likely it would have been just one more way to ruin everything.

"You have access to billions of people, though, right? Can't you just connect with the good ones?"

Esme frowns, concentrating as she tears off a corner of the white paper tablecloth. I hope she doesn't start to cry. "It doesn't work like that," she says. "I'm at school with them. You have to play by their rules, but the rules change every day. You can't win."

"Do you want me to talk to Mom about transferring schools?"

"She's never going to listen to you," Esme says, rolling her eyes. It's a little harsh for her to put it like that, even if it's true.

"Does she know that we hang out . . .

sometimes?" I ask.

Esme shrugs, and then shakes her head.

"I think it would hurt her feelings," she says, and I don't ask anything else.

The waitress arrives with our seafood platter. She places it on the table between us, and we both just stare as the dry ice steams off it like a cheap special effect.

"I just shouldn't have sent that photo," Esme says miserably. "I wish I could go back in time."

I watch her, trying to figure out how to word what I say next, even though I'm losing confidence in the idea that felt so perfect when I thought of it last week. The right words feel just out of reach, and I feel stupid for thinking I'd be able to find them.

"I think I wanted you to have the camera so you could use it to tell your side of the story. I thought maybe it could help," I say slowly.

"You know I can just film stuff on my phone."

"I don't know, I thought it could help to keep something separate from what's happening in your phone. Is that naïve?" I ask, realizing that this could be the equivalent of when I sliced the tip of my finger off during a shoot and my homeopathic on-set guardian gave me a cup of cinnamon powder to manage the pain. When Able found out, he fired her on the spot and called a doctor to come straight to the set. He waited with his arm wrapped tightly around my shoulders while the doctor gave me stitches, and he had such a gentle, fatherly expression on his face that I thought maybe everything would be okay after that.

"Kind of," Esme says, and I pull my attention back to her because the memories of him being kind to me are always the worst ones.

"I'm just saying, I understand that sometimes the worst part of it all is that you lose control of your own story."

Esme frowns and then holds the camera up to me. The red light is blinking.

"How do you know so much about this?" she asks, and I put my hand out to cover the lens. "Seriously, sister, tell all."

"Come on, Esme."

She wriggles away from me but flips the camera shut and puts it back on the table next to her plate.

"*I'm* just saying you seem to know a lot about this shit."

I pick up a ring of calamari while I decide what to do. I put it in my mouth and chew it quickly, the hot oil inside the batter burning my tongue. Esme folds her arms across her chest, waiting for me.

"Do you remember back home in England when we used to lie on the grass and look up at the sky on Hampstead Heath?" I ask suddenly.

"I guess so, kind of," Esme says, watching me strangely.

"Didn't everything seem just so possible back then? Like we could do anything we ever wanted?"

"I guess?" Esme says, humoring me, and then she shrugs. "Remember I was just a kid, Grace."

"Okay. Well, I remember, and the world felt pretty fucking big back then. But what if every time something bad happens, it just makes your world a little smaller." I take a deep breath in because the words are tumbling out now, racing to catch up with each other. "Until some days, you can't even see the sky anymore."

"No, Grace. That's not possible," Esme says, looking at me as if I'm losing my mind. "Do you mean figuratively? What are you saying?"

I tear off a corner of the tablecloth, balling it up until it's just a damp shred of paper in my palm. A silence stretches between us while I wonder whether we'll ever understand each other implicitly again, or whether too much time has passed.

"Is this because of Able?" Esme asks quietly, and the air stops dead around me.

"What are you talking about?" I ask, each word a sliver of glass. I watch them float in between us for a moment before Esme meets my eyes defiantly. The shards fall onto the table.

"I heard you and Mom the night before you left," she says, her voice soft. "You know you never say his name, Grace."

"You don't know what you're talking about," I say, and as Esme's face crumples, I understand that I'm letting her down, and that I have a chance to fix something in her that is already broken in me. My heart climbs into my throat at the thought that I might actually be about to say the words out loud for the first time. I know that I'll never be able to explain it all to Esme, but I take a deep breath anyway, trying to harness the quiet fury or the fear or anything else he left in place of everything he took from me.

"I was hurt, in a different way from how those kids are hurting you, but, in another way, it was also the same. He took all of my power away from me, and then he left me alone to deal with it. To deal with the shame."

Esme is watching me carefully.

"Is that why you're so weird?"

"Thanks, Esme," I say, but my words are already twitching with relief because I've almost said the truth out loud and nobody told me I had to take it back

"Are you angry at him?" she asks.

"Sometimes," I lie, thinking about the constant low-level dark thrashing in my mind, and how occasionally the anger bursts through to the surface and I have to do whatever I can to make it go away again, and how I have no idea what my life would actually be like if it weren't there, had never been there, taking and taking, draining and draining.

"It sounds like you might need the camera more than I do," she says, studying me.

"It's more complicated than that," I say after a moment. "I've been asked to present him with an award."

"The one Mom was baiting you about?" Esme narrows her eyes.

"Exactly. Lifetime achievement at the IFAs."

"So you don't need the camera because you'll already have an audience, and an entire fucking TV crew," Esme says slowly.

And of course I can imagine it, have been imagining little else since Emilia suggested that I present the award. I'm standing on-stage while the audience applauds my return on its feet. The glitter on my gown dances under the stage lights as I talk into the microphone, shakily at first, growing in confidence until my voice is loud and force-ful. When I've finished, the audience is standing again, applauding my bravery. Able is frozen in his seat, every ounce of power drained from his body. I try not to think about Silver and Ophelia at home with their babysitter, Emilia's pale face as she watches me from her seat next to Able, the inevitable mauling my family and I would receive from the media in the aftermath.

Esme picks up a lobster claw and she seems lighter, as if she's been reassured at last that order will be restored. Underneath all her teenage cynicism, I can tell that she still believes in the good guys and the bad guys, in retribution and happy endings, and I envy her for it. I already sort of wish I hadn't told her about it, because I know that in doing so, I've finally made myself accountable to someone. Maybe I figured I would lose my nerve if I didn't, or maybe I just wanted to make her smile at me like she is now, her eyes bright and wicked. I ignore the tiny bit of white flesh that lands on my arm as Esme cracks her lobster claw.

"Maybe their turn for winning is over, Grace. Maybe it's our turn now."

CHAPTER THIRTY-THREE

I try to hold on to Esme's words as I stand on the doorstep of the peach house the next morning, waiting to meet Emilia for a coffee. After a minute, Emilia flings open the door and stands in the doorway with one hand on her hip and the other holding a bowl of sliced apples. She looks flustered, but she breaks into a wide, grateful smile when she sees that it's me. I try not to feel guilty as she throws her arms around my neck like a little kid. She smells of peanut butter mixed with her peppery Le Labo perfume.

"I am so *beyond* pleased that you're here. You wouldn't believe the morning I've had already," she says into my hair as she hugs me. "The nanny, Marla, broke her leg last night, and we've all descended into absolute chaos as a result. It's also the worst possible timing with this trip to Salt Lake in a couple days."

"You're going this week?" I ask, pausing in the doorway as Emilia nods.

"Yes, I'm sure I told you. For Able's screening? At least I've somehow convinced my husband to fly home with me afterward," Emilia says, rolling her eyes. "Do you mind doing coffee here instead?"

I nod woodenly in response and turn around to close the door so that she can't see my face. I tell myself that I always knew Able would be coming home at some point, and that at least this way I can arm myself with the knowledge and keep one step ahead of him.

The twins are sitting at the kitchen table, chattering like excited monkeys with cheeks red from exertion and sticky hair stuck to their foreheads. I sneak glances at them when they're not looking, relieved to find they look more like their mother than Able.

"Will you two just stop screaming for a second? Come and sit with us."

"I'm sorry to hear about Marla," I say as I take a seat at the table.

"So was I. She'll be out for weeks," Emilia says brightly, smearing the apple slices with thick peanut butter. Her hair is damp and pulled into a messy bun at the nape of her neck, and she looks different without her glossy shield of hair, as if she's been exposed in some important way without realizing it.

"Girls, do you remember Grace?" she asks, and they both look up at me. Silver lets out a grunt and Ophelia waves before they lose interest again. Emilia seems to have given them each an early Christmas present to distract them — two new baby-pink Polaroid cameras.

Emilia turns to stare at the shiny, industrial-looking coffee machine and then shrugs, stumped.

"I'm really sorry about this," she says.

"I already had a coffee, it's okay," I say, but I don't know if she hears me.

"Do you know how much sugar peanut butter has in it?" Silver asks, glancing up from her camera long enough to squint at her mom. I try not to recognize any of Able's mannerisms in the nine-year-old.

"It's the kind without the sugar." Emilia rolls her eyes at me and ruffles Silver's hair.

"And the kind without the palm oil? Because you know that they have to destroy the rain forests to —"

"I know, Silver. It's also the kind without the palm oil. And I'm really still so pleased that Marla teaches you about this sort of thing," Emilia says smoothly, miming shooting herself in the mouth behind Silver's head.

"Can I take a picture of you?" Ophelia asks me quietly while they're talking, and I nod. I stick my tongue out just as she presses the button, and she giggles, a low gurgling sound that makes me smile. When the Polaroid comes out, she grabs it and waves it in the air.

Emilia already looks exhausted, but she tries to make conversation anyway, rambling about a movie the girls' school had tried to ban after they'd already seen it. Watching her struggle to maintain control of everything, I feel a jolt of sympathy, but then her phone rings a few minutes later and I see a photo of Able appear on the screen, dimples flashing as he leans against a palm tree. My whole body tenses, but Emilia doesn't seem to notice, apologizing as she glides past me to answer the call in the living room.

While Emilia is out of the room, I try not to think about the voice on the other end of the line, so I pick up the Polaroid Ophelia took of me from the table instead. In the picture I look carefree and easy, and I wonder if this is what Emilia sees when she looks at me. I have no idea how I fit into her narrative, whether she really does see me as an extension of herself or whether she still just pities me for being so alone.

When Emilia comes back into the kitchen,

she looks unsettled, those red blotches that very pale people get climbing her neck.

"What's wrong?" I ask her, and she looks at me, taking a moment to focus.

"Oh, nothing really. Able just reminded me that our financial adviser is coming over this afternoon, but I have to take the girls to school for their final holiday pageant rehearsal. I also have this deadline that I've been putting off." Emilia breaks off and smiles at me. "You know, it's fine. Millions of people do this every day. I'll figure it out. I just need a moment to catch my breath."

I stand up and walk around to her, putting my hand on her shoulder. I can feel the damp heat of her sweat through her thin cotton top, and I feel a snap of guilt for what I'm about to do to the only person who has actually wanted to be around me since I've been back in Los Angeles.

"Why don't I drop the girls off at school?" I ask slowly. "I have something I need to do at home, then I can come pick them right up."

Emilia looks up at me for a moment, and the expression on her face is pure and grateful. "Are you sure you don't mind?"

"Of course not."

"Where on earth did you come from, Gracie?"

I try to concentrate as Emilia tells me the address of the school, and how I need to ignore Silver when she tries to sit in the front of the car, but my mind is already somewhere else. Sometimes, things start to fall into place so naturally, so neatly, it's as if you have been planning them that way all along, without ever realizing it.

I'd like to tell you that I didn't go straight home and put on an eighties-style red bodysuit with a pair of vintage Levi's jean shorts and a Gucci belt. That I didn't run a brush through my hair, choose my best pair of sunglasses, the black ones with the gold rim, or that I didn't apply a slash of bright red lipstick just before I left the house. I'd like to tell you that I didn't wave to Emilia from the car as if nothing had changed, that I didn't text Laurel with the address and time of the school drop-off. That I didn't smile directly into the lens when the photographer started taking photos. That it didn't cross my mind that the image would be circulated instantly, tearing through social media like the Napa Valley wildfires. That I had no idea Able would see them.

But I would be lying, of course.

Am I angry? All the time.

314

■ ■ ■ ■

Once I've handed the girls over to a blond teacher I think I recognize from an episode of *CSI,* I drive back to my rental. I make myself some scrambled eggs the way Emilia taught me, and then I sit on the porch and stare at the plate, waiting. At five p.m., Laurel messages me a link. There is a story online about me being back in LA and looking better than ever. The main image is a photo of me holding each of the girls' hands and leading them from my car, followed by smaller images of me handing them over to the teacher. I do look good, smiling widely with my white hair glittering under the LA sunshine, my eyes covered in black sunglasses. The girls' faces have been blurred, but you can clearly see Silver's sparkly sneakers and the twins' bright red hair.

Laurel sends me a couple more links, the last one a piece reporting that I left town because Able and I were having an affair. The photo they've used is one from the *Lights of Berlin* premiere in London, Emilia and I on either side of a frowning Able. Emilia's mouth is open because she's in the middle of a sentence, and her makeup is wrong for the lighting — her skin coated in a bright white powder that catches the flash. I look relaxed on the other side of Able, and my perfectly made-up lips are pulled into a small, glossy smile. I try to remember the dread I felt when I was posing for the picture, but the memory feels out of reach now that I'm looking at the evidence.

The story is from a trashy, disreputable website, but the thought that Able could be reading it, too, that he might be the one who is scared, powerless to stop whatever move is next, makes me feel more alive than I have in years. That's when I receive a message from a number not saved in my phone, the only one I will never be able to erase.

What are you doing???

The inevitability of his words nearly winds me, because isn't this what I've been waiting for this whole time?

I delete the message before I can count the question marks or think about where he is, whether he can get to me again. Maybe from now on, Able can be the one to wait, to have to guess my next move. Maybe my time for winning has only just begun.

CHAPTER THIRTY-FOUR

"How did you find me?" I ask when I open the door to find Camila, the journalist from *Vanity Fair*, standing on my doorstep the next morning. I have just woken up from a night of fractured, adrenaline-laced sleep, and I'm unconfident in my ability to handle this interaction. I look around for someone to save me, but the other residents of Coyote Sumac are all either already in the water or still in bed.

"I asked around," Camila says, and she seems calmer than when I first met her. "Don't worry, your secret is safe with me."

I smile wryly because we both know why she's here.

"I'm actually on my way out," I say then, even though I'm clearly still in my pajamas.

"I saw the stories about you and Able."

"It's just trash, Camila," I say, folding my arms across my chest.

Camila studies me for a moment before

changing tack. She leans in toward me and starts to speak softly. "Look, I want to be clear with you. I am going ahead with a story about the systemic abuse of power in Hollywood, and it is up to you whether you want to be part of it or not. I don't need you, but I would like your voice to be heard. I have a former colleague of his implying that your relationship with Able wasn't strictly professional. I also have an eyewitness account that he bullied you on the set of every movie you worked on together."

I curl my trembling hands into fists by my sides.

"Without my side of the story, that's just conjecture. I thought *Vanity Fair* had higher journalistic standards than that."

Camila watches me, sensing my hesitation.

"You're still trying to force me to do something, you know," I say quietly. "I still don't have control over it."

Camila pauses. "I'm trying to give you the choice. Can you understand that?"

Of course I understand that Camila isn't trying to catch me out. She's just like the rest of us, trying to match her job to her ambition, without thinking about the fallout for anyone else. It's just, when I think of the message from Able last night, the thrilling sensation that ran through me at the sight of those four words, it makes me wonder something . . . Why am I always the one who has to jeopardize everything I've built for myself? Why can't Able suffer in silence for once while waiting for my next move, as his loved ones quietly pull away from him like he's a virus nobody wants to catch? Why should I be the only person with nobody in the world to turn to?

What are you doing???

I'm closing in on you.

"I'm not ready," I say slowly. "But I might be able to give you something else. Do you want to come inside?"

We plan the shoot in under twenty-four hours. Emilia instantly agrees to let me use the peach house for our location, as I knew she would. She is due to fly to Salt Lake City for Able's screening that evening, so the twins are already at a sleepover with a friend from school, and she jumps at the chance to help me out. I wonder what Able will think when he sees the interview and photos of me in his house. Whether he can feel me circling ever closer to him even from all these states away.

When I arrive at the peach house, Emilia throws open the door. She looks immaculate again, more than ready to charm whomever I need her to.

"Did you see the stories about us all?" she asks, laughing, and I wonder what it would be like to feel so sure of your own place in the world that you never once paused to question anybody's intentions.

"I'd hoped you hadn't seen them," I say, because it isn't necessarily a lie.

"Oh, trust me, we've all been in this business long enough to know that reporters just tell whatever story they want to tell. It will blow over, just try not to worry. They can sense your fear."

"I'm not scared," I say, wondering whether it could be true this time.

"I know, darling, of course you're not," she says, and I immediately feel embarrassed, like I'm a sulky teenager whose ego needs to be stroked. Somehow I always seem to say the wrong thing around Emilia, even though she tries her best not to let me realize it. I force a smile, trying to piece my facade back together.

"Thank you for letting me do this here. Honestly, I couldn't let anyone see my dump of a house," I say, and Emilia instantly waves her hand in the air.

"Oh, please, don't mention it again."

I have promised Camila an exclusive on the reason I left Los Angeles, the state of my marriage and a vague confirmation of the demons everyone now suspects I have. It's not exactly what she wanted, but it's an exclusive all the same: a rare glimpse into the life of someone notoriously private. As I wait for her to arrive, I sit cross-legged on the sofa and give myself a pep talk: *Make yourself seem fragile at times but never broken. Don't demand anything of Camila, or the people who are going to read the profile. There's nothing more desperate than a celebrity seeking the validation of strangers. Forget the notion that she wanted to talk to you and therefore you don't need to sell yourself. Remember that you always need to sell yourself. Keep your jaw pushed forward to avoid a double chin, and don't frown too much. Seem uncomplicated and appealing and, above all, grateful for everything the public has given you. Never mention how quick they were to take it away.*

"Are you feeling okay about this?" Emilia says as she passes behind the sofa, touching me gently on the shoulder.

"I think so," I say, shrugging. "The media

have been hard on me lately, so I don't want to make anything worse."

"That's how it works, isn't it? They gobble you up, then shit you out when they're done with you," Emilia says, and I would laugh if it weren't true.

She sits down next to me. "You can turn this around. You just have to pretend to be suitably chastened, as galling as that might be. Everyone will want you to have *learned something* from your transgressions, as if life is ever that simple."

I pull a face and she laughs.

"Have you run through the questions with this person in advance?"

"Most journalists don't do that," I say, which isn't entirely true since I've already told Camila exactly whom she can't mention.

"You'll be fine. Would you like me to stay in the room in case you don't like the direction she's taking? I feel slightly uncomfortable that you don't have a publicist here or anyone to support you."

I'm about to decline her offer, but I stop myself when I realize that having the physical reminder of Emilia's presence might just stop me from revealing too much about myself. I nod, trying to look grateful.

"Thank you, Emilia."

■ ■ ■ ■

The shoot is straightforward enough. I am wearing a white shirt and ripped jeans with Emilia's diamond and sapphire Bulgari necklace that she insisted I borrow. I choose the living room as the location because it's dark enough that the photographer will have to use a flash without me asking, and it will be more flattering for me. Before we start, I make Camila promise not to airbrush any of the shots, knowing that she will include the surprising request in her story and that it will instantly endear me to thousands of normal Americans who will now take it upon themselves to defend my appearance. I pose in front of Able and Emilia's extensive book collection with a small, sad smile on my face that says it all: I may be fragile but I am brave, and more importantly, I am learning.

The interview is trickier to navigate. Even though I have told Camila she needs to focus on my hiatus and return only, and to avoid the subject of Able, her questions are still probing, and they affect me more than I thought they would. I try not to let her see that she's getting to me, becoming more creative with my diversionary tactics as the hours pass.

"Everyone makes out like I was literally plucked off the streets and rescued from this depressing existence, but I had a good life in England, too, you know? I've always had a family who love and support me," I say at one point, smiling amiably. "I'm aware that I've been incredibly lucky in that respect."

Camila nods, but I can tell from how she shifts in her seat that she is frustrated by the uninspiring answers I've been giving her since we started.

"And what about the drinking? There have been rumors that you've had a problem with alcohol for a number of years."

I take a deep breath and stretch out my hands in front of me, palms up. The picture of openness, honesty, asking for forgiveness.

"Yes, I was absolutely overindulging at one point. I'm trying to understand how it happened, and I think that it was because I never had to learn who I was when I was alone. Being back home with my family this past year has really grounded me. I've been sober for over a year now," I say, nodding graciously when Camila congratulates me, as I knew she'd have to do. I think of the bottle of pills in my bag, and hope I closed it before leaving it by the foot of the kitchen table. "I don't want anyone to feel sorry for me, and I promise you that I'm hyperaware of my own privilege. I know that I'm not saving any lives. I'm just trying to be the best version of myself."

I wonder if Camila is trying not to roll her eyes.

"And what about Emilia? Can you tell me about what this relationship means to you?" she asks then, watching me closely as she changes tack, and I understand that I have already backed myself into a corner by choosing Emilia's house for the shoot. If I deflect in any way, I will be flagging up to Emilia that something is wrong.

"Emilia," I call, and Emilia smiles from her position behind Camila. I pat the sofa next to me and she takes a seat.

"Camila was asking about you," I say, before turning back to the reporter. "Emilia is my rock. I'm proud to call her my friend."

Emilia smiles at me and takes my hand.

"We would do anything for this girl. Woman. She's a member of our family."

The photographer takes a photo of us, and just like that, our affection for each other is immortalized. *Snap.*

Camila nods and scribbles something down. I narrow my eyes and then smile when she looks up.

"And Dylan? What role does he play in the life of this new and improved Grace Turner?"

Hyde.

"Dylan will be in my life forever. Our souls have known each other for a really long time now."

"Are you talking about past lives?" Camila asks, her pen hovering over her pad.

"Absolutely," I say, widening my eyes slightly. "We have the strongest karmic connection."

Emilia sneaks a look at me. I know it's a good deflection even if I sound like a fantasist. Camila frowns and puts her pen down.

"And right now? Are you still together? And I'm talking physically as opposed to spiritually," she stresses, smiling blandly at me.

"Dylan is my best friend," I say carefully. "And he supports every step I'm taking to rediscover who I am, and what brings me peace."

I check my watch and realize the interview should have been over twenty minutes ago. I feel vaguely irritated that nobody told me, and I stand up to stretch.

"Have you got what you need?" I ask brightly.

Camila shrugs and stands up too. She's

probably terrified that I'm going to tell her more about my past lives. I silently thank Margot for that one.

"For now, Grace. Like I said, I'm planning on turning this around quickly, but I'll be in touch if I need you to clarify anything."

I kiss Camila and the photographer on each cheek and lead them to the front door. At the last minute Camila turns back and hits record again on her device. She holds it out between us, and I stare down at it. Emilia is standing protectively next to me.

"One thing I forgot to ask. Have you got anything to say about Able's influence on your life? What it's like being known as his 'muse'?"

I freeze and it takes everything in my power not to open the door and push her through it. I think of all the things I could say that would be a lie, and I hate Camila for being so casual with the secret that has forced its way so violently into my sense of self.

I paste a rigid smile on my face.

"What can I say about Able? He made me who I am today."

Camila's eyes burn into mine for a second before she nods once. As Camila and the photographer finally turn to leave, Emilia asks Camila to send her a copy of the candid shot of the two of us on the sofa. She wants to frame it and put it on her wall.

CHAPTER THIRTY-FIVE

I sit on Emilia's bed with a glass of iced tea and watch her pack for her trip. I have made her late and she is stressed, although she's trying not to let me see it. I have also been in a strange mood since Camila left, as if there were two versions of my life dangling in front of me for a moment, and somehow I chose wrong all over again. I look at Emilia and wonder if, in the long run, I'm going to end up hurting her more than I am Able.

"Are you okay, darling?" Emilia asks at one point.

"I'm fine," I say, nodding, but I must not be convincing enough because Emilia pauses, clutching a change of clothes for after the flight in her hand, including a modest black silk bra. The intimacy of it all, that I now know what Able will be touching, unclasping, later that night, makes me flinch.

Emilia notices my discomfort and sits

down next to me on the bed.

"I'm sorry. I should have asked if you were okay earlier. Today was a big deal, wasn't it? It was the first time you've spoken publicly about your . . . sobriety. I know we've never spoken about it before."

I nod slowly.

"You're doing so beautifully, Grace. I want you to know that I see you."

I want to ask Emilia why people are always lying to me like this, what purpose it serves when they make special concessions for me. Not having a drink in my hand or an opioid in my blood isn't *doing beautifully,* it's just doing what other people do every day without ever having to think about it.

Emilia puts her arm around my shoulders, and we sit together like that for a while, my body eventually softening into hers. And then, with a clarity that makes my chest feel tight, I realize why I don't want Emilia to go to Salt Lake City. I don't want her to go because Able doesn't deserve her. He doesn't deserve to feel safe or loved, to be told that everything will be okay whatever happens. I want Emilia to stay here with me instead, and I want her to choose me over Able, time and time again, until he feels as alone as I do.

"I guess it feels like there are just more

people to let down this way," I say after a moment, an idea slowly unfurling in my mind.

"You won't let anybody down," Emilia says firmly. "Remember that you aren't accountable to anyone except for yourself. You need to keep your head down and focus on your own recovery. Fuck everyone else."

"Can I be honest with you, Emilia?" I ask, and my whole body is trembling now. Emilia reaches over and takes my hand.

"Of course."

"I've never wanted a drink more than earlier, when I was saying those words out loud."

Emilia makes an anguished sound as she turns toward me.

"Oh, darling, I'm so sorry to hear that. I wish I could stay and look after you."

I shrug, waving my hand at her, realizing as I do that it's the exact way that she does it.

"I'll be okay. I've been through worse than this."

"Is there someone we can call? Do you still have a sponsor?" Emilia murmurs.

I shake my head, and then I feel a rush of disappointment as Emilia stands up anyway, dropping the clothes from her hand into her overnight bag and zipping it up.

"Well, you know both Able and I will be home tomorrow night if you need us," she says gently.

"I'll be fine," I say, forcing a smile. Emilia is watching me now with a sad look on her face, and I can see that she's teetering on the edge of making the right decision; she just needs a little nudge.

"I should go," I say as I stand up. Then, as I lean in to hug her good-bye, I dip my hand into the pocket of my bag and flick the bottle of Percocet out onto the bedroom floor. We both watch as the bright orange bottle rolls along the rug, stopping underneath Able's bedside table. Emilia looks at the bottle and then back at me. I can't tell whether she knows I did it deliberately or not, but either way it serves the same purpose.

"Excuse me, Grace. Give me a minute."

I pick the bottle up and hold it in my clammy hand as I wait on the bed. I wonder what I've done, if I've gone too far this time. I take my phone out of my bag to distract myself, and find a message from Esme asking when we can meet again. I ignore it and put my phone away. After a long while, maybe twenty minutes, Emilia walks back in and stands in front of me. She looks flushed, unhappy, but she forces a bright smile.

"What do you say to a night of Katharine Hepburn movies and hot chocolate?"

"What about the screening?"

"I've spoken to Able, and he agrees that I should be with you tonight," Emilia says, not looking at me anymore. "This is more important than his ego. Come on, let's go downstairs."

"He doesn't need you there?" I ask as Emilia wheels her suitcase back into her walk-in closet.

"You need me here," she says, and I feel a stab of guilt that I've manipulated her like this, but mostly I am relieved that she chose me over him, even though I forced her to. I comfort myself with the notion that I'm actually protecting her, because if she knew what he was really like, she would never choose him again.

We sit together on the sofa with a mug each of creamy hot chocolate and a bowl of buttery popcorn to share, and we don't speak another word about the interview, or Able, or my sobriety for the rest of the night. Instead we watch *Stage Door* and *The Philadelphia Story,* and just after midnight Emilia hands me a pair of brand-new silk pajamas before showing me to the guest

333

room. I climb into the giant oak bed and, for once, fall asleep almost as soon as I close my eyes.

In the morning Emilia cooks me a heap of scrambled eggs with a smiley face made out of pine nuts, and, with her back turned to me, she tells me that she heard from Able overnight.

"He's canceled his flight home," she says, and I can't quite read her tone. "He said he needs more time to work on the edit, whatever happens at the screening today."

"I'm sorry," I say, because I understand that he's punishing her like he used to punish me.

"It's not your fault," she says, but there is an edge to her voice that I haven't heard before. Emilia puts her own plate of eggs on the table and sits down opposite me, but she doesn't eat. Instead she rests her chin in her hand, studying me.

"He won't be back until the twenty-third," she says after a moment, and the hardness is already dissipating. "Breezing back home just in time for Christmas with the kids."

I feel a jolt of energy at Emilia's words, but I try to keep my face neutral as I swallow my mouthful of food and place my hand over hers on the table. Emilia's engagement

334

ring is sharp against my palm as I smile at her comfortingly.

"Well, you know I'm always here if you need me," I say, and I can almost feel her gratitude for my presence.

CHAPTER THIRTY-SIX

Wren walks down the stairs of the glass house in a short black dress and snakeskin Louboutin shoes, with her glossy hair tumbling perfectly down her tanned back, her skin glowing with youth or goodness or Glossier highlighter or *something,* but Dylan still hasn't looked at her once.

I'm wearing a silk Saint Laurent dress I bought in Paris, and I want to believe that I only remember I wore it on the first night of our honeymoon when I see Dylan's face, but maybe I knew all along. Dylan stands for a few minutes staring at me on the doorstep, forgetting to invite me in, and I have to slip past him into the foyer of the house so that Wren doesn't notice how strange the atmosphere is.

"What do you think?" Wren asks Dylan eventually, doing a self-conscious shake. She turns to me and explains, "I'm hardly ever out of my work clothes, so this is a big deal."

Dylan nods and then glances at me again quickly before turning back to answer his girlfriend.

"Beautiful. You both look beautiful."

Wren's face crumples for one tiny second before her smile slides right back, and I already wish I were anywhere but here.

The taxi drops us at the top of an alley, right in the dirty heart of Hollywood. Wren and I walk past a snaking line of beautiful people of fluid gender and indeterminate age, and she takes me right to the front, where a man stands flanked on either side by two strikingly beautiful women in leather jackets and tight neon dresses. The bouncer frowns at me for half a second before waving us in, lifting the rope so that we can shuffle past him.

"I don't want to eat anything tonight. We're not eating, right?" Wren says, and I recognize her steely determination already, remembering how many times I've begged someone not to go home just because I need a warm body next to me while I self-destruct. She threads her arm around my waist and rests her head on my shoulder for a second as we walk, and the small gesture makes me want to try harder to make her happy.

The club is small and almost empty, despite the massive line outside. It is decorated like an old circus with neon lights and distorted mirrors lining the walls, and a bar at the back. Wren heads straight to the bar to order two dirty vodka martinis, her pale hand holding the back of the bartender's head gently as she speaks.

"Filthy. I'm talking super, super dirty. Like how dirty you're thinking right now, times a thousand," she says loudly, and I wonder if she's already drunk.

When the drinks arrive, Wren holds up her glass to cheers me before she downs half of her drink in one sip. I look down at my glass and imagine the vodka slipping down my throat easily, familiarly. I touch my glass to my lips and then take it away again when I remember Emilia telling me how beautifully I was doing. I'm finding it harder to remember whether I'm lying when I say I've never had a drinking problem, or when I say I have one.

"We should get another order in now. That felt like it took ages," Wren says, taking another long sip of her drink.

"Wren, you know that's just straight vodka and vermouth."

"You're right, not nearly enough olive brine. Can we get two more of these, please?

Extra brine," Wren shouts to the barman, and he nods. We stand, moving slightly to the music as the venue fills up around us. The music is louder now, and I'm grateful that neither of us has to make conversation because we really only have one thing in common.

"You look good," Wren shouts at one point, studying me.

"I feel okay," I say, but even as the words leave my mouth, I'm scared that I'm leaving myself open for it all to be snatched away. It turns out that Wren wasn't talking about my emotional well-being, though, as she reaches out to touch the ends of my hair softly before we're interrupted by a beautiful boy dressed as a leopard asking Wren to take a picture of the two of us. Wren smiles and obliges, snapping a few photographs of us on his phone. Before he leaves, the leopard boy asks me to say the line from *Lights of Berlin,* but I pretend not to hear him and pat him gently on his furry shoulder instead.

After he's gone, Wren stares at me as if she's still seeing me through a lens, frowning slightly and studying me.

"Who is the friend you were with last night?" Wren asks, and before I can change the subject from Emilia, the lights dim and a strange, frenetic drumming starts to thrum from the speakers. I subtly place my drink down onto a table next to us as we all move toward the purple spotlight in the center of the room, beaming down on a circular drum stage. A woman climbs onto it, holding a chainsaw in midair, inches away from the crotch of her lace thong. Her pale, teardrop breasts are covered only by small sequined nipple tassels that glitter in the purple stage lights. I watch with the rest of the crowd, both horrified and mesmerized until I can't watch anymore, but when I turn to Wren, she is no longer next to me.

I find her back at the bar, whispering in the barman's ear. By the time I make it through to her, I've already watched her do a shot of tequila with the barman, sucking on the lime like she's eighteen and in Cabo for spring break. Before I can stop her she orders two picklebacks.

"Can we get some coke?" Wren asks, her eyes glassy and blank. It looks like the numbness has finally set in, and it's miserable to watch.

"Have you ever done coke?" I ask her, aware that I'm being everything that someone who wants to self-destruct would hate most in the world.

"Never," she says, just as the barman

places two shots of whiskey in front of us, and a shot each of pickle juice to chase them. He grins when I glare at him over the size of the whiskey shots. They're practically in tumblers. I grab Wren's arm but she's already downed the whiskey and is retching into her hand. I stick my middle finger up at the barman and lead Wren through the crowd, ignoring our distorted reflections in the mirrors as we pass.

I sit Wren down on the curb outside In-N-Out and instruct her not to move. She's already been sick in the gutter four times, maybe five. I drew the line at holding her hair back from her face because I never went to college and we're not sorority sisters.

"I want to dance on the counter," she mutters as I leave her, but she doesn't move. Her upper body is slumped, now too heavy for her to hold up, and one of her false eyelashes is loose at the corner.

I order more food than we will ever be able to eat, then I sit down on the curb as Wren methodically works her way through each Double-Double burger and grilled cheese as if she hasn't eaten in weeks.

"Thank you. I feel better," she says, still slurring softly.

"We're idiots. We should have eaten before we went out," I say generously.

"I used to have an eating disorder, you know," Wren says, unwrapping another burger.

"What kind?"

"All of them."

"I'm sorry."

"Want to know what kills a relationship faster than plutonium? Watching your girlfriend eat seventeen Oreos, three tubs of ice cream, two bags of Funyuns and a wheel of brie in one sitting," Wren says.

"Obviously, Dylan has been a gem about it," she adds after a beat, but there is an edge to her voice. She stretches her legs out in front of her restlessly, her leather shoes in the road. I stare down at the grilled cheese sandwich in my hand.

"You know he'll always be in love with you. I just have to decide how much it bothers me," she says. "Did you see his face earlier? It would be funny if it wasn't so awful. And it's not your hair, before you try to say it. He can't even look at you. Or me."

I put the grilled cheese down on the curb next to me and figure out what I need to say.

"I made him so unhappy." The truth.

"Do you think you could ever unmake

him unhappy?" Wren asks, staring at the gutter under our feet.

I think about it for a second before I shake my head.

"Probably not."

She nods slowly, closing her eyes for too long when she blinks.

"I don't think I can either," she says miserably.

"Why are you doing this, Wren?" I ask. "Trying so hard to be friends. You know you really don't have to pretend to like me." *I barely even like me,* I add in my head.

Wren studies me for a moment before shrugging.

"I don't know. Maybe I thought if I could see what Dylan saw in you, I could be enough for him too. Maybe I thought some of your magic would rub off on me. Or maybe I'm just a nice person, Grace, and you seemed like you needed a friend."

I think about that for a moment, wondering if it's true. I haven't felt so lonely lately, or at least nowhere near as lonely as when I was surrounded by people who were paid to spend time with me.

"Can I give you some advice as a friend then?" I say slowly.

Wren nods.

"Don't let Dylan get away. It will be the

biggest mistake you'll ever make."

A Range Rover pulls up in front of us then, the tires crackling over the old burger wrappers by the side of the road, and Dylan rolls down his window. He breaks into a smile, his eyes creasing at the corners when he sees us both sitting on the curb, surrounded by In-N-Out wrappers. I look at Wren and she shrugs.

"I texted him," Wren says hollowly.

"All right, you reprobates. Jump in," Dylan says, and if he thinks this is weird, or if he's annoyed that Wren got so drunk and is surprised that I'm not, he doesn't let either of us know it.

I pick up our trash and dump it into the nearest trash can, because I don't want Dylan to think we're complete animals, and then I get into the back of the car. I figure Wren is going to sit in the front, but she climbs shakily into the other backseat instead, clipping her seat belt on silently. She stares out the window the entire drive to Malibu, so that after a while I have to open my window to drown out the silence.

CHAPTER THIRTY-SEVEN

I get out of the car at Coyote Sumac, telling Wren to call me tomorrow. She nods wordlessly in response. I watch Dylan drive back up the dirt track slowly, and I very nearly convince myself that watching them leave together is the easiest thing in the world.

I drink some cloudy water straight from the tap before collapsing onto the sofa. I turn on an old episode of *Friends* and try not to think about the intensity in Wren's eyes all night. Maybe getting fucked up has been misunderstood this entire time, and it's actually the only thing some of us can do to live in the moment.

I'm about to switch off the TV when there is a knock at the front door. I creep toward it and look through the peephole at the distorted figure in front of me. I open the door and stand in the doorway with my arms folded across my chest.

"Can I come in?" Dylan asks, wincing

slightly, probably at the obviousness of it all.

I turn around and walk back to the sofa, leaving him to close the door and follow me in. He leaves a gap between us when he joins me on the sofa.

"I think Wren just broke up with me. I mean she passed out at a pivotal moment, but I got the idea," Dylan says, rubbing his eyes.

"I didn't do anything," I say, staring straight ahead at the TV, my stomach in knots.

"I know you didn't," Dylan says gently. "But she did say that you might have some shit to say to me. Or maybe she knew I had some shit to say to you. She's pretty smart like that."

We watch in silence as Phoebe gives birth to triplets on mute. After a while, Dylan shifts over so that our arms are touching, and he says my name so softly that I turn to him. He looks serious, older than I remembered, as he reaches over and turns off the TV.

"When you first left . . . I didn't believe that there was a version of my life without you. Sometimes I still don't," he says slowly.

I nod wordlessly, willing myself not to cry. I want to say that the problem was I could never believe there was a version of my life *with* Dylan. It seemed inconceivable that I could ever be so normal. So likely to have three kids and two rescue dogs and retire happily to a beautiful ranch in Montecito. I remember how Dylan used to kiss the top of my head each morning before he left for work, and how, like everything else we did that had become a tradition, at some point I instinctively started to pull away from him so that there would be one less habit to break when it was over. I wonder now why he's here, what he needs to get off his chest. The problem is that I can remember, in photographic detail, his face the night I tried to tell him about Able. He would deny it if I ever tried to tell him what I saw, but maybe I just know him better than he knows himself.

"Look, the end of us was just stupidly dark, and I wouldn't want to revisit it or even, like, spend a long weekend there, but I do know that we were nearly perfect once. I remember it." Dylan has been staring intently at the floor in front of his feet, but now he looks up at me again. "And I'm so fucking sorry for the part I played in the end. I just wanted you to know, whatever that means to you at this point."

"We were miserable," I say. "Or I was

miserable, so I made you miserable, which made me more miserable, which made you more miserable. Our relationship was one never-ending clusterfuck of misery."

"Can I take you out for dinner?" Dylan asks suddenly. I shake my head, smiling despite myself. He holds his hands up and shrugs.

"Look, I could be losing my mind, but what you just described didn't sound like the worst to me," he says, and a smile plays on his lips that would just need the smallest amount of encouragement to spread across his face. I wonder then what Dylan still sees in me after all this time and whether it's something that is actually there or not. All I know is that on the first night of our honeymoon, we stayed up all night on a deserted beach in Andros, and for once I didn't need any vodka in my veins or anything else but him to reach the sunrise in the morning.

"There were good times too," Dylan says as if he's reading my mind, and I just nod in response, not trusting myself to speak for a moment.

"Did you know that when we were together and you went away anywhere, I'd plan your eulogy?" I ask, after a while.

"What?"

"Like, I wouldn't even realize I was doing

it, and then I'd be midway through composing a funny but heartbreaking speech in my head, about how classic it is that you would choose to die in the most polite, least messy way possible, when I'd realize what I was doing. That's not normal, is it?"

Dylan is trying not to laugh, seemingly at a loss for anything to say.

"Nobody's normal, Grace."

"Except for you," I say, and I've got him there because we both know that Dylan isn't planning anyone's eulogy in his head.

"So how did I go?"

"What?"

"When you used to picture it. How did I die?"

"Ventricular fibrillation in your sleep. It was always very peaceful."

"Thanks, Grace. I guess that's something."

We sit in the dark, smiling for a few moments.

"This has been a weird day," I say. "You *just* got dumped."

"I did," Dylan says, but he doesn't move, and I don't want him to. We sit next to each other, and my heart is drumming in my chest. Then Dylan stands up and stretches, his T-shirt lifting to expose the tattoo on his stomach that he let me do for him one morning in a New York hotel. A jagged, uneven heart filled in with solid black that kept getting bigger because I messed the lines up. And that's when I remember. I remember when Dylan had just arrived in LA and was renting that studio apartment in Los Feliz with one gas hob for a kitchen and a toilet with a flush you had to stand on to make it work, but he saw it as his palace. I knew from that first night that all he wanted was to love me and I that if I could just let him, I might actually feel safe for once in my life. I remember how I felt on our wedding day, my hair tumbling down my back with a silk ribbon plaited through it, when I thought maybe I could be the person he wanted me to be. I imagine what would happen if I kissed him right now. We'd probably end up fucking against the wall within seconds.

I stand up and I hug Dylan good-bye instead, breathing in his warm, familiar smell at the base of his neck, and for the first time in a while, I let myself believe that everything might actually work out okay.

CHAPTER THIRTY-EIGHT

I wake up to the sensation of my phone vibrating next to me. I pick it up and squint at the caller ID. I feel an unpleasant, complicated flicker of guilt when I see Emilia's name and I wonder why I'm always the one feeling bad about everything. I pick up the call.

"Darling, I'm calling to see whether you want to come to the girls' Christmas pageant this afternoon. Actually, who am I kidding, I don't even want to go, but you would be doing me a massive favor. I hate doing this sort of thing alone."

"I have a plan . . ." I say slowly, because I already told Esme she could come over. "But I think I can get out of it. I owe you, anyway."

"Ugh, thank you!" Emilia says, ignoring my reference to the other night as I knew she would. "But please wear a disguise so nobody recognizes you. I don't want to have to share you with all the Stepford wives at school."

I promise her I will before hanging up the phone.

"Oh, Grace, what was the one thing I said?" Emilia asks when I slide into her car a couple of hours later. I look down at my ripped black jeans and black sweater and shrug.

"I'm disguised as a normal person," I say, and when Emilia lets out a loud laugh, I feel guilty over how much I could ruin her life if I found the words.

"Aren't we all," she says after a moment, and she's still laughing as we drive up the dirt track.

"Thank you so much for coming with me to this," Emilia says as she pulls into the driveway of the girls' school. "I always end up doing this sort of thing by myself."

The car wheels shriek as they roll over the gravel. We pass the drop-off zone where I handed the girls over earlier in the week, heading instead to the underground parking structure.

"After all these years, I still hate being alone. Could you tell? You're much more self-sufficient than I am, and I envy you for it," Emilia says, but I ignore her generosity because we both know it's not true in the slightest.

"Is Able still mad that you missed his screening?" I ask as Emilia slows down to let another car pass.

"He doesn't exactly have a leg to stand on when it comes to missing important life events," Emilia says lightly.

"Do you ever get angry about it?" I ask, surprising myself as soon as the words are out of my mouth.

"What?"

"Being by yourself," I say, my voice steady.

"How could I be angry about that?" Emilia says, and I can tell that she's about to change the subject.

"Well, it's just . . . Able's priorities," I say, as if I don't want to be the person pointing this out to her. "That he never shoots a movie in LA, they're all on location. It was a running joke on set that he couldn't stay in the city for more than six weeks at a time."

Emilia pauses for a moment without looking at me, and even though I know I'm being unkind, I feel a jolt of satisfaction. "They have better tax breaks elsewhere. We're looking for space E9."

I point to an empty spot in front of us,

and Emilia pulls into it. She turns the engine off.

"I'd never really thought of it being a choice," she says.

"I didn't mean —"

"No, I know," she says. "The truth is of course he could shoot here. But he needs his space to work, and I have a good life, so I really can't complain."

"Of course not," I say, smiling at her, but I can feel that I've hit a nerve. We climb out of the car and take the elevator up to the grounds in silence.

The doors open up to the sprawling school campus, consisting of a cluster of log cabins that have been decorated by the kids, and a horse stable, an indoor swimming pool and three tennis courts. A goat attached to a long rope greets the parents by nuzzling at their pockets.

"I can promise you that this won't be your typical nativity play, at least. We chose this school because it's very . . . progressive," Emilia says, any trace of uneasiness now gone. "They're all lunatics."

We walk past the tennis courts and follow signs to the playhouse. Before we get there, Emilia stops and ducks around the corner of the toilets, beckoning me to follow her.

"Judging by Silver and Ophelia's rehearsals, we're going to need a little help," Emilia says as she roots around in her bag. She pulls something out and inhales deeply from it, the smell of fresh weed filling the air. She coughs slightly and then holds out the little stick to me. "The best OG Kush you'll ever find. Want some?"

I look down at it and she immediately flinches, closing her hand so that I can no longer see the vape.

"I'm so sorry. I'm clueless sometimes."

I shrug. "Weed was never one of my problem areas."

"Even so," Emilia says, and then she smiles. "Able hates that I do this."

Something about the wistful way she says it makes me wonder if she's still thinking about what I said in the car.

"How long is this play?" I ask.

"Two hours," Emilia says, making an apologetic face. I hold my hand out and after a moment she drops her vape into it. I run my finger over her initials embossed in gold.

"Thanks," I say, taking it from her. I inhale once, and then twice, three times, only blowing out afterward. I immediately feel something happen, the warm tingling sensation growing as it spreads through my body. The world around me takes on a hazy, dreamlike quality, as if I can only really focus on one thing at a time.

When we walk back onto the path, the goat is staring at me. I nod at it and I'm not surprised when it politely nods back. I stifle a giggle as I follow Emilia through to the playhouse, an outdoor amphitheater with stone tiers around the stage and fairy lights laced around each level.

"The kids take most of their classes outside in the tree house. They have a goat-milking rotation," Emilia informs me as we climb the steps, both of us struggling to keep a straight face. We choose seats near the back, and I can feel the effect of the weed even more now that I've stopped moving, a strange, warm feeling of contentedness slipping over me despite myself. I'm just wondering why I never really got into weed when, with the sun still high in the sky, the golden fairy lights flick on and I have to close my eyes because it all becomes too much of a moment.

The play starts, and I understand what Emilia meant. The story is hard to keep up with, an elaborate mix of Hanukkah, Christmas and Diwali celebrations, but when I recognize Silver and Ophelia shuffling on-stage dressed as two candles in a human menorah, I find that I'm smiling, both corners of my mouth stretching even wider when Silver breaks character to wave at us.

For the nativity section, instead of frankincense, gold and myrrh, Jesus is given the gifts of acceptance, equality and kindness, as personified by three small children inexplicably dressed as two mermaids and a lobster. "Oh, sweet Jesus, spare us," Emilia murmurs under her breath when the older kids, playing the shepherds, start a debate about the immaculate conception, which spitballs into a rap song about women's reproductive rights over the years. When a boy comes out proudly dressed as a *Roe v. Wade* newspaper sandwich board, I can feel Emilia finally lose it next to me. She starts to laugh, and, when she lets out a loud snort, I can't stop myself from grinning too. It could be the weed, but suddenly everything seems so insanely, improbably funny, and we're both shaking with laughter. People eye us with a mixture of distaste and envy, and I feel like one of the lucky ones for a moment. A woman on the tier below us turns around to shush us, looking horrified. Her face changes instantly when she recognizes me, which only makes us laugh more. It's the most I've laughed in a long time.

■ ■ ■ ■

On the car journey home, I feel weightless, like I did in the swimming pool my first morning back at the glass house. Silver and Ophelia are staying with friends, so it's just the two of us, and when Emilia turns the radio up loud for a Beach Boys song it feels as if I'm hearing music for the very first time, the harmonies crisp and clear, suspended in the air around us.

I sneak a peek at Emilia, stupidly grateful for something I can't name. My mood isn't even dampened when Esme rings and I have to fumble to send the call to voicemail before Emilia sees. I tell myself that I'm protecting my sister, but I know I'm just being selfish because I would never be able to answer a single question about Esme without revealing too much of myself.

"I actually need to talk to you about something," Emilia says when we're nearly back at Coyote Sumac. She looks sheepish, and a flurry of apprehension steals a piece of my high.

"I hope you don't think I've been meddling, but you seemed so excited the other day about the John Hamilton project, and I couldn't resist having a little word with him about it. I don't know if you know, but he's a dear friend of the family. He's actually Silver's godfather," Emilia says, grinning like a fool. "And he said that he wants to meet with you. Soon. Do you hate me?"

"No," I say, surprised that I somehow forgot that everyone is a dear friend of anyone in LA. "But I heard they'd already cast the role he wanted me for."

Emilia frowns slightly. "Oh, you know this kind of thing is always changing."

"He figured I was a liability and pulled out," I say, and Emilia flinches before smiling ruefully.

"I think he was just worried, but I've spoken to him and he's excited to meet you. He's going to call Nathan to arrange it all."

"Thanks, Emilia," I say, and Emilia waves her hand dismissively, causing the car to swerve slightly.

"I did next to nothing, trust me," Emilia says. "Although once it's announced, we should get you on a late-night talk show, or maybe *Ellen*? We need to truly mark your return somehow."

"Why are you doing all this?" I ask before I can stop myself.

Emilia pulls up outside my house and turns the engine off, before turning to study me.

"If it's because you still feel guilty about not looking after me when I was younger, then it's fine. You had the twins, you were busy, the last thing you needed was another charge. I get it."

Emilia shakes her head.

"I'm doing this because we're friends, Grace, like you told Camila the other day," she says. "And friends help each other out."

I pause, my hand on the car door handle.

"Thank you," I say, turning away before Emilia can notice the stricken look on my face.

CHAPTER THIRTY-NINE

"You look like a deranged elderly runaway," Esme observes, frowning at me in the mirror, and I'm already regretting her presence.

"Or an extra from *Les Misérables*," Blake offers from behind her impossibly small sunglasses. I glare at them both as I pull off the dress, even though they're not wrong — the dress is the color of wet sand with elbow-length sleeves and a ragged hem. I'm not sure it's exactly what Laurel had in mind when she scheduled the fitting for me.

"I didn't ask you here for your styling advice. I'm already paying someone way too much for that," I say at the exact moment my stylist, Xtina, walks back in from the bathroom. Esme snorts and I glare at her.

"Actually, I didn't even ask you here. Why are you two here again?" I ask, rolling my eyes.

"Therapy was canceled," Blake says. "Some sort of celebrity hypno-birthing emergency."

"How much longer do you have to be in therapy for?" I ask, turning around to look at her.

"I guess until I'm *cured*!" Blake says, doing jazz hands for a second before dropping them back down to her lap. "Or at least until I leave for college."

Esme shakes her head sympathetically. "You have to meet Blake's mother to understand. Talk about deranged."

"Have you met ours?" I mutter. "I'm not even sure she's aware that therapy exists."

"Why do you think we're such good friends?" Blake asks, and Esme shoots her a look in the mirror, but I think it's half-hearted and only because she would be betraying our mother if she didn't.

"Are you coming home next week?" Esme asks me, and I turn to face her, confused. "For Christmas, Grace."

Shit. I turn back around and pretend to assess my reflection in the mirror again. It's always been easier to lie to myself than to my sister, and I still feel guilty about blowing her off on the weekend.

"I'm figuring it out."

Xtina hands me a black dress, and I unenthusiastically put it on, even though I can already see that it will wash me out.

Xtina is a stylist based in New York, and every year leading up to awards season she takes over a suite in the Four Seasons to clothe her clients in beautiful, overpriced dresses and jewelry loaned to her by different designers. The IFA dress code is different from the Oscars in that you don't officially have to wear black tie, but I've been warned that I need to play it safe, as the fashion blogs will already be gearing up to put me on their worst-dressed lists.

"That interview you did was pretty sick," Blake says, shifting positions in her chair.

"Did you really like it?" I ask, ever the needy actress. I even turn around to study her face to see if she's telling the truth. The *Vanity Fair* interview was published online yesterday morning, and it appears that I hit the perfect note of contriteness, spiritualism and strength to satisfy the baying masses. Laurel told me she had already fielded dozens of requests for more interviews or TV appearances off the back of it. *"The tide is turning!"* she'd added, just before we hung up. After we spoke, I reread the interview alone in my house with a growing sense of dread: Camila had included everything except for my quote on Able, and the omission felt ominous rather than generous —

as if she could be saving it for a different story.

"Yeah. I also heard my mom and her friends talking about it. They kept saying how brave you were to talk about your issues like that. They're also *really* hoping you get back with Dylan."

I nod slowly, turning to Esme. "Did our mom read it?"

"If she did, she didn't mention it to me."

"Cool," I say, not wanting to ask outright what Esme thought of it, even though I'm sure she would have read it. I unzip the ugly black dress and pull it over my head, instinctively assessing my half-naked body in the mirror as I wait to be handed something else to try. When I look up, Esme is watching me over her phone.

"Hey, Grace. Do you think maybe *I* was the vain sister in a past life?" Esme asks then, grinning smugly at me. I roll my eyes at her. Of course she thought my interview was idiotic.

The next dress Xtina hands me is yellow with long sleeves and a cream silk bow at the neck. I raise my eyebrows at Esme in the mirror, and she shakes her head slightly back at me. It's too fussy, too prim.

"What about that one," I say, pointing to a slithery gunmetal dress hanging at the end of a rail Xtina hasn't touched since I've been here. The rail has been pushed into the corner of the room behind another rail filled with fake fur coats and brightly colored stoles.

Xtina shakes her head, playing with the end of her braid. "I'm sorry, that one doesn't work."

"What do you mean?"

"It's hard to explain, but only certain designers are available for certain clients and events."

I wonder if someone else is wearing it, and that makes me want to wear it even more. Esme smirks at me in the mirror.

"I think she means that whoever designed it doesn't want you to wear their clothes," she says, trying not to laugh.

"Look at all this other stuff though!" Blake says loudly, pointing to the pile of dresses I've already tried on.

I walk over and touch the gunmetal dress, the heavy material surprisingly soft in my hand. It is made up of thousands of tiny sequins that give the overall impression of an impenetrable suit of armor.

"Can I try it on at least?" I ask, and Xtina nods at me, because even though my value is currently somewhere around basement level, she still works for me. I slip into the dress, and the fabric settles onto my skin, cool and slithery. The dress is skintight around my breasts and waist before skimming off my hips and around the softness of my belly, ending exactly at my toes. It is the first dress I've tried on today that hasn't been chosen solely to mask my new "fuller" figure; dresses with sleeves that cover my upper arms, or capes cascading over my shoulders and down to the hem of the dress. As I stare at my reflection in the mirror, Xtina smiles reluctantly.

"It does look cute." She holds her phone up and takes a photo of me. "I'll send it to their PR and we'll see what we can do, okay? No promises though."

"Thank you," I say, and I think they'll let me wear it once they read the *Vanity Fair* interview.

Esme and Blake are watching me in the mirror.

"I'm loath to admit it," I start, smiling at them both, maybe because I think my sister might even be impressed for once, "but this feels good."

I turn slightly in the mirror so that the dress catches the light and shimmers back at me like a snake.

"Are you still going to do it?" Esme asks

then, catching my eye. "Like we talked about?"

I frown at her and turn back to Xtina instead.

"Do you have anything I could wear over the next few days? I've got a couple of lunch meetings and things."

"Let me think about it. I have another appointment now, but I can get some looks together and courier them over to you later? I feel like white is really working on you with that hair."

I can feel Esme's eyes on me as I change out of the dress and into my regular clothes, but I ignore her. I try not to think about her question, about what it would mean for the baby steps I've been taking to reclaim parts of my life I thought I lost years ago. I think about Emilia's fierce, seemingly unconditional belief in me, and I know that its value is something my sister would never be able to understand because she's never lacked it from my parents, and I try not to resent her for it.

"What?" I ask eventually, when we're in the elevator going down to the lobby, because Esme is still studying me as if she's trying to work something out.

"Nothing. I just thought you said that none of this stuff was real," she says.

"Of course it's not," I say. "It's all bullshit."

"You sure seem to be enjoying it a lot for someone who thinks that," Esme says sort of smugly, as if she's won a debate I didn't even know we were having.

CHAPTER FORTY

"In my experience, women who don't say a lot are one of two things — exceptionally stupid or exceptionally smart. I figure you're the latter, but nobody has given you the chance to show it," John Hamilton says as he leans back in the wicker chair on his deck. We are at his house at the very top of the hills, so high up that the air feels thinner and the city unfolds beneath us like a game of Chutes and Ladders. John claims that the house was owned by a famous pop singer before him, the evidence to prove this being four Grammys left behind, because wherever she was going, she didn't need them anymore.

"Mmm," I say. The hot tub is bubbling away next to us, but I pretend not to notice. "And that's just women?"

"Well, women are more extreme than men, wouldn't you agree? There are a lot of mediocre men in this town, and not enough brilliant women." John smiles winningly at me, and I can't work out if what he said was actually an improvement because I'm blinded by his little marshmallow teeth, incongruously set somewhere in the middle of his large, fleshy face.

"You must have met my agent and manager then," I say, and he just stares at me.

"What?"

"Mediocre men?"

"Ahhh. Ha. Ha ha, that's funny," John says, folding his arms across his chest. "See . . . ? You're smart."

I nod, wondering if I'm supposed to congratulate him on being smart enough to notice my smartness.

"Speaking of smart, that was a great interview you did," John says then, and I look at him, surprised that he bothered to read it.

"It's already *Vanity Fair*'s most shared piece this week," I say, remembering now that Nathan told me to mention this. I hope I worded it correctly.

"That's great. Like I said, it was a good move. So tell me . . . how much weight have you actually put on . . . ten, fifteen pounds?" John asks, his eyes narrowed as he assesses me. I can't quite believe that this was his only takeaway from the interview, but, then again, maybe I can. I try to keep my face open, even though John must weigh nearly three hundred pounds himself and hardly seems qualified to be making this assessment. He smiles approvingly after a moment.

"Emilia told me it suited you and it does. Some women can't carry it off, but your face is . . . I don't know. Less harsh. You look like you could play a suburban mom now instead of the school drug dealer. A beautiful, young suburban mom, but you know . . . Hey, it's a compliment," he adds when I don't respond, because I'm thinking about how glad I am that everyone feels so qualified to comment on my appearance in this way. I wonder whether all women are subjected to the same running commentary on their weight, or whether it's reserved solely for the complicit, those of us trading in our looks for cash.

"So the project . . . ?" I say after a moment.

"Are you single right now?" John says, leaning back in his chair.

"Excuse me?"

John is sitting with his knees spread wide and his arms behind his head. He is both excessively comfortable in his own space and assured of his own power. I should stand up and thank him for his time, then walk out before he has the chance to demean me any more, but instead I am leaning toward him, my ten-to-fifteen-pounds-overweight body curving in on itself while I work hard to keep my tone light, my forehead uncreased, my jaw defined.

"You and Dylan . . . you guys broke up, right? I was sorry to hear it. I thought about hiring Dylan on this movie, give him that step up into features, but then I heard you guys were done, and I wanted you for the project more."

"I think Dylan wants to stick to documentaries, actually," I say, and I can hear how defensive I sound. I start again. "Tell me about the project, John. I really can't wait to hear about it."

"All right. You're focused, that's a good start. So it's called *Anatopia*, and it's this epic love story set in space. There are four planets that make up the dystopian galaxy of Anatopia: Neutron, Hydron, Platon and Euron. You're Sienna, queen of Euron, and you're at war with the other planets, only you've fallen in love with the son of the leader of Neutron. Your sworn enemy —"

"What are we at war over?"

"What?" he says, unimpressed at having been interrupted.

"What are we fighting about?"

"We're still finessing the details," he says. "We had a script but we weren't happy with some parts of it, so we're looking at some different names for a rewrite. Big names."

"Big names! The biggest names you've ever seen!" I say, and he frowns at me.

"What?"

"Trump?" I say, grimacing. "I'm sorry, I think I'm nervous."

John starts to laugh, thumping his hand against his thigh so animatedly that the housekeeper comes out to check on him.

"Agnes, great. Another La Croix for me — you want one, Grace? And can we get some of those smoked almonds, the ones with the low sodium? Don't bring them out if they're not low sodium — I'll be able to tell."

Agnes nods and heads back into the house. I watch her retreat, sort of wishing I could follow her.

"So isn't that wild? Does that sound wild to you?" he asks, grinning at me as he runs his hand through his hair, and the way he says *wild* makes me feel embarrassed for him.

"It does sound . . . wild," I say, thanking Agnes for the can of La Croix she has brought out and poured over ice for me.

"There was some talk of a feminist angle. Where is that?"

The drink crackles as I wait for John's response. He doesn't answer my question until Agnes has gone back inside.

"Sorry, I don't like talking about work in front of the staff. You never know who they're talking to, you know? Everyone in this town is working on a fucking script."

"Mmm . . ." I say lightly, hoping Agnes doesn't have to stay in this job for too long. "So the feminism?"

"The feminism is all in the way your character — that's Sienna of Euron — how she's this badass ruler of this entire planet, you know? But she never really wanted any of it, she nearly gives it all up for this Neutron guy, even kind of loses it for a while after he dies in battle, but it ends up being this fury that propels her to beat the other planets. When she emerges as the victor, you think the movie is over, but the real ending will totally destroy you. It makes the hair on my arms stand up just thinking about it," he says, and he pauses to show me his large arm. I try to appear impressed, even though I can't see anything happening in his follicles.

"Once she's won, Sienna destroys the entire galaxy because it's become so corrupt, and greedy, you know. She literally kills everyone, including herself, leaving only this one couple and their dog, who are left with the entire future of civilization in their hands. It's this incredibly important comment on what we're doing to the planet, but you don't realize that until this shot at the very end of the movie. I'm telling you — it's subtle, but it's brutal. Nobody is going to forget how it made them feel. It's going to be one of those. Like *Titanic.*"

I find myself nodding along with him, and by the time he's finished talking and said the word *Titanic,* I realize that I actually want to be in this stupid movie. I want to be Queen Sienna of Euron. I know that, as dumb as it is, it's the exact kind of thing I would need to seal my freedom from Able. I sit up straighter in an attempt to appear more regal.

"That sounds amazing. Inspiring. I'm very into the environment too — saving the dolphins and whales," I say, nodding seriously. John seems pleased, waiting for me to elaborate. *Ugh, Grace, why haven't you done anything good in your entire life?*

"I actually volunteered at the sea-life center near my parents' place when I was home this year," I say, willing him not to ask me where they live. If he does, by my count, it would only be the third question he's asked me after "How much weight have you put on?" and "Are you single?"

"That sounds great, Grace," he says, clearly thinking about something else. He taps his fingers on his knee before leaning forward. "Do you know what? I'm doing some reshoots over the next few days on location downtown. Could you drop by tomorrow to screen-test?"

I pause. "Screen-test tomorrow?"

"Sure. You're okay with that, right? It's an insurance thing, everyone we cast had to do it," John says, and I feel weirdly grateful to him for lying to me.

"Sure, okay," I say, trying to smile in the way that doesn't weaken my jawline.

"How about I also take you out for dinner tonight? To talk about the project some more?" he asks, pursing his lips as if to show me how serious he's being.

"Why don't we get the screen test out of the way first," I say smoothly. "Then we can go for dinner with Nathan and Kit in the New Year."

"Sounds great, Grace," John says good-naturedly, and I'm sickeningly relieved that he's not going to make a big deal about being turned down. He stands up, stretching a little.

"So I'll get Nathan to email you later about the screen test?" I ask as he walks me through the house, and I try not to notice that he moves like a man who is used to people getting out of his way. I repeat my question again in my head, without the question mark, for next time.

"Sure, we'll get it booked in for the morning. I assume I'll also be seeing you at the Globes?"

"Undecided," I say vaguely, because I haven't been invited. "I usually only go when I'm nominated. And sometimes not even then."

John laughs as he opens the front door for me. He kisses me good-bye on the cheek, leaving a warm, wet residue that I have to resist the urge to wipe.

"I'm excited about the project," I say, one more time, before I leave.

"I'll see you tomorrow, Grace. Send my regards to Emilia if you speak to her." John leans in again, this time to speak quietly in my ear. "Paparazzo by the black Jaguar."

I nod and walk down the steps, holding my head up high so the photographer catches me sliding gracefully into my car and driving away.

CHAPTER FORTY-ONE

I ring the doorbell of the peach house, and the twins answer it together. They seem disappointed when they see that it's me, and I figure I should bring them a present next time, since that seems to be what sustains them.

"That was a great play the other day," I say, smiling. "Hands down the two best menorah candles I've ever seen."

Silver ignores me but Ophelia smiles back at me shyly. Emilia walks into the hallway to greet me, wearing a pair of glasses I didn't know she needed.

"Darling, thank you for coming! Come on in," she says, wiping her hands on her jeans.

I follow her into the kitchen and take a seat at the table. Emilia immediately puts a plate of shortbread in front of me.

"Sorry about the mess," Emilia says, gesturing to three shopping bags sitting in the corner of the room. "I'm so pleased that you're here. Girls, do you want to move into the playroom?"

The twins, who are playing a game on their phones, ignore her. They chat loudly and unselfconsciously, telling each other what they have achieved in terms of gold rings or makeover points in their game. Emilia raps her knuckles on the table, and Silver stands up and runs out of the kitchen in one movement while Ophelia hangs back.

Emilia puts her arm around her. "Can you make sure your sister doesn't get too worked up? You know what she's like."

Ophelia nods and follows Silver out of the kitchen. Emilia pulls up a seat opposite me, tilting her head to one side as she watches me.

"Tell me everything," she says, leaning toward me, and for a moment I forget that she's asking about my meeting with John.

"It went well . . . I think, although obviously you never really know," I say, choosing my words carefully. "John seems like a very interesting man."

Emilia lets out a loud peal of laughter and she claps her hands together as if I've just said something utterly charming, as opposed to paying her dear friend a disingenuous compliment.

"He's not as bad as he seems, I promise,"

she says. "We all know that there's worse out there, particularly in this industry."

I take a bite of shortbread so that I don't have to comment, but my stomach turns when I realize it's the exact same kind that Able used to give me when I was younger.

"I have to audition for the part," I say. "It's been a while."

"Oh no, I think that's perfect," Emilia says, sounding pleased. "It means that you'll be able to silence all the people saying you're not up to it, in one go. Nobody can deny that you earned the role."

My discomfort at her words must be obvious, because Emilia immediately puts her hand over mine.

"I just meant . . . Look, try to think about it this way . . . At the moment, however brave they think you are, however much they respect what you said in the interview, however much they may *like* you, they are still just waiting for you to slip up again, because that's how it works. They don't want you to win. And I don't just mean John, I'm talking about the industry as a whole, the press, even the public. But what you're going to do is take that negativity and turn it into something you can use, let it become the thing that fuels you. And if you do that, then you're not only going to win the part, but you're going to win everyone's hearts by the time this movie is finished. You're going to be America's sweetheart, darling." Emilia says the last sentence in a Katharine Hepburn mid-Atlantic accent, satisfied that she has put my mind at rest. I struggle to swallow the lump of shortbread still in my mouth.

"That reminds me, actually, we need to talk about the IFAs," Emilia says as she pushes her glass of water across the table to me. "I meant to ask you about your decision the other day, but it must have slipped my mind somewhere during the story of the Maccabees, as told through interpretive dance."

"What does Able think?" I ask after I've dislodged the thick biscuit coating the back of my throat. My armpits start to prickle with sweat.

"We want it to be a surprise," Emilia says, looking lost for a second. "Do you think he'll hate it? He hates surprises."

"I don't know," I say uncomfortably.

"You must let me know if you're not up to it," Emilia says, watching me closely.

"Why wouldn't I be up to it?" I ask quietly, and as the words come out of my mouth, I realize that I'm giving Emilia the chance to tell me that she knows something was wrong. With a force that nearly stuns me, I understand what this has all been about: I want to believe that Emilia already knows what Able did, because if she can forgive me, then I will have all the proof I ever needed that none of it was my fault. I blink back hot tears that sting my eyes as I wait for my friend to answer my question.

"You know, I tried to explain something the other day, but I think I wasn't entirely honest with you," Emilia says, and I can hear the sound of my blood rushing in my ears.

"You asked why I wanted to help you, and, the truth is, I *do* feel responsible for you. I was the one who promised I'd look after you at the beginning. I was the one who went to your parents' house to get you to sign up for *Lights.* At the time, I thought it was the best thing for you, but now I'm not so sure. You would barely talk to me after that, and I just let you drift away. Then when Able didn't sign you up for the next one . . . I don't know, it must have felt like we abandoned you."

"I don't know if that's entirely accurate," I say, my voice tight.

"Gracie, I know that you ended up in the hospital. After you . . . overdosed," Emilia says softly, embarrassed for me. "Able told me about your . . . issues with your mental health. I knew they were working you too hard and I felt so guilty for not having said so at the time."

I don't know why I'm so surprised by her words. I've never owned my own story.

"We actually sent a gift basket when we heard . . . Did you get it?" she asks now urgently.

"I never went back to the house in Venice," I say, my voice strange sounding.

"Oh, darling, I've upset you," Emilia says, looking stricken herself but recovering quickly because she doesn't like to think about sad things for too long. "You've come so far since then, it really is so incredible to see."

I stare at a framed photo on their wall that wasn't up last time I was here. It's a picture of Able standing in between two beautiful chestnut horses with Silver and Ophelia sitting proudly on top in full dressage outfits.

"You're angry at Able," she says then, and I feel instantly dizzy, unspooled by the unexpected accuracy of her words. "I realized it when Camila asked you about him the other day. He hurt you."

I swallow hard because now that the moment is here, my throat feels as if it's closing up.

"You know there was a time when I was jealous of you. You and Able always had that connection that nobody else could get near. Not that I'd have even wanted to be involved, it wouldn't have been healthy. It just seemed unfathomable to me that there was this huge, important part of his life that I couldn't be a part of," Emilia says, thoughtfully. I study the chipped black nail polish on my hands, trying to shield myself from her words. The light behind Emilia warps slightly as she struggles for the right words.

"What I'm trying to say is that sometimes we forget that we can never really know someone else, you know, all of them. And that's okay, we're all allowed our secrets, but it does mean that occasionally we mistake our own perspective, our own *narrative,* for theirs. All it took was Able explaining that he saw you like a daughter and that you were the one who asked him to guide you, to nurture your talent where your parents couldn't seem to, like his grandmother did for him all those years ago, and my jealousy just . . . shifted."

I swallow, unable to meet Emilia's eyes as her words float into me instead, settling in even the darkest places I've worked so hard to protect. I search for some secret subtext in them but all I hear is that Emilia has no

384

idea about anything that happened to me. She has no clue who I really am at all, and how could she when Able had already started his campaign against me years ago?

"Anyway, I didn't want to make this about me, but maybe you should talk to Able, see what he has to say. He will have his reasons for whatever happened between the two of you after *Lights*. You just might not have been able to understand them at the time."

I nod, slowly.

"We were, close, you know," I start, my heart hammering in my chest. "Able and I. We were always close."

"Of course you were, anybody could see that. I don't think you could have done the work you did if you weren't," Emilia says, then she stops abruptly and something in her face changes.

"What are you saying, Grace?" she asks, and I swallow hard, understanding that this is my final chance to tell her what happened while still protecting myself. To brush over it now would be to deliberately lie to her for the first time, and if the truth ever came out, we would both always remember the moment in her kitchen when she left me room to tell her my story.

Emilia's pale eyes hold mine as I think of everything I could say, both now and onstage at the IFAs, how even if I somehow managed to say the right words out loud, each one would only ever bind me tighter to Able. When I think about him, it's as if I'm being dragged back down to my knees, only this time I'm pulling everyone around me down with me. For the first time since we met, I am the one with the power to threaten *his* happiness, but the power is all wrapped up in that threat, and as soon as I actually say the words, that power will be released into the world for others to claim, fight over, apportion blame. After that, I would never be anything more than Able's victim, to the rest of the world too.

I think about another type of revenge — the quieter, less explosive kind I could inflict just by living my life in spite of him. And what could be more galling for Able than watching me become happier, more successful without him? To know that I always held the power, I just never believed I could do anything without him. I could work again, maybe even on *Anatopia,* and this time it would be without any of Able's conditions. Maybe I could learn to relax around Emilia, could learn to accept some of her small acts of kindness toward me, and maybe the way Dylan occasionally still looks at me, as if I am someone good and important, wouldn't have to change beyond recognition.

"Nothing," I say after a moment. "Just that maybe it's too soon. I'm not sure I'm ready to be back in public just yet."

Emilia nods without meeting my eyes, and I'm relieved when she changes the subject after that, telling me that Silver has been begging her for a retired greyhound for Christmas. She turns away from me as she talks, changing the water of a vase of exotic, fleshy flowers that have wilted in the heat. *This is enough,* I tell myself as I pick up a fallen petal from the table, scrunching it up in my hand until it's unrecognizable. *This has to be enough.*

CHAPTER FORTY-TWO

"I'm sorry to interrupt, but could you move your hair out of your face?" the casting director asks, not unkindly. "It's obstructing your words."

"Sorry, yes, of course," I say, tucking my hair behind my ears. I want to point out that it's more likely the sound of hundreds of cars rushing down the freeway underneath the parking structure that is obstructing my words, but I wouldn't be doing myself any favors if I did. I'm already on the back foot, clearly having held everyone here for longer than they expected.

"And can you direct your dialogue more to me?" the producer says, folding his arms across his chest. He is standing slightly to the left of the camera. I look at John for confirmation, and he nods encouragingly.

"Sure," I say, wiping my damp hands on my jeans. Even though it's my first screen test in nine years, I think it's unusual for the director, casting director and producer to all be here in person instead of watching the tape at a later date. I'm not sure if that means they're taking it more seriously or they just happened to be on set today for the reshoots, but for the first time in years, I feel sickeningly nervous. Even though I memorized the lines last night, I'm still gripping the script in my hand, my fingers leaving damp marks on the paper.

I start over again but the entire time I'm trying to concentrate on the lines, I can already hear his voice in my head telling me how badly I'm fucking it up, that I'm too much of a liability, too fat, too broken to be given the job, that I lost my light years ago and the whole thing is a waste of time.

"I never asked for any of this, don't you understand that?" I read, but this time the producer puts his hand up for me to stop.

"I'm sorry, something still isn't working. Can we take the makeup off?"

"Sure," I say as an assistant appears to hand me a face wipe. I can tell by the slight grimace on his face that his empathy levels are too high, that he probably feels things too strongly for this industry.

I turn around and wipe my makeup off, trying to compose myself. I know this is the thing I can do, the one thing that always came naturally to me. The assistant holds his hand out, and I drop the dirty face wipe into his palm.

"Do you mind if I go to the bathroom quickly?" I ask, and John checks his Rolex before waving me in the direction of the public toilets. I walk past him, ignoring the crew setting up on my way, some of whom stop what they're doing to stare at me.

The toilet seat is yellowing, cheap, but I never actually learned to squat, so I unzip my jeans and sit straight onto it. I try not to cry out when my skin gets caught in one of the cracks in the seat. I feel like I can't get enough air into my lungs, and I wish I'd listened in all those meditation classes Laurel made me do, but I could never seem to get the right parts to expand when they were supposed to.

While I'm peeing, two women walk in. One is wearing a red latex bodysuit and a tiny matching mask over her eyes, and her hair is scraped back into a ponytail heavy with extensions spilling down her back, nearly to her waist. The other one is dressed normally, and from the way she hovers around the first woman, I figure she's probably her assistant or an old friend from school she brings with her for support.

I watch them both through the gap in the

door, realizing that the woman in the mask is the lead actress in the film they're reshooting in the parking lot. She was on a huge network TV show for a couple of years, and Nathan told me she had left it to make the move into features, booking John's action movie as her first role. She's a couple of years younger than me, and she seems glossy, uncomplicated, enjoying it more than I ever could, but maybe I'm too quick to judge.

"Did you see her?" she says, addressing her friend, while still staring at herself in the mirror.

"She looks different. Kind of like a caricature of herself?" the friend says, her words peeling up at the end as she watches the actress for cues.

"Right," the actress says, leaning in and dusting something from her cheek. "But I think she's still kind of beautiful. There's something eerie about her."

The friend leans in closer. "You know I heard they've already cast the role she's auditioning for. I think they're only seeing her today as a favor to someone."

"Shit. And I heard she overdosed last year," the actress says, making a sympathetic noise at the end.

"Did you read that interview she did? She

seemed kind of unhinge —"

I cough loudly before flushing the toilet and unlocking the toilet door. The two women are horrified but they recover quickly, and the actress holds her arms out to embrace me even though we've never met and I haven't washed my hands yet. I stand stiffly and let her hug me anyway, catching the eyes of my reflection in the mirror as I do. That's when, from nowhere, I hear Emilia's voice, as clear as if she were standing next to me in the bathroom.

They don't want you to win.

I walk back into the corner of the parking lot and stand on my mark. Nobody is looking at me anymore, punishment for wasting their time while I was in the bathroom.

"I'm ready," I say. "Give me one more take."

The assistant turns the camera back on, and the producer stands behind it. I drop the script onto the floor at my feet and inhale a deep, shuddering breath.

They don't want you to win.

I let the negative energy bubble up inside me, summoning it, trying to mold it into something else: a protective shield of armor around me. *They don't want you to win.* I breathe in and out, every nerve in my body firing until I start to fill the whole fucking parking lot with my light, soaring above these people and their impatience, their passive-aggressive power moves and their time commitments. I channel Sienna, queen of Euron, gathering her strength to defeat the final galaxy, her reluctance to lead ending up being the very source of her strength.

"I never asked for any of this, don't you understand that?" I start, and my voice rings out, clear and perfect through the air. I can see the assistant glance quickly at me out of the corner of my eye, but I keep my gaze focused on the producer, burning into him with every word I say. "I've always seen it as a sign of weakness. That people who want too much of anything are flawed."

My words cut through the open structure like flaming arrows, pulsing out of my body one after the other at lightning speed until they create a ring of fire around me. The casting director puts her phone down and watches me with interest. The hairs on the back of my neck stand up as the power flows through me in intense waves.

"But after what they've done, do you think I have any choice? That I have any other possible life to live?" I continue, my eyes filling with tears as I say the lines because at least I know now that nobody can take this away from me, however hard they try. This is what I do.

"So you ask me why I want to win this war, and I'll tell you this: I never once *wanted* to rule over Anatopia. It is my destiny."

When I'm finished there is a silence, before the casting director turns off the camera and John nods approvingly.

"Great job, Grace," he says warmly. "Do you want to watch any of it back?"

I shake my head. I already know I nailed it from the look on his face.

CHAPTER FORTY-THREE

I park on a side street off Melrose, underneath a blossomless jacaranda tree, and check the directions to the restaurant that Laurel texted me. I feel invigorated from the audition, as if I've just remembered who I am after the longest time away. As I walk, I call Emilia to fill her in on my screen test, but it rings through to her voicemail. I haven't heard from her since our talk in her kitchen yesterday, but I feel so relieved about that now, too, safe in the knowledge that I made the right decision in not telling her the truth. Maybe the past really is just that, something to forget ever existed. I feel wildly happy all of a sudden, like maybe if I run fast enough I could even take off from the ground. The feeling is vaguely familiar to me but in the past it was only ever drug induced and not caused by something that genuinely has the power to save me, like this god-awful, beautiful fucking movie.

There is a magazine stall on the corner of Melrose and I slow down, scanning the titles. My face is on the cover of at least five magazines, but only one of them is still leading with the deranged photos from PCH. The rest have followed *Vanity Fair*'s lead in recasting me as a survivor, traumatized by a life spent in the spotlight. I lift one up so that I can read the headline: "Grace's Tragedy: The Real Reason She Left LA."

I drop the magazine without reading it and walk into the restaurant. A woman on her way out recognizes me and digs her daughter in the ribs, but she's too late, I've already passed them.

Roots is a new vegetarian restaurant, right in the heart of Melrose, with swaths of outdoor seating so that everyone can see you from the street. Green cacti swing in macramé planters above jewel-toned velvet sofas, and trays filled with brightly colored food decorate the gold tables. Everyone is beautiful and tattooed and locked in intense conversations, but they all still stare at me as I make my way through the restaurant. Laurel is already waiting at a table just inside, set back behind a giant cactus.

"Didn't they have a table outside? I'm worried nobody will see us here."

"Wow, hi to you, too, Grace. Since when

do you care about being 'seen'?"

I sit down opposite her and roll my eyes. "I was talking about the servers, obviously."

"Sure you were," Laurel says, studying her menu. "How was the audition?"

"I think it was good. It felt good. You were right, it turns out I don't know how to do anything else."

"And John? I've heard he's kind of a creep."

I think about it for a moment. "I guess kind of, but in a nonthreatening way."

Laurel raises her eyebrows. "Thank heavens for that."

"I mean, at least it's all on the surface with him," I say, thinking of Able's perfect white teeth that will drain your blood faster than a leech, before I quickly add, "I did feel a little like he was pushing for a date more than the movie at first . . . Do you think that's crazy?"

"Probably not. As I said, he doesn't have the best reputation," Laurel says.

"Yeah. I think I actually felt grateful that he didn't make a big deal when I rejected his dinner offer. Isn't that fucked?"

"Sounds like the patriarchy," Laurel says, signaling the server, who comes straight over. We order a few different plates, and then the server asks us how successful we've been at manifesting our goals this year, and Laurel laughs in her face until she leaves, because apparently only she's allowed to ask me that type of thing.

"So do you think you'll do the movie?"

I look down at my nails and then back up at her. "If they offer it to me, yeah. It's kind of earnest, but I think that could work in its favor. It's like *Game of Thrones* meets *Titanic,* set in space."

"They'll probably want you to get your tits out," Laurel says, swiveling around to check something behind her.

"Are you okay? You seem distracted."

"I'm fine. Did you talk to the paparazzi today?"

"I thought you did that for me. Are they here?" I ask, but Laurel is still looking around. "Are you sure you're okay?"

"No, no, great. I actually forgot to call them. Maybe they just got a tip."

"Yeah, I guess so, or maybe they followed me from the audition? They were outside waiting when I left."

The waitress brings over our food, and a matcha smoothie for each of us.

"Do you want to order anything else? My manager said it's on the house," the waitress says, smiling widely, her eyes not leaving mine.

"I think we're okay," Laurel says at the same time I say, "Can we get some more beetroot raita?"

"Everyone's being nice to me again," I say, once the waitress has left.

"It's because you don't look like you've escaped from a psychiatric ward anymore."

"It cannot just be the hair. Or one interview. This fucking city," I say, rolling my eyes so hard I can nearly see my brain.

"It's not just the hair, or the interview, it's what they both represent. You've got your shit together. You're not running across three lanes of traffic holding gas station pizza. *In Crocs.*"

"I was hoping you hadn't noticed the Crocs. And it was actually four lanes," I say, semi-proudly.

"I took the Crocs with me last time I was over. They're somewhere in a dumpster in Echo Park."

"You know, I'm going to call Crocs and ask them to sponsor me, just for you."

"I wouldn't," Laurel says, chewing her way through a mouthful of charred brussels sprouts. "My contact at Lancôme says they're considering you for the face of their new fragrance."

I pause, my fork suspended in the air.

"What? Do you think it's true?" I ask, only

399

slightly unsettled to realize how excited I am by this news, and by how thrilled Emilia will be when I tell her.

"It would make sense. You're everywhere again. In a good way this time."

I smile at Laurel, still pleased for reasons I don't even understand. I feel something rippling through me — if not happiness then at least pride, or maybe gratitude. I am slowly rebuilding Grace Turner, only this time I'm doing it without Able.

"The thing I like about you is I can tell where I'm at, in terms of public perception, just by hanging out with you. You're my one-woman litmus test. If you're being nice to me, then I know that everyone else must like me again too," I say, still smiling.

"The difference being, I still hang out with you even when you're acting like Britney Spears before her meds. Don't forget that."

"Best friends forever," I say faux sweetly.

"And ever."

I take a sip of smoothie and think I can taste the deactivated charcoal.

"So Emilia thinks I need to build on the momentum of the *Vanity Fair* piece. She suggested a couple of awards show appearances and a late-night talk show once I've signed on to *Anatopia*. What do you think?"

"*Anatopia* won't even start shooting until

the middle of next year, so you need to do something before that," Laurel says, frowning slightly. "I guess you could do a talk show. But you should check which one with Emilia, obviously. She seems to know best."

I let the resentment hang in the air instead of trying to appease her.

"What are your plans for Christmas?" Laurel asks, but she still seems distracted.

"Honestly? I haven't even thought about it," I say.

"It's six days away, Grace. You can't just sit in that house. Jesus."

I shrug, not wanting to tell her I don't have many other options right now.

"Look, you can come over to my place if you need somewhere to go," Laurel says hesitantly, in a way that makes me think she might be regretting the offer already.

I smile at her anyway. "Thank you."

"So, how are you feeling at the moment? Like really?" Laurel asks after another pause, but I can tell she's still in a weird mood. I consider adjusting her energy in the way she would if this was the other way around.

"I actually feel okay. Maybe even more in control, I don't know," I say, smiling over Laurel's head at the photographers crowding around the entrance to the restaurant.

"And it's not my fucking hair."

"Grace —"

"I know what you're going to say — one day at a time, blah, blah, but I haven't even thought about having a drink or doing any drugs in weeks. To be honest, I'm sick of everyone treating me like I'm damaged," I say, drinking some of my green smoothie and frowning, but not in the way that gives me the "eleven" lines between my eyebrows.

"I think that's great, and I'm so happy you're feel —"

"I don't even necessarily just have to stick to acting, if that's what you're worried about. What are those people called that do a bit of everything? Maybe I'll write a book on mindfulness or something," I say, grinning as I swirl my straw around in my glass. "Or a vegan cookbook. I really should have kept it up, but did I tell you what my dad made me the first night I was home?"

"The salad with cheese and bacon bits," Laurel says, and I think for a second that she's bored or maybe just miserable.

"And ranch dressing! I couldn't —"

"*Grace,*" Laurel interrupts at this point, basically shouting. I look at her, surprised.

"I'm sorry, but I've been trying to tell you that I have to go for fucking ages," Laurel says, sounding sheepish. "I didn't tell Lana

I was with you, and I'm kind of freaking out that she's going to see that I'm with you before I have a chance to explain, because of all these fucking cameras. You're not her favorite person after our night in Coyote Sumac. I hadn't done coke in six months until I saw you."

"I'm sorry, who?" I ask, not understanding.

"Lana. My partner."

I can feel my shock register on my face. I don't even try to keep my features neutral for the photographers this time. "Your what now?"

"We've been together two years, Grace. You've met her. What the fuck."

"I didn't even know you were gay," I say, and then there's a moment where I think Laurel might smash a plate of blackened eggplant over my head, but instead she starts to laugh, her eyes filling with glossy tears as she reaches across the table to take my hand.

"Never change, Grace," she says, and even though I think I can hear genuine affection in her voice, I'm still embarrassed.

"I'm the pits," I say, and Laurel nods.

"Can I meet her?" I ask. "Again, I mean?"

"Sure. But not right now. Like I said, she hates you."

I look down at our setup, the table for two filled with sharing plates piled with vegan food, and matching matcha smoothies, surrounded by photographers calling out my name.

"What the fuck are you still doing here then?" I ask, smiling and putting my sunglasses over my eyes. "Go home."

I climb into my car, pulling my baseball cap over my head once I'm inside. One of the photographers taps on my window, and I open it two inches so that I can hear what he's saying. He is older than the rest and is smartly dressed in a sky-blue linen shirt. He drops something through the window that lands on my passenger seat. It's a business card. I turn it over in my hand. *Mario Gomez — Professional Photographer.*

"Call or text me whenever you need me, okay? I'll be there," he says through the window as I reverse away from him.

CHAPTER FORTY-FOUR

I leave three messages for Emilia over the next few days, but she doesn't return any of my calls. Even when I tell myself that she must be busy getting everything ready for Christmas without Marla, I still check my phone a few times an hour to see if she's been in touch. I want to tell her how I think I finally understand what she meant about sifting through the shit life deals you and holding on to the good stuff with everything you have. Maybe I'll even find the words to tell her how much more grounded I've been feeling since I started spending time with her, like she might be the kind of person I could grow up to be like, if I can just stay on track.

The late December sun is blazing hot, hotter than I can ever remember it, and the beach below my house is filled with tourists shaded under bright umbrellas and mismatched towels bought on Venice Beach. I collect the binoculars from the kitchen drawer, and point them toward the peach house. The house is dark, with no movement, but Emilia's car is still parked in the driveway. I consider walking up the back to surprise her, but instead I settle into the beige lawn chair and wait.

After an hour or so, I see her blond head bobbing across the driveway, and then her car starts to move. I race to my own car. The drive down to PCH from Emilia's takes longer than from mine, so I drive up the hill and wait at the opening until I see her Porsche turn onto the highway. I follow her car, keeping at least three car lengths between us as she drives south on PCH for about twenty minutes. She turns off just before we reach Venice, and I follow her, telling myself I just want to share the story of my audition with her, since she was the one who got it for me. I turn the radio up loud to drown out everything except the golden sun, the song and the white Porsche in front of me.

Emilia parks on one of the side roads behind Abbot Kinney but I drive on, opting for the paid parking just off the main street instead so that I have a head start on her. I can't figure out how to use the payment machine so I just leave my car and hope that I don't get another ticket.

Abbot Kinney is buzzing with Christmas tourists and local girls gripping iced coffees along with their car keys and sparkly phones. Christmas lights are strung over the storefronts, and trees glitter in the windows. I duck into Le Labo when I see Emilia ordering something from a juice truck parked in front of the Butcher's Daughter across the street. I make a big thing about smelling the different perfumes in case she's coming in here, but then I find one that is actually familiar — the one Emilia wears. Thé Noir 29. I spray it on my neck, turning my back on the pretentious man behind the huge oak counter. I clocked the exact moment he recognized me, his face softening disingenuously.

"That one is actually my favorite," he calls to me, and I smile as if that's just sealed it. What a salesman.

"I'll take a bottle. I also want to buy a gift for my friend — does this come in candle form?"

"We have something you'll love even more, let me grab it for you," he says, running around the other side of the counter and trailing his finger across the candles until he settles on one.

"You can personalize the message on the

label — what would you like it to say?"

"How about . . . Emilia, Thank you for everything, Love, Grace x," I say, picturing the candle in the middle of the table in the dining room, or maybe on the mantelpiece behind the toilet in the master bathroom, a surprise for Able every time he takes a piss. I watch out the window while the man rings up my order. Emilia is no longer at the juice truck.

"Hey, can I film you saying that line for my friend?" the man asks, waving his phone at me. "You know —"

"I know," I interrupt him. "But I'm kind of in a rush."

After that, the man takes an unholy amount of time mixing my perfume and creating an individual label for both the perfume and the candle, before gift wrapping them both so slowly that I'm convinced he's actually moving backward at one point.

I pay quickly and rush out the door. I walk down Abbot Kinney, smiling politely back at anyone who recognizes me or nearly does. One girl says hi to me, thinking I'm a friend of a friend or maybe someone from her yoga class, before realizing her mistake and looking mortified. I say hi back graciously.

I peer into every store that I imagine Emilia could be in, the eco-friendly jeans store, the Scandinavian jewelry store, even the weed dispensary, but in the end, I find her in the one place I didn't expect — the spiritual bookstore. She is wearing a cream cashmere sweater and jeans with a pair of tortoiseshell sunglasses, and is scanning the spines of books about astrology. I touch her on the shoulder lightly, molding my face into an expression of casual surprise when she turns around.

"What are you doing in here?" Emilia asks accusingly, but then she recovers and pushes her sunglasses up on her head so that I can see her eyes. "Actually, what the fuck am I doing in here?"

She leans in to kiss me on the cheek, but none of it is quite right.

"Are you wearing my perfume?" she asks, narrowing her eyes again slightly.

I sniff at the collar of my vintage T-shirt. "Oh yeah, someone gave me a sample of it. It smells better on you," I say, hoping she won't ask to look in the Le Labo bag.

Emilia smiles politely. "You're so sweet."

"Do you want to go for a coffee? I've already had one, but it's the only high I have left so . . ." I say, trying to make her smile. "Unless I'm about to sit through a two-hour interpretive nativity play, of course."

Emilia checks her Cartier watch quickly. I

409

stand like an idiot, waiting for her to respond, and when she eventually looks back at me, it's like she forgot I was there.

"I did the audition — for *Anatopia*? I think it went well," I say, desperately trying to keep her attention. "It felt amazing."

She smiles again. "I'm so pleased for you, Grace. Really, that's great."

I wait for her to say something else, but she has turned to the display of books on moon cycles, picking one up and turning it over in her hand. When she notices me waiting for something, she shrugs apologetically.

"I'm sorry, this isn't a great time. I'm getting some last-minute presents and *then* I have to go to the British store in Santa Monica to get some disgusting culinary invention called Marmite." She rolls her eyes. "*Your* people invented it, and Able likes me to make the gravy using it, just like his grandma used to."

"Able's coming back?"

Emilia looks at me strangely. "Of course he's coming back. Christmas is three days away."

I nod and try to appear as if I knew that, and I'm just having a bad day too. I tuck my hair behind my ears.

"I actually have some Marmite at mine. I can drop it over if you want?" I say, trying

410

to sound casual.

Emilia narrows her eyes. "You do?"

"I do. I haven't even opened it yet," I say. "I can drop it over tomorrow?"

"That would be great. Thanks, Grace," Emilia says, turning back to the books.

"Are you . . . is everything okay?" I ask, hating how desperate I sound.

"Of course it is," Emilia replies, but her voice is clipped and tight, and she must hear it, too, because her eyes soften a little. "I'm sorry, I've just got a lot going on at the moment."

"I understand completely," I say, my voice dipping like my mother's does when she's lying, and reminding me that I haven't called my parents since I've been back in LA. "The Marmite is the least I can do, Emilia. I'll drop it over tomorrow."

I walk out of the bookstore with my Le Labo bag swinging by my side, but the smile drops from my face as soon as I'm out the door.

I have no place to go other than my depressing rental, so instead I walk down onto the sand with my baseball cap pulled low on my head. All the locals know that you don't actually swim or sunbathe on Venice Beach because of the weird sewage foam that rolls in with the tide, but there are still hundreds of tourists lying on the sand beneath the cornflower-blue sky and unseasonably blistering sun.

I pull my phone out of my bag and look down at it. For some reason my encounter with Emilia is making my chest heavy and tight, and I feel lonelier than I have in a long time. *What is* wrong *with me?* I think as I scroll through my contacts and call Nathan.

"Nathan, hi!" I say enthusiastically.

"Hi, sweetie. I've actually been meaning to call you."

"You have?"

"I think John Hamilton is going to offer you this role. He said your screen test blew them all away."

"Okay," I say slowly, surprised by the validation I still feel at his words. "So when do we sign?"

"It doesn't exactly work like that," Nathan says, sniffing. "He'll be trying to get you for cheap now, so we'll have to negotiate. He did seem to like you though. Thinks you're smart."

"Who was it that said women and dogs are the only two instances where too much intelligence is a bad thing?"

Nathan snorts. "Probably John Hamilton."

412

"So can we meet with him next week? After Christmas?"

"Yes, I'll get Dana to email him and arrange it."

"Thank you. I've got your support with this . . . comeback, right?" I say needily, hating myself.

"As long as you don't call it a comeback. Remember, you took one year off, to spend time with your parents."

"That's what *I* told *you.*"

"You didn't have to miss the goddamned Golden Globes, Grace," Nathan says, but his voice isn't nearly as scathing as it was when we were in his office.

"And there will be at least one topless scene. It might not say it in the script, but you could be topless for the entire one hundred and twenty minutes, if it's John making those decisions."

I swallow. "I'm ready for it all."

"You're a lucky girl, Grace, if you manage to pull this off," Nathan says, just before we hang up.

I look down at my phone and flick through my contacts until I reach my sister's name. Esme has called me three times since I last saw her. My finger hovers over the call button for a moment, but then I just lock the phone instead. I should really check that I don't have a parking ticket.

I think I'm going to drive home to Malibu, but somehow I end up on Grand Boulevard, my body making a series of unsolicited turns that bring me right to the doorstep of the glass house. I ring the bell and wave into the security camera. Dylan opens the door, and I didn't realize how much I missed him until I see him standing there in his navy swim shorts and an old Bob Dylan T-shirt. He looks tanned and his hair is ruffled on one side where he must have been lying on it.

"Have you been sleeping?" I ask, surprised.

"Swimming," he says, and he's not even trying to hide how pleased he is to see me. "Come in."

We sit around the kitchen island, and I remember how much I loved this house, even though nothing in it was ever really mine. It's less showy than Emilia's, with ivy tumbling down the kitchen cupboards, and colorful books propped up against every surface. It's the kind of house where you could believe that someone has actually read the books.

"Did I ever tell you about the pimp and

414

the . . . girl I saw at a launderette downtown years ago?" I ask, before we can start any of the painful small talk that has been our trademark since I've been back. I don't know why the memory came to me, but now that it has, I'm finding it hard to think about anything else.

"I don't think so." Dylan shakes his head.

"So, it was the second assassin movie, and we were filming this intense scene where I had to shoot and kill my fellow assassin, my former best friend, but I kept doing it wrong. I was getting tired and restless, and after about thirty takes, Able stood up, furious, and ordered the complete closure of the set for the day. I thought he was going to send me back to the hotel alone, but he drove me to downtown LA instead and pulled up outside this depressing strip of stores. I got out of the car and watched this sweaty, shiny-suited man walk into a launderette with a skinny blond girl who had these bruises all over her arms and legs, and lips covered in scabs like mosquito bites. The man was dropping a pile of old clothes off with the launderette owner, I guess to be altered to fit her, and this girl was trying on these dresses that were five sizes too big for her, like sequined ones with big eighties shoulder pads that hung off her. At some point she caught me staring at her, and all of a sudden she came to life, coiling up and spitting at me through the window like a snake," I say, shaking my head at the memory of the spit trickling down the window, right where I stood. "Afterward, Able took me to this divey diner next door for a milkshake, and he said, 'The differences between your life and someone like that are less substantial than you think. *Never* forget how lucky you are to be where you are,' and for the first time in a while, I really *felt* it. On set the next day, I stared my former best friend in the face and thought of the girl as I shot her in the forehead. I nailed it in one take, and the crew gave me a standing ovation when I left."

I look up, and somehow Dylan is still watching me with interest. I stand up and take a box of water from the fridge because I need a moment to catch my breath more than anything.

"The thing was, this girl was clearly just fucked, like she knew her entire future was going to be sleeping with disgusting creeps in shitty cars and getting to keep like two dollars from whatever she made, and we just left her there, trying on these dresses, and now I can't understand why I didn't do anything to help her. I was just so content for the whole exchange to be about me; I actually remember thinking how *lucky* I was that I'd been able to witness it, but it should never have been about me at all. It was about her — it was her *bad luck* that she was there."

I look at Dylan and then shrug apologetically. "I don't really know why I'm telling you this. But, honestly, what the fuck?"

Dylan frowns slightly, probably trying to work out what I'm really asking, which is already a nonstarter because I don't even know.

"Do you think she'd still be around?" I ask, pulling a face when I remember the bruises on her arms and legs, as if she was already decaying.

Dylan shrugs because he will never be someone to assume the worst. "I mean, I don't know. You could try to find her. Or, do you think it's not actually about her?"

"If you're going to tell me that I'm the little girl, I'll kill you," I say, and he grins. "I've had a compassionate thought about someone else for the first time in five years, so let me have this moment."

"That's bullshit, you're one of the most compassionate people I know," Dylan says, shaking his head. "If anything, you just overthink everything to the point of paralysis."

"I'm so relieved that we're talking about *me* again," I say, and he laughs.

"I'm just saying, it's a good thing you haven't forgotten about her. I wouldn't question your own motives too much," he says. "It's good to feel strongly about something, so you know what you want to change."

"I've been spending some time with Esme," I say then, and Dylan looks surprised. "She's going through some stuff. I've been trying to help her."

"She's a good kid. She's lucky to have you," Dylan says, and as he smiles at me, I experience the rare feeling that, for the first time in a long while, things might actually be working out for me.

"Do you want to get dinner tomorrow night?" I ask him suddenly, and Dylan nods, his eyes creasing slightly.

"Sure."

CHAPTER FORTY-FIVE

I open an email from Laurel with a link to the John Hamilton photos once I'm back in my car. In the photos I am walking out of his house wearing the white jeans and white sweater that Xtina picked out for me, John's fleshy hand pulling the back of my head toward him as he whispers a secret in my ear. My lips are curved in a hint of a smile, my eyes hidden underneath lemon-yellow Kurt Cobain–style sunglasses. For a moment, I consider going back into the glass house to mention the photos to Dylan, but I'm pretty sure I don't need to explain myself, because we've both been in this business for a while now.

On my way back to Malibu, I stop by the English shop in Santa Monica to pick up the Marmite, as well as some orange squash and Jammie Dodgers for the twins. While I'm paying at the checkout, my phone vibrates in my pocket. I pull out my phone, but it's just Laurel.

Are you okay? Are you still coming over for Christmas? Lana is almost looking forward to it LOL.

I click my phone off and put it back in my pocket without replying.

When I get home, Emilia is sitting on the steps of my front porch, smoking a cigarette. I tuck the Marmite into the glove compartment before I get out, steeling myself for her to reveal whatever it is she's been hiding from me.

"Why do you have binoculars?" Emilia asks, holding up the pair I left lying on the lawn chair in my haste to follow her to Venice.

"I like to watch the dolphins," I say calmly. I reach out to take the binoculars from her, but Emilia moves them out of my reach. She holds them up to her eyes and stares out at the ocean, pivoting at the last minute so that she's looking up at the peach house through them.

"I'm not stalking you," I say. "You're the one who's always on *my* porch."

The joke hangs between us until, after a

long silence, Emilia drops the binoculars back onto the seat. She looks different, her eyes unfocused and oil collecting on either side of her nostrils. This is it, I think. This is when it ends.

"It turns out Able isn't going to be home for Christmas," Emilia says before I can say anything. "All flights out of Salt Lake City have been canceled. The runways aren't safe."

I don't trust myself to speak, so I stay silent.

"The good news is that there's no fucking danger of any storm happening here, because it's the happiest place on earth."

"I'm sorry," I say carefully.

Emilia stubs her cigarette out on the ground. "And who even knows who he's with this time?" she asks. I stand very still, keeping my face neutral as Emilia walks to the edge of my porch and leans against it. Her eyes never quite land on my face as she talks. "I never have any idea what he's doing at any given moment and I'm not allowed to ask, because that would break the code."

"The code?" I ask, my voice steady.

"The code that says he can do what he wants because he makes all the money. The code that says I'm not *allowed* to feel like shit because my life is so fucking great."

She shakes her head, looking embarrassed for a moment, and I realize that I rarely hear her swear. I wonder if it's something she has to make an effort not to do.

"So I'm stuck by myself with the kids in this soulless, make-believe place where everyone pretends to be happy all the time, just because the sun won't stop shining long enough for them to realize they're not," Emilia says, each word soaked with contempt. "Why can't it *at least* rain here?"

"Tell me about it," I say as we both watch a pelican dive into the calm water. "It's like living in Disneyland."

Before I can think of what to say next, Emilia turns to me and puts her hands on my shoulders so that she's looking directly into my eyes. I force myself to maintain eye contact, keeping my face light and open even though her palpable, uncharacteristic neediness is making me uncomfortable.

"Gracie, would you be able to do something for me?" she asks, and we're so close that I can see the beads of sweat forming on her upper lip.

"Of course. Anything."

"Would you come up to our place on Christmas Eve?" she asks, her tone now softer, almost wheedling, catching me off guard. "It's just me and the girls, but it would really take some of the pressure off with Able not making it back."

I pause, unsure of how to respond.

"Of course, Emilia. If that's what you want," I eventually say as relief burns through me.

She nods once, satisfied as she turns away from me, her car keys in her hand. Then, at the last minute, she turns around on the top step and smiles a small, sad smile I haven't seen before.

"Where did you come from, Gracie?" she asks, and for the first time, I wonder if she actually wants an answer.

As I stand there on the porch steps, watching her leave, a strange feeling spreads through me, and I allow myself to finally wonder how this is going to end. On one side, the white houses of Coyote Sumac are twinkling under the pink light of the sun, and on the other, the ocean shimmers gold and turquoise like a mermaid's tail. That's when I realize that, despite what I said to Emilia, this dusty hellscape of a city has never felt so much like home to me, and I'm not ready to give it up without a fight.

CHAPTER FORTY-SIX

After Emilia has left, I go for a run along the beach. I haven't run in years, but I push myself forward, each step making me feel more powerful than the one before it. Energy surges through my body, and it feels good to drain myself on purpose for once. The cool December air burns my lungs, and by the time I get back to my house, I am doubled over, my chest heaving satisfyingly with the effort.

I'm still out of breath as I dial Laurel's number from my sofa. As I wait for her to answer, I justify pulling out of Christmas at her place by telling myself that it was only a pity invite anyway, and I would have been crashing her and Lana's celebration. I'd probably even be expected to grovel to Lana, which sounds tiresome for all of us, and like something I could do at any other time. The difference is that Emilia really needs me.

"Sure, that's fine, Grace," Laurel says when I tell her, but she sounds slightly put out, which catches me off guard. "Got a better option, huh?"

"I'm seeing Dylan tomorrow, so I figured I'd wait and see what happens," I say, but I'm not sure why I'm lying. "Actually, Emilia wants me to go over. Able's been held up and she's worried about the girls' reaction."

Laurel doesn't say anything for a moment, and I think of how distracted she was in the restaurant the other day. She's probably not even listening to me. Lana's probably got her tongue in her phone-free ear as we speak.

"What is this thing with Emilia?" Laurel asks, seemingly choosing her words carefully.

"She's my friend," I say defensively.

"Yeah, but I thought you didn't want anything to do with Able after *Lights.*"

"It's not quite that simple," I say brightly, skimming the surface of the truth like I always do. At the time, I'd told Laurel that Able and I had parted ways, but I didn't go into any details. Now I wonder how much she could have guessed.

"Grace, are you okay? You sound weird."

"I feel great, actually. Better than I have

in a long time."

"I guess that's good to hear," Laurel says, still sounding unconvinced.

I'm about to hang up when she says my name again.

"Yeah?"

"Look, are you sure you're okay? You're sounding a little . . . I don't know. Manic, I guess," she says softly, and it's the closest she's come to mentioning the hushed discussions about the state of my mental health my team held whenever they thought I couldn't hear.

"I'm fine," I promise her, before hanging up. "Stop being so nice, it's freaking me out."

When Esme turns up the next morning, I'm halfway through making an apple pie to bring to Emilia's for our Christmas Eve dinner. I found a recipe on Google, and am disproportionately pleased with myself for not having had to call anyone for help at any point. I move gracefully around the kitchen, feeling a rush of adrenaline when I work out how to use my new digital scale with an ease I didn't know I had in me. The molten apple mixture is bubbling away, and the buttery smell of pastry fills the small house, transforming the entire place.

The loud knock on the door comes just as I'm checking how the pie is coming along, and I end up burning my finger on the yellow Le Creuset pie dish Emilia lent me. My good mood instantly evaporates, and it doesn't recover when I see who is waiting on the porch.

Esme strolls in, throwing her phone on the sofa before sitting down.

"You forgot about me," she says matter-of-factly, and I don't lie to her and pretend that I didn't.

She folds her arms across her chest. "I've been calling but you never answer. Where have you been?"

"Sorry, I've been busy. It's nearly Christmas," I say, even though I have no idea what that means for someone like me.

Esme narrows her eyes at me. "Are you coming home for it? Mom was asking."

"Does she know you're here?" I ask, caught off guard.

"She freaked out that I had a boyfriend in LA, so I had to tell her the truth."

"How did she react?"

"She was fine. Whatever. Look, I need to talk to you about something," she says, leaning forward. "I've been using the camera."

She's waiting for my reaction, her eyebrows raised, and it's the most excited I've

427

seen her.

"That's great news! Are you feeling better about everything?" I ask, speaking loudly to cover up the fact that I'd forgotten to ask her before.

"Much better. But I'm using it in a different way from how we discussed," Esme says innocently.

"What does that mean?" I ask warily.

"This girl from my school, August, is having a party for New Year's up at her parents' house in Ojai, and I've already been messaging Jesse to tell him that I want to hook up with him again. So, the day of the party, we're going to set the camera up in August's parents' bedroom, and I'll lure Jesse in once he's drunk. I'll get him naked, and then I'll just leave him . . . I'm basically going to have footage of him naked, trying to get with me, that I can use to bargain with him to stop spreading the nude. The fake nude."

"Hmm . . . I don't know how . . . experienced you are. But logistically, he might think it's a little strange if you're making him strip completely naked while you keep all your clothes on," I say as neutrally as possible.

"You clearly don't remember sixteen-year-old guys," Esme says, rolling her eyes. "It's the only time they actually do anything you ask them to do."

"Okay, sure. So Jesse is naked, you're film-ing him, then you blackmail him with the footage," I say, pausing for a moment. "And then we're done. Right?"

"Wrong," Esme says slowly. "Totally wrong. I was thinking about what you said about taking control of the story, and I'm going bigger. Much bigger. I'm going to make a movie about how social media has basically turned into another way for men to control women and their bodies, but that girls are the ones buying into it and perpet-uating it ourselves, and *then* it's going to be about *everything* that sucks about being a girl. So we'll start with me and Jesse, and then we can interview Blake about her experience growing up trans in Anaheim, then we'll move on to you."

"Me?" I ask nervously.

"Yeah. We'll use footage of you taking down Able at the awards show. It will be our Spartacus moment."

"Okay, let me think about this," I say, panicked and stalling for time. "Do you want a drink? I have La Croix or apple kom-bucha."

"Hello? Earth to Grace? What is wrong with you today?"

"I'm just thinking it through," I say, walking over to the sink and turning it on. "While I think it's great that you're so passionate about this, I just don't know how realistic some of the logistics are going to be. Plus, you know I haven't heard any more about the awards show, so I'm not really sure what's happening with that."

"Well, why don't you ask?" Esme says, watching me from the sofa.

"I'm not in a position to chase right now," I say.

There is another knock at the door. I walk over to it, grateful for the interruption until I realize who is standing on my porch. It's Camila.

I open the door slowly, and I can feel my sister moving behind me.

"Wow, you're brave coming back after what you pulled last time," I say quietly, remembering her parting question the day of the shoot. When I turn around, Esme is hovering a few feet behind me, trying to hear what I'm saying. I wave at her to sit back down on the sofa, then I step out onto the porch, leaving the door open only a couple of inches.

"Can I come in?" Camila asks, but she doesn't try to explain herself or say she's sorry. I wonder if she's remembering my comment about women apologizing too much.

I shake my head, and, to her credit, she doesn't try to look past me into my house. Her expression is set like a linebacker at a championship game, and I figure that she must really need whatever she thinks I have to say.

"I'm here to ask you one final time if you have any statement to give on Able Yorke winning the lifetime achievement award at the Independent Film Awards in a little over two weeks," she says slowly, her eyes never leaving mine. The sound of his name still has the power to wind me, but I try not to let it show.

"I already gave you the interview," I say. "Didn't you get what you wanted?"

"Did you?" Camila responds instantly.

I study her face, a quiet intensity written all over it, and I wonder how different the roads were that led us both here.

"Are there others?" I ask after a moment.

Camila pauses, debating how to answer my question.

"I don't know," she says, and my face must tell her how much hinged on her answer, and that maybe her words prove exactly what I never wanted to face: there was just something bad about me. Camila

431

steps forward then and leans in so close to me that I can smell the coffee on her breath. "Look . . . I've heard about other women who are coming forward . . . not about Able but about someone else, and . . . I think something is building, Grace."

For a moment, time stops on the porch, a cool breeze slipping through the heat of the sun and lifting my hair off my shoulders. I think of everything I could tell this woman, wondering how I could ever reduce it to a statement. I'd have to distill it, purify it, erase any of the nuances that could cast me in an unflattering light because I know what people would say about me. People would want to blame me, too, and the worst part is, I wouldn't know how to stop them. Able doesn't look like a monster: he's not slithery or lecherous, foaming at the mouth like a rabid dog. He's not racist, or homophobic, or any of the other labels I know how to use. His is one of the most beloved faces in America, yet another example of how hard work and perseverance can triumph over adversity any day, further proof that if you fail here, maybe it's just because you never tried hard enough. I wish it was as clear-cut as I made it out to Esme, but I have never been able to separate myself from any of it, and in my darkest moments, I wonder if I don't actually want to face up to what it would mean if I did. Whether I say the words today or at the IFAs, I will never be anything other than Able's victim. He will still own me, just in a different way, and I would never move on from my past because it would be all anyone saw when they looked at me.

Camila's expression is determined, but I can see something else now too. Is that empathy? Of course not. It's pity. She pities me.

"No comment," I say quietly, and I'm turning around to go back inside when she reaches out and puts her hand on my forearm. My skin burns where her fingers touch it.

"Everyone would be listening to what you had to say," she says softly.

"I wish I was stupid enough to believe that," I say, shaking her hand off. I close the door without looking at her again.

When I turn around, Esme is standing next to the open window, watching me. She is holding the video camera, and the red light is flashing. She swings it around to follow me.

"Turn that off," I say as I walk into the kitchen and turn the kettle on, more to drown out the words still hanging in the air than anything else.

"What was that about?" Esme asks slowly, holding the camera up. I make a big thing about choosing a specific mug from the two options I have, eventually settling on the baby-blue one Emilia gave me, and then I remember the apple pie. I grab the rubber mitt, but by the time I've opened the oven door, smoke is already pouring out around me. When it clears, I can see that the pie is black, ruined.

"You're still going to do it, right?" Esme asks, the red light still flashing on the camera. "Confront Able?"

"Turn the camera off, Esme," I say, aware of how cold I sound. I can feel everything I ever wanted slide further out of reach every time I hear his name.

Esme turns the camera off and throws it onto the sofa.

"You know, I really need to do something for work. This just isn't a good time for you to be here."

Esme folds her arms across her chest. "You hardly have a job. What, did you forget to get a spray tan?"

"Esme," I say, my voice intended as a warning.

"You promised me you'd do it, but you've forgotten already," Esme says, her voice shaking slightly. "You've forgotten who you are."

"Esme, please," I say, not in the mood for her theatrics. "Look, I know that Mom and Dad have made you feel like you're the center of the universe, but you're not. Life isn't always black-and-white, and things don't always end up exactly how you planned."

"Mom was right about you. All you do is let people down."

I walk toward the front door and open it, waiting for my sister to leave. Instead she stays put, watching me as if she can see through me to my blood, and I feel so angry suddenly, because she was given everything I ever needed and she's still giving me a hard time about it.

"I have been by myself since I was fourteen years old and I have worked, and fought, for every single thing I have. You would never understand that. I'm not going to reduce my entire life to being a footnote in someone else's legacy."

"You said it was all bullshit."

"It's no more bullshit than pretending to be someone I haven't been for nearly ten years. Esme, this is all I have left, so please don't make me feel bad for wanting to protect it. You can't go up against someone like that and win. Not in the long term," I say, my voice quiet. I can feel my sister's disappointment in me, and I suddenly want to be anywhere but here.

"Why are you so scared of everything?" Esme asks, looking at me as if I'm a stranger. Every emotion I am feeling is reflected in such excruciating detail on her face that I have to turn away.

"You know that I didn't ask for you to follow me around, right? In fact, I have never invited you over, not even once. I don't know how to help you and I can't tell you that everything works out in the end, because it doesn't, and the truth is that you will never get what you actually want, because by the time you do, you won't want it anymore. That's the secret of the fucking universe that nobody wants to admit to themselves. Do you feel better for knowing it?"

I fold my arms across my chest and stare at my younger sister as her eyes fill with tears, and I remember now that she's just a kid, that it's not her fault everything is so fucked. I remember how she used to stare at the broken limbs of her dolls in her small hands, trying to work out how to put them back together, somehow believing that things were always better when she could control them, even if she ended up breaking the thing she loved. I have to swallow the lump rising at the back of my throat without my permission, and I want to tell her that I understand. That I tend to break things before they can hurt me, too, that I'm sorry, that I have the emotional intelligence of a fucking slug, that it's probably our mom's fault, when she stands up roughly.

"I actually feel sorry for you," Esme says. "Because you lie to yourself every single day, and you lie to everyone else too. Your life is just one big fucking lie, and I wish you weren't my sister."

Esme pushes past me roughly, and I watch her walk away even though I know I should stop her. The saddest part is that, unlike me, I know my sister never lies.

CHAPTER FORTY-SEVEN

I get dressed slowly for my dinner with Dylan, putting on a baby-blue vintage silk shirt with a ruffled neck, a pair of black leather pants and tiny gold hoop earrings. My hair is creamy and smooth, tucked behind my perfect ears. I put on a slick of lip gloss before I leave, and, of course, it's the only makeup I need. I've always looked like someone I'm not, and tonight it's truer than ever. It's at its most obvious when I smile, two rows of perfect white teeth promising good, wholesome things I will never be able to fulfill.

Dylan sends a car to pick me up at eight thirty, and I slide in, nodding at the driver's eyes in the rearview mirror. I stare out of the tinted window as the city slides away from me, until we arrive on a side street somewhere south of Venice. The car turns up an alley, and we pass the exits of an Ethiopian restaurant and a BDSM store.

We pull up behind a third establishment, which has bags of trash covering the parking spaces and red lightbulbs around the back door.

I climb out of the car and push open the heavy wooden door. It is a Mexican restaurant, dimly lit other than multicolored lights strung across the ceiling, and candles scattered across empty tables. Dylan is sitting in a booth in the otherwise empty restaurant, music playing softly through the speakers. He stands up and gives me a kiss on the cheek when I reach the table. He's wearing a white T-shirt and jeans, and he's happy to see me.

I slip into the booth opposite him.

"What's that smell?" I ask, because he smells different.

"I don't know. The woman in the store told me it would make me irresistible to all men." He grins at me, his eyes warm and easy.

"I prefer your normal smell," I say. Dylan is still smiling but I'm annoyed at myself for being prickly already. I feel hot and guilty after my fight with Esme, but I try to soften the angles of my face, removing the sharp edges from my voice.

"So what's been happening? What have you done today?" he asks, and then he stops himself. "Actually I already know. Paparazzi are all over you at the moment, huh?"

I shrug. "It's not so bad."

Dylan studies me for a second before looking down at the menu. "Did they follow you here?"

"I don't think so . . ." I lie, not telling him that I already texted Mario the address and that he is waiting to capture a photo of Dylan and me leaving the restaurant together as soon as I send the go-ahead. I realize now that it was a mistake.

"So what is this place? It's cute," I say, staring up at the fresco painted on the ceiling. It's a Day of the Dead scene showing skeletons wearing mariachi costumes and vivid red and purple dresses, painted in thick acrylic.

Dylan looks at me strangely and then he shrugs.

"Just a restaurant I like," he says.

The server places a plastic bowl of tortilla chips and salsa on the table. I ask for some guacamole as I pull out my phone, scanning the new messages and emails. One from John telling me he is looking forward to our next meeting, and one from Nathan. I put the phone facedown on the red-and-white tablecloth next to my water glass. After a couple of moments, I flip it back again so

440

that I can check the screen subtly from now on, instead of making a big deal out of it.

"Are you okay?" Dylan asks. I turn my phone facedown again.

"Yeah, why?"

"I don't know, you seem a little different." Dylan chooses his words carefully.

"I feel good," I say, stretching my legs out under the table and flashing him a big smile, the kind I use to shut people up, forgetting that he knows all my sleights of hand. I take a deep breath and start over because even I can't tell when I'm lying anymore.

"I'm about to be offered a part in this movie, but I can't work out if it's going to be awful or not . . ." I say, searching for something honest that isn't too revealing.

"Want to talk it through?" Dylan says. "I don't know about the movie, but I know you pretty well."

"Mmm, yeah, maybe," I say, checking my phone quickly again. A message from Laurel asking if I was doing okay. "Did you know Laurel is a lesbian?"

Dylan laughs. "Of course — I've met Lana. We both have."

"Was I a worse friend or wife?" I ask, just before I realize I'm talking about myself again.

"How are you anyway? How's the single

life treating you?" I ask, shooting for funny but landing somewhere between awkward and belligerent. Dylan grimaces.

"Sorry. How are the surfers?"

"They're all right," he says, having a sip of water and still watching me carefully. "The story isn't doing what I want it to do, but I know I just have to roll with it."

"That's how it works, right?" I ask. Dylan's hair is still wet from a shower. Some of it is falling in his eyes, and I'm finding it difficult to concentrate on anything other than how good he looks. I imagine pushing him into the bedroom and fucking like we used to, always like it was going to be the last time. Despite everything, I always enjoyed sex with Dylan more than I ever deserved to. "I thought that was the point of working with real people."

"No, it is. The story is never what you think it is. I'm just hoping I'll be able to see it soon," he says, shrugging. "It's been a long shoot."

"The story is never what you think it is," I repeat. "I like that."

I have another sip of water, sort of wishing I could have a tequila soda to relax a little instead. Maybe it was being around Dylan that made me drink more. He listens too closely, expects too much. It's unnerving when you're not used to it.

"I've been working on this . . . project with Esme, but I think she feels like I've let her down. Maybe I just need to tell her that we were chasing the wrong ending all along."

"I'm sure she can't be mad at you for long," Dylan says. "That's cool, by the way."

"What is?"

"That you're helping her out like that."

"Oh. I think it might be the other way around," I say, digging a tortilla chip into the guacamole. "It's hard to tell sometimes."

I wipe my salty fingers on the tablecloth, and when I look up, Dylan is watching me like he used to, as if I'm some rare, beautiful thing, which instantly makes me want to do something to ruin it.

"You seem different too," I say after a moment.

"Different how?" Dylan asks warily after a pause.

"I don't know. Like less innocent or something. I mean you came to my house minutes after your girlfriend broke up with you."

Dylan swallows a tortilla chip and doesn't say anything for a moment. A mariachi version of "I'll Be Home for Christmas" is playing softly through the speakers.

"We came here the night we got engaged,"

he says eventually. "We literally sat right here."

I look around again, but nothing about this restaurant is even remotely familiar to me. The server hangs back by the entrance to the kitchen, looking about as pained as I feel. I try to remember the day we got engaged. Dylan woke me up with blueberry pancakes and his grandmother's wedding ring, and while I was still crying, he showed me his ring finger with my name already tattooed around it in black, scratchy ink. The tattoo was raw, and I cried because that was exactly how I felt when I saw it, so in awe that this person wanted to share his life with me. It was one of those rare spring days when I thought everything would be okay, but I still supplemented the glasses of champagne with secret bumps of coke whenever Dylan left the room. After that, I remember the beach at sunset, and maybe a flat tire. Was there a dinner too?

"I'm sorry. I really don't remember it." The expression on his face is making my chest hurt, so I don't want to look at him anymore. "I think this was a bad idea."

"Luckily, I already ordered everything we ordered that night, and it's only going to get more and more fucking awkward as the night goes on. What did you call it? A clusterfuck of misery?" Dylan asks, running his hand through his hair. "I mean, you did warn me."

"What did we order?"

"It's okay, we don't have to do this for my benefit."

"Remind me of what we ordered."

"All right," he says slowly. "We drank jalapeño margaritas, but I got mine with vodka instead of tequila because you put me off tequila for life the night we met. You couldn't choose between burritos and enchiladas so you got them both, and they made a heart out of sour cream on top, and for some reason you loved that. For dessert we had the Mexican wedding cookies with coconut and chocolate ice cream because we were celebrating. So what, were you high or just drunk that night?"

"Don't be mean, it doesn't suit you," I say as the server places a pitcher of margaritas in front of us, with jalapeños swimming in it. I might have remembered the margaritas if Dylan had mentioned them earlier.

I take a sip, and when I realize it doesn't have any alcohol in it, I feel instantly, uncomfortably disappointed.

"You know I *can* drink, I'm not going to kill myself in one night," I say, folding my arms across my chest.

"Go ahead," Dylan says wearily, signaling for the server. "Can we have a bottle of tequila on the table for my friend?"

The server brings a bottle of Don Julio, and we both just stare at it. I try to remember how it felt when we liked each other.

"Grace, I'm sorry. I'm not trying to be a dick. I'm exhausted. I want to work this out, but I can't figure out if you want to be found anymore."

"I don't want to be found?" I ask, my voice tight. "You think I don't want to be found."

Dylan tenses, sensing something different about my tone. I lean toward him and speak quietly.

"Do you want to know why I left you? I left because you never wanted to see who I really was. You had this image of me as this little lost girl who you could rescue with your love, and you panicked when it turned out not to be as simple as that. Your love suffocated me because it was a love for somebody else. You never took the time to get to know who I really was, and the one night I tried to tell you, you didn't want to know. That's why I fucking left."

Dylan listens to me, a weird expression I don't recognize on his face.

"You do know that everyone feels like

that? That it's actually really hard to feel worthy of anyone's love because we all know how shitty and selfish and fucked up we are on the inside, but we still work at it. You did the exact same thing to me. You always think I'm this honest, hardworking, genuine *good* guy, just the total opposite of everyone else in LA. You know that person doesn't exist, right? But it never mattered to me, it just made me want to work harder to be the person you thought I was. People can change if they want to, Grace. I thought that's how it worked."

The server brings over a sizzling plate of enchiladas dripping in green sauce and melted cheese, with a sour cream heart dripping over it all. We both stare at the food in front of us but neither of us moves. I can feel the Percocet throbbing in my bag next to me, and I have to fight the urge to take one out and shove it down my throat at the table. I just need to wait for Dylan to go to the bathroom or look away for a couple of seconds, then I can at least try to blur the edges of this awful fucking day.

"What night was it?" he quietly asks instead.

"What?"

"You said you tried to talk to me. What night was it?"

447

"The night before I left. On the balcony."

For a second I think that Dylan is actually going to laugh, but then he closes his eyes briefly, and when he opens them, he looks sadder than I've ever seen him.

"Do you want to know what was running through my mind that night?" he asks.

"That I'd fucked up, yet again? And you didn't want to hear it?"

Dylan shakes his head.

"That I cheated on you, Grace. The night before. And I could say that I did it because I knew I'd already lost you, and it might even be the truth, but mainly I was lonely and I just wanted to be with someone and it not be so fucking complicated and sad all the time."

After he's finished talking, he slumps a little. I sit perfectly still and we're something out of an Edward Hopper painting, the two of us sitting in front of a table of untouched food, trying our hardest to prove we were never good enough for each other.

"Was it with Wren?" I ask when I trust that I can speak without a shake in my voice.

"With a waitress at the Good Life. I thought you found out," he says, realizing exactly as I do that we are always having a different conversation from the one we think we are having. "But you really did just leave."

"Oh, please. Are you going to tell me how you cheating on me shows how much you love me?" I say. "So you win?"

"It's never been a game. Neither of us is winning."

Dylan is staring down at the table. I look at him for so long that the lights start to flare around him. I realize now that I have no idea who the person in front of me actually is.

"I know I shouldn't have done it, but don't pretend that you were perfect," Dylan says quietly, and I know he's referring to the nights I came home late and couldn't remember where I'd been.

"You were never supposed to hurt me, Dylan. That's the whole point of you."

"People don't have points. It doesn't work like that."

"Are you even sorry?" I ask, my voice searing.

"I don't know right now, Grace," he says after a moment, and it infuriates me even more because now that I know he's not actually incapable of lying, why can't he do it now, when I need him to?

I push myself out of the booth and stand up.

"That night, I was trying to tell you that Able sexually assaulted me," I say. "Repeatedly."

I leave before I have to watch the horror spread across his face.

I never texted Mario, so when I walk out the back of the restaurant, I don't expect to find him there, hidden in the darkness, waiting for me. He raises his camera and takes over a thousand photos of me standing alone, tears streaming down my face. I scream at him to stop but it turns out I never really controlled any of it.

CHAPTER FORTY-EIGHT

I take three pills as soon as I'm home, then I sit on the sofa in the living room, waiting for the morning to come. When it finally does, the sun casting streaks of white gold across the blue sky, I have to close the blinds because everything seems too hopeful with them open. It's Christmas Eve and this is a city for people who wake up every morning believing that today could be the day their life is transformed, not for people like me. I should have known that everything I touch eventually gets destroyed, like a curse Able handed down to me.

I decline Dylan's calls, and I keep the blinds down so that when he inevitably comes over to try to talk to me, which he does at around ten a.m., I can pretend not to be home. He knocks on the door and says my name softly, as if he can feel that I'm just feet away from him, my back pressed against the wall. When I don't answer, he

451

stands outside on the porch for a while, before his car engine starts and he drives back up the hill.

I try to muster some relief, or anger, or self-pity once Dylan has gone, but I can't even pretend to myself that any of this is about what he told me last night. This is about what I told him, and how I can't bear to see the truth reflected in his open, familiar face because, without ever meaning to, he'll show me what I really am, which is a powerless, scared little girl. A victim. Everyone always tells you that the truth will set you free, but now that I've said the words out loud, I feel more alone than ever. I should have listened to Laurel when she tried to talk to me yesterday. It turns out some people aren't supposed to have anything for themselves. I take another pill and wait for the clouds to slip over me. I will tread more lightly from now on.

The day slides past without me noticing. Darkness falls and I come to slightly, realizing that it's time for me to go to Emilia's. I consider messaging her to tell her I can't make it, but I can't admit to myself that it was all for nothing in the end.

I get dressed in a daze, putting on a vintage Smiths T-shirt and a faded pair of

Levi's. My body feels heavy and sluggish, and I stare at myself for so long in the mirror that I can almost see what I'd look like if someone were meeting me for the first time. Anemic skin, purple slugs under my eyes from lack of sleep, and that much-discussed extra weight padding out my belly and thighs.

I walk up to the peach house via the beach steps, something I haven't done since that first day. I count eighty-six steps, and I'm out of breath by the time I reach the top. My boots are covered in a fine dusting of sand as I walk alongside the peach house until I'm standing in front of the entrance, holding the Le Labo bag and the small jar of Marmite I brought with me to remind Emilia that Able let her down.

Now that I'm here, I understand that the plan has changed. Expensive cars line the cul-de-sac, people just leaving them in the middle of the street as I stand there. The peach house is lit up from every room, a warm, inviting light that promises only beautiful people and golden-hued memories. I walk up to the front door as a feeling of snaking inevitability wraps itself around my insides.

I ring the doorbell, trying to disguise my trembling hand. Emilia answers the door and pauses for a moment when she sees that it's me, one slender hand on the door frame.

"Grace. Thank you for coming," she says rigidly. Already everything feels worlds apart from when we spoke on my porch yesterday, and I wonder whether I imagined the entire exchange.

"Of course I came . . ." I say, holding up the Marmite.

Emilia leads me into the thick of the crowd, and of course she has curated the ideal ratio of beauty to power, and I already recognize many of the guests from movies I've worked on or publicity tours I've done. I keep my head down as I follow her, and a pressing sense of dread falls over me.

I stop walking and Emilia does too. Her fingernails dig into my flesh, and there is something different about her, too, an undercurrent of something I can't identify. The ghost of Frank Sinatra croons from the speakers, barely audible over the heavy thrum of conversation. I turn around but there is a smiling stranger there, poised to greet me, blocking me from the exit. I turn back to Emilia and search her face. She looks dazed, untethered.

"Are you okay?" I ask quietly.

"Able wanted to celebrate, so he invited a few friends over. You'd think that these people would already have plans on Christmas Eve, but you know Able. He snaps his fingers and people come," Emilia says shrilly, snapping her own fingers. I turn away from her so that she can't see the stunned look on my face. Despite her efforts to appear normal, Emilia seems as unsettled as I am by Able's unexpected return, even vulnerable, and instinctively I want to protect her as she has tried to protect me.

Emilia hands me a glass of champagne before catching herself and apologizing. She swaps it for a glass of water and then introduces me to a few of her friends, all publicists. When I reach for her arm, she slips away from me, and I'm left trying to catch my breath alone.

"I hear you're not working with Nan anymore?" one of the women asks me, and even though I'm still reeling, trying desperately to scan the room and locate Emilia, I pull my attention to her. They are all indistinguishable to me, these women with their glowing skin and haircuts as blunt as their questions.

I excuse myself as soon as possible and lean against a wall on the other side of the room. You can see the whole living space from here, even through to the expansive deck that overlooks the ocean. And that's when I see him. The man who both created and destroyed me. He stands with his back against the doors that lead onto the deck, telling a story to his crowd of fans. He speaks quietly so that those around him have to lean in toward him to catch each word. People are drawn to him like this. They hover around him and laugh too loudly, even when he's not being funny, which is most of the time. I remember how important it felt to remain in his glowing orbit, to do whatever it took not to be cast back into the dark. He controls everyone around him, refusing to acknowledge my presence because he doesn't have to, even though I know that he's spotted me from the deliberate way he will look anywhere but at me.

The fury comes now, the force of it buoying me up instead of pulling me under for the first time since the day I met him. I watch him from afar, blood pumping through my veins, my fingers tightening around the glass in my hand. I watch him so intently that everything else around us starts to blur, the lights flaring and everyone else fading into the background. Able's blond hair is thick and perfectly tousled. His skin is golden, his red lips plump and his incisor teeth sharp.

A hand snakes around my waist and I turn quickly, ready to knock someone out. When I see that it's John Hamilton, I step deftly back, angling my face so that he can kiss my cheek with no risk of him getting anywhere near my mouth.

"Publicity already kicked in on the movie, right?" he says, and I stare at him blankly. "The photos? Outside my house?"

"Sorry, of course. Yes, exactly," I say, trying to focus on him. Even in the dim lighting, I can see the film of sweat covering his skin, his lips slick with spittle. John is cumbersome, even repellent, seemingly a different species from Able. I think how different it might be if his was the face of my nightmares instead of Able, whether people would understand it more, maybe even want to believe me.

"I'm going to pay my respects to the man of the hour. I hear this new one is his best yet," John says, before he claps me on the shoulder. "No offense."

"None taken," I say, stepping out of the way so that he can sail past me, settling in next to Able.

Silver comes up to me then, wearing a polka-dot dress and clutching a pack of Lucky Strikes like it's an Oscar.

"What are you doing with those?"

"I heard someone say that smoking is so uncool, it's actually cool again," she says, and I should probably stop her, but I let her wander off instead, still holding the pack of cigarettes. I put my glass straight down on the vintage butler's table Emilia traveled to an auction in New Haven to pick up. I don't take my eyes off Able for a second.

When he and John slip outside with a couple of cigars, I move closer, into the living room area. An aged rock star sits in the emerald velvet armchair, his tobacco-stained fingers twitching on the armrest. A young actor, tipped to clean up this awards season, sits in the other chair, comparing vapes with his older cast mate. The porcelain caroler figurines that were once Emilia's grandmother's line every surface of the room, and I try not to look at them for too long, each of their shiny frozen faces pulled back into an eternal scream.

Someone else taps me on the shoulder, and I turn around. The woman standing there already feels familiar; her lips are fleshy and slick with glossy lipstick.

"Grace, it's me. Lorna," this woman says, her mouth stretching wide into a smile. Lorna. I shake my head, no, too disoriented to feel bad for not knowing who she is.

"From the first two movies?" she says, embarrassed now.

"I killed you in the second movie," I say, because of course, she was the other female assassin. I try to concentrate while also making sure that I know exactly where Able is. He's still outside. Where's Emilia? I shake my head and try to form something resembling a normal question. "What are you up to now?"

"I'm working in script development," Lorna says self-deprecatingly. "We can't all be famous, I guess."

"I would swap it with you," I say honestly, and she shrugs, maybe because she's one of the only people who would believe me and wouldn't want it either. I'm about to turn away when I remember something. Another piece of the puzzle that was in the wrong place.

"You know the day we shot your last scene . . . the day that Able shut down the set," I say, and Lorna nods. "What did the rest of you do? I never even thought to ask."

"Oh." Lorna puts her head to one side, remembering. "You know, we went to Disneyland. One of the makeup artists told me it had been planned for weeks. Able just has to make a big deal out of everything, doesn't he?" she says, chewing a loose piece of skin

459

off one of her nails. "It was good to see you anyway, Grace. Good luck with everything."

I think of the girl in the launderette, and my memory warps, flickering slightly like an old movie reel. There is no such thing as luck. Everything about my life has been inevitable, predetermined from the moment I cried onstage during the audition at my school. Suddenly, it's as if I'm looking down on the room from above, watching myself ricochet from person to person, each encounter taking something different from me, diminishing me slowly until eventually I am the size of one of Emilia's carolers, my face frozen in a silent scream. For the first time in a long time I understand with a near-blinding urgency what I need to do in order to rebuild all that was lost.

I need to get out of this house.

I'm nearly at the front door when Emilia intercepts me. She grabs me, her nails digging into my arm again. I struggle slightly, but her grip only tightens.

"Gracie, I thought you'd want to speak to our surprise guest. Or maybe you're the surprise guest, I can't keep up anymore," she says, and I can tell that she's drunk from the way her pupils can't focus. She takes a step back, leaving me and Able staring at each other. Each synapse in my body is firing, screaming at me to get away from him, but I force myself to step toward him instead because Emilia is watching and I don't want her to see how scared I am. I kiss Able stiffly on the cheek, and his golden skin is still papery and rough up close, just like it is in my nightmares.

"Grace," he says quietly, formally, as we step back from the embrace.

"You must have been relieved the storm cleared up," I say, my voice tight, and Able frowns, seemingly both confused and irritated by me.

"The storm?" he asks, and we both look at Emilia. I understand now that she lied to get me here, in front of him, so that she could see for herself. I have to watch it happen on her face after that, the confirmation that nothing is what she thought it was, that everything she feared most in the world is here, in this room between us.

Emilia grips the back of the sofa, and there is a moment when I think she is going to sink to the floor, but of course she recovers beautifully, straightening up to smooth a piece of hair behind her ear before she focuses somewhere above my head and touches Able gently on the arm.

"Darling, you must introduce me to Jennifer. I've heard such wonderful stories."

They float away from me, and I'm left standing alone among the hundreds of stricken carolers, trying to remember how it is that we breathe.

CHAPTER FORTY-NINE

I'm in Able's office. I was going to leave, but instead my body led me here, and I don't know what I wanted but my heart is racing fast in my chest and I feel sick and scared, and it's clear to me now that everything is exactly the same as it was back then, that I am exactly the same, and that I always will be.

The lights in the office are low, hidden in the walls above the mahogany desk. The walls are still lined with books chosen to make Able seem smart, informed: Stanislavski, Chekhov, Miller and Williams, most of which I know Able will never have touched, let alone read. With trembling hands, I pick up the photograph still on the desk. Able and Emilia stand proudly behind the girls, frozen in time at age three with Able's hands on their shoulders.

The door to the office swings open, and I jump behind the desk, dread tracking heavily through my veins. Emilia. She closes the door behind her and she looks exhausted, sadder than I've ever seen her.

She starts to make her way over to me, but I flinch and she stops moving, somehow understanding that I can't have her near me right now. She smells of champagne and cigarettes, of good times, but her eyes are drained of all signs of life.

"The other day, in my kitchen. Your face," she says quietly, and in her I can see my own rawness reflected back at me. "Just tell me one thing. And I will never ask it again."

I nod, and the ringing in my ears gets louder with every passing second.

"Were you ever in love with my husband?" she asks, and I understand she's asking me what I have asked myself every single day since I was fifteen in my own attempt to do what she's trying to do right now.

"No," I tell her.

Emilia's body deflates like a balloon, her shoulders curving in as if she can't support herself anymore, and I can see how hard she's worked to keep everything together over the years. I can see all the rumors, the late nights, the self-deprecation, the fake smiles. A whirling dervish with a martini in her hand and lipstick on her teeth. I feel sad for her now, this stranger who tried to help me when she thought I needed it the most. She didn't know she'd already been cursed, just like I had.

Emilia straightens, and picks up the photo from Able's desk.

"I didn't think so," she says, turning it facedown.

I'm on my way out of the house, knowing that it will be for the last time, when I become aware that something is happening in the kitchen, and that everyone else is pretending not to notice. I make eye contact with a tall man in a green velvet smoking jacket who is standing closest to the kitchen door, and he raises one eyebrow back at me. I frown at him but I'm listening now, too, my back pressed against the cool wall.

Emilia's voice is taut but shrill, cutting over the ambient Christmas music and hum of polite conversation.

"Why aren't they leaving?"

"Emilia, please. You're embarrassing yourself."

I don't hear what Emilia says in response to that, but Able's voice gets quieter, his tone rougher. I have turned to stone, my feet rooted to the floor, and maybe I want to tell her my story before he does, or maybe I want to protect her from him, or maybe it's always been something more complicated than that.

Emilia opens the kitchen door and pushes past me. She walks straight upstairs without looking at anyone. Most of the guests notice her but nobody wants to go home yet, even though the alcohol ran out at least an hour ago. I consider following her, but I don't know what I could say.

When Emilia emerges again, she is wearing cream silk pajamas, and her hair is pulled into a scrappy knot on top of her head. She has removed her makeup, and her eyebrows have disappeared completely, replaced by smooth skin that is shiny and raw, like the rest of her face. She walks down the stairs slowly, coming to a stop at the foot of the staircase, then she sits on the bottom step, her arms folded across her chest and her face set, unreadable. Silver runs over to her.

"Mommy, what are you doing?" she asks loudly, clearly panicked. Emilia brushes her away. She sits in silence, glaring at everyone until they are forced to acknowledge her presence. The music stops and the guests finally start to make their excuses, shaking Able's hand firmly, then bending down to kiss Emilia's clean cheek without quite meeting her eye. They trickle out the door steadily, already gossiping about the night as they leave. The coat check girl is the last to leave, and I stand by the door, holding it open for her too.

Once she's gone, I follow Emilia like a ghost into the kitchen, where the girls are sitting. Ophelia is playing with the cheese board in front of her, but Silver is anxious, watching her mother closely.

Able storms into the kitchen and opens all of the cupboards, searching for something.

"I'm sorry, why are you still here, Grace?" he asks as he slams another cabinet door.

"Don't be rude," Emilia says sharply. I think of her, sitting on the steps in her pajamas, still lifting her cheek for everyone to kiss good-bye because the worst thing in her world would be to be impolite.

"I'm tired, I just got back, and I would like to spend some time alone with my family," Able says quietly, leaning against the counter and folding his arms across his chest. I recognize the pattern of behavior instantly: the steely quiet before he blows up.

Silver tugs at her mom's sleeve, but Emilia is still staring down at her hands.

"The hands are the first thing you notice. People say it's your neck but it's your

467

hands," she says quietly.

"Okay, Lady Macbeth," Able says, always irritated by the oblique. "I need another drink. Girls, why are you still up? Where the fuck is Marla?"

"Marla broke her leg," Ophelia says, not lifting her eyes from the piece of Brie she has wedged her fingers into.

"I told you that twice," Emilia says.

"Can I have some wine?" Silver asks, trying to get anyone's attention. Her cheeks are flushed, and she's on the verge of a tantrum. I sit frozen, watching the family portrait unfold around me, despite me and because of me at the same time. I am unable to move.

"We're out of everything," Emilia replies to Able coolly.

"I'm going to go and pick something up then."

Able pushes off the counter too quickly and has to grip the back of a chair to steady himself.

"You can't go anywhere in this state."

"Daddy's drunk," Silver sings desperately, willing even to sacrifice herself to change the dynamic in the room.

"Well, then you go get me something," Able says challengingly.

"I've drunk too much too. It's enough.

We've had enough. Able, sit down. The night's over. It's over."

Emilia's voice is hard and Silver starts to cry. Emilia turns to comfort her.

I stand up then, slowly and deliberately.

"I can drive you, Able. I haven't had anything to drink."

Emilia looks between the two of us, her expression unreadable as Able finally meets my gaze.

"Yes, Able. Why don't you let Grace drive you?" Emilia asks tautly, daring her husband to say something. The air stops moving around us all.

"Fine," Able says as he turns and walks out of the room, knowing that I will, of course, follow him.

CHAPTER FIFTY

Able tosses me the keys and slides heavily into the passenger side. My heart is pounding, but I try to steady my hands as I turn the key in the ignition. A Tom Petty song plays softly through the speakers. I pull out onto the road.

"I hear you're speaking to John Hamilton about *Anatopia*," he says, tapping his fingers on the console between us. "It's a smart move for you."

I shake my head. "I know what you're trying to do. It's not going to work."

He shrugs. "Whatever you want."

Neither of us speaks for a moment.

"Do you ever feel bad about it?" I ask, my voice tight.

He stares out of the windshield and pauses for long enough that I think he must be considering it at least. "I try not to feel bad about anything."

"No regrets," I say, thinking about how

my mom has always said the same thing, and neither of us has ever lived by it.

He touches the car audio system, skipping a couple of tracks before he lands on another Tom Petty song. That he feels the need to even control what song is playing infuriates me so much I can't think for a moment.

"You need to leave my family alone, Grace. I know you know that."

"Emilia is the one —"

"Emilia feels sorry for you because you're lonely, and you're mentally unstable," he interrupts, holding up his hand to stop me.

"Don't pretend this is about her. You still need me," he says, so simply that I almost believe him.

"I don't need you." Almost.

"Why are you hanging around my family then? Always in my house? You can't keep away from my life."

"That isn't what I'm doing."

"You don't know yourself like I know you, Gracie. You never have," Able says. "You want me to notice you. That's why you're doing all of this."

My breath is coming thick and fast now as I try to wade through his words, unpicking them like I always have to. He moves his hand up to my head and starts to gently stroke my hair as panic floods through me, its icy claws gripping my heart.

"After everything you've done to me, please, please don't make me feel like I'm crazy too," I say. My memory of the assaults are sometimes razor sharp, but at other times they break and shatter like a strobe light. I can't quite reach any of it right now, when I need to believe in myself the most. My eyes fill with tears but I blink them away.

"Can you speak to someone about this? Or would you like me to? Maybe Nathan, or your parents?"

"I'm not a child," I say.

"Then stop acting like a lovesick teenager. It's embarrassing," he says as he snatches his hand away, and the thing that gets me is he doesn't even look at me once after that. He just stares out the window at a view he's seen a thousand times before. He's bored with the conversation.

"Was the girl at the launderette an actress?"

"Can you watch the road?"

"Tell me the truth," I say.

"I don't know what you're talking about," he says.

"Was the girl at the launderette an actress?" I repeat. "The girl trying on the sequined dresses. The broken girl who spat at me, who you chose to use as a lesson in my good fortune."

"Of course she was an actress," Able says after a pause. "What were the fucking chances? Open your eyes, Grace."

"I was just a kid, you know," I say, and my desperation is rendering the gaps between my words nonexistent. The lights on the road ahead flare in my tears. "And I couldn't admit that I never wanted any of it, because then I would have to be a victim. I couldn't afford to be a victim."

"So you're here because you want me to absolve you? If what you just said was true, then you wouldn't need me to do that," he says, still staring out the window. I push my foot down harder on the accelerator and turn left onto Malibu Canyon at the last minute. As always, the truth is slipping further out of reach with every word he says.

"Don't do that. That isn't what this is about," I say, and I can see that he's getting nervous about the speed I'm driving at because he's looking at me again now.

"I know. I know exactly what this is about, because I *know* you, Gracie, better than you know yourself. You're upset that I stopped needing you. I understand that, nobody likes to feel rejected. Especially not an actress."

"This is not about rejection. This is about

473

how I am unable to have a relationship because of you, and I don't have a single person in the world to talk to. This is about how you ruined me. Not as an actress, but as a person," I say, my voice thick.

"Will you at least fucking look at me?" I say, driving even faster now. I feel like I'm underwater again, kicking and flipping in the black, pressure building in my lungs. I want to break the surface, but I don't know how to make it all stop.

"Pull over, Gracie, and let's try to talk about this like adults. I get it. I've always cared about you more than your own parents do. But right now I'm the embodiment of everything you hate about your life, and I'm willing to take that blame until we can get you the help you need."

I press my foot onto the accelerator and swing around a bend, near blinded by my own tears. The drop on the side of the winding road cutting through the mountains is at least two hundred feet. I can feel Able tense as we climb even higher, approaching a tunnel.

"Where the hell are you going? For fuck's sake, Grace, pull over." Able's calm facade is slipping and his knuckles are white as he reaches over and grips the steering wheel. I swerve and he lets go instantly. Adrenaline rushes through my body.

"Not until you admit what you did to me." I push down harder on the gas when he tries to grab my arm. He closes his eyes and speaks through gritted teeth so that I have to strain to hear him.

"You're a fucking psychopath."

We enter the tunnel at seventy miles per hour, and I turn the headlights off so that the road ahead is lit only by the dim strip of lights lining the roof above us. Able is breathing heavily next to me and I can smell his sour, whiskey-laced breath in the dark. He turns to me and grips my thigh, speaking quietly but quickly, each word burning a brand onto my body.

"Do you want me to actually fuck you? Is that it? You never once said no, Grace. Remember that when —"

I never do get to hear the end of Able's sentence, because by this point we are out of the other side of the tunnel and soaring through the night, pausing in midair for one pure, perfect second before we fall three hundred feet into the foothills of the Santa Monica Mountains. Funnily enough, it's at that exact moment that I think maybe LA is quite beautiful after all.

Things I remember from the accident: his

voice — low and gentle, despite everything else about him. The feel of his hand on my leg just before I do it. A familiar something prickling through my body, too complex to label. The full moon hanging cleanly in the sky for the first time in a while. When I finally turn to look at him, he laughs because he doesn't think I'll go through with it. If I really think about it, this is what makes me do it. One small jerk of the wheel and then that perfect in-between moment just after we clear the road but before we start to fall. The sound of Tom Petty's voice as we crash down, down, tumbling to the bottom of the earth. A piercing, jagged tear, and then nothing but stillness.

AFTER

CHAPTER FIFTY-ONE

I wake up on Christmas day with a tight, four-inch gash above my right eyebrow, a broken nose, a fractured patella and a mouth as dry as Death Valley in August. It turns out I was both unoriginal and ill prepared when I drove off Malibu Canyon at that particular moment. If I'd looked into it, I would have discovered that, in 1964, a couple walked away untouched from a wreck in the exact same three-hundred-foot ravine, and, more recently, in 2012, a car of six teenagers survived a crash in the same spot. I should probably have known I'd be invincible — I always get the things I don't want.

I tell the hospital that I don't want any visitors, and the doctors and nurses fall over themselves to tend to me over the next couple of days, to tell me how lucky I am and how well I'm recovering. They list other actors with facial scarring, and tell me that they'll put me in touch with the most prolific cosmetic surgeons for my second rhinoplasty. Every hour a new delivery of flowers or presents arrive. Even from my hospital bed, I understand that I'm infinitely more interesting after surviving this crash.

I have to give a statement to the police, a simple process that ends when one of the detectives asks me to record a video message for her daughter. I shouldn't be surprised anymore, but somehow I still am.

"Why are you sorry?" I ask the male one after he apologizes for what happened to me for the fourth time. His skin is fleshy and pink, like a rare steak.

"We know you were just doing the guy a favor. His blood alcohol level was through the roof."

"Through the roof," I say, forcing a smile. "I get it."

I've always hated puns.

The officer shifts uncomfortably in the plastic hospital seat, and the other cop takes over. She's small with bad skin and perfect hands. I can't stop staring at her hands, which become self-conscious under my gaze, twisting and eventually slipping underneath her legs. I force myself to meet her eyes instead.

"Guys like this think they can just do what

they want, huh? He was lucky you were there. You must be his guardian angel or something, mama."

I stop in at Able's room on my way out of the hospital. My nurse told me that he has a cut that is almost an exact mirror image of mine, over his left eyebrow, acquired when a large piece of the windshield flew into the back of the car, slicing us both neatly on its way. Mine needed exactly two more stitches than his, twelve in total, but other than that they are almost identical. We will now forever be bound by our scars, along with everything else.

Able's room is filled with flowers and cards, most of them also identical to my own. We each received an enormous bunch of blooming white lilies from John Hamilton that are nearly indecent in their fleshiness. Able is asleep, secured to the bed in a web of needles and tubes. The nurse told me that his recovery has been slower than mine because of the alcohol in his blood, despite the angry pain that fills every nerve in my body when I put any weight on my right leg.

Even though the gauze dressing on his head is spotted faintly with coppery blood, Able looks peaceful, maybe even well rested.

This is probably the longest time he's taken off work in decades. I didn't kill him, I gave him a vacation.

I watch a monitor showing his heart rate and brain activity, and I figure that he's just pretending to be asleep when he licks his lips quickly. I don't get any joy from thinking he may be scared to be alone with me now. Whatever happens, he always wins.

Laurel comes up behind me and tells me it's time to go. I walk out of the hospital slowly, trying not to show my limp as I grip her arm. The wall of paparazzi, who have been camping outside the hospital for days, calls out for me like I'm a war hero.

"So how about this weather?" Laurel says, once we're in her car, and I look at her blankly, because of course the sky is forget-me-not blue, impossibly blue, always exactly the same blue in LA. My head is throbbing and it feels like the worst hangover I've ever had, squared. Or it could be approximately 980 percent of the worst hangover I've ever had, a hangover to the power of infinity, if I were a different person and had no respect for the rules of math.

"It's a joke, Grace. What the fuck were you doing?" Laurel says wearily, when I don't respond.

"I guess I lost control," I say, and then when she turns to study me, I add, "of the car."

Laurel turns the engine on. I tightly grip the bag of prescription painkillers the doctor sent home with me, my fingertips leaving damp patches on the paper.

"Are we really not going to talk about why you did it?" Laurel asks.

"Were you really clean for six months before I came back?" I ask in response, remembering something she told me.

Laurel shrugs and keeps her eyes on the road ahead.

"Yeah."

"Why did you come over that night? What a dumb move."

"You've always been my blind spot," Laurel says, and I shift in my seat because I can't help but remember all the times I've either blown her off or used her since I've been back in LA.

"I'm sorry," I say, and she looks like she wants to say something else, but she doesn't.

"Thank you for picking me up," I say, watching the smoke shops and trashy lingerie houses of Hollywood Boulevard slide past in the window. "But I'm so fucking exhausted."

■ ■ ■ ■

We pull up outside Laurel's house, a white craftsman bungalow just off Sunset in Silver Lake. Laurel's girlfriend, Lana, is sitting at the kitchen table doing a sudoku or something on an iPad, her long fingers wrapped around a mug of coffee, and for some reason, when I walk in, I have to swallow a thick, unexpected lump in my throat. I lean against my crutches as Lana assesses me over her iPad in a not-unfriendly way. I wonder whether Laurel has told her to be nice to me, since I'm possibly both suicidal and homicidal at this point.

"I'm Grace," I say, holding up my hand.

"We've met," Lana says, smiling slightly. "At your house in Venice?"

"Of course we have," I say, pushing any thoughts of that house or my husband somewhere far away. Dylan seems as if he belongs to yet another version of me, a long time ago.

Laurel pulls up a seat at the table and gestures for me to sit down.

"Thanks for letting me stay, are you sure it's okay?" I ask, directing my question at Lana. She nods.

"Of course."

"That was close, Grace," Laurel says, and she's testing the waters, trying to assess my psyche at the time of the accident and also now, since I'm going to be staying with her for a while. She keeps her eyes on me as she speaks, tracking my reaction to every word.

"TMZ said that if you'd lost control before the tunnel instead of after, a tree would have impaled the car and you'd have both been killed instantly. Some expert did all these diagrams to show all the ways you could have died, and they've been circulated everywhere. They're even on the news. If you'd been going slower, something about the trajectory being altered, I don't know, you'd also have been killed. It's kind of insane, actually, there was really only one way you couldn't die, and you happened to —"

"Laurel!" Lana interrupts, frowning at her. "Don't be so macabre. I don't think Grace needs to hear about all the ways she could have died. The important thing is, she didn't, and —"

"You know, I am so tired. Do you mind if I rest?" I interrupt her, even though I know I'm being rude. I just couldn't bear it if either of them told me how lucky I was.

Laurel shows me to the spare bedroom, a

485

pale yellow room with a monkey mural on one wall and a gray elephant mobile hanging over the bed. I stare at her and she shrugs, trying not to smile.

"What? Maybe one day. Kids are Lana's thing. Stop looking at me like that. One day at a time. And as you know, I really am back at day one."

Once I'm alone, I pull my phone out of my bag and scroll through the messages I received when I was in the hospital. Frantic texts from Dylan and Laurel checking that I'm okay, a couple from Nathan and Kit wishing me well, the last of which saying that they want to schedule a John Hamilton dinner for as soon as I've recovered, as if that will be some sort of incentive for me to speed the process up. Another one from Nathan, unable to resist an addendum about my name being the most searched for on Google on Christmas Day. A text from Esme saying only: What did you do!?! Two voicemails from my parents, both asking when they can come to the hospital to see me. I text my mom to tell her that I'm out and staying at Laurel's, and that I'll call her soon. No message from Emilia. I turn my phone off before shutting it in the bedside table. I'm embarrassed I ever believed I could be anyone else.

486

CHAPTER FIFTY-TWO

Time moves differently at Laurel's. It creeps and cowers in the morning, slithering along until it's time for dinner and I realize that I've forgotten to do anything all day. Now that I have no purpose other than to heal my bruised body, I spend most of my time in bed, aside from the occasional shower or slow shuffle to sit by the mossy pool in the backyard if I'm feeling adventurous, or trying to make Laurel feel better about my productivity levels. I take six painkillers a day, and I make sure not to mistake the warm glow they elicit for anything more than it is. I know it isn't real.

I think of Emilia sometimes, of what she wanted when she sent Able out with me that night. I wonder if she had any idea what I was going to do, if perhaps she wanted him to be punished for what he did to us both too. I try to imagine how she felt when she got the phone call about the accident, if a tiny part of her thought that some justice had been served, or if she just grieved for the father of her children, unconscious in a hospital bed at Christmas. Most of all, I wonder if any of our friendship was real.

Laurel and Lana try to give me space, but they also spend a lot of time watching me closely, as if they are trying to work out what I'm thinking at any given moment. I want to tell them not to bother, that most of the time I feel like I'm still trapped at the bottom of the ravine, but I can't quite make myself do it.

I change my own dressing every morning like the doctor taught me, avoiding touching the raw skin unnaturally strung together with stitches. Every night I stroke the tender, yellowing flesh around the wound with arnica cream. My nose was cracked in the accident and it is now slightly off center, bulbous in the middle. I stare at this new, distorted face in the mirror and understand the irony of it all, that I'm no longer either Grace Turner or Grace Hyde.

On New Year's Eve, Laurel holds a Native American smudging ceremony in the living room, which I can't help but feel is solely for my benefit. She waves a burning white sage bundle around the room and talks about cleansing our auras for the year to come, dispelling the negative energy that surrounds us, while Lana and I alternate trying to act as if we're taking it seriously so as not to hurt her feelings, Lana working harder at it than me.

My knee is throbbing, so I go to bed before the clock strikes midnight, but Laurel and Lana are still shuffling around the living room when it does. I can hear the warm murmur of their voices and the quiet jazz music playing from the speakers, and I think that they might be dancing with each other, even though I have no way of knowing for sure.

CHAPTER FIFTY-THREE

We spend the first few days in January watching horror movies on the sofa as the world outside carries on without us. I try to ignore the way Laurel and Lana watch me instead of the gruesome scenes most of the time. I've become their own personal horror story, one about the monsters and demons you don't ever want to think about.

I'm brushing my teeth later that evening when a memory hits me, nearly winding me with its force, and I have to grip the edge of the sink to catch my balance. The memory hurts more than it should, and I know it's because it's not the weddings or the funerals or the dark offices, but one of the everyday, forgotten memories that can get you in a place you didn't even remember existed.

Dylan and I were in the glass house, and it wasn't the first day we were there, or even the first month, but it was a good day, and we were eating breakfast around the island in the kitchen. Dylan was talking about how many children we would have, he wanted at least four, and I suggested names that became more and more ridiculous, trying to make him laugh like I always did because it somehow made me feel as though everything was going to be okay, just for a couple of seconds. It's weird to think that I could have pretended to be that person for so long, that I hadn't already ruined it all by then.

I put the toothbrush down and walk into the bedroom. When I'm sitting on the bed, I take my phone out of the drawer, turning it over in my hand like it's a relic of a different time. I turn it on, and the messages start to come through, but there is nothing from either my sister or Emilia. I don't read any of the others. Instead, I type out a number from memory and hold the phone up to my ear, my chest already tight.

"Happy New Year," I say softly, when he answers.

"Grace," Dylan says, and his voice causes a ring of pain to burn through my chest. "Are you okay?"

"Do you remember when we made a pact to name our children after famous movie villains?" I ask, ignoring his question.

"Yeah," he says, and I can hear that he's

smiling. "You were pretty excited about little Leatherface, from what I can remember."

"I don't know why I just thought of it."

"I'm fucking sorry, Grace."

I don't say anything back, and after a moment he speaks again. "I wish you'd killed him. Can I kill him?"

"I think I have to go," I say, because my throat is closing up and the feeling is too much for me right now and it's making me want to take another painkiller, or maybe three.

"Everyone's acting like your life is another one of his movies," Dylan says. "Like it's a miracle you're both still alive."

"I really need to go, Dylan," I say, waiting for the familiar shame to seep through me once again.

"Can you just tell me something . . . ?" Dylan asks, desperation in his voice.

I wait for him to speak again, but he pauses for long enough that I figure he doesn't actually know what he wants to say to me.

"Are you going to be okay?" he asks after a moment.

"I have no idea," I reply, and because it's the truth, I already know it's not what I'm supposed to say.

I hang up and my eyes sting with tears.

I'm still trying to fall asleep when the unmistakable scent of weed slips underneath my bedroom door. I walk into the living space and then through the unlocked door into the backyard, where Lana is sitting on a deck chair, smoking. She opens one eye and holds the joint out to me, but I shake my head, sitting on the damp chair next to her instead.

"Apparently it's going to rain," Lana says after a moment. "Can you smell it?"

I sniff the air to humor her, and it does smell slightly heavier than usual.

"Everyone says it never rains here, but that's a lie," I say. "It's like collective amnesia or something. A pact the locals make with each other to preserve the myth that it's perfect in LA, you know?"

Lana smiles. "I like it when it rains here."

"Me too."

She takes another drag of the joint and then holds it out to me again. I take it this time and inhale, feeling the burn on my lips. I have to try not to choke when it hits the back of my throat.

"This one's a tickler. I don't smoke often, but we're all allowed our vices, right?" she says, holding her hands out in front of her and then turning them over as she starts to laugh.

"Hey, who am I to judge?" I say. "I once did crystal meth with the guy who did the voice for Scooby-Doo."

Lana laughs harder but I'm feeling a little nauseated already, light-headed, and am about to go back to bed when I remember something Laurel said.

"I just want to say that the other night, when Laurel . . . relapsed, it was entirely my fault. I didn't know, but I should have . . ." I say, but the words are eluding me. "I haven't been a good friend to her for a while."

Lana smiles at me gently, and in her smile I can see her affection for Laurel. I'm about to turn inside, satisfied that my friend is luckier than most people, when Lana puts her hand on my arm to stop me. I stare down at it because it's the first time anyone has touched me so gently in a while.

"Can I say something now, Grace? I don't want you to think that I'm being patronizing, but I know how important you are to Laurel, and I think I'd feel bad if I didn't say it."

"Go ahead," I say. She drops the joint into an ashtray, and it sizzles under the water she pours onto it.

"I don't exactly know what's happened to you, but I know that sometimes you can't change other people, you can only change how you respond to them, and that has to be enough. Does that mean anything to you?"

"That's what I figured," I say as I stand up. "But it turns out they control that too."

CHAPTER FIFTY-FOUR

Laurel walks into my bedroom the next morning, her iPhone pinned between her ear and her shoulder. "No, I know, of course. Olivia, naturally, I think that's totally normal given the situation." She mouths *sorry* at me, and I understand that she's on the phone with my mother. I shake my head violently and wave my hand at her, but she perches on the end of my bed.

"Tell me about it, I had to learn that the hard way too," she says, holding her hands up at me as I scowl at her. She mouths *what?* at me before speaking again.

"No, I'm with her. Like I said, she promised me she would call you the minute she felt better. She didn't want to have to lie and pretend that she was okay when she wasn't, you know. Although, she's actually looking marginally less deathly than she was, so it's perfect timing. Okay, I'm handing you over to her now. I know, okay, bye."

She passes the phone to me as if it's burning hot and shakes her head, mouthing *Jesus* to me as she leaves the room. I scowl at the back of the door and take a deep breath.

"Mom."

"Oh, so you do remember me," my mom says, her voice high and charged with something. She must have been gearing up for this phone call for a while. "You're going to have to jog my memory, though . . . your name is familiar . . ."

"Grace Hyde. You gave birth to me. I ate my twin sister in the womb and my head was in the ninety-eighth percentile for size in the country?" I say, because this part has always come easily to us both.

"We don't know that it was a sister," my mom replies instantly. "It could have been a boy twin. Your father would have been so pleased."

"I'm fine, Mom, thanks for asking."

"I know you're fine, but do you know how I know that? E! News. And Kim Kardashian tweeted to say how relieved she was to hear it. I've been trying to get ahold of you for a week."

"I'm sorry, Mom. I wasn't allowed visitors, and then I just . . . switched my phone off. Wait, are you on Twitter now?" I ask, already exhausted.

"Can I just ask you one thing?"

"Go ahead," I say, waiting for the coins to clatter into the gutter like they always do.

"What have I done to deserve this treatment?" my mom asks, and her voice has a rawness to it that it didn't before. I squeeze my eyes shut, my forehead throbbing with the extra exertion of sparring with my mother.

"Mom, come on. I was going to call."

"No, please. Tell me exactly what I did wrong." My mom's voice is getting louder again, and I feel safer, because at least her indignation is familiar ground. "First I lose you, and now Esme doesn't want anything to do with me. How either of you can be happy in that city, breathing all that smog, talking about what a dreadful mother I am, how I always ruin everything . . ."

"What are you talking about?" I ask. "What about Esme?"

"What?"

"Where is Esme?" I ask slowly, fear rendering me stupid.

"I wouldn't know, Grace, because she's with you," my mom says after a pause.

"When did you last see her?"

"New Year's Day . . . She spent the night with a friend from school, and when she came home she told us that you'd asked her

498

to stay with you for a couple of days, before school started up again. She just texted me yesterday, saying she was with you at Laurel's."

I don't respond. New Year's Day was three days ago. My mom starts to speak again, and her words tumble out, overlapping, grappling with each other for space.

"She'd been in such a good mood since she started visiting you, but she was a complete nightmare again over Christmas. We didn't know what to do with her. It was like having you back, at your very worst. She didn't want to be here, and we thought it couldn't hurt for her to stay with you, especially as we knew you were out of action. How can I stop her anyway? You try telling a sixteen-year-old anything. You should know better than anyone how imposs—" She breaks off.

I rest my head in my hands and try to understand what my mom is telling me. Three days. Esme's been by herself for three days.

"Maybe she went to stay with a friend instead," I say, trying to keep my voice calm. There is silence on the other end of the line.

"Grace?" my mom asks eventually, her voice barely above a whisper. "Where's your sister?"

CHAPTER FIFTY-FIVE

I put Laurel's car keys in the ignition and take a deep breath. I didn't consider when I asked to borrow it that I hadn't been behind the wheel of a car since Christmas Eve. I stretch my knee out carefully and then turn the engine on with a roar, pulling the hand brake off quickly, before I can change my mind. I ignore my heart rattling in my chest and the deep, glowing pain in my knee, and I keep my eyes focused on the road ahead, taking one stop sign at a time, just like my mother taught me.

I pull up outside my parents' house, which has been painted a pale blue since I was last here, and make my way to the front door as fast as I can in my incapacitated state. I ring the bell and my dad opens the door within seconds. When he sees me standing there on my crutches, with my battered face, he takes a step back, gripping the wall to steady himself.

"Grace," my mother says quietly from over his shoulder. She's standing behind him in a purple velour tracksuit. "You look awful."

I shuffle toward her, every single bone in my body still sore. She hugs me for longer than usual, and I try not to pull away too early, even though all I can think about is finding my sister.

"How are you feeling?" my dad says, patting me on the shoulder. I try to smile reassuringly and then end up shrugging instead.

"Still kicking," I say, and it seems to be enough for them.

I turn to my mother. "What exactly did Esme say before she left?"

"I already told you. She said she was going to stay with you for a couple of days. You weren't answering our calls, but there isn't anything out of the ordinary there," my mom says, but her heart isn't really in it. She seems even smaller when she's frightened.

"Mom, please."

"She'd been staying with a friend in Ojai, and then she came home in the morning and just started packing."

"How did she seem when she got home?" I ask my dad. He looks at my mom, but neither of them seems to know how to answer.

"I think she seemed fine," my mom says helplessly. "But maybe I don't know her anymore. Do you really think she's at a friend's house? Do I need to call the police? How am I supposed to tell them we just . . . *lost* her?"

We all stand in silence, and I can hear my dad's watch quietly ticking on his wrist, each extra second a reminder that Esme is missing, until I can't take it anymore. I turn back toward the front door.

"Where does Blake live?" I ask, and my mother looks up at me in surprise, as if she forgot I was even there. Her cheeks are flushed, and I think she's about to start crying. I can't remember ever having seen her cry before.

"Five houses down on the left," she says dully instead.

I hobble out of the house and down to a bungalow that is identical to my parents', but a pale yellow. I ring the bell and it plays "The Star-Spangled Banner." A small woman with blond curly hair opens the door.

"Grace Turner!" she says, her delight palpable. She is wearing a pearl necklace, drawing attention to her sun-damaged décolletage.

"Hyde," I say, forcing a smile through my impatience. "My parents are your neighbors? The Hydes?"

"Oh, I know. Esme's parents," she says, nodding with recognition. "What can I do for you?"

"Is Blake in?" I ask, peering past her into a house filled with taxidermy and American flags. A framed copy of the Second Amendment hangs on the porch next to me. I'm having trouble picturing Blake anywhere near this house.

"By the pool," Blake's mom says, shaking her head. "He's always by the pool."

I follow her through the house, trying not to touch anything, and I step through the screen door leading out to the backyard. Blake is sitting in a baggy black T-shirt and khaki shorts, with her legs dangling in the pool, even though the sky is now a threatening shade of dark gray. I think Lana was right, that the drought might be about to break.

Blake's mom hovers by the inside of the door, and I smile at her politely even as I slide it closed, shutting her back in the house.

"Wow," I say.

"I know. Meet Anaheim Blake," Blake

says, pointing to something next to me. Resting against the glass window are two pro-life placards, one of them showing an unborn fetus in the womb, and another filled with the words SMILE! YOUR MOM CHOSE LIFE! in hot-pink letters filled with gold glitter.

"My mom's really thrown herself into this pro-life campaign," Blake says. "It's almost like she's trying to make up for something."

"I'm sorry," I say. I rest on my crutches and squint at her. My knee is throbbing in the damp air, sending waves of pain up to my hip and down to my ankle.

"What can I do for you?" Blake asks, as if she's just realizing how weird it is that I'm at her house.

"Blake, do you know where my sister is?"

Blake looks at me sharply.

"Like right now? I thought she was with you?" Blake asks.

"What happened at the party?" I ask, not really wanting to hear. I feel exposed when I think about Esme, about that short tuft of hair in front of her ear, as if my chest has been ripped open and my heart is on the outside.

"It was bad," Blake says, shaking her head.

"Blake, come on."

"It was a dumb plan. I wish she'd told me

504

about it first," she says.

"I knew about it," I say, and something in my voice makes Blake start to talk. As she does, fat drops of rain start to fall down onto us, but neither of us moves.

"Everything was going how she thought it would, like she spent ages setting the room up — finding the perfect angle so that she couldn't possibly miss the shot of Jesse without any clothes, and then the time came when they were supposed to meet. Esme went into the room, and Jesse was in there, only it wasn't just him. All of the girls from her school were there, too, hiding under the bed and behind the curtains, and *they* were livestreaming *her.* She didn't get the chance to tell them what she was doing. They made out like she was so crazy to have thought he wanted to hook up with her again, and she ended up running out of the house and hitchhiking all the way back to Anaheim. When she got here, we talked about everything and I thought it was okay, like maybe she had calmed down and was going to be able to forget about it? I even dropped her at your place in the morning," Blake says, looking at me hopefully. "Are you sure she wasn't with you?"

I've already turned around, my hand on the screen door.

"Thanks, Blake," I say, looking one more time at the placards propped against the window and Blake's drab clothes. "How much longer have you got before you go to college?"

"Two hundred forty-three days, seventeen hours and" — Blake checks her watch — "twenty minutes."

The rain tumbles down as I leave Blake's house, making up for months of baking sunshine. The sky is a thick blanket of charcoal gray, and I am already soaked by the time I get back into Laurel's car.

It's the first rainy day in months, and we are all sliding across oil-slicked lanes that shimmer like rainbows in the car headlights, but I drive as fast as I can. I wish I could communicate to the other drivers that I'm not just another person on the road racing to a spin class or a lunch meeting in Santa Monica, but I know it doesn't work like that. Everything feels like it's the end of the world until you're actually faced with the end of the world.

I pull up outside my house at Coyote Sumac, the wheels of the car skidding across the sludgy dust. I swing myself over to the porch on one crutch, holding my other hand above my head so that I can see through the pounding rain. When I reach the top of the steps I freeze, horror spreading through me.

The front door is wide open.

I drop my crutch and run into the house, ignoring the bolt of pain in my leg. An empty box of Lucky Charms has been knocked over onto the kitchen table, surrounded by garish, brightly colored marshmallow shapes and cereal loops. My clothes are everywhere, covering the floor and the kitchen counters, my black Valentino dress hanging from a light fixture over the sofa. The TV is on and showing an episode of *Friends* at full volume. Flies buzz around an open bottle of Coke, and a slice of half-eaten pizza rests on the back of a DVD case on the floor.

"Esme?" I shout, running to the bedroom. It's empty. I push open the bathroom door, and a turquoise wash bag with a cartoon of a cat on it saying *You're PAWfect* is open on the floor. I try not to think about my sister's solemn face, the way she takes everything so literally, her infuriating honesty, and the weird noises she makes when she's embarrassed, or frustrated.

I limp out onto the porch, scanning for any signs of when she was last here. When I get down onto the beach, I stop in my tracks

507

and the world flickers around me for a moment. My rose gold slip dress and Dylan's Ohio State sweatshirt are in a wet heap on the sand in front of the house, the waves already licking them. When I get closer I can see Esme's phone resting on top, raindrops skimming off her glittery Union Jack case. I run toward the ocean, fear like I've never known it propelling me through my pain.

My sister is bobbing in the ocean, about twenty yards out, her hair fanning around her. I fall onto the wet sand, the word *no* caught at the back of my throat as fear tears through me. The feeling is primitive, raw, unlike anything I've ever felt before. Before I know what I'm doing, I'm up again and running into the icy water as thick raindrops continue falling from the sky. Seaweed snakes around my ankle, and I trip over a large rock embedded in the sand, landing on my bad knee as the waves crash over me. I propel myself forward with my arms until I'm swimming, the wound above my eye stinging from the salt as the water whips my face. I push through the fiery pain until I'm slipping underneath the waves, swimming like a mermaid through the darkness. I must be close. I break through the surface again and look around. I can see Esme's black hair drifting in the water around her. She's so close. I reach out and grab my sister by the shoulder, pulling her toward me. She gasps for air as I wrap my arms around her.

Esme shouts something over the sound of the rain hitting the water, and I think she's fighting me off, splashing and writhing under my grip.

"Come with me," I say, tears streaming down my face. I wrap my arms around her again.

"What are you doing?" she shouts in between coughs, but I won't let go and we both sink beneath the waves again. I kick hard, my arm gripping Esme around the waist, and I only let go of her when I feel the sand beneath my feet. We break through the surface at the same time, and Esme spits out salt water while I rub my eyes.

"We're okay," I say, breathing heavily as Esme shakes her head, staring at me as if I've lost my mind.

"You're psychotic," she says, but she lets me throw my arms around her neck.

"I'm so sorry. I should have told you. It was a really bad plan," I say, half sobbing and half laughing with relief.

My sister lets me hold her for a minute, and then we both sink onto the sand as the rain tumbles down over us.

Chapter Fifty-Six

Esme doesn't speak to me for most of the journey home, closing her eyes and pretending to be asleep almost as soon as we get inside my car. It's just as well, as the adrenaline-fueled fight through the waves has left me drained, and I don't yet know how to form the words I need to say to her.

We're on the freeway when my sister opens her eyes again.

"Where are we going?" she asks quietly, because the gunmetal sky and the rainwater rivers flowing next to the freeway have rendered Southern California unfamiliar, turning it into anywhere else on the planet.

"Home. I'm taking you home, of course," I say, and maybe because she knows I don't have one, she doesn't argue with me.

"Do you remember when I used to make up stories about Patrice the mermaid for you when you were a kid?" I ask when we're almost at my parents' house.

Esme is quiet for so long that I think she's asleep, but after a while she shifts in her seat.

"Yeah, except I thought Patrice was a pirate," she says.

"No! Patrice was a mermaid. She stole from the pirates," I say, horrified.

"Doesn't that make her a pirate too?" Esme is staring at me strangely. "She even had her own ship. Her name is practically an anagram of 'pirate.' "

"Patrice used to steal the booty from the pirates to hide in her shipwreck under the ocean," I say, trying to remember. I shake my head. "Shit, I guess maybe she was a pirate."

Esme smiles slightly and closes her eyes again.

My parents nearly buckle at the knees when we walk into the house, and I don't think I'll ever forget the look on both their faces when they see my sister. Even through the protective shield of my own relief, I understand that I will never be the person to trigger such a simple, primitive response from them — that too much has happened, or hasn't happened up to this point.

Esme already seems panicked by the display, frozen in the hallway with her hair hanging in clumps around her shoulders and her mascara smeared down her face in spindly spider legs.

"What happened to you?" my mom asks, horrified. She turns to me. "What did you do to her?"

"Mom," Esme says loudly before she slides down against the wall in the hallway, ending up next to a pile of shoes and the old newspapers my parents keep forgetting to recycle. We all stare down at her, none of us knowing quite what to do with our love for this small, broken girl. I meet my mother's eyes, and a flash of recognition passes between us.

My dad steps forward to scoop Esme up, and, to my surprise, she lets him. He walks with her down the hallway to her bedroom, leaving my mother and me alone by the front door. My mom stands with her arms hanging by her sides, like she doesn't know what to do with them if they're not reaching for my sister.

"Thank you for bringing her home," my mom says quietly, and even though her words are simple, I'm surprised by their force.

"You're welcome," I say, then, after a moment: "You painted the house."

"Your father did it after you left," she says.

"I kind of miss the pink."

"I knew you would say that," she says. My dad has appeared in the hallway, and my mom turns to him. "I told you she'd say exactly that."

"I'm not getting involved," my dad says, and we all just stand there for a moment because none of us has the energy to keep it going.

"Is she okay?" my mom asks, making a move toward Esme's bedroom.

"We have to let her sleep," my dad says, gently steering my mother back toward the kitchen.

We sit down together at the kitchen table, and nobody offers to make tea.

"Is this about the suspension?" my mom says, staring blankly at me. "Because I can email the school about it. I'm sure it was all a misunderstanding."

"Not really," I say, and maybe it's cowardly, but right now I can't handle being the one to tell them that they couldn't protect their daughter. The thing is, I've spent my whole adult life trying to shield them from that very realization, and I suddenly feel exhausted, as if all the years of effort have caught up with me at once. I don't know how to pretend anymore.

"I'm so tired," I say. "I think I have to rest

for a while too."

"How long is a while?" my mom asks, and both the hopefulness that has crept into her voice and the guilt it elicits are too much for me to bear right now.

"I don't know, Mom," I say, and I start to limp down the hallway to my old room. My parents follow me right up to my bedroom door, and I can hear them hovering in the hallway, between the two rooms, as if they can somehow now protect us both from the intruders and monsters and evil spirits that have already chewed us up and spat us out.

My dad brings my dinner to me on the beanbag tray with the spaniels on it, softly knocking before he opens the door and places it at the foot of my bed. On the way out he squeezes my shoulder as he passes, but he doesn't ask anything of me and for once I'm grateful for it.

After he's left, I trail down the hallway to Esme's room with my tray. I knock before opening the door with some difficulty because of the crutch hanging from my arm.

My sister is sitting up in bed, eating an identical dinner of grilled cheese sandwich and tomato soup, off my mom's tray with the poppies on it. Her hair is scraped back and she has no makeup on, and she moves her legs slightly so that I can slip onto the foot of her bed like she used to sit on mine when we were kids. The walls of her bedroom are covered with posters of boy bands and Olympic ice-skaters, and there is a framed photo of the four of us at Disneyland on her bedside table. I wonder if I'd been in her bedroom before I left, whether I would have realized how young she still is and have spoken to Mom about what she told me. I like to think it would have changed things, but it probably wouldn't.

"Do you wish you'd killed him?" Esme asks before I've swallowed my first mouthful.

"I don't know," I say, trying not to lie to her anymore.

"They said that if you'd crashed in the tunnel, you would have both been killed instantly," Esme says, pretending not to look at me.

"I really didn't think it through that much," I say, and she lets out a snort.

"It's still raining," I say, and Esme ignores me, dipping the corner of her sandwich into the soup. "Do you want to talk about what happened at the party?"

"No," Esme says through a mouthful of cheese. "I guess it's like you told me, sometimes the bad guys were always supposed to win."

"When I found you, Esme, were you . . . trying to hurt yourself?" I ask, because I have to.

"I don't know," Esme says quietly, taking her mood ring off and turning it over in her fingers. "I don't think so. I just wanted to feel anything, I guess."

"I'm so fucking sorry. I should have stopped you from going to that party."

"It's okay," Esme says.

"It's really not," I say. "I messed up."

"Why are you making this about you?" Esme asks, rolling her eyes.

"Because I'm your sister," I say, and I wipe at my eyes roughly with my sleeve, embarrassed. "And I'm an adult and I let you down."

"Well, you're not exactly an adult," Esme says, shifting a little next to me. "Remember you froze in time when you became famous. So you're actually younger than me."

I smile gratefully at her, and she concentrates on her food for a moment.

"I did catch their setup on camera," Esme says dully, after a moment. "They said some pretty enlightening things about me. Really pushed the English language to its limits."

I turn to her, something snapping in my chest. "Can I kill them? I will literally kill them if you just say the word. I've got money, I can pay someone to do it."

Esme looks at me like I'm completely and hopelessly insane, and for just a moment, everything slots perfectly back into how it always was. The moment only passes when I remember that it's raining outside, and that everything has changed, and that Esme and I will probably always have the scars to prove it, visible or not.

"I'm so sorry. They're cretins."

Esme closes her eyes.

"At least you can use that footage for the movie," I say.

She opens her eyes for a brief moment before closing them again.

"There is no movie."

"What do you mean? Of course there's a movie," I say slowly.

"There is not going to be a movie," Esme repeats. Then she raises an eyebrow. "Are you going to the awards?"

I shrug, but after a moment I shake my head because I don't want to lie to her again.

"See? It's over. All of it," she says, just before she closes her eyes.

I think she's fallen asleep when Esme speaks again, softly. "Grace?"

"I'm here," I say.

"Your apology wasn't entirely horrible. I think you could be growing up," she says, and there is a faint shadow of a smile on her face.

CHAPTER FIFTY-SEVEN

"So you were just swimming," my mother says, frowning at my sister and me over a breakfast of Lucky Charms with diced strawberries.

"I was just swimming," Esme says authoritatively.

"In the torrential rain."

"In the torrential rain," Esme repeats.

"Like your sister was *just* driving off a mountain on Christmas Eve."

My sister and I exchange a look. I swallow a mouthful of milky, powdered chemicals.

"Just like that," I say, shrugging.

"I don't know how we raised two such thrill seekers," my dad says, pouring more cereal into Esme's bowl, "when I've never even smoked a cigarette."

There is a long moment of silence before Esme and I start to laugh, and it's the kind of laughter that comes after a funeral, loud and grateful, checking you're still alive.

519

While I'm laughing, I have this strange notion that one day we might discover how to stretch time, and if we do, I would be happy to just live this one little moment over and over again.

"Will you be staying over again tonight, Grace?" my mom asks, once we've stopped laughing.

"I don't know," I say, looking down at my hands. "I should probably get back for . . ."

"Nothing?" Esme says, staring me down.

"I guess nothing."

I find my dad in the kitchen later, preparing lunch. He's standing in front of the oven, frowning down at a stick of homemade garlic bread. The outside of the loaf is dark and crispy, but there is a hard lump of butter stuck in between each groove he has made in the baguette.

"The butter won't melt," he says, looking up at me.

"I think you set it to broil instead of bake," I say, switching it over. My dad smiles gratefully and I sit on the chair by the window, stretching my bad leg out in front of me.

"Why didn't you guys ever make friends here?" I ask.

My dad breaks the baguette into smaller sections and then puts it back into the oven,

520

burning his hand on the way out. I hear his skin fizzle, but he doesn't even make a noise. He just walks over to the sink and runs his hand under the cold water.

"We were at a different stage when we moved here; it gets harder to meet people as you get older. Neither of you were at school in the area, and we couldn't work at first because of the visas, then your mother just never started up again." He shrugs. "You know she doesn't like many people anyway."

"How's she doing?" I ask. "Current drama aside."

"Good, actually. She's started Pilates classes with one of the neighbors. Joined the local theater company against all the odds."

"Is she eating more?" I ask my dad.

"A little more," he says, shrugging.

"We're all going to be okay," I say, even though we both know that I have no idea.

"She was upset when you didn't call," my dad says, moving his hand from under the tap to open a can of tomatoes. "We both were."

"It was only six weeks," I say, but of course I'm aware that I'm in the wrong. "I'm sorry."

"It's okay. We never asked you and your

sister to be perfect, but we do need to figure out how we can rub along together as a family. Keep talking, keep moving forward," he says, emptying the can into a saucepan. "I know it's not easy coming home."

He starts to messily chop an onion. It's the opposite of watching Emilia cook with her measured movements, each piece of onion precisely the same size and shape as the one next to it. I try not to pull a face when he squeezes a generous portion of tomato ketchup on top of the chopped tomatoes.

"You know I sometimes catch your mother in here sneaking chocolate and cakes, so maybe it's just my cooking she doesn't like," he says, smiling, and then he puts the knife down and stares at the pile of different-sized onion pieces in front of him.

"I hate cooking," he says after a moment, more to himself than to me, and, as I watch him pick the knife back up to start chopping again, I feel a surge of love for him that nearly knocks me over with its force.

CHAPTER FIFTY-EIGHT

After lunch, I tell my parents that I'm going out for a couple of hours. I hobble to the Ralphs at the end of their street in the rain, my face slick with sweat by the time I reach it. I collect the ingredients I need as quickly and economically as I can, scanning the signs in between the aisles carefully before I commit to anything. Once I've paid, I slowly make my way back to my parents' house. When I get there I sit on the porch for five minutes, until all signs of pain are erased from my face, and then I let myself in and join my mom and Esme on the sofa.

We all watch a made-for-TV movie together, and I try to focus on the awful storyline without thinking about Emilia's fictional vets falling in love with cowboys in Montana. If I stop to think about it, I might have to admit how hurt I am that she hasn't been in touch. I should have known she wouldn't believe me for long.

When I see my dad stand up to head into the kitchen, I stop him.

"I can make dinner tonight . . . if you want."

My parents and sister stare at me as if I've just offered to raise, kill and roast a suckling pig for them for dinner with my bare hands.

"Nothing spectacular, just scrambled eggs," I say, rolling my eyes. My dad smiles and sinks back into his armchair, relieved.

"That would be wonderful."

Once I'm in the kitchen, I get to work making eggs the way Emilia taught me. I remember how she cracked them softly because it takes less force than you think, and that way you're less likely to get the gritty fragments of shell in your mixture. I can see the way she spun across the tiled floor of her kitchen to drop the shells in the food disposal and then back to whisk, season and pour the eggs, practically in one seamless movement. She could maintain a conversation with me while she was looking after the girls and cooking, and I still always felt as if I had her undivided attention.

I toast the bread until it is golden on both sides, then I spread the wafer-thin pieces of butter I've already prepared onto each slice. I dish the eggs onto the toast before garnishing each plate with a sprig of parsley and some pine nuts.

I walk into the living room holding the tray with the poppies and a plate of eggs, but my family isn't in their usual spot by the TV. I turn around and they're all sitting at the table tucked around the corner of the living room, the one we never use. The gingham tablecloth is out, as are four straw mats I recognize from when we lived in England. I put the beanbag tray down on the sofa and place the plate of food on the mat in front of Esme, then I bring the other three plates out.

"Please don't make a big deal out of this," I warn them as my parents start to make appreciative, over-the-top noises when they take a bite. "It's scrambled eggs. Don't make this weird."

"This is delicious," my dad mumbles, wiping some egg from the corner of his mouth.

"Very, very tasty," my mom says.

"Good job, Grace!" Esme says overenthusiastically.

"Shut up, all of you," I say, rolling my eyes.

After a moment, my parents start talking at the same time. Naturally, my dad concedes and my mom starts again.

"You know, Grace, I went into CVS the other week, and I noticed that this checkout girl's wedding ring was very similar to yours. It was a small opal, set in a band of tiny diamonds," she says, in mock surprise. "What are the chances!"

"She didn't steal it, Mom," I say, hoping beyond measure that she didn't make a scene in the middle of the store in one of her velour ensembles.

"Yes, I'm aware of this *now*. The girl explained that her aunt had met some insane red-haired woman in the street, and that she had given all of her jewelry in the world away to her," she says. "I knew that it had to be *my* insane, formerly red-haired woman as soon as she said it."

"Thanks, Mom," I say, rolling my eyes. "I'm glad that it's gone to a good home."

"Actually, she said that opal is bad luck and that she was only wearing it to scare off the nasty men, so I took her to buy another one," my mom says, pleased with herself. "A diamond this time."

"You shouldn't have —"

She waves her hand in the air. "It's all your money at this point anyway, as you so graciously reminded us last time you were here."

I pull a face, and my dad shakes his head.

"Leave her alone, Olivia."

"Leave her alone? I just got her ring back. A ring that she gave away to some cleaner

526

like a mental person. I hope you didn't tell Dylan," she says, her eyes shooting up to the ceiling in despair. "Anyway, I have it if you want it."

I watch as she pushes the eggs around her plate some more before putting the fork, loaded with toast and eggs, into her mouth. She chews slowly and then she swallows. She finishes the entire plate while my dad, Esme and I watch her in amazement.

"What?" she says, smiling to herself.

I'm nearly asleep when I hear a soft knock at the door. I assume it's Esme and am already making room for her at the foot of my bed when my mom pushes open the door. She seems tiny, standing in the middle of my room in her bathrobe, lit only by the moonlight.

She waves her fingers and I move over so that she can sit on the edge of the bed next to me, even though there's not enough space. She takes my hand and presses something cool into my palm. My wedding ring. I close my fingers around it.

"We need to talk," she says, her chin set resolutely. "We should have had this conversation years ago, but I didn't know how, and I would hate myself if we didn't have it before you left again."

"Mom. I'm twenty-three years old in one week. Please don't let this be the moment for our first heart-to-heart," I say, raising my eyebrows at her then immediately wincing because I forgot about the gash on my forehead.

"Just hear me out, Grace, and how did you become such a wiseass?" My mom takes off her glasses and cleans them with the hem of her bathrobe.

"Please," I say quietly, but my mom's jaw is already set, and the expression on her face is one I can't identify. She opens her mouth to say something but then she stops. She doesn't know anything, I tell myself, clutching the ring in my palm so tightly that the veins on the back of my hand become engorged.

"You outgrew us when you were still just a kid, and I'm not proud of how easily we let you go, or that I didn't think about what happened to make you change like that. I was too busy thinking about myself."

"I don't want to talk about this," I whisper, and I don't know what my face is trying to tell her, but my mom has to look away from me.

"Grace, you drove yourself off a cliff on Christmas Eve. We have to talk about this, because if not now, when? Not when you've actually killed yourself."

My mom's breathing is rough and jagged, and that's when I realize how hard this is for her, to admit that she failed at something too. After everything that's happened, I think the discovery that I couldn't even protect my parents will be the worst part of all, and I suddenly want to be out of this room, out of my own skin, under the water, flying off the mountain again, anywhere but here.

"We let you down," my mom says, even her hands trembling under the weight of her words.

"I'm sorry I didn't come home. I didn't mean to outgrow you," I say quietly.

"That's what kids are supposed to do. Outgrow their parents," she says, her voice wavering only at the end. "As I said, I'm not proud of how we dealt with it, but also I can only be who I am. Same goes for all of us."

The veins on the backs of my hands have turned a deep blue.

"You know you can never go back," my mom says then, but I just stare at the baby-pink nose of a cuddly toy koala peeking over the desk in the corner of my room.

"You just have to keep going forward instead."

The koala stares back at me with dark, glassy eyes.

"I know that you're scared, Grace, but you need to face up to what happened. To whatever he did to you," she says quietly, and that's when my heart really drops. I try to quell the shame that comes crashing over me. Suddenly, I'm right back where I was when I was fifteen, confused and alone, trying to make sense of what was happening to me.

My mom hovers above me, unsure of what to do next, perhaps waiting for me to finally tell her about it, for me to set the secret free in the way that everyone believes will instantly fix you, like taking a Tylenol for a fever, or compiling a list of pros and cons before you make a big life choice. Only I know that it doesn't work like that. My secret is already out, trapped among the leaves of the palm trees that line the streets of Los Angeles, lying in the dirt at the bottom of the Santa Monica Mountains, and nobody feels any better for it. I look down at the blanket covering my legs, and all I feel is trapped, more entwined in Able's web than ever.

"I can't," I whisper, and it's when I see the disappointment register on her face, too, that I have to look away. My mom strokes

530

my hair as the tears finally fall, slipping down my cheeks and soaking the collar of my T-shirt as my body racks with grief for everything I've ever had to break before it could break me first.

"Then you're just going to have to forget it ever happened."

CHAPTER FIFTY-NINE

The day of the Independent Film Awards, I wake in the middle of the night sweating, my pillow soaked. I dreamed Able was in the room with me while I slept, but I couldn't move or call out because his knee was on my neck, pinning me down all over again. I reach for my painkillers before remembering I left them at Laurel's. After that, I sob into my pillow until I can hardly breathe, while the sky lightens around me. I don't know how to be normal, how to stop him from being able to reach me.

In the morning, I slip out early to go for a walk. I'm wearing one of my mother's velour tracksuits because it fits perfectly over my knee brace, and it is nearly soaked through with rain by the time I get back to the house, holding a coffee in my crutch-free hand.

"Gracie."

I freeze at the bottom of the porch steps.

Emilia is sitting on a lounge chair, smoking a cigarette with her hair coiled into a low bun like she's Carolyn Bessette-Kennedy reincarnated. She is dry as a bone and a soaking white umbrella lies on the deck next to her Gucci loafers. I remember now that I don't trust anyone who remembers to carry an umbrella in Southern California.

"How are you?" Emilia asks softly.

I shrug, not wanting to move any closer to her but needing to rest my leg, which is currently sending white-hot signals of pain to my brain.

"Okay," I say, climbing up so that I'm leaning against the porch railing, my leg extended in front of me.

"It really is a miracle that you are okay," she says. "That you're both okay."

"When did you start believing in miracles?" I say, refusing to play the game with her.

"Look, Gracie. I came here because I wanted to . . . ask you something," she says, looking down at her cigarette and then back up to me. "It's not easy for me to say, but I hope that you'll understand."

I watch her stub her cigarette out on the deck, and then she just stares at it for a moment, unsure of what to do with it. She takes a deep breath, collects herself and meets my eyes again.

"I'm so sorry for what happened to you. I have tried over and over again to work out if I could have stopped it in some way," Emilia says. "And you know I will never try to excuse it."

"The thing about saying you're not trying to excuse something is that you kind of already are," I say, folding my arms across my chest.

Emilia blinks. "Able is in recovery in Utah as we speak."

"Recovery," I say, trying to wade through her words.

"He's in therapy. He's coming back for the awards ceremony tonight, and then we're going to pack up the house and move to Greenwich to be nearer to my family. Permanently."

I start to speak but she holds up a perfectly manicured hand to stop me. I look down at my own hands. My fingers are red and raw, the nails bitten down to the quick.

"It's over, Gracie. We want to leave this here. You have my absolute word that he will never work in the industry again, or try to contact you. We won't be coming back to LA."

"Well, I'm so relieved that you've taken this opportunity to finally get what you want," I say to her. "I hear Connecticut is beautiful in the spring."

"Gracie . . ."

"You know that only you and Able actually call me Gracie, and it's only ever when you want something from me, or when you're trying to make me feel like a child."

Emilia takes a deep breath before turning back to me.

"Please let me help you, Grace. Able wants to press charges against you for the accident. He has a statement ready to say that whatever happened between the two of you was when you were of legal age, and to his knowledge, fully consensual. I can stop him."

I shake my head, and for just a moment, I think I must be dreaming.

"Did you know that he molested me when I was underage? Did he tell you that part?"

"It's highly unlikely that your case would even make it to court. It's not like in the movies," Emilia says quietly. "There wouldn't be enough evidence to sustain the molestation charges, and there are hundreds of people to testify how much you were drinking and doing drugs around that time, how you'd followed him around like a lost dog for years."

"Were we ever really friends?" I ask her,

because while she's been talking, I realized how much we must have hurt each other.

"Don't oversimplify things, Grace. You're smarter than that. What did you expect to happen?"

"What do you actually want from me?" I ask, not able to look at her anymore.

"Do I need to tell you that I'm sorry again?"

"You're not the one who should be sorry."

"He's the father of my children, Grace, and he made a mistake. He misread your feelings, and he was weak, and stupid, but what else can I do? What would you do if you were me? Of course I am so deeply, painfully sorry that this happened to you."

"You keep apologizing for what 'happened to me.' Nothing happened to me. It wasn't an accident. He did it to me," I say slowly. "I know that you don't like to think about bad things, but sometimes you have to."

"Please, just tell me that you'll think about what I'm saying."

"You know, I really have to think that you don't understand what you're asking of me," I say.

Emilia watches me, and then something crosses her face. "Of course I know exactly what I'm asking of you, and you may not see it now, but this is the only solution for any of us. If it even made it to court, which isn't likely, the case could take years to build, and you'd be in career purgatory for that entire time — nobody would hire you while it was pending. The trial would then be covered on news channels around the world, and you would turn up to court every single day to find that every minute, private detail of your personal life now exists solely as material for the jury and the public to judge you on. You think you're being judged now, but you can't even imagine the things they'll say about you. Every text message to Able, questions about your sex life with Dylan, even the medical report from the time you overdosed. I've heard your own team wanted to commit you because they thought you could be bipolar. Do you really want to put your parents through that? Do you want to put Dylan through that? You have to admit that you're not the most reliable witness."

It starts as a tingle, but by the time she's finished, every single nerve in my body feels as if it's on fire. I am roaring from the inside out, a lioness gathering myself up and protecting myself against the predators trying to ruin me.

"I need you to get away from me right now," I say, and I hope my voice sears deeper into Emilia with every word as she stands on the porch in front of me. I hope she never forgets this moment, just like I know I never will. After a couple of seconds, she starts to climb slowly down the steps, stopping when she's at the bottom, her umbrella forgotten as the rain skims down her face too.

"We can't all be heroes, Grace."

And who knows, maybe if she didn't look so sad while she was saying it, I might have actually been able to do what she was asking of me.

CHAPTER SIXTY

I watch from the side of the stage as the young actress introduces Able simply, ridiculously, as the man who saved independent cinema. She's never been in one of his films, and I can't figure out the connection between them. When her introduction ends soon after that, I realize it's because there isn't one, that she's just one more person desperate for the chance to be somebody else. I can tell from the surge in applause that Able has started to make his way up to the stage from his table in the middle of the floor, and that's when I stroll past the event organizers at the side of the stage who are holding clipboards and timing everything perfectly down to each second. A woman in a headset puts her hand out to stop me, and I shake it off. "I'm Grace Turner," I say scathingly. "I'm Able's surprise guest."

The woman sighs and waves me on, because her only other option is to physically remove me herself before I make it onstage, or to wait for security to escort me offstage when everyone is watching and the cameras are rolling. She knows who I am, and the risk is too high for her.

I showed up late to the awards show, missing the specific time slot that Nathan texted me for my entrance. I called Camila before I came, figuring if I lied my way through my last interview with her, at least I could give her the real story now. Camila escorted me down the red carpet, understanding implicitly how to sidestep the inane chatter from TV presenters about my dress, and other questions about my miraculous escape and appreciation for the man of the hour. I moved slowly on one crutch, and was stopped many times by my peers who wanted to tell me how brave I was just for being there after what happened. I kept my mouth closed, and I posed in front of the IFA branding for the pit of photographers, my gunmetal armor dress catching the light of their flashes and glittering perfectly. The paparazzi called out for me like I was already a legend, and I tried not to believe them this time.

When I think that Able is close to the stage, I limp out into the spotlight, joining the actress behind the podium. She is confused, blowing a kiss to Able before she sashays off, leaving me alone in front of the audience.

"Hi, everyone, please excuse the change of plan. I only decided to come half an hour ago," I say, and the audience titters politely. Able has stopped on the stairs next to the stage, gripping the handrail. His head has been shaved all over, and he has the gash over his left eyebrow, the perfect mirror image of my own.

"Come on up, Able," I say, and after a moment's pause, he climbs the rest of the stairs, his face ashen.

My hands are shaking so I slip them out of view, behind the podium.

"So I think this is the part where I introduce Able, and thank him for his unending commitment to giving independent films a platform, for his tireless contribution to our industry as a whole and, most of all, for everything he's done for me. This is definitely what I'm supposed to do," I say, my voice shaking. I clear my throat, and the audience is so quiet I wonder if they can hear my heart beating through the microphone.

"I have spent years trying to work out what I could have done differently, or maybe what my parents could have done differently. I should have told someone after the first time he made me touch him, or when he told me I was mentally unstable for the hundredth time. Maybe I shouldn't have waited until every part of my life was already destroyed before I tried to kill myself. Maybe I shouldn't have worked so hard to become, as I was told just this morning, such an unreliable witness. But it was never really up to me, was it?" I say, and then I pause because, look, there is the queen of Hollywood, watching me with growing interest, her hands still folded on the table in front of her. She's nearly eighty now, and sitting at a table that is further away from the stage than she used to sit, but in Hollywood, not so much a town as a social construct, she still reigns. At the next table over is the actor who just got caught sleeping with a sex worker in Canada, and he doesn't know what to do with himself in his reluctance to look anywhere near me. And there is John Hamilton, watching me with an expression of vague horror. He knows I'm about to fuck everything up, but it doesn't really matter, as there are a hundred other girls like me who will get their breasts out in his film, and they're probably younger and thinner than me anyway. He's already eyeing up the nineteen-year-old actress at the table next to him, the one who wore the latex catsuit in his last movie and who, despite still sort of thinking about how she said the wrong designer's name on the red carpet, already understands implicitly what I'm about to say. They all do. Whether they have guessed the truth about my story or not, they have all known stories like mine. And with that, I'm finally ready for this to end. I'm ready for this to be out in the world, blazing and soaring its way across news sites and text messages and conversations in bars, gyms, restaurants and offices all over the country. I'm ready for it to be anywhere other than just within me.

"So, actually, I am here to thank you, Able, in a way." I turn to look at him, for just a moment, and I can see that he would kill me right now if he could. I take a deep breath.

"Thank you, for making me aware that there are an infinite amount of ways to get hurt, every day of my life, even when you are nowhere near me."

The room is more than silent — it is frozen in time. I am suspended above them, my words floating and falling around us all like blossoms, settling into the darkest, loneliest crevices of Hollywood.

"Because knowing what I know, and still getting up every single day, despite it? That makes me stronger, and braver, and better than you. So, Able, you don't get to have ruined me. Not even one tiny part of me."

Able is looking away from me, into the wings behind me, and that's when I see Emilia standing there. She turns and walks away from both of us. The audience is silent because, like the good, docile actors they are, they are waiting for someone to tell them what to do, some director or publicist to tell them whose side they are on. Then the queen of Hollywood starts to clap, slowly at first, but it rings out like thunder in the silent auditorium. A few others join in, but I'm already walking off the stage and straight out of the back of the building, past the photographers who don't know what's happened, past the crowds of fans waiting to catch a glimpse of their favorite actor, and past the black town cars and SUVs that are lining Highland, waiting to take the stars inside back to their real lives. I walk past them all, limping alone down the eerily quiet stretch of Hollywood Boulevard, the hem of my dress dragging over the names of everyone who came before me, encased in stars for eternity.

EPILOGUE

I hold my twenty-fourth birthday dinner at Musso and Frank, right where Hollywood's heart would be if it had one. Photographers are still waiting outside, but I'm a different kind of celebrity now, and we all know that I'm not theirs in the same way anymore. I smile at them as I pass with Esme, and I remember what it was like at my first public appearance, where so many strangers were calling my name that it turned into a sound I didn't recognize anymore. Maybe that's how I forgot who I was.

At first it feels strange to watch my friends and family interact with each other, but when I notice my mom and Laurel sparring happily in the corner, or Esme quizzing Dylan about licensing music for the movie she has now nearly finished, I feel a flicker of hope that overpowers my need for control. At one point I try to stand up to thank everyone for coming, but my voice becomes thick and my eyes fill with tears, and I have to sit right back down again. Laurel and my mother spare me any further embarrassment by pretending not to notice, but Esme quietly takes my hand in hers, and my dad smiles at me from the other end of the table. Dylan signals for Lana to bring my birthday cake out then, a towering rainbow sponge cake with a large 24 on it, and I hide my face while everyone sings "Happy Birthday" to me. As I close my eyes to blow out the candles, I think about second chances, how maybe I am one of the lucky ones after all. Then, just when I think it's time to leave, Esme stands up and taps her spoon against her glass.

"To my big sister," she starts, grinning at me and holding her glass out. "The most infuriating, bravest and probably the best person I know. Happy birthday, you cretin-buster."

I raise my glass until it meets hers.

Dylan is driving me home, and we're listening to our favorite The Cure song, the one that we nearly danced to at our wedding before someone told us it was about death not life. He's sneaking glances at me to check that I'm okay, which is something people around me have been doing a lot since the IFAs.

I watch as the city that gave me everything and took it all away from me slips past in the window. I'm slowly taking some parts of my life back, not in the same way I was before, but steadily, carefully, in a way I sometimes think might just last.

"When I was blowing out my candles earlier, do you know what I was thinking?" I say to Dylan, and I've been trying to work out how to word it without worrying him or seeming like I'm being dramatic, but now I just think *fuck it* because it's the truth, and for some bizarre reason, he seems to want to know this kind of thing about me.

"What?" Dylan asks, and he slows down a little because we're nearly at my new house, a few miles up the coast from Coyote Sumac.

"So we're there, with all my favorite people in the world, and I know that I'm feeling something that's like . . . the most obvious, uncomplicated happiness that I can remember experiencing. I'm trying to just soak it up, and be present, but *then* I start thinking, isn't it fucked that you will never know if you're *actually* living the happiest moment of your life until you've lived them all? Isn't that some sort of massive flaw in the human experience?"

Dylan is shaking his head and laughing at me, about to say something, but I hold up my hand to stop him.

"*But,* then I thought about it some more, and maybe there are some things you just don't need to know. Maybe it's all right that there's always the potential to outdo your best. Plus, there is no way you'll actually be trying to work that shit out when you're dying."

"You thought all of this while you were blowing out your candles."

"Yep," I say, shrugging. "I'm quite the existential multitasker."

"So what was your takeaway?" Dylan asks, pulling to a stop outside my house even though I can tell he wishes we weren't here yet.

"Takeaway was, maybe it's okay not to be okay all of the time," I say, smiling slightly because even though it sounds like a bland inspirational quote from a coffee mug, I still think I mean it. "Maybe it's okay not to be perfect, or the best, or even special for a while."

Dylan shakes his head but he's looking at me like I'm magic, and for the first time in my life, I actually want to believe him.

"Are you going to be all right?" Dylan asks

while I'm reaching for my jacket and bag from the back of the car. I understand that he still has to ask me this question because just over a year ago I drove off a cliff into a ravine at the bottom of the Santa Monica Mountains, and I have the scars to prove it. Because after I faced the source of all of my nightmares at the IFAs, I then had to endure hours of questioning at the police station about the emotional abuse, the sexual assault and, finally, the crash, so that by the time they let me go, I didn't know if I felt weightless or drained of everything I had. The state won't press charges against me for the accident, but are still deliberating over what to do about my claims against Able. My lawyer told me that Emilia was right, the reality of Californian law is that my case is unlikely to make it to court, and if it does I will have to endure weeks of attacks on my credibility by Able's lawyers that, best-case scenario, will result in a couple of months in jail and a small fine for him. Some days, just knowing that there are names for what he did, things that at one time seemed so horrifyingly unique to just me, feels like it could be enough. Other days I want to stand up in court and testify against the man who abused me in so many ways, fire roaring in my veins. I change my mind every day. And I'm allowed to.

"I think so," I say. The truth.

I kiss Dylan on the cheek before I climb out of the car, and he smiles because it has to be good enough for the moment, while we're still figuring everything out.

I'm a couple of feet away when Dylan winds down his window.

"Do you think it's an appropriate moment to . . . say the line?" he says, grinning so widely I start to laugh.

"I'm not sure that it's ever appropriate to say the line."

"Come on . . . it's kind of perfect."

I stand for a moment, hands on my hips, trying to remember what it felt like to play a homicidal sex worker in an orange jail jumpsuit, rage pounding through my veins in every scene. I think about the line that strangers still shout at me when I pass them in the humid city streets; the line that I once believed could get me an Oscar, but that I now know just means a part of me will always belong to other people, whatever happens next. The line that Able wrote just for me. I take a deep breath as I turn the words over in my mind, and then I just drop my hands back down to my sides and shrug.

"You know, I think I've officially earned the right to never say the line again in my life," I say, grinning at Dylan unapologetically. Our eyes meet for a second and I feel that familiar kick, low in my belly.

We're both still smiling as Dylan drives away, his waving hand nearly lost in the Malibu dust that billows behind him. And that's when I notice the sky above the Pacific. Have you ever seen a sunset like this one? I hope you have, the wild pink sky slashed with flaming streaks of gold, the kind of sunset that makes you feel lucky, golden; the type that has the power to tell you that perhaps, for one small moment in time, you are exactly where you need to be.

THANK YOU

To my parents and Sophie, for your support in me and for being the funniest (and best) family in the world. D — thank you for always encouraging me to write and be creative, and for leading by example. I promise I'll read *Dracula* now. M — thank you for all of your thoughtful advice and for being the first person I trust with anything, in both writing and life. S — thank you for being my best friend and my memory, and for having enough enthusiasm for us both. I am so BEYOND lucky to have you all.

To Jen Monroe, for being the smartest editor I could have dreamed of. Thank you for understanding me (and, more importantly, Grace!) implicitly, and for excavating the heart of the story. Working with you has been a dream.

To Julia Silk, for seeing something in my writing early on and for setting everything in motion. Thank you for your patience and for your wicked sense of humor — some of the lines exist only to make you laugh.

To David Forrer, for choosing to take me on and transforming my life almost overnight. I could feel your warmth and magic from the first time we spoke.

To Jin Yu, Jessica Brock, Diana Franco, Craig Burke, Jeanne-Marie Hudson and Claire Zion at Berkley, for your ideas, enthusiasm and support — I'm so grateful for all that you do. To Colleen Reinhart and Emily Osborne, for the beautiful cover. To Angelina Krahn, for being a truly talented copy editor and making me look better than I am.

To Lola Frears, for being my first reader, my hype man and my therapist all in one. I can't wait to see what you do next. WE STILL GOT THIS, RIGHT?

To Tilda and James Napier, who believed I could do this even when I didn't. Thank you for being such positive forces in my life, and for Jackson and Jeanne.

To Rachael Blok, for the early edits and emotional support, as well as the much-needed punctuation lessons. And to everyone at CBC, particularly Anna Davis, for the early reads and advice.

To Tim and Martha Craig, for the early lessons in confidence and kindness, and to

Nora Evans and Mark Owen at KAS, for fostering individuality and creativity above all else.

To Christian Vesper and Rustic Bodomov, for your invaluable insight into the respective worlds of film/TV and stunt work — any errors are entirely my own. To Christine Louis de Canonville — thank you for your tireless efforts to reform the laws around coercive control until they reflect the realities of so many.

To Jacqueline, Lili (and Bodhi!), Mary, Dan, Jazz, Charlie, Lottie, Athina, Claire, Vikki, Maggie, Jenni, Ed, Vanna, Will, Sarah, Nenners, Merry, Janet, Dave, Hannah, Owen, Rach, Emma, Bonnie, Kim, Paul and Ben, for your friendship and stories, and for keeping me (relatively) sane. I hope I didn't steal any of your best lines!

To Rocky, because it would be weird if I didn't mention you once in 100,000-odd words. A true angel.

And finally, to James. Thank you for your unwavering belief in me from the moment we met, as well as your love. Thank you for always falling asleep with a smile on your face. I couldn't have done this without you.

AUTHOR'S NOTE

I started writing *The Comeback* in February 2017, and I understood from the start who Grace was, and what she'd experienced in a male-dominated environment of toxic power that had gone unchecked for too long.

This was eight months before the *New Yorker* and *New York Times* articles exposing the systemic sexism and chilling sexual abuse allegations in Hollywood came out. I watched in awe as the Me Too movement, started in 2006 by the relentless and inspiring Tarana Burke, took hold. At first it was stories from people like Grace, their words filtered through the mainstream press and given coverage because of who they were, but soon enough the stories took on a life of their own: thousands of secrets fighting their way out of bedrooms and offices and refuges across the world. The tireless work of Burke and the reporters who broke those initial stories — Megan Twohey, Ronan Farrow and Jodi Kantor — as well as the thousands of brave survivors who came out in the following months has been a beautiful, rallying example of how the Internet can be used for good, as well as showing the power that comes when we remove the secrecy and stigma from sexual abuse.

I made the editorial decision to leave Grace's story as I had first envisaged it, choosing not to reference the developments that were happening in the world around me and the effect these would have on Grace's story. While aspects of Grace's experience are familiar, it is, like every instance of abuse, ultimately a very personal story about the shame we can carry in the aftermath of trauma.

I stand with the survivors of abuse of every gender, whether that abuse is sexual, physical, emotional or any other type, and I hope that in telling Grace's story, I have done them a small justice.

ABOUT THE AUTHOR

Ella Berman grew up in both London and Los Angeles and worked at Sony Music before starting the clothing brand London Loves LA. She lives in London with her husband, James, and their dog, Rocky. *The Comeback* is her first novel.

The employees of Thorndike Press hope you have enjoyed this Large Print book. All our Thorndike, Wheeler, and Kennebec Large Print titles are designed for easy reading, and all our books are made to last. Other Thorndike Press Large Print books are available at your library, through selected bookstores, or directly from us.

For information about titles, please call:
(800) 223-1244

or visit our website at:
gale.com/thorndike

To share your comments, please write:
Publisher
Thorndike Press
10 Water St., Suite 310
Waterville, ME 04901